Books by John Clarkson

REED'S PROMISE

JOHN CLARKSON

A TOM DOHERTY ASSOCIATES BOOK
NEW YORK

This is a work of fiction. All the characters and events portrayed in this novel are either fictitious or are used fictitiously.

REED'S PROMISE

A Forge Book
Published by Tom Doherty Associates, LLC
175 Fifth Avenue
New York, NY 10010

www.tor.com

Forge® is a registered trademark of Tom Doherty Associates, LLC.

ISBN 0-812-56538-X
EAN 978-0812-56538-6
Library of Congress Catalog Card Number: 20010480

First edition: December 2001
First mass market edition: May 2004

Printed in the United States of America

0 9 8 7 6 5 4 3 2 1

To Adam and Everett,
two very important parts of my life.

ACKNOWLEDGMENTS

Many people helped me with this novel. Whatever rings true is because of them. Whatever doesn't is because of me. Among them I'd like to thank the Koshman for his unflagging interest and his willingness to connect me with whoever could contribute. And Bruce Jonas, Jack Faer, and particularly Larry Jonas, not just for information on technical matters but also for their wonderful enthusiasm. A special thanks to the eminent Dr. Anthony Blau, who helped in more ways than I'm sure he remembers. Finally, I'd like to thank Bill Herman for connecting me with Bernard Murphy. There have been times when I told someone I couldn't thank him enough. This is one of those times. The contribution made by Bernard and his colleagues went far beyond any kind of thanks I can extend. In the most natural and unassuming way imaginable, they helped me experience the truth that all people are indeed precious beyond measure.

ONE

Bill Reed had three seconds.

Time enough to see the big, black sport utility vehicle backing up, blocking the intersection. Time enough to crush the motorcycle's handbrake, to curse, to realize there wasn't a damn thing he could do to prevent the accident about to happen, and just time enough for Bill Reed to hope that he might get away with only broken bones and torn skin.

Three seconds. Then the wheels locked, slid, and five hundred pounds of motorcycle slammed down on a slick city street, spinning counterclockwise at forty-five miles per hour.

Reed's left elbow, shoulder, head, back, hip—banged onto the asphalt hard enough to crack bones. His jacket disintegrated. Then his shirt, then his skin. The pain screamed through his body, but okay, okay, just skin and bones, the wind knocked out, can hardly breathe, but just skin and broken bones. And then the leg, his left leg, ended up under the sliding machine, the side of his knee grinding into the pavement, but the engine guard taking most of the weight, not too bad, not too bad.

He could take this; he could survive this. The bike began to slide away from him. In another second, he would be free of it, yes, tumbling, bouncing, skidding down the hard street, maybe banging into a parked car or a curb, but still free of the five hundred hard pounds sliding along on top of his leg.

And then, hope ended.

The bike crashed into the SUV, slammed back into Reed, onto his leg, catching his foot, twisting it, breaking the ankle, ripping the foot off, twisting the knee with horrible force, all in a fraction of a second, tearing apart the knee with such massive torque that the joint disintegrated and his femur splintered like a fragile, useless stalk of bamboo.

Three seconds to go down.
Three seconds to stop.
Six seconds to change a forty-two-year-old life, forever.

When Bill Reed woke in the intensive care recovery unit, two thoughts penetrated the haze of anesthesia and pain medication: I'm alive. I hurt.

Reed closed his eyes and let the medication take him back under.

Nearly seven hours later, he woke in fits and starts, until finally he forced himself awake. He understood that he had survived the crash, but he felt as if his body and his mind were enveloped in a thousand pounds of medicated gauze. He felt encased, deadened, the pain somehow suppressed. But what had happened? He tried to move his head. His neck hurt, but okay. Then he noticed his left arm encased in a fiberglass cast. Understandable. His left shoulder hurt, too, and his hip. He moved his left leg. Then his right. Okay, not paralyzed. His mouth was dry. He managed to work up just enough moisture to swallow. He reached over and felt the bandages on his shoulder, hip. Okay. Okay, he told himself. It's all right. He lay back letting the morphine take him back under. He never even thought to prop himself up to look down at his legs. After all, it felt as if they were both still there.

Six months and seventeen days later, Bill Reed rolled down the pathway leading to his new favorite spot in Central Park, the model sailboat basin on the east side of the park off Seventy-fifth Street. The push rims of his custom-made Para-Glide wheelchair spun through his cupped hands. He grasped the rims lightly, slowing the chair, then gripped them to stop at the end of a park bench facing the north end of the pond. He locked his wheels and wiped the shoulder of his T-shirt across his forehead to keep the sweat from dripping into his eyes. Breathing hard, he pulled off his finger-less gloves and waited for the burning ache to seep out of his arms and shoulders.

The acre-size pond, surrounded by a wide walkway, benches, and trees, provided an oasis within the oasis that was Central Park. A breeze rippled the surface of the water, as if searching for model sailboats, but in the months of mornings Reed had been coming to his spot near the park bench he had never seen anyone sailing the boats with their remote control devices. He arrived too early in the morning for that, just a few minutes past eight.

A flurry of air passed over Reed, cooling him, the breeze holding both the night's chill and the promise of an unseasonably warm New York November day. Fall temperatures had somehow been held in abeyance. Soon chill winds would pounce on the city, but not yet. Not today.

Reed pushed aside the thought of his first winter with one leg. He reached into the carry-bag attached to the back of his wheelchair and pulled out a blue windbreaker, wrestled his way into the light jacket and zipped it up to cover his soaked T-shirt.

He fidgeted in the nylon cradle seat of the wheelchair. His khaki pants were wet with sweat, too, but he would never have considered wearing shorts. Nearly seven months after the accident, he still detested seeing his stump. The notion of it being on display for any passerby to stare at mortified him.

From his gym near Sixty-fifth Street and Central Park West, to the deli on Columbus Avenue, over to the park entrance on Seventy-second Street took twenty minutes pushing steadily on the oversized twenty-six-inch wheels attached to the rigid but very lightweight tubular frame that comprised his high-tech wheelchair. The chair had been built for speed, maneuverability, and strength. It looked more like a small straight backseat with large wheels on the sides and hardly noticeable wheels in front. There were no armrests, nothing for his remaining foot to rest on except the bare tube that comprised the wheelchair's frame. The only extra item on the chair was Reed's carry-all bag hanging on the back.

Reed considered the trip from gym to deli to park entrance the transition between his weight training workout and his aerobic workout, which commenced once he entered the park. As soon as he crossed Central Park West, he bore down, pushing hard on his twenty-six-inch wheels, increasing the effort with each rotation of the wheels, building speed, making sure his arms and shoulders burned with the effort. There were only two downhill sections on the route to the pond, and even on those Reed still pushed hard.

He'd even gotten to the point where he could time his crossing of the two roadways where traffic ran through the park on weekdays. His best time clocked in at just under twenty-three minutes. When he'd started four months earlier, it had taken over forty minutes.

Now that his morning workout was over, Reed twisted around, reached into the carryall bag attached to the back of the Paraglide, and extracted a sixteen-ounce cup filled with ice, a pint of Tropicana orange juice, a poppy seed bagel with cream cheese, and a five-hundred-milliliter bottle of Ketel One vodka.

The routine had become familiar: pop open the cup top, slide it back just a bit so he could pour out the melted ice, pour in the vodka, then the orange juice, replace the top. Punch the straw through the cross-hatched slit in the top, settle back, unwrap the bagel, and watch New York's two-legged citizens pass by while he enjoyed his breakfast.

Reed had been coming to this spot long enough to pick out a few familiar faces: the Hispanic housekeeper walking the two golden retrievers; the thirty-something couple who ran together in matching Nike jogging shoes; the heavyset young woman in a business suit and briefcase who strode purposefully through the park, heading south toward midtown.

Reed watched the early morning passersby, swirled the contents of his cup, sucked up a mouthful through the straw, feeling the early dose of alcohol and orange juice hit his stomach and begin to numb him slightly. Content, he bit off a hunk of bagel and cream cheese, wiping the corner of his mouth with the back of his hand, and turned his gaze to the boat pond. His peripheral vision caught sight of a figure coming toward the bench next to him. Reed had an immediate sense that the person intended to sit near him.

Reed stared straight ahead, looking at the pond, stubbornly holding his spot and concentrating on not turning toward the uninvited guest who for some reason came over and sat right at the end of the bench, as close to Reed as possible.

Reed muttered a curse to himself, just loud enough for the uninvited visitor to hear. He shoved the icy cup in his crotch, unlocked the wheels of his chair, preparing to leave.

"What's the rush, boss?"

Reed turned, stifled a smile, shaking his head.

"You gotta be kiddin' me."

Irwin Barker filled most of his end of the park bench. In the early morning chill air he wore no coat. Just a brown suit, 50 Long, a white shirt, modest tie, and sensible shoes. But the tie was undone, the suit rumpled, and his dark stubble hadn't been scraped with a razor in at least twenty-four hours. Barker squinted at the morning sun.

"Yeah, it's great to see you, too, Bill."

Irwin reached over and took the cup from Reed's hand, popped off the top and nearly drained it. He let out a sigh of pleasure, ran a hand through his thick black hair, and smacked his lips.

"No, go right ahead, don't worry about it." Reed took the cup back.

"Thanks."

"What happened, Irwin, tough night?"

He pulled out a creased pack of unfiltered Pall Malls, lit one with a Bic lighter that nearly disappeared in his meaty hand, and said, "About the usual." Irwin exhaled, taking in the tranquil scene. "I don't think I've ever been in the park this time of day."

"No kidding."

Reed mixed himself another cup full of screwdriver. Irwin watched him and said, "Nice way to start the day."

"Thanks."

Silence descended between them. After a few more moments, Reed asked, "So what's this, Irwin, you worried about me or something?"

"Could be."

"Why?"

"Oh, shit, I don't know, maybe 'cause you lost a leg in a horrible fucking accident, haven't shown up at the office in over six months, your answering machine is turned off, and you start your day with about a half pint of vodka."

"I don't have an answering machine. I have automatic call answering."

"You ever fucking check it?"

"Sometimes. And don't grab my cup again."

"Is that better than Gatorade after working out?"

"Hell yeah." Reed looked sideways at Barker. "What do you weigh these days, Irwin? Two-fifty, two-sixty?"

Barker took another long drag from his Pall Mall. "Sumpin' like that." He looked over at Reed. "Shit, you do look in good shape."

"I am."

"How's your head?" Reed didn't respond, except to take another sip of his screwdriver. "You don't drink all day, do you?"

"Not lately."

"Right."

They both looked out at the pond, watching the breeze play across the surface. Irwin tossed his cigarette in the bushes behind him. "So how bad is it, Bill? I been keeping my distance for a while now, but I figured I'd drop by and see what's up."

"How'd you know where to drop by?"

"Same way I know about your morning workouts."

"Yeah, all right Nanuck, but why now? Are the clients getting restless?"

Irwin shrugged. "I don't know. I doubt it. Adele's so goddamn buttoned-up. She's spreading the work out with a couple of freelance guys. I jump in when asked. So far everybody seems comfortable with the sixth-month sabbatical thing."

"Uh-huh. Who said it was six months?"

"I don't know. Adele, I guess." Irwin looked over at Reed. "So is it six months or what?"

"It's already been six months."

"So?"

"So what?"

"So you don't give a shit, is that what I'm getting?"

Reed sucked up another mouthful of his screwdriver, deciding whether to answer.

"I sure as hell don't give a shit about locating some philandering husband's assets or figuring out the latest corporate twist on hiding profits."

Irwin shrugged. "Sometimes it's fun."

Reed didn't respond.

After a moment, Irwin quietly asked, "So one more time—how bad is it?"

Reed fidgeted, uncomfortable in his utilitarian chair, suddenly wishing the chair had armrests so he could brace himself. He hunched forward, resting his forearms on his thighs. Then, staring at the ground, talking as much to himself as to Irwin Barker, he began.

"It's pretty bad. I don't know what I expected, but this is fucking bad, Irwin."

"It ain't getting better?"

"Not the way I want it to."

"What do the doctors say?"

"Fuck the doctors."

"Why?"

Reed snorted with disgust. "It's all a bunch of bullshit. A bunch of compartmentalized specialists each doing their little jobs. That's the way it was in the hospital, that's the way it is now." Reed took another sip, feeling the vodka now seeping through him, relaxing him. "The medical system is a very sophisticated operation that works very stupidly sometimes, Irwin. You've got some really smart people on top, and a massive amount of advanced technology and equipment, but mostly it's a bunch of intimidated underlings carrying out orders given by people who are too busy or too lazy to give a shit about what's really going on."

"I'm not sure I follow you."

Reed waved a hand as if to dismiss the whole issue. "It's not important."

"Yeah it is. What's the main problem?"

Reed sat up. "All right, it started in the hospital. In my situation, my amputation, I didn't have time to prepare for it. Most amputations, people know it's coming. They set things up, get their head straight. I didn't have that. Plus, I had this raft of other problems—the busted arm, screwed-up shoulder, banged-up hip—basically everything on my left side torn up or broken. So in addition to not being ready for it, I couldn't use crutches or a walker. I couldn't even stand on the temporary prosthesis. There was no way I would walk, but they just kept pushing along with the exercises and stump care, the prosthetic fittings, and their infuriating advice."

"Didn't they make adjustments?"

"Nobody seemed able to get that concept." Reed paused, as if remembering it all again. "Except for one person, an older woman, but she wasn't really part of the medical team. She was a social worker named Mrs. Carpenter. Sarah Carpenter. Feisty little bird. She didn't take any of my crap. She could see I was just pushing to get up and out of there. Finally, she sidled up to my bedside and looked me in the eye and asked me how long did I think it took her to get comfortable walking on her leg."

"Oh, she was an amputee, too?"

"Yeah, AKA like me, but right side."

"Also Known As?"

"No, Detective. Above Knee Amputee."

"Oh. So how long?"

Reed gave Irwin a rueful grin. "Hell, I figured she wanted me to guess on the high side, right?"

"Yeah?"

"So I said, three years."

"Three years?"

"Yeah. That's what I said. She looks at me and says—thirteen years."

"Thirteen! She was serious?"

"Yeah. She really wasn't exaggerating. She went through three different prostheses, two surgeries, and she tells me she's still faster on her crutches."

"Christ."

"Obviously that's not the norm. And the technology is a

hell of a lot more advanced than when she went through it. And her initial surgery was screwed up."

"Was yours?"

"No. At least they said it wasn't. You know, there's more to it than just chopping off a limb. If they fuck up your nerve endings or don't leave enough padding, you're screwed."

"So how're you doing now? You look all healed."

Reed bent and flexed his left arm, rolled his neck and shoulders.

"Yeah. The left hip still feels a little twingy, but the working out helps. I'm doing the crutches and chair and all. You'd be amazed at how much walking on crutches takes out of you."

"I never thought about it."

"You never broke a leg, sprained an ankle?"

"Been shot twice, but never been on crutches."

"Big as you are, Irwin, even with your strength, you'd be screwed hauling that weight around."

Irwin thought about that for a few moments, then asked, "So getting back to the booze, why fuck everything up with drinking?"

"What is this, some sort of half-assed intervention?"

"Just a question."

"I'd rather medicate myself with alcohol than the goddamn painkillers and mind-benders they're so anxious to give me."

"You sure you don't need 'em. For depression or something."

"Hey, you lose your fucking leg, you're supposed to be depressed."

"You sound more pissed off than depressed to me. So how long until you're actually walking?"

"I am walking. I use a crutch to hop around the house. Two crutches for up to a few blocks or so. I can stand the leg for maybe three, four blocks, tops. I use the chair when I'm going farther. Or carrying stuff. But to be up and around on the prosthesis all day, I'm figuring a year. The problem is basically the stump. It keeps changing. Getting smaller. We keep doing fittings. There's this pressure thing, a liner, it's got to be just right. The goddamn prosthesis is pretty complex. The knee joint, the Flex-Foot. You go through all this physical therapy and working with the prosthetist. It's very trying. Fittings, castings, measurements, deciding on hardware and mechanical devices. It's trial and error and pain. You can't really get the prosthetist to decide anything until he's tried something, every time he tries something, it takes time." Reed absent-mindedly massaged his left thigh, as if gauging the status of his stump. "The first socket was too tight. Then too loose. The thing slipped around. I got blisters on the back of my thigh. And then, of course, there's the lovely little zing of phantom pain when I take a wrong step."

"Phantom pain?"

"Not to be confused with phantom sensation."

"What's that?"

"That's when it feels like your leg is really there, but it's not. For a while, when I'd be lying in the hospital bed, it would feel like my knee was bent and my leg was going down through the mattress hovering above the floor." Reed bent his arm into an L shape pointing down. "It wasn't there, but I had this horrible urge to straighten out my leg."

"Shit. So what's the phantom pain thing?"

"Oh, that's a beaut. That's when it feels like someone shoved an electric cattle prod into my shin . . . which isn't there."

"No shit."

"It usually happens when I take a wrong step with the prosthesis on. Something to do with the nerve endings. They say it resolves over time." Reed waved a hand. "Fuck it. It's boring. You don't really want to hear about all this, Irwin. I know you."

"Yeah, I do. I mean, I know you're not exactly in the swing of things, but you are coming out of it, aren't you?"

"Yes and no."

"What's the no part, what's the part that's still fucking you up?"

Reed grabbed the sides of the wheelchair seat, hunching over, concentrating on trying to come up with the right words. Finally, he said, "The goddamn finality of it, Irwin. The damn, never-ending permanence of it. One second I have two legs, the next, just one. Forever. It's very hard to resist obsessing over it. Believe me, I know all the arguments, all the techniques, but you know, you just keep getting reminded of it too often. Every time you make any move, even shifting in your chair, every time you turn over in bed, you can't escape it, and I don't really think that you, or anybody who hasn't experienced it, can grasp the forever part of it."

Irwin leaned toward Reed, asking. " 'It,' being the—"

"The loss. The permanent loss. With no fucking warning, no chance to relegate yourself to it and no way to ignore the stupidity of it." Reed motioned with his hands as if pointing out the SUV that backed up in front of him. "Some idiot backs up through an intersection to get a parking space, and I lose my leg. Maybe it's just the stupidity of it that I can't shake. I don't know."

"Yeah, well, maybe we ought to find that prick and—"

"Hey, I've thought about that, believe me. It's not the right move."

"No, I suppose not."

"Okay, so that's my report. Now why are you really here? You look like you've been up all night thinking about it."

Irwin flipped his second Pall Mall into the bushes behind them and stared out at the boat pond. "Sort of. I ended up hanging around at Tommy Burns's bar until closing, so I just figured I'd stay up."

"Okay. So what's going on? Somebody suing us? Some pain-in-the-ass client looking for me?" Irwin shook his head. "Did Adele badger you into having a sit-down?"

"Ah, you know Adele, she's always buggin' me about you. But no, that's not it. None of that shit." Again, Irwin turned to face Bill Reed. He nodded, more to himself than to Reed. "Okay." And then he reached into the breast pocket of his suit jacket and extracted an envelope. "I didn't want to lay this on you if you were all fucked up or something. I mean, I know you have a shitload of problems right now. And I didn't want to add onto the pile, but I figure unless you're a lot worse off than I think you are, you have to see this."

Irwin extended the envelope toward Reed, who didn't look at it, but simply asked, "I see you've opened it. What's in it?"

"A message from your cousin."

"My cousin?"

"Yeah."

"I only have one cousin, Irwin, and I assume you recall his situation. He is not able to write a letter."

"It's not a letter."

Frowning, Reed reached out slowly and took the envelope from Irwin's outstretched hand. He turned the envelope over and examined the outside. The address read: Bill Reed, c/o Reed & Barton, with the New York address of Reed's office written clearly underneath. The return section on the envelope bore the initials JBR, but the crude printing was as much a picture as a set of initials. The three scrawled letters had little to do with writing, but everything to do with revealing the very limited mental capacity of the writer.

Reed stared at the envelope.

"The address . . . it's written in a woman's hand. No zip code. I'll bet she got it from a phone book or a telephone operator. John certainly couldn't have given it to her."

Irwin Barker nodded in agreement.

Reed extracted a single sheet of paper and unfolded it. His head jerked slightly at the sight of it, a confused expression clouding his face. After a moment, he looked up at Irwin and asked, "What do you make of this?"

Irwin turned to look at the page for a moment, as if to expose himself to the image again, but only briefly, then he returned his gaze to the placid waters of the model boat pond.

Someone, presumably Reed's cousin, had painstakingly glued about a hundred tiny individual letters and numbers onto the page, randomly, spread out in no particular pattern. The six point letters and numbers were all the same type font, carefully cut from the same page of print. Drawn over many of the pasted numbers and letters was a ragged blob of tortured lines comprised of pencil, crayon, paint, and black ink. The colors were almost all earth-toned with some swirls of yellow and red. Every line and all the colors had been drawn from the four edges of the paper, converging toward the center of the page, all meeting and clashing in a mass of twisted, writhing colors and strands. Buried under the lines, barely visible, but surrounded by a bright yellow highlight, there seemed to be a tiny stick figure with a round circle for a torso. The overall impression was that of a small figure attacked by the elements on the rest of the page.

Reed continued staring at the page. Finally, he said, "What do you make of it?"

"Hell if I know. Whatever it is, it don't look like good news to me."

Reed asked, "I don't suppose you looked into this at all."

"No. I didn't know how you'd want to deal with it."

Reed sat back in his chair and closed his eyes for a moment. Irwin asked, "You had any contact with him lately?"

"Not since before my accident. Actually, not for a long time."

"What about his family?"

"There isn't any family. His father, my Uncle Leonard, has been dead for almost seven years. His wife was—is—a psycho. She's been out of the picture for years. A long time. About a week after John Boyd got placed in that residence, she took off to somewhere in England. I doubt if she's even sent him a Christmas card in the last fifteen years."

"Is that how long he's been institutionalized?"

"Yes. Two days after they finally got him placed, *two days* mind you, she ran off. My uncle didn't bother to try to convince her otherwise. Or go out of his way to stay in touch with her. It was good riddance. I'm John's only family, but obviously, we're not that close."

Once again, Reed stared at the strange message. Irwin Barker sat with him in silence for a few moments, ran a hand through his hair, pursed his lips, rubbed a forefinger under his nose, then stood up from the park bench. He turned to Reed, facing him now, leaning forward slightly as if to compensate for the fact that Reed remained seated in the wheelchair.

"Well, I'll be on my way. When you figure out what you want to do, call me. For whatever. You hear me?"

Distracted, Reed nodded. "Yeah. Sure. Thanks, Irwin. I will. I will."

"You fucking better."

Irwin turned and walked off. Reed watched him go. Then suddenly, he called out, "Irwin."

The big man stopped and turned.

"Thanks."

A tight, quick smile, another small nod, and the big man shambled off.

Reed slowly folded the strange page from his cousin and replaced it in the envelope, holding the envelope as if he didn't know what to do with it.

Instead of the day becoming warmer, it had cooled off. Reed felt sticky and stiff from his workout and would have preferred to be home, but he didn't move. The tortured lines and scrambled print on the bedraggled page had immobilized him.

He thought about his cousin, John Boyd Reed, a short, stocky, dark-haired, middle-aged man whose face and body bore the indelible features of a person with Down syndrome.

Reed had known his cousin ever since they were both children, but they had never formed a deep relationship. Reed had always excused himself from making the effort to form a relationship by telling himself his cousin was retarded and could not relate to him in any meaningful way. But somewhere in a place Reed never examined too closely, he knew that his excuse was exactly that—an excuse, an evasion. He had never formed a relationship with John Boyd Reed because he never wanted to work past the difficulties. Certainly not as a child. Perhaps, as an adult, Reed had been more inclined to try, but he had never followed the inclination, ignoring it until it withered away.

So why follow it now? he asked himself. I've got enough damn problems of my own. Who knows what the hell this means?

But as he sat in the park, the picture-letter in his hand, the image on the page would not leave him. The message was too clear, too stark.

He muttered a simple curse. "Shit." And then Reed asked himself, "How the hell did he get this to me?"

Reed knew part of the answer. His cousin was retarded, but that didn't mean he was weak or passive. As a child, John Boyd had always been good-humored and affectionate. He almost always responded to any attention given him with a smile. Even as an adult, John Boyd had a habit of reaching out and patting you on the shoulder or hugging you for no apparent reason other than spontaneous affection, asking nothing in return.

But Reed had never considered his cousin just a simple, puppylike person who smiled whenever you spoke to him or patted his head. He saw a complexity in John Boyd, a willfulness. John Boyd was retarded, but he was not simple. Bill Reed could well imagine him pestering and agitating and persevering until he found someone to help him find Reed's address, write that address on an envelope, stamp it, mail it, keeping at it until somehow that letter arrived in Reed's hands, a letter that instantly and efficiently communicated a chilling sense of pain and trouble.

Reed ran a hand through his thick brown hair, stiff now from dried sweat.

"So now what?" he said out loud.

He shoved the letter into the pocket of his windbreaker. Reed began the uphill push out of the park to Fifth Avenue.

Reed made it out of the park and pushed over the sidewalk and cobblestone to drop down the curb into Fifth Avenue where he could hail a cab.

He sat hunched over in the chair, morose, waiting for a familiar yellow cab to come into view. And he sat, waiting, thinking, This is the last goddamn thing I need now.

TWO

In 1958, Mathius Ullmann founded the Ullmann Institute. A strict but compassionate man, Mathius believed he had devised a reliable method for housing adults suffering from a wide range of learning disabilities and mental retardation. He provided a clean, safe place to live and required that his residents work at a job, engage in rigorous daily outdoor activities no matter what the weather, and follow guidelines and procedures designed to instill a sense of order, obedience, and responsibility. Mathius Ullmann believed even the most severely impaired could understand those concepts on some level if presented consistently and fairly.

In 1983, his son Matthew Ullmann joined the institute's staff after graduating from Wharton Business School. Matthew immediately assumed the mantle of heir apparent to his father. The senior Ullmann died of pancreatic cancer four years later, leaving the institution to his son, Matthew, and his daughter-in-law, Madeleine.

Outwardly, little else about the institution had changed since its founding. It occupied a two-hundred-acre campus, mostly woods. On twenty acres of land at the south end of the property were located three two-story dormitories, a clinic building, an administration building, a woodworking shop, the kitchen/dining hall, vegetable gardens, a barn, various outbuildings and sheds, and four run-down but functional houses used by staff, most of whom were required to live on campus.

One place on the institute campus that was decidedly not run-down was Matthew Ullmann's office in the administrative building. It occupied a corner of the single-story, brick structure situated near the entrance to the institute. The office's furnishings were suitable for an executive: a large cherry-wood desk with a return for Matthew Ullmann's computer and printer, a credenza for his books and records, two leather guest chairs, and a wrought-iron coffee table with glass top and a leather couch.

The office afforded Matthew Ullmann a nearly panoramic view of the North Country landscape lying to the south of the institute, but instead of looking out his double-wide set of corner windows, Ullmann sat staring at his computer screen, occasionally sliding and clicking his mouse and stabbing at the keyboard. When he heard the knock on his office door, he did not turn away from the screen.

"Yes?" he yelled, elongating the word to convey his annoyance.

Gladys Richards opened the office door slowly and extended her pudgy hand toward Ullmann, "The phone messages, sir."

Now Ullmann swiveled to his left, peering at Gladys through his wire-framed glasses. Matthew Ullmann was a stocky man of average height, square-faced. He had large eyes and bushy eyebrows, thick lips and thinning dark hair combed to the right to cover his balding pate. He tried to hide his girth under expensive sweaters, with limited success. Ullmann spoke rapidly, almost always impatiently, and treated nearly everyone with disdain, particularly Gladys Richards.

He motioned for Gladys to bring him the batch of phone messages. Gladys, a short woman whose obesity had grown to the point that her support hose rubbed audibly as she walked, headed for Ullmann's desk.

Ullmann motioned for her to hurry up.

Gladys tried to move her considerable weight more quickly, but the attempt only irritated Ullmann more. He sneered at the *swish, swish* sound of her nylon stockings rubbing against her formidable thighs. Seeing his expression, Gladys tried to walk in such a way as to reduce the noise, which caused her to walk more slowly, irritating Ullmann even further.

Gladys handed Ullmann the carbonless copies of phone messages that had been entered into a logbook. She patted her hairspray-stiff hair, standing in front of Ullmann, waiting. Hardly bothering to look at his secretary, Ullmann took the phone messages and without expression said, "Thank you."

Gladys smiled at her boss, then retreated toward the door. Ullmann sneered at her back while she exited, then turned his attention to the messages. The pile of slips covered yesterday, Wednesday, and the first half of today, Thursday.

Each message had been written on a form that told Ullmann a quick story—the caller, the time, the purpose of the call. He required that every call to the institute pass through the main line. No one received calls directly. Every call had to be entered into the message book, even if it had been immediately put through to the proper party. Matthew Ullmann believed nobody at the institute had the right to speak to anybody outside the institute without him knowing about it.

There were twenty-seven phone messages. Not many for an operation that housed one hundred twelve residents.

Three entries quickly caught his attention. As per his orders, they had been circled because they indicated contact between a family member and a resident of the institute. The first message indicated that Erica Park's mother had phoned. Mrs. Park, a frail woman approaching eighty-two, called every Wednesday evening without fail, despite the fact that her fifty-one-year-old daughter Erica spoke not much more than single syllables and a few words she remembered from watching a great deal of television at a young age.

The second and third circled message drew more attention from Ullmann. The messages simply stated: William Reed for Johnny Boy Reed. The callback box on the forms had been checked. Ullmann stared at the messages. The first call from William Reed had been received at 2:20 P.M. on Wednesday. The second, 11:00 A.M. on Thursday. Ullmann could not conjure up any image of William Reed, although he had a vague recollection of another family member besides Johnny Boy's father visiting around Christmastime several years ago.

Ullmann checked the phone numbers. The area code told him the calls had originated in New York City. Ullmann swiveled back to his computer, pulled up his database program, and typed in the name Reed. A screen appeared showing him Johnny Boy's records. He tabbed down to the section that recorded visits and hit the enter button, bringing up another screen. Johnny Boy Reed had received regular visits from his father for a little over eight years. They ceased with the father's death seven years prior. In the past seven years, he had received three visits, the last one four years prior, all from William Reed. No other contact of any kind, except for a Christmas card and gift every year after the last visit, also from William Reed.

Ullmann chewed the nail of his right thumb as he reconfirmed that Johnny Boy Reed had for years been without family contact of any significance. So why the sudden interest now?

Ullmann turned away from the computer screen and scanned the other phone messages. Nothing else interested him. He yelled out, "Gladys."

When his assistant came hurrying in, Ullmann simply held the phone message slips out to her, facing at his computer screen, saying nothing. She took the slips and left the office without a word. Ullmann knew she would now dutifully walk to a file cabinet in the outer office and file the phone messages in the proper place. Ullmann also knew that in the six years Gladys had been filing the messages away, he had never asked her to retrieve one. He took particular pleasure in knowing that Gladys would never have the temerity to ask if she could stop filing the messages or throw any of them out.

Later that same day, Thursday, another call from William Reed came in for Johnny Boy Reed. Another message was dutifully entered in the logbook.

An hour later, when Reed called for the fourth time in two days, the switchboard answered as usual. "The Ullmann Institute," she said. "How can I help you?"

"Yes, this is Bill Reed, again. Can I ask you a question?"

There was a hesitation on the line before the female voice said, "Uh, yes."

"How come you keep asking how can I help you, when you don't seem to be helping at all?"

"Excuse me?"

"I've been calling for two days. I ask to speak to my cousin, you tell me he's not available, then take a message. I haven't heard back from anyone. Has he been getting my messages?"

"Oh, sir, all the messages get forwarded to the administration building."

"And then what?"

"Well, uh, they . . ."

"They what? What happens to the messages? Do they give them to the residents?"

"Oh, I, I . . ."

"Do you know?" A few moments passed. *"Could you transfer me to the administration building?"*

"Who did you want to talk to?"

"Whoever is in charge. Mr. Ullmann, let me talk to Mr. Ullmann."

"Mr. Ullmann?"

"Yeah, Ullmann. Is he still running that place?"

"Oh, yes, sir."

The voice sounded surprised at the question.

"Is he available?" Reed asked.

"Uh, I'll see. Hold on."

"Thank you."

Gladys Richards picked up the call, "Hello, Mr. Ullmann's office. How can I help you?"

Reed, trying to control his growing irritation, answered, *"Mr. Ullmann, please."*

"May I ask who's calling?"

"Bill Reed. John Reed's cousin."

"Just a moment."

The line went silent as he was put on hold.

Gladys Richards pushed the intercom button on her phone and said, "Uh, Mr. Ullmann, there's a Mr. Reed on the phone for you."

Inside his office, Matthew Ullmann officiously waved a hand in the air, refusing to turn away from his computer screen and shouted back, "Tell him I'm in a meeting."

Reed listened to the woman's voice come back on.

"Sir, Mr. Ullmann is in a meeting."

"A meeting."

"Yes."

"Oh, really. Who is he meeting with?"

"What?" asked Gladys, her voice registering surprise.

"Who is he meeting with? And when do you expect the meeting to be over?" asked Reed.

"Oh, I don't know," said Gladys.

Reed sat in his living room overlooking Central Park. Scattered lights in apartment buildings on the east side of the park gleamed against the twilight descending upon the city. Reed had yet to turn on any lights in his apartment. He sat slumped in a deeply cushioned club chair, the phone to his ear. He pictured the person at the other end of the phone line, forming an impression of her by the way she spoke and the words she used. She sounded tentative, easily flustered when made to vary from her stock phrases. He imagined her as a person who mostly took orders, not as a self-appointed gatekeeper, not as someone who took it upon herself to screen the boss's calls.

Reed's voice softened.

"Excuse me, who am I talking to?"

"I'm Gladys Richards," she said without hesitation. Reed noted the lack of dissembling in the response.

"Gladys, could you do me a favor?" Reed asked.

"Yes?"

Reed heard a hint of question in her voice, making Gladys

sound like a vulnerable person. He made an effort to sound friendly.

"Could you give Mr. Ullmann a message for me?"

"*Oh, yes,*" she said. "*Of course.*"

"Could you please tell him that I would like him to call me back as soon as he's finished with his meeting." Reed emphasized the word *meeting* just enough so as to convey to Gladys that he didn't for one second believe Mr. Ullmann was in a meeting, and that she and he now shared a pact with each another, both silently agreeing to accept the lie for the moment.

"*Call you back,*" repeated Gladys. "*Yes. I'll tell him.*"

"Tell him, please, it's very important that he call me back. Tell him this is my fourth call to you folks in two days. Tell him I need to hear from him today. I'll give you my number."

"*Okay,*" said Gladys.

She asked him to repeat part of his phone number twice, but Reed didn't mind because it meant she was actually writing the number down. He thanked her and hung up the phone, wondering exactly why the people at the Ullmann Institute were making it so difficult to contact his cousin.

Reed stared out at his view of Central Park, shaking his head. Are they incompetent? Confused? Or just don't give a shit?

Gladys Richards hefted her bulk out of her office chair and took the message to Matthew Ullmann's office. She knocked on the closed, solid wood door.

"What?"

She opened the door, holding out the slip of paper.

"A Mr. Reed called. He said it was very important that you call him back."

Ullmann, still staring at his computer screen, raised his voice, "What?"

Gladys opened and closed her mouth without saying a word, holding out the slip of paper with Reed's phone number in her hand.

"Go," said Ullmann.

She returned to her desk.

Ullmann logged off the Web site he had been checking and once again brought up his database program. He continued moving his cursor and tabbing down to successive fields and screens, moving through information about Johnny Boy Reed until he found what he was looking for.

Talking to himself he said, "Who the hell is this idiot?" He grunted as he read the entry on the screen . . . William Reed, cousin.

"A cousin?"

Ullmann highlighted Reed's entry and stabbed the enter key. Reed's name and business address came up on a separate page: Reed & Barton, Inc. No home address.

Reed & Barton, Inc.? wondered Ullmann. What the hell is that?

Ullmann picked up the phone and dialed the number displayed on his screen for Reed & Barton, Inc. Adele Simpson answered on the first ring, speaking briskly, *"Good afternoon, Reed and Barton."*

"William Reed, please."

"Mr. Reed is not in, may I take a message?"

Ullmann hesitated, realizing he must have called a number different from the one given to Gladys.

"When do you expect him in?" asked Ullmann.

Adele answered crisply, *"Who's calling, please?"*

"Matthew Ullmann."

"Mr. Ullmann, we don't give out Mr. Reed's schedule. May I take a message?"

"Do you have another number where I can reach him?"

"What is the nature of your call, Mr. Ullmann?"

"I'm returning his call."

"If you give me your number, I'll have Mr. Reed call you when he checks in."

At his end of the line, Ullmann sneered and said, "Goodbye," abruptly hanging up on the woman who apparently thought she could tell him what to do.

Adele Simpson, a trim woman in her sixties, dressed in one of her impeccable business suits with perhaps a simple string of pearls, sitting in the office adjacent to his, her antique leather-topped desk in front of her, a workstation behind her on which sat a state-of-the-art computer, a color scanner, a fax, and a high-speed laser printer. She frowned at the rude response, pushed the flash button on her console, and speed-dialed Reed's home phone, expecting to leave a message on his call answering. To her surprise, Reed picked up the phone on the first ring.

"Yes," he said, with just enough inflection to make it sound almost like a question, as if someone had tapped him on the shoulder, interrupting his thoughts.

"Mr. Reed, it's Adele."

"Oh," he said, sounding surprised.

"Mr. Reed, I just had a call for you from a Mr. Ullmann. He said he was returning your call."

"Yes, Ullmann, but why is he calling me there?"

"I don't know."

"Did he say anything else, Adele?"

"Nothing. No message. Then hung up rather rudely."

"Oh?"

"I asked for his number so you could call him back and got a curt 'good-bye' and a hang up."

"Really? How charming."

"Yes."

"Well, I'm sorry about that, Adele. I'll take care of it."

"Not your fault, Mr. Reed. Some people are just that way."

"Yes, they are, aren't they? Okay, Adele, thanks."

"Call me if you need me."

"Right."

Reed hung up softly, knowing that Adele would have liked to prolong the conversation, to find out how he was doing, what he was doing.

He sat back in his comfortable club chair, gazing out his

window, the living room darkening in the fading daylight. What the hell is going on? he wondered.

Reed picked up the phone receiver and started to dial the Ullmann Institute's number, but stopped. *Four damn phone calls, and he calls back to a different number I didn't give them? The guy must have ignored my message. Just looked me up in a file.*

Reed punched in the number. This time, he didn't wait for the receptionist's standard greeting to end. "Connect me to Mr. Ullmann's office, please," saying it in a way that cut off any response.

As soon as Gladys Richards answered, Reed said, "Gladys, it's me, Bill Reed. Let me talk to Mr. Ullmann. He just called me."

Reed waited on hold. He reached over and switched on the light next to his chair, clenching his teeth slightly, waiting, making an effort to give Matthew Ullmann the benefit of the doubt.

Matthew Ullmann came on the line, *"Hello?"*

"Mr. Ullmann, Bill Reed here."

"Yes?"

"John Reed's cousin."

"Yes?"

The man on the other end sounded as if he were in a hurry and had little time or patience for this call. Reed's voice hardened, getting right to the point.

"How is he?"

"Who?"

"My cousin. John Reed. How is he?"

"He's fine. Why do you ask?"

"There are no problems? He's well?"

"Yes, of course. Why do you ask?"

"Because I've been trying to talk to him for two days now and I can't seem to get through to him."

"Is that why you called my office?"

"Yes."

"I just called you back."

"I know. You didn't call the number I left. You called my office."

Ullmann said, *"Yes,"* but not in any way that acknowledged Reed's point. He asked Reed, sounding annoyed, *"Is there a reason you're calling me? Is there some sort of emergency?"*

Reed, making an effort to keep from shouting, said, "No, but how do you know there isn't? This is my fifth phone call."

"I wasn't aware of that. So there's no emergency."

"Why hasn't anybody given John my messages? Why hasn't he called me back?"

"Sir, most of our residents need help with that. You should call when he's available to come to the phone. His proctor will bring him to the phone. You have to call when he's at his dorm. I don't have your cousin's schedule memorized. I'll put you on with my assistant. She can give you his schedule."

Reed heard the line go silent as Ullmann put him on hold. He yelled into the line, "Hey! *Hey!*" And then Reed heard a stuttering click and a second later the infuriating hum of a dial tone. Reed cursed and slammed his phone down.

Reed picked up the phone and punched the redial button, the anger in him rising so strongly that he felt his neck and jaw tighten. But before the call went through, he hung up the phone.

"Calm down," he told himself.

He slid to the edge of the club chair and braced his right calf against the chair. He pushed himself up, balancing on one foot, grabbed a single crutch resting against the end table, and hopped over to his window, expending the effort as much to release his anger as to give himself time to calm down.

"Asshole."

The hell with it, he told himself. He said John was all right.

But Reed couldn't shake the anger he felt at Ullmann's officious, cavalier treatment of his call. The infuriating disdain—particularly considering the person involved—a person with Down syndrome.

Reed saw the face of his cousin, John, a round, eager-to-please face smiling at him, a retarded man who couldn't read, couldn't speak very well, and yet for some reason had painstakingly constructed a complicated picture message, found a person to help him, had explained about a cousin in New York, and had persuaded the person to look up Reed's address, address an envelope, stamp it, and mail it.

Reed grimaced. Suddenly a flux of emotions welled up in him: shame, guilt, anger, not a single emotion, not even an emotion he could identify. It was a surge of feeling, an overpowering sensation comprised of guilt and defeat, anger and frustration, shame and ineptitude, all of it cascading inside, culminating in a profound sense of regret.

His retarded cousin could get a message delivered into his hands, and he couldn't even get a simple phone call put through to him. With a half snarl, half curse, Reed headed toward his bedroom.

He recalled the location of the institute . . . far up north and west in New York State, up past the Thruway, up the North Way a good distance and then fifty miles west, near an isolated, nowhere town called Dumphy.

Reed leaned on his crutch, stepping through his dark bedroom toward the desk that occupied one wall of his bedroom. He sat down and booted-up his computer, propped his crutch against the desk, pushed a pile of papers out of his way, flipped on his printer, moving methodically now, compelled to feel productive, to feel as if he were accomplishing something.

He logged onto the Internet, sliding and clicking his mouse until book marked pages took him to a site that would provide a map to Dumphy, New York. He quickly typed in his point of origin, his destination, staring at the screen, waiting for an illustration of the roads that would lead him to the Ullmann Institute.

"Come on," he said.

The screen blinked. The route appeared. Reed squinted at the road numbers, remembering now, his finger hovering in front of the screen.

"Yeah, okay, asshole, you don't want to talk on the phone, let's see how you like talking to me face-to-face."

THREE

Johnny Boy Reed sat in the dayroom of his dormitory, Davis Hall, staring out the window, his thick legs crossed, his chin resting in the cup of his right hand, ironically mimicking the pose of Rodin's *The Thinker*.

He wore a red-plaid flannel shirt, brown corduroy pants secured with a wide, black leather belt, white socks, and crepe-soled brown Hush Puppies shoe-boots. Johnny Boy Reed had dressed himself that morning, as he did every morning, proud of the fact that he could do so without assistance, including tying his own shoelaces.

Johnny Boy sat staring out the only window in the twenty-by-twelve-foot room. In another chair that had been carefully placed near Johnny Boy ten minutes earlier sat a thirty-eight-year-old woman with Down syndrome named Pauline Trainor. When Pauline had come into the dayroom and taken her place next to Johnny Boy, she had smiled at him. Johnny Boy was her boyfriend and she his girlfriend, so being together usually made Johnny Boy happy. But Johnny Boy had returned her smile only briefly, saying just, "Hi Pauline."

Pauline had answered, "Hi Johnny." He smiled again, briefly, but hadn't reached out to touch her elbow or squeeze her hand gently as he normally would.

Pauline blinked at Johnny Boy and sat next to him saying questioningly, " ''Tomach?"

Johnny Boy's tight smile told Pauline everything she wanted to know. Pauline nodded once and contented herself with simply sitting quietly next to Johnny Boy Reed.

Once settled in next to Johnny Boy, Pauline did not attract attention. At not quite five feet tall, Pauline was even shorter than Johnny Boy. And although Pauline's figure definitely could be called pudgy, her movements were very economical, almost dainty. She could occupy a space and hardly move at all, sitting with a contented half smile, dressed in her white blouse and an ankle-length green corduroy jumper, corduroy being the Ullmann Institute clothing of choice, as it provided the extra warmth needed to North Country residents with winter coming on.

In ten more minutes, Pauline would be off to barn duty, and Johnny Boy would join the work crew heading out to stack wood behind the dining hall. So for those ten minutes, Pauline would just be with Johnny Boy.

Not much happened in the dayroom. A 1984 seventeen-inch television sat on a shelf bolted to the far wall of the room. The TV's reception depended on an antennae attached to the roof. There were no cable or satellite stations broadcast to the residents of Davis Hall. Only three network stations. And there were no Ping-Pong tables, craft supplies, books, or records in the day room. Only three wooden tables and a half-dozen chairs, the kind made out of fiberglass-colored neon shades of yellow and red, with scooped out seats and spindly iron legs.

Four other women, none of them with Down syndrome but all with varying levels of mental retardation, sat in a tight little group, nestled in a corner of the dayroom. Three of the women spoke mostly at each other rather than to each other, using the phrases they relied on to communicate, speaking in tones of voice nonretarded people would consider too loud. The fourth woman sat with the others, but did not speak.

Johnny Boy faced away from them, sitting on the edge of his plastic chair rocking slightly in an attempt to comfort himself. Occasionally, while he rocked, he absentmindedly straightened his shirt collar or hiked the wide black leather belt firmly cinched around his pants up over his soft, round stomach. Johnny Boy didn't have much of a waist. He was a short, square block of a man, his forty-one-year-old body thickening around the middle. His less than flattering appearance had little effect on Johnny Boy. He maintained a stubborn, concentrated effort to stay neat and clean, and keep his unruly raft of black hair combed. Every morning he slicked his hair down with water and combed it into place.

Johnny Boy also kept close watch over and took good care of his possessions. In fact, he was slightly compulsive about it. His normal voice had a slightly nasal quality as Johnny Boy tended to speak through his nose. If anyone disturbed his belongings, he became distinctly whiny when he chided them about it. He neatly stacked his socks and underwear in a foot locker at the base of his bunk bed. He carefully hung his wardrobe, which consisted of a second pair of corduroy pants, denim blue jeans, three shirts, and a wool pea coat, in a long cubbyhole set in the wall between his bed and his roommate Melvin's.

Again, Johnny Boy hiked at his belt, trying to relieve the discomfort in his abdomen. The bothersome, achy feeling accompanied by nagging constipation had become increasingly more acute. Johnny Boy had gone to the institute's clinic so many times that he did not want to go anymore. But the aches continued, especially in the mornings when he tried to have a bowel movement. Then it really hurt, often making Johnny Boy's eyes tear with pain.

Which was why Johnny Boy had sent the picture message to his cousin Bill. Johnny Boy knew his father was in heaven and couldn't help him. And he knew his mother was gone, although he could not remember where she had gone or why. He had a vague recollection of their housekeeper, a black woman named Emily, but that seemed so long ago and so far away from him as if to be in another lifetime spent in another country.

But Cousin Bill—Cuz'n Bill—Johnny Boy had remembered his Cuz'n Bill. He could still recall an image of his cousin's ruggedly handsome face and thick brown hair and white, perfect teeth. Cuz'n Bill's teeth mesmerized Johnny Boy. And his voice—Johnny Boy remembered Cuz'n Bill's strong, confident voice. Cuz'n Bill's size and voice and manner had sometimes frightened Johnny Boy, until Johnny Boy remembered Cuz'n Bill liked him, and then Cuz'n Bill made Johnny Boy feel safe, his voice and manner casting an aura that made Johnny Boy feel as if everything would be all right; and not just all right, but sometimes even fun. A voice and manner that made Johnny Boy smile and feel relaxed and happy.

Johnny Boy's recollection of Cuz'n Bill was almost enough to take him out of a life that almost always felt crimped and constrained and robbed of joy by ever-present apprehension.

Johnny Boy never really knew enough about what went on around him to feel comfortable and in control. But he knew enough to realize that he didn't know, and worst of all, would never know.

So Johnny Boy sat in his ugly fiberglass, dayroom chair, rocking slightly, shifting to relieve the ache in his abdomen, quietly garnering his memories of Cuz'n Bill, thinking Cuz'n Bill could help make the pain go away, if he would come. If only he would come.

The door at the far end of the dayroom opened and Eddie McAndrews, the Davis Hall proctor, entered. Johnny Boy stopped rocking, stopped thinking about his Cuz'n Bill, turned from the window, and stared at the floor. Pauline stood and walked toward the door, as did the other four women.

"All right," yelled Eddie McAndrews, "let's get on it, boys and girls."

Johnny Boy waited a moment, letting the women go ahead of him, then stood up and joined the exodus.

Eddie McAndrews remained at the doorway. Over a foot taller than anyone else in the room, McAndrews gazed over the heads of those filing out, as if he were looking for someone in the far corners of the dayroom. Johnny Boy kept his head bowed as he shuffled toward the door, but he raised his eyes surreptitiously watching Eddie as he continued to walk toward him.

Johnny Boy heard the high-pitched voice of Eddie McAndrews suddenly call out, "Johnny Boy. Where's my main man, Johnny Boy Reed?" speaking Johnny Boy's name quickly as if it were all one word, looking away from Johnny Boy as if he couldn't find him in the small, nearly empty room.

Johnny Boy did not respond. He continued to walk toward

Eddie, who continued to look above Johnny Boy's head calling out, "JohnnyBoyReed, JohnnyBoyReed, where the hell are you, man?" all the while watching Johnny Boy with his peripheral vision, just waiting for Johnny Boy to reach him.

As Johnny Boy came closer, Eddie let out one more shout directed away from Johnny Boy.

"Yo, Johnny Boy."

Eddie McAndrews reminded Johnny Boy of one of those shouting wrestlers on TV. Eddie wore a white shirt stretched tight over his muscular chest, but loose over his narrow waist and washboard stomach. His sleeves were rolled halfway up his thick forearms. A stringy black tie hung from his thick neck matching his black jeans. Eddie had big hands and big muscles and big veins in his arms. He wore his hair tied back in a long ponytail and always spoke loudly, with an accent, just like a lot of those wrestlers on TV.

As Johnny Boy approached the doorway, he kept his head down and edged past Eddie. And then, just as Johnny Boy made it out the door, just as he thought he made it past his tormentor, McAndrews viciously flicked his middle finger against the top of Johnny Boy's right ear.

The pain shot through Johnny Boy like an electric jolt. He twitched away from the proctor, making a noise that sounded like the yelp of a dog that had been kicked. Eddie acted surprised, as if he had nothing to do with the sharp, burning pain.

"Johnny Boy! There you are, you sum'bitch! Goldammit, you hidin' out on me, boy?"

Johnny Boy had to clench his eyes shut to stop from crying. What had happened? Why was Eddie acting like he hadn't seen him? Hadn't he just hurt him?

And now Eddie changed his manner again, now sounding angry, yelling, "What's with that? You think you're slick enough to slip past me, goddammit?"

Johnny Boy rubbed his ear and frowned at Eddie defiantly.

McAndrews, now friendly, lightly punched Johnny Boy's arm and said, "Hey, don't get pissy with me, shithead. Ise just fucking with ya. Be a sport."

Johnny Boy stepped away from his tormentor. His mouth moved involuntarily as if trying to form a word, but his confusion and frustration prevented any words from forming.

Eddie cupped his ear. "What? What'd you say? I cain't hear you, Johnny Boy."

Johnny Boy just shook his head from side to side.

"What? What's that? You didn't say nothin'?"

Johnny Boy kept shaking his head.

"No? Well if you didn't say nothin', smartass, you must have said something, Johnny Boy. Ain't you ever heard of a double negative? Huh? Huh?" Eddie poked insistently on Johnny Boy's shoulder. "So what did you say, Johnny Boy? What did you say?"

Johnny Boy twisted away from the poking finger, instinctively putting his hand up to ward off the painful prods. Eddie backhanded Johnny Boy's raised arm, his knuckles stinging the edge of the bone just above Johnny Boy's wrist.

Finally satisfied he had extracted his quota of pain, McAndrews magnanimously grabbed Johnny Boy around the shoulders, almost playfully, and said, "All right, take it easy. Come on, forget about the work crew, we got someplace better to go. Come on, straighten up and let's go, or you know what's gonna happen. Come on."

Johnny Boy did not try to shrug off Eddie's grip around his shoulders. He bowed his head, staring at the top of his Hush Puppies while he walked down the hall in Eddie's fake friendly embrace, rubbing the side of his wrist where Eddie's knuckles had smacked him.

"Know where we're goin', Johnny Boy old boy? Huh?"

Johnny Boy kept walking, but he didn't answer. No answer ever satisfied Eddie McAndrews.

"We're goin' to see Mr. Ullmann, Boy."

At the mention of Ullmann's name, enough fear and tension hit Johnny Boy that he thought he might urinate. He did not want to lose control of his bladder. If that happened, Eddie would be very mad.

Eddie released his grip around Johnny Boy's shoulders and

elbowed him lightly on the side of his shoulder. "So what did you do, Johnny Boy? Huh? Come on, what did you do?" With each question, McAndrews poked a bit harder. "Huh? What did you do? You might as well tell me now, Johnny Boy 'cuz you know I'll find out. You better tell me, 'cuz you're gonna get it, Johnny Boy. Mr. Ullmann's gonna give it to you now, Boy, so you might as well tell me."

Johnny Boy Reed had to grab his crotch and squeeze to stop the urine from staining his pants.

As Johnny Boy Reed walked the long walk to Matthew Ullmann's office, Bill Reed sat back in his desk chair, looking at his printouts of maps, tracing the way from Manhattan to Dumphy, New York.

Reed stared at the maps, calculating how many times he would have to stop for gas, and the near impossibility of finding a full service gas station, meaning he would have to maneuver around on his crutches to fill his gas tank. He thought about wearing his prosthesis, just to make pumping gas and using rest rooms more convenient, but he knew he could never endure sitting hour after hour with the artificial limb attached to his stump.

He thought about packing his weekend bag, which would mean crutching his way over to his hall closet and somehow getting the bag off the shelf. And packing food so he wouldn't have to deal with trying to eat in one of those awful, crowded, eternally hectic highway rest stops that nowadays had abandoned any idea of a sit-down restaurant in favor of fast-food franchises that required standing in lines that crawled to the counter.

And then what? Reed wondered. I just show up unannounced looking for John? What if the poor guy doesn't even remember me?

The more Reed thought about the trip and all it would involve, the less he felt like actually doing it. The more he thought about actually traveling to the Ullmann Institute, the more his previously motivating emotions evaporated under the heat of the apprehensions that plagued him.

"The hell with it," he said, thinking to himself, It's stupid to just go up there half-cocked. I'll call them again in the morning, early. I'll make them wake up John if I have to. Find out what the hell is going on. Just get him on the phone and talk to him, try and figure out what's going on before I travel way the hell up there for no reason.

Reed straightened up the papers on his desk, held on to his desk, and stood up on his one leg, grimacing with the effort. Hungry now, he made his way to the kitchen, trying to figure out what he would prepare for his dinner, and trying not to think about how he would make himself understood over the phone to a severely retarded cousin he hadn't spoken to in four years.

FOUR

Matthew Ullmann watched Eddie McAndrews walk Johnny Boy Reed into his office, holding the much smaller Down syndrome man by the left arm as if he were in need of constant control.

Ullmann assumed McAndrews would be squeezing Johnny Boy's arm hard enough to cause at least some pain, but Ullmann did not see any discomfort registering on Johnny Boy's face. As McAndrews pushed Johnny Boy into a straight-back chair that had been placed in front of Ullmann's desk, Ullmann tried to gauge what that meant. Some of them didn't seem to register pain as easily as normal people. Was that it? Or was this one just being stubborn? As with most of the residents, Ullmann had had so little interaction with Johnny Boy Reed that he had no way of judging.

He motioned for Eddie to leave the room. Eddie pushed Johnny Boy's head and told him, "You listen to Mr. Ullmann, you hear?"

Johnny Boy did not respond except to jerk his head away from Eddie. An action that Ullmann interpreted as defiance.

Ullmann waited for his office door to close, then sat on the edge of the desk, hovering over Johnny Boy hunched over in his chair. Ullmann wore expensive wool slacks, a burgundy cashmere V-neck sweater, blue button-down Oxford shirt, and a striped tie. Ullmann brushed an imaginary piece of lint from his slacks, waiting for Johnny Boy to look up at him, but Johnny Boy kept his gaze downward.

Ullmann smiled, but it looked more like a grimace. They usually understood a smile.

"Johnny Boy?" he asked, waiting a moment for Johnny Boy to raise his head. "Johnny Boy, look at me."

Johnny Boy sat resolutely keeping his head down.

The smile left Ullmann's face and he raised his voice, still sounding friendly, but firm.

"Johnny Boy, come on now, look up. I can't talk to you unless you look at me. That's the rule, come on now."

Still, Johnny Boy refused to look up at Ullmann. Once more Ullmann tried, speaking louder, insisting.

"Johnny Boy! I said look at me."

Johnny Boy looked up, startled into doing it, but then quickly bowed his head, avoiding eye contact with Mr. Ullmann.

Ullmann pushed himself off the edge of the desk and calmly walked to a bookshelf, his mouth pursed into a frown. He picked up a cloth-bound copy of the *Physician's Desk Reference,* a sizable book. Ullmann gripped the book by the spine, walked back around his desk, and with one sudden, swift move slapped the book across the side of Johnny Boy Reed's small, round head.

Johnny Boy did not even see the blow coming. A searing, jolting pain exploded along the side of his head and face, made worse by being so unexpected. Johnny Boy grabbed his head, hunched over, squeezing his eyes shut to fend off tears, stifling a keening wail.

Ullmann's voice now turned unctuous, the false sincerity belied by the casual cruelty he had just committed on the small retarded man hunched in front of him.

"Okay, Johnny Boy, I'm sorry I had to give you a treatment, but you really have to look at me. Now stop your crying and look at me, I have to talk to you."

Ullmann placed a crooked forefinger under Johnny's chin and slowly but firmly lifted his head. Johnny Boy did not resist. When they finally made eye contact, Ullmann said, "Okay, that's a good fellow. Now listen carefully. Are you listening?"

Johnny Boy nodded yes.

Ullmann's voice rose again. "I can't hear that, Johnny Boy. Are you listening?"

"Yes," he said, just managing to get out the single word.

"Okay, now, Johnny Boy, I want to know if you've been making any phone calls lately. Did you push the O on the phone and ask the operator to help you call somebody?"

Johnny Boy hesitated, then answered with a quick, sharp "No," the fear and tension in him making the word sound even more nasal than usual.

"Did you ask somebody else to call for you?"

He repeated, "No," inflecting the word now, trying to make it sound emphatic.

"Johnny Boy, you'd better tell me the truth or I'll be very mad at you."

Johnny Boy shook his head, steadfast in his denial. "I didn't."

"Didn't what?"

Johnny Boy struggled with the question, his face contorted by the effort to understand his tormenter.

Ullmann stared at the stocky, middle-aged man with Down syndrome he called boy, making sure to intimidate him, but also looking closely at him, uncertain about Johnny Boy's capabilities. He couldn't gauge Johnny Boy's ability to lie. Ullmann took another tack.

"You have a cousin, right, Johnny Boy?"

Johnny Boy looked at Ullmann, slightly wary. "Yes."

"What's his name?"

Johnny Boy answered slowly, "Cuz'n Bill." His answer sounded like a question.

"That's right, Cousin Bill. Do you know where Cousin Bill lives?"

"New York."

"New York, right. That's right. And you're sure you didn't call him?"

"I didn't. I don't know the phone."

"You don't know the phone? What do you mean? You don't know how to use the phone? Yes you do, Johnny Boy. I think you know how to use the phone."

"I, I, I don't know the phone."

"What do you mean you don't know?"

"I don't know."

"You don't know *how* to use the phone, or you don't know *if* you used the phone?"

Johnny Boy's right leg began to bounce nervously, he grimaced once, then repeated what he had said, only more quickly this time, his voice even more nasal now, pitched higher with tension.

"I don't know the phone."

Ullmann's face pinched with anger and frustration. This was beneath him, this dealing with the retarded. He gripped the thick book. He knew another blow would elicit nothing more, but he wanted the satisfaction of striking out to assuage the offense he endured.

Instinctively sensing the possibility of another blow, Johnny Boy repeated his answer, "I don't know the phone, the phone. I don't know the phone."

There was something strange about the tone of the answer, as if Johnny Boy couldn't finish the sentence. Ullmann had a flash of insight. "You mean the phone number? You don't know the phone number?"

"I don't."

Ullmann, proud of himself, repeated his question more slowly, encouraging Johnny Boy with a knowing smile. "You don't know the phone *number,* right? You don't know the number."

Johnny Boy shook his head. "I don't know it."

Ullmann nodded, closely watching Johnny Boy respond. It seemed like Johnny Boy had understood him. But that brought up an even more remote possibility.

"Johnny Boy," Ullmann asked, "can you write?"

Johnny Boy looked down again.

"Johnny Boy, I asked you something, can you write?"

Slowly, without raising his head, Johnny Boy said, "Yes."

"All right, look at me, Johnny . . . when did you learn how to write, Johnny Boy?"

Johnny Boy quickly looked up. He knew this answer. "When I, when I got my glasses."

"Your glasses?"

"My reading glasses."

Ullmann nodded. "Ah, your reading glasses. So now you can read and write."

"Yeah."

Ullmann frowned for a moment. It was ludicrous, but mostly out of curiosity, Ullmann reached over to his desk and picked up a legal pad and a pencil, handing them to Johnny Boy.

"Write something for me."

Johnny Boy slowly reached into his shirt pocket and pulled out a pair of black framed glasses. He carefully put on the glasses, blinking at the yellow pad of paper as if he didn't quite know where to start.

Ullmann said, "Write, 'Dear Cousin Bill.' "

Nothing.

Ullmann raised his voice, "Go on, write it."

Johnny Boy twitched and turned his attention to the paper, gripping the pencil awkwardly, making circles and curves and lines. It looked as if he were writing in a very large, very or-nate script, but none of the lines formed actual letters. After a few moments, Johnny Boy stopped his elaborate scribbling and concentrated on etching something at the bottom of the page.

When he finished, Ullmann took the pad back and gazed at the page. Other than the painfully drawn letters JBR at the bottom of the page, nothing else resembled a written word.

Ullmann returned to his desk, sat down, and swiveled away from Johnny Boy. He gazed out the window of his corner office. It afforded him a view not of his institutional buildings, but of the back lawn that stepped down to a forested region. The view extended almost five miles through scrub forest and far-off fields, finally ending at the foothills of a choppy range of mountains. A high pressure zone had pulled cold, clear Canadian air into the region. In the fading twilight Ullmann gazed at a landscape dominated by dull brown late fall foliage and scattered maple trees that dotted the landscape with fading red.

Ullmann swiveled back around and looked at Johnny Boy Reed, recognizing the blank gaze that often characterized the mentally retarded. Not a care in the world, Ullmann thought.

"Go on out and tell Eddie we're done."

Johnny Boy bolted out of the office, grimacing as he touched the side of his head. Ullmann watched him leave, surprised at his quickness.

Eddie McAndrews stuck his head into Ullmann's office.

"I take him back?"

"Yes. But wait a minute . . ."

"What?"

Ullmann's antennae had twitched. Ullmann knew defiance when he saw it. A fearful defiance, but defiance nonetheless. Repeated phone calls did not come in from a relative after a four-year silence for no reason. Somehow, some way, Johnny Boy Reed had contacted his cousin. Ullmann could not fathom how he did it, but the defiant act had been committed.

Ullmann turned to look at the calendar hanging next to his desk. Thursday. The weekend approached. Distant, uncommunicative relative suddenly makes contact.

"What's up, boss?"

Still pensive, Ullmann looked up at McAndrews.

"I don't like relatives, Eddie."

"Pains in the ass."

"I especially don't like relatives who show up out of nowhere."

"Right."

"Eddie . . ."

"Yeah?"

"Tonight . . . give Johnny Boy a treatment. A towel treatment."

A grin creased Eddie's horselike face. "*The* towel?"

"Yes."

"You got it, boss."

"Do a good job of it, Eddie."

"No problem."

FIVE

When Eddie McAndrews brought Johnny Boy back to his dormitory room after his meeting with Ullmann, he didn't push at Johnny Boy or torment him. He seemed satisfied to simply tell him, "Stay out of trouble, you old fart."

Johnny Boy lay down on his iron-framed, single bed, his head aching from the blow Ullmann had struck him, his stomach aching from the usual discomfort he felt, both pains intensified by the fear Ullmann had instilled. Matthew Ullmann was the bogeyman, the unseen power, the ultimate authority figure of the institute. He rarely spoke to the residents, and when he did, it always had repercussions, positive or negative. In a world that existed only inside the confines of the Ullmann Institute, Matthew Ullmann occupied the center. For years, Johnny Boy's contact with the outside world had been virtually nonexistent. He could not read or write. He often had no understanding of the words he heard. For Johnny Boy, a television news broadcast was mostly just sound and movement. No one visited him. No one spoke to him except his fellow retarded and the too-busy or too-harsh staff members. He barely remembered his mother. He knew he would never see his father. No one and nothing protected him, comforted him, contacted him.

But now, as Johnny Boy Reed lay in his bed, hurting, rolled into a fetal ball, a smile came to him, a warm feeling stole over him. The ultimate authority figure in his life had spoken the words *Cousin Bill*. Johnny Boy could not perceive the logic of Ullmann's questions. At that moment, he did not even connect the questions to the picture/message he had sent. He did not know why Ullmann had uttered the words, but none of that mattered. Mr. Ullmann had said *Cousin Bill*. Mr. Ullmann had verified that Cousin Bill existed. Cousin Bill was not gone forever like his daddy. He had not been imagined. He was real. Cousin Bill would come. Johnny Boy Reed felt it, knew it, allowed the warm balm of the knowledge to seep into his being and comfort him, telling him that he was not alone in the world.

Johnny Boy fell asleep remembering the image of his daddy and Cuz'n Bill sitting with him in the dayroom of his dorm on a cold North Country day, clean snow blanketing the grounds, colorfully wrapped boxes of Christmas gifts arrayed on the table between them. It felt so long ago to Johnny Boy. So long ago as to seem like a dream.

Two hours later, Eddie McAndrews's foot banged off the steel frame of the bed, startling Johnny Boy out of his already fitful sleep.

Eddie yelled, "Come on, moron, get up. What're you doin' hiding out here, I gotta come looking for you?"

Johnny Boy sat up quickly, not wanting another kick to shake his bed, not quite knowing where he was or what time it had become.

"Come on, Johnny, it's time for your shower. You already

slept through dinner. No more laying around, git your clothes off and git in the shower."

Johnny Boy responded automatically, unbuttoning his shirt, on his feet now, but still in a daze, not realizing that it was Thursday, not Friday, his regular shower day.

He looked in the direction of his tormentor, seeing now that Eddie McAndrews stood with Raymond Boggs, another dorm proctor who worked with McAndrews in Davis Hall where Johnny Boy resided. Boggs stood shoulder-height to McAndrews, but he was thickset, powerfully built. He had a mastifflike head, dark hair glistening with pomade, and despite his shorter-than-average height, Boggs always seemed to be looking up at you with dark eyes, set deep and hooded with thick, black eyebrows. Boggs wore the Ullmann Institute proctors' uniform: a white shirt and tie. But Boggs favored short-sleeve white shirts that emphasized his large biceps and revealed the tangle of crude blue-ink tattoos on his thick forearms.

Boggs stood now, glaring ludicrously at Johnny Boy as if a brute such as Boggs might be needed to control the thoroughly dominated Johnny Boy Reed.

They stood watching Johnny Boy strip down to his baggy briefs, a pair of shorts that had gone through the institution's commercial washing machines so many times with so many colored items of clothing that no amount of bleach would ever turn the underwear into anything but a dingy gray.

Johnny Boy had little perception of his soft, blocky body, but the way Boggs and Eddie looked at him, he instinctively felt a queasy sense of embarrassment mixed with the ever-present feeling of dread whenever McAndrews or Boggs or most of the other male proctors turned their attention to him.

McAndrews, Boggs, and some of the other Ullmann proctors could have just as easily worked as prison guards. Their rough ways and use of force were rarely needed except for a very few, very disturbed residents. But without anyone to restrain them, force and intimidation had become a habit at the Ullmann Institute.

McAndrews yelled at Johnny Boy to take off his shorts. He complied, standing naked, his skin white and soft, almost hairless except for the dark patch of pubic hair that nearly enveloped his stubby penis.

"Go on, git down to the showers. I ain't got all day."

They followed Johnny Boy as he walked down the hallway to the dorm bathroom. When he reached the doorway, McAndrews pushed him inside saying, "Take a shower. You know how."

While Boggs and McAndrews waited in the hallway, Johnny Boy stepped into the dank shower stall, one of two in the bathroom. He turned on the faucets. The restricted institutional showerhead concentrated the stream. Johnny Boy winced as the water hit the side of his head where Ullmann had slapped him with the book.

Johnny Boy followed a routine as he washed, one that had been pounded into him years ago at the institute. Start at the top . . . hair, head, face, pits, crotch, ass, feet. Hair, head, face, pits, crotch, ass, feet, remember the ass. Hair, head, face . . . one of the old proctors, a black man by the name of Peterson, would stand in the bathroom and intone the commands until he was sure his orders were being followed. Mr. Peterson had been hired by Mathius Ullmann. Mr. Peterson had possessed little education or training, but he had taken his job seriously, working hard at it, following the rules, and making sure all the residents followed the rules. Johnny remembered that Mr. Peterson never hit him. Maybe a push once in a while. And he yelled. But he never hit him. And Mr. Peterson had never called him Johnny Boy. He had used his real name, John Boyd, John Boyd Reed, a strong-sounding name that had been taken away and replaced with a child's name.

As the old staff died out, so did John Boyd's name. The newer staff referred to him as Johnny Boy, a name they felt better suited somebody with Down syndrome. It had started so long ago that Johnny Boy had almost forgotten his real name, but he still remembered the wash commands . . . hair, head, face, pits, crotch, ass, feet.

Before Johnny Boy could finish his feet, Eddie McAndrews pounded on the shower stall.

"That's enough, Johnny Boy. Let's go."

When Johnny Boy emerged, still slick with water and soap, he balked at the two who stood with him in the bathroom.

McAndrews in particular looked outfitted to handle toxic waste. Both McAndrews and Boggs wore thick rubber gloves. Not the type they used in the kitchen, not the yellow gloves they made Johnny Boy use when he worked kitchen detail. These were thick black gloves, the ones used to protect against harsh chemicals and acids. In addition to the gloves, McAndrews wore a rubber cap, the kind swimmers use, pulled down low just above his eyebrows and covering both ears. The lower part of his face and neck were protected by a polyester neck warmer pulled up just under his nose. Finally, he had smeared a coat of petroleum jelly around his eyes and in his eyebrows.

Boggs stood off to the side. McAndrews stood in front of Johnny Boy who felt like running, who would have run except that he was cold and naked and knew that he would have to get past Raymond Boggs standing in the doorway.

McAndrews told Johnny Boy, "Don't move, motherfucker. Just stand right there."

And then Johnny Boy saw the plastic Tupperware container placed on one of the sinks set against the wall opposite the showers, a rectangular, plastic container, large enough to hold several quarts of dry food.

McAndrews peeled off the lid, telling Boggs, "Stay back. Just grab him if he moves. This fucker is crawling with 'em, trust me."

McAndrews carefully extracted a large, yellow bath towel from the container, being very careful to hold it away from him. The towel was stiff, as if it had dried in the Tupperware container. It smelled faintly of must and mildew. McAndrews carefully unfolded the towel, moving slowly so as not to stir up the microscopic insects that infested it. Without any warning, McAndrews pushed the towel against Johnny Boy's wet chest, rubbing it roughly against the skin.

"Lift your arms up," he yelled, his voice, muffled by the neck warmer, sounding almost panicky as if he wanted to get this over with as soon as possible. He rubbed the towel under Johnny Boy's armpits, down to his waist, back up the chest, then down again. He ground the towel into Johnny Boy's genital area, barking, "Turn around."

When Johnny Boy complied he rubbed Johnny Boy's rear end and back, pushing the towel into Johnny Boy's head, gathering it up into a ball and grinding it into Johnny Boy's scalp.

McAndrews stepped back, gingerly folding the towel, still keeping it at arm's length. He replaced the towel in the plastic box, pushing down the top, making sure to seal it tightly.

He told Boggs, "All right, hand him his stuff, but keep your distance."

Boggs tossed a set of pajamas at Johnny Boy. They fell to the wet floor.

"Put 'em on, Johnny Boy, and don't you fuckin' move from there 'til I tell you to."

Johnny Boy bent to retrieve his pajamas. McAndrews reached over to the sink top for a brown bottle containing a viscous liquid. He poured Lindane onto his rubber gloves and proceeded to lather up as if he were thoroughly washing his hands. He turned on the hot water, letting it run until it came steaming out of the faucet before he rinsed the gloves.

Johnny Boy dressed slowly, the thin pajamas sticking to his still wet arms and legs. A cold breeze stole into the bathroom through a partly open window, lifting off some of the medicinal odor of the Lindane, chilling Johnny Boy's wet skin.

SIX

Bill Reed woke at his usual early hour on Friday, but he did not wheel to the gym. He had allowed his previous resolve to subside under his doubt and disability. He had told himself, don't go off half-cocked, don't be stupid. Find out what's going on first.

It had sounded correct, rationale, the right thing to do, but even though Reed felt the lie underneath it, he wouldn't allow himself to admit that he was simply conjuring up another excuse, another rationale to avoid the obligation.

He simply did not want to go, so he had decided to call once more. This time, however, he would make sure he spoke to John Boyd. This time, he would brook no excuses, no being put on hold, no transfers to another person.

He waited from 4:00 A.M. until 8:00 A.M. to make the call, his resolve and determination building hour after hour.

He dialed, ready, focused, determined—and sat listening to an infuriating mechanical voice offering him two options: call back later, or dial the number of a security company in the case of emergency.

Reed slowly put down his phone. He knew he could have waited, called back. But he knew even more certainly that it wouldn't make any difference. He wouldn't get through to his cousin today. There would be some reason, some excuse that would leave him yelling impotently at a dead telephone, or a dial tone, yelling ineffectually far, far away from where his cousin resided.

He saw it all very clearly now. Bill Reed would not do this over the phone.

He braced his hands on the arms of his club chair, pulled his right foot under him, and made the tedious effort—pushing with his arms, standing with one leg, grabbing his crutch. Then he stepped/hopped out to the hallway and down to the closet. He maneuvered himself into the cramped space and braced his back against the wall behind him. He pulled his crutch out from under his armpit and used it as a prod to lever a weekend bag off the top shelf of the closet, dropping the crutch just in time to catch the falling bag.

Today, he would pack, plan, prepare, steel himself, get in his car, and drive to the Ullmann Institute. Today, now, not tomorrow. Tomorrow, Saturday, one way or another, he would see his cousin and bring the tortured page back to him, show it to him, tell him he had received it, and find out how he had composed the message and why.

After his Thursday night shower and toweling with the stiff, infested towel, McAndrews and Boggs had taken Johnny Boy down to the basement under his dormitory. Johnny Boy had never been to the basement before, not in the fifteen years he had lived at the Ullmann Institute. The steps down were metal, pebbled to prevent slipping, but the hard points of the stairs dug into Johnny Boy's bare feet, making him wince at the pain.

Johnny Boy kept his head down, making sure Boggs and McAndrews didn't see his fear. However, it wasn't difficult to avoid their gaze since they walked well behind him, keeping their distance to avoid infestation.

When Johnny Boy reached the bottom of the stairs, McAndrews told him to turn right and walk forward down a long corridor. The walls were made of brick, painted a dozen coats of semigloss institutional green. Johnny Boy walked far enough to feel as if they were taking him away from everybody else at the institute. He passed by a closed door behind which a boiler rumbled softly.

The floor felt gritty and dirty under his feet, and Johnny Boy worried about the soles of his bare feet becoming soiled. They yelled at you if you were dirty, and he knew his feet were getting dirty.

Johnny Boy smelled the dank, dusty basement smells. He shivered, becoming more and more tense because he knew that now he could not find his way back to his room. He sensed that Boggs and McAndrews were going to be mean and leave him in the basement. How would he ever get back? And how would he explain why his feet were dirty?

Suddenly McAndrews said, "Hold it."

Johnny Boy stopped, head down, looking to his right and left, but not focusing on anything.

Standing a few feet behind Johnny Boy, McAndrews reached to his left and opened a door. McAndrews backed away from the open door and told Johnny Boy, "All right, genius, turn around and go into this room here."

Johnny Boy did as he was told, walked back toward McAndrews, and entered the room.

He wanted to see somebody else in the room, anybody else, any of the other residents, but the room was too dark. The only light came from the corridor outside. Was anybody here? He tried to think why he was in this room. Were they moving him? Would he have a new roommate now? What had he done wrong? Johnny Boy had the sense that he had been doing wrong things, but he could not think of what, could not grasp it, could not form an image of himself doing anything that would connect him with this dank, dark, faraway basement room.

Still standing out in the hallway, McAndrews reached into the room and flipped the light switch. A single, bare bulb in a ceiling outlet filled the room with light so bright that Johnny Boy ducked away from the glare, squinting.

After a moment, Johnny Boy saw the wall in front of him, much closer than he expected, on his left, a plain metal bed frame, a bare mattress, a stained pillow. On his right, another bare wall, nothing else. There wasn't room for anything else.

He immediately grew more anxious. How could he have a roommate now? Where would he put his clothes? Where would he keep his things? How could he find his way back to the dorm? If he had a roommate he could do it, but the idea of doing it alone, all alone, frightened Johnny Boyd. Where were the stairs he had walked down? Could he open the door? Why did he have to stay here alone? All alone, away from everybody else. What had he done wrong? What were they doing?

"Eddie?"

"What?" barked McAndrews.

"Eddie?" That was all Johnny Boy could say, one vast, confused question represented by saying the name of the person doing all this to him.

"All right, don't worry about it. It's just temporary. You gotta sleep here for a couple of nights. Don't worry. Just go to sleep you dumb son of a bitch. Quit being a baby. I'm gonna leave the light on so you don't start crying and shit. Go lay down. And don't try the door. I'm gonna lock it. You gotta stay here tonight."

Johnny Boy watched McAndrews pull the door shut behind him. Johnny Boy stared at the closed door.

Temporary. What did that mean? Temp, tempry. Johnny Boy tried to repeat the word in his head, but he couldn't quite remember it.

Johnny Boy turned and looked down at the bed, then stepped over to it and sat on the edge. After a moment or two, he lay down.

There was nothing else to do. Or to see. He turned toward the wall, pressing his head against the cold cement brick simply to feel some form of contact. There were no sheets, no pillowcase, nothing to cover or comfort him. Johnny Boy pulled the pillow onto his face to block out the overhead light, to cover his face against the terrible dread and loneliness that overwhelmed him.

SEVEN

After three hours of awkward preparations, at eleven o'clock Friday morning, Bill Reed rolled toward the door of his apartment. His two crutches were bungee-corded to the back of his wheelchair. A book of maps and a bottle of Evian water were stuffed into his carryall bag hanging on the back. In his lap were a shearling coat and a weekend bag, both of which he intended to toss into his car trunk.

Despite his careful preparations, Reed felt like a nervous kid all packed up and heading off to his first dreaded day of school.

"Jeezus Christ," he growled. "You fucking baby. What's the worst that can happen? You fall down trying to take a piss at the Mobil station on the Merritt Parkway?"

The question made him stop and reverse his wheelchair

back toward his kitchen. He pulled open the refrigerator and lifted a quart jar of cranberry juice from the lower shelf. He emptied the remains of the jar in the sink, firmly replaced the cap, and shoved the empty bottle into his carryall sack.

"All right, enough," he told himself.

When Reed rolled into his garage two blocks from his apartment, a silver BMW 740iL stood waiting for him. Reed had driven frequently since his accident, usually out to Long Island to meet with his prosthetist. Since he still had his right foot, driving the car had changed very little for him. Behind the wheel of the luxury car was one of the few places where Reed felt totally in control. However, getting in and out of the car invariably made him feel like a cripple.

When the Jamaican garage manager approached him, Reed made it clear that he did not want help loading up. This was the first time he had taken the car out for a trip requiring luggage, but Reed had already envisioned the loading procedure, pictured it, planned it, much as he did many activities prior to actually doing them in order to work out problems before they embarrassed him.

He wheeled around to the back of the car and popped the trunk lid, tossed his coat and weekend bag in. He had brought only enough clothes for the weekend. Get up there, check it out, stay overnight, one night, get back. That was the plan. One bag was sufficient.

He grabbed the lip of the trunk and pulled himself up on one leg, twisted and sat uncomfortably on the edge of the large trunk. Bending forward toward the wheelchair, he went through the actions he had rehearsed in his mind. Slip the crutches out from the bungee cords, prop them against the bumper so he could use them to get to the driver's seat, pull off the carryall bag, set it in the trunk, detach the quick-release chair wheels one by one, lay them in the trunk, fold the chair, lay that in on top of the wheels. Bending, twisting, fumbling with the bungee cords that seemed to have a mind of their own, Reed cursed to himself quietly so the garage attendant would not think any of it directed toward him.

Reed grabbed the crutches, made it to the driver's side door, lowered himself into the seat, was just about to pull in his crutches when he remembered he'd left his bathroom bottle in the carryall bag.

"Shit."

He pulled himself onto one leg and crutches, retrieved his bottle, found it too awkward to carry the bottle and use the crutches so he tried stuffing the empty quart bottle into the pocket of his sport jacket. It wouldn't fit, so he ended up pushing the bottle along the roof of the BMW, stepping after it. His anger almost drove him to yell at the garage manager, you got anything better to do than watch me hobble around with my piss bottle? But Reed held his tongue, making an effort to calm down, reminding himself that no matter how many times he rehearsed it, this kind of unforeseen stuff always happened.

Just take it easy, he told himself. He remembered the advice the social worker Sarah Carpenter had repeated more than once during her visits, You can do it all, it just takes more time.

Once behind the wheel, Reed finally felt secure and in control. Now if anyone looked at him, what would they see? A handsome, formidable-looking man, fortyish, fit, dressed in a burgundy, cashmere polo shirt and expensive Paul Stuart tweed sport coat, sitting at the wheel of a luxury car few could afford. They would see success, confidence, money. They would not see the stump.

Reed fired up the powerful engine, selected a Vivaldi concerto on his CD player, and headed out toward Seventy-second Street, which would lead him west to the Henry Hudson Parkway.

"All right," he said out loud. "It's about time you got up off your ass and did some good." But as he accelerated onto the Parkway he asked himself, "Since when did you need a pep talk?"

Almost six hours later, Reed finally saw a Chamber of Commerce sign that announced he was entering Dumphy, a town big enough to have a traffic light at the intersection where Main Street started. He rolled right through the main part of town in about twenty seconds, reaching a familiar-looking corner gas station/convenience store/video rental store. About a hundred yards ahead, on the outskirts of the little town, he spotted a round white sign glowing in the glare from a floodlight set in the ground. The sign hung suspended from the branch of a large maple tree. The Maple Inn looked about as he had remembered it, a four-story, wood-shingled building, trimmed in ornate molding, set back from a picket-fenced lawn. A wraparound front porch surrounded the inn on three sides.

Reed drove into the parking lot situated behind the inn, shouldered open the driver's door, and pulled himself up onto his right leg, balancing one arm on the open car door, the other on the roof of the BMW.

Reed had been sitting for most of three hours, having stopped twice for gas. Now, suddenly upright, he felt the blood rushing into his stump. He grabbed the stump with his left hand, lifting at the hip, trying to keep the stump level, but it was too late. Phantom pain hit him, feeling as if someone had lashed his nonexistent left shin with barbed wire. He hissed and winced, pulling his stump higher, holding it up, trying to stop more blood from rushing into it. He sat back down in the driver's seat, waiting for the weird pain in a nonexistent part of his body to subside. He yearned to rub the shin that no longer existed. Instead he rubbed and massaged his stump. After about three minutes, as the circulation slowly returned to his stump, the pain ebbed away. Only then could he get upright on his crutches and retrieve his wheelchair and bag out of the trunk. Reed went through the routine of assembling the chair and gathering his belongings, intent on finishing before anyone else pulled into the parking lot.

He wheeled through the lot, trying to shake some of the tension and stiffness from his shoulders and neck, grateful for the chance to work his muscles. Twilight had grown into a deep gloom. Suddenly the high-intensity lamp atop a pole in the middle of the small lot began to buzz and flicker to life.

Reed had planned to leave his wheelchair on the front porch, use his crutches to enter, and ask one of the inn staff to bring everything to his room. But to his surprise, he saw that a simple but serviceable handicapped ramp had been built leading to a side entrance. The ramp had been assembled in two sections, zigzagging to conserve room, making the pitch of the ramp fairly steep, which didn't bother Reed at all. Between his long excursions in the wheelchair and his fanatical early morning workouts, Reed's upper body and hand strength had reached the point where he could easily and quickly roll up the two turning segments.

Reed pushed himself through the entrance that opened onto a bare hallway that ran past the kitchen area. At the end of the hallway, double swinging doors opened up near a small gift shop. Reed pushed his way through the doors and turned left, wheeling the short distance to the lobby. He sat patiently at the counter while a young woman checked him in, allowing her to fawn over him to the point of annoyance. She made a big deal out of providing him with the one and only ground-floor room, the only wheelchair accessible room in the place since there was no elevator.

His chair barely fit through the doorway to his room. He had to pull himself in, hands on the door frame. He surveyed the room. Everything looked as if it had been made sometime shortly after World War II. The carpet, wallpaper, and furniture were all in dark colors. One double-hung window afforded him a dismal, ground-level view of the parking lot.

He wheeled over to the bathroom and peered inside. A sink and shower stall, no tub. Great, he told himself, picturing himself showering standing on one foot leaning against the wall.

He unpacked his bag. He used the bathroom, surprised that he ended up not minding the cramped size of the room since it meant that no matter which way he turned, he could reach out and brace a hand against one of the four walls.

He hadn't eaten anything during the trip except a ham sandwich he had brought from his kitchen, wolfing it down between gulps of warm diet Coke. He felt stiff and tense from the long trip, disgruntled about the dark, closed-in room, and uneasy with being in such a remote, isolated area. He craved a drink and a hot meal.

Just before dawn on Friday morning, Johnny Boy woke with a start. It felt as if McAndrews and Boggs had come down to the basement to burn him with lit matches. He had seen McAndrews do that to Walter Philips. One morning during barn chores, McAndrews had badgered Walter, pushing him, goading him until Walter finally yelled at McAndrews, telling him to fuck off. It amused McAndrews when one of them fought back. And it gave him an excuse to enact another cruelty. This time, he pulled out a pack of matches, lit them one by one, pulling them across the strike pad and directing them at Walter's face, all in a single motion. Walter swatted at the burning matches coming at him and ducked. Most of the matches fell short. The few that hit him burned very little, but all of the matches terrified Walter Philips.

Johnny Boy thought McAndrews must have figured out a better way to do it because it felt like dozens of matches were hitting him, all at once. The horrible sensation made him jack-knife up off the bed. But it wasn't matches. McAndrews and Boggs weren't standing there. They had already done their job, having rubbed Johnny Boy down with a towel infested with scabies, horribly torturous mites that had dug under Johnny Boy's skin, attacking him with stupefying virulence.

Seeing that Boggs and McAndrews weren't there terrified Johnny Boy even more. Now he no idea why it felt like burning matches were hitting his crotch, under his arms, at the nape of his neck, on his back, his waist. In seconds, every thought left him, replaced by a panic. He began scratching, digging at himself, quickly tearing through his skin. The scratching brought only moments of relief so he had to scratch more and more. By midday Friday the horrible itching had spread between the fingers on both hands, making scratching his burning itches even more horrible since moving his hands now made them throb with nearly unbearable tingling and itching.

Johnny Boy scratched until the heat and tingling reached a crescendo of pain, almost like an electric current running through him, and then he would stop, wincing, waiting for the tingling to subside, only to be met by another round of biting, itching, scratching.

As the scabies spread and burrowed under Johnny Boy's skin, welts appeared on his face, neck, and most of his upper body. His pajamas became streaked with blood. He pressed the warm blood into the burning itches, and then the cold wet blood, anything to change the feeling. Even tearing at his rent flesh felt better than the deep, constant, biting, burning itching.

By two in the afternoon, after nearly eight hours of torture, Johnny Boy sat on the edge of his bed, his arms wrapped around him, his head pressing down on his arms to create pressure, to create another feeling, anything to counter the horrible, burning, tearing itching. He had descended to a level of pain where he felt no single thing, but felt everything. Not one itch, but an avalanche of tingling, burning itching that made his entire body ache. Mercifully, the overload of pain short-circuited some receptors in his brain and he slid into a state of semiconsciousness, knowing only that he could not move, could not open his eyes, could do nothing but be alone and cursed and abandoned like a stray dog dying of the mange.

EIGHT

Traveling from his ground-floor room to the dining room took Bill Reed about thirty seconds, making him slightly less resentful of his room's location near the lobby.

He wheeled to a lectern set up at the entrance to the dining room. A tall, painfully thin blonde woman stood behind the lectern writing in her reservation book, a pile of menus resting next to the book. Reed was not at all surprised to see a hostess seating guests. Labor was cheap in rural areas. Jobs tended to get created when someone could always be found to work them for low wages.

The blonde wore a white blouse, a string of pearls, and a pale yellow suit jacket and skirt that hung on her bony frame. But the suit wasn't made well enough to hang gracefully on her body, so the clothes tended to make her seem awkward. She had an attractive face, although somewhat elongated, but wore no makeup except for a gloss lipstick. All the pale colors and her demeanor made Reed feel as if the spirit had been leeched out of her. But despite her fatigue or depression or the toll it took on her to put together a hostess's wardrobe on a Kmart budget, she gave Reed the impression she was determined to do her best.

Behind her Reed saw a barroom off to the left, occupying a corner. Reed wouldn't have been surprised if a sign over the barroom said Cozy Corner Bar.

The woman twitched a smile at Reed, greeting him mechanically, "Good evening, sir."

"Dinner for one," he said.

She replied, but too softly for him to make out what she had said, particularly with her so tall and him sitting in his wheelchair. Reed didn't attempt to answer the hostess and she didn't repeat herself. She simply turned and led the way to the dining room, a menu and wine list tucked under her arm.

The dining room reeked of country inn with rough-hewn wooden tables, a stone fireplace, exposed beams. The hostess deftly removed one of the wooden captain's chairs at a corner table for two, as if she were accustomed to dealing with people in wheelchairs. Reed rolled into position, pleased to find the table at a comfortable height.

Again she spoke softly, but this time she leaned close enough to Reed so that he could hear her as well as breathe in her too-floral perfume.

"Can I get you a drink?"

Ah, thought Reed, no small talk. Right to the point. You have redeemed yourself.

"Yes, thank you. Do you have any Ketel One vodka?"

The look on her face told Reed she had never heard of it.

"That's all right. How about Absolut?"

"Yes."

"An Absolut martini, rocks, with a twist. Please."

The hostess went for his drink, showing no interest in any conversation beyond the required.

Reed looked around the dining room. Out of about twenty seats, six were filled with other diners, a pair of white-haired ladies at one table and two couples, also senior citizens, at a table against the far wall of the room.

Reed glanced at the menu and wine list . . . distinctly American food and modest wines.

He shifted in his chair. Pulled a napkin onto his lap. Sooner than he expected, a waitress arrived holding his drink. Both looked so impressive that Reed's eyes actually widened for a second. The vodka martini, chilled to condensation, filled a generously sized old-fashion glass right to the brim. And the waitress—even though she wore a unisex outfit comprised of a white shirt, black vest, and black slacks, the clothes couldn't hide her figure—tall, slim, long arms and legs, full chest. She had an oval-shaped face with strong but feminine features, engaging eyes and full lips. Her brown hair had been piled haphazardly on the top of her head, fastened with a single large clip as if she had just stuck it up there when she came to work. She smiled easily as she set down the drink, a smile that seemed both friendly and slightly seductive.

"There you go," she said, sounding as if the martini had been her idea.

"Thanks."

She pushed a stray strand of hair back behind her ear and Reed noticed a delicate filigree of tattooed lines surrounding her right wrist. There wasn't enough time to make out the design of the tattoo before the cuff of her white shirt hid it from his view, but the ink work seemed much more intricate and artistic than the usual tattoo. Reed figured her for mid-thirties. Her manner, her figure, her nonchalant attitude about her looks, the tattoo, all gave Reed the impression this woman should have been waiting tables in a chic New York bistro or SoHo restaurant rather than in a nowhere North Country inn.

"You want to hear the specials?"

"Not really," Reed answered. "What's good?"

His answer seemed to please her. She smiled again, making Reed smile back.

"You like fish?" she asked.

"Yeah."

"Try the cod. It's actually fresh. It's good."

"I'll take it grilled with whatever vegetables you have."

"You got it."

"And do me a favor?"

She looked at Reed, eyebrows raised as if she anticipated a come-on or an unusual request.

Reed pointed to his drink. "Just before that's empty, could you get me another one?"

"Sure. Just for that one, or for the rest of dinner?"

He held up his hand and said, "No, I think just one more of these will do it."

She held her hand up, mimicking his gesture, once again revealing the intriguing wrist tattoo, and said, "Right. Want anything to start? A salad?"

"Why not?"

After the second martini, Reed switched to white wine.

Each time the waitress came, Reed found himself acting overly friendly. The vodka and her attractiveness prompted him, but so did a sudden, insistent need for a woman's attention. Reed became annoyed at himself, particularly since the waitress pointedly maintained the right social distance, making sure to be friendly, but not flirty. Working for the tip, but not for untoward attention.

After dinner, Reed felt like a brandy so he headed for the small barroom he'd noticed off to the left of the dining-room entrance.

The old wooden bar accommodated only four stools, but there were three tables in the barroom, two on one side, one on the other near a small fireplace set into the wall. A heavy-set, balding man who looked to be about sixty stood behind the bar polishing glasses. He too wore a white shirt, black vest, and dark pants. Reed couldn't remember ever seeing anybody polish glasses behind a bar except in an old movie. It made him feel warmly toward both the bar and the bartender, especially when the bartender perked up as Reed rolled in and parked his wheelchair at the table closest to the entrance.

"Good evening, sir."

"Good evening. Can I get a Rémy and a glass of ice water?"

The barman nodded and smiled, apparently pleased to have someone interrupt his polishing. Reed watched him pour a generous amount of brandy in a large snifter and fill a tall glass with ice water. Reed appreciated the generous pours at the Maple Inn. The barman came out from behind the bar, carrying the glasses on a small cork-bottomed tray. Reed dropped a bill on the tray, raising a hand that signaled, keep the change.

"Thank you, sir," said the barman. "Anything else?"

"Not right now."

Reed took a sip of his brandy and looked up at a single shelf of books set into the wall opposite him at eye level. The shelf ran across the entire width of the wall. He noted a title that interested him, hesitated, then pushed himself out of his wheelchair, up on his one leg. He considered hopping to the opposite side of the room, figuring he could brace himself on the table near the far wall, then forgot about the idea. Instead of sitting back in his chair, he twisted and maneuvered so that he sat on the bench against the wall, leaving his wheelchair empty, trying to make it appear as if that was what he had intended all along.

Just then, the dining-room waitress entered the bar. She wore a tan leather jacket that reached below her hips, the same black slacks and white shirt but no vest. She had a large leather purse over her shoulder. She slung one long leg over an empty bar stool and straddled it, tossing her purse on the bar. She fished out a pack of Camel Lights, lit one, and pulled the clip out of her hair, letting it fall down as she ran her fingers through it. The bartender poured her a Jack Daniel's on ice without being asked.

Reed watched her, acutely aware of how attractive he found her. For months, he had banished even the idea of a woman in his life. He might be able to overcome the mechanical problems of getting around, escorting someone to dinner or even a movie. But sex? No, impossible. The thought of being naked with someone, the thought of a woman looking at his stump, mortified him.

But now, being so far away from home, knowing he would be gone in a day, two at the most, Reed let go of his inhibition, allowing his gaze to linger on the waitress, for the first time in a long time allowing himself to enjoy the view.

A long sip of bourbon and a deep drag from the cigarette were her first priority. Then she turned and saw Reed sitting with his brandy. An involuntary smile flickered, but she quickly turned away.

Reed sipped again from his snifter. No fraternizing with the patrons, hey?

With her head still turned away, Reed said, "You were right."

She couldn't avoid turning back to respond.

"About what?"

"The cod. You were right. It was good." And then, without thinking much about it, just doing it quickly while he had her attention, because Reed knew if she turned back to the bar he'd have to call out to her again which he would never do, Reed impulsively waved her over and said, "Join me."

He watched her hesitate, thinking it over; then she stood up off the stool, her long legs reaching the floor before she left the seat, and came over to his table, drink and cigarette in hand.

When she reached his table, she matter-of-factly moved his wheelchair out of her way and pulled a chair into place across from him. Reed shifted over so he sat opposite her at the table, happy that the move also put his empty trouser leg more out of view.

"Cool chair."

"What? The wheelchair?"

"Yeah."

"You familiar with wheelchairs?"

"No, I just like the design of that one. I haven't ever seen one like it, made out of one long tube like that. All curves and nothing extra. What is that, aluminum?"

Speaking more softly now than in the dining room, her voice sounded sultry and slightly husky. Maybe it was the bourbon and cigarette, thought Reed.

"I don't know," he said.

Reed's answer seemed to surprise her, perhaps even disappoint her.

"Uh, actually, I seem to remember it's molybdenum, something like that. I don't think about it much. I don't expect . . ." Reed stopped himself with a shrug, deciding what he was about to say would be too complicated.

"Don't mean to pry," she said.

"Nah, hell, that's okay. Not at all. I just don't concentrate on it much because I'm not planning to be in it for all that much longer."

"Ah," she said, nodding, seeming to understand without any more information than that.

The waitress transferred her cigarette to her other hand and reached out to shake Reed's hand.

"Angela. Angela Quist."

Reed shook her hand. "Bill Reed." She had a large hand, even for a woman of her size, with skin surprisingly rough for a woman's and a grip almost as strong as a man's.

"So continuing with my usual lack of tact, what happened? How'd you lose the leg?"

"Motorcycle accident."

Angela grimaced and shook her head. "Man, that's like so . . ."

"So typical?"

"No, that's not the word I'm looking for. Expected. So expected. When you hear it, it seems like, yeah, of course, a motorcycle accident. You know, they're so damn dangerous aren't they?"

"No, it's the drivers who are dangerous. I was going too fast. And I wasn't completely sober. I wasn't drunk, but I wasn't completely, one hundred percent sober. Which you should be when you ride."

She nodded, frowning sympathetically.

Reed frowned, too, but not in concert with the waitress. He frowned at how easily that fact about his level of sobriety had come out. He had never mentioned it to anybody.

"Did that make the difference?" she asked.

Reed pursed his lips and shook his head. "Nah. I couldn't have stopped in time. Just going too damn fast for what happened."

"What kind of bike? A Harley?"

"No. I seem like the Harley type?"

"You do and you don't. You look like you can afford one."

Reed let that comment go and simply answered, "No, it was a Jap bike. Nice one. Too fast, though."

Angela stubbed out her cigarette and took another sip from her drink.

"So what brings you to the North Country?"

"I'm visiting a relative."

"Up here? Whereabouts?"

"At the Ullmann Institute. You know the place?"

Angela nodded quickly. "Sure. I know the place."

"Well, he's . . ."

"I know the place," said Angela, "for retarded people."

"Yes," said Reed.

Angela took a long swallow from her drink, tipping it back to get the last measure of whiskey past the ice cubes, draining it.

She flexed her shoulders and neck as if to dispel the tension from her waitress shift, letting out a half grunt, half sigh of fatigue. "Well, that's it. I'm out of here. Friday night, done for the week."

"Right."

"You're around for the weekend, I assume."

"Yeah."

She stood now, looming over Reed who remained seated.

"Well, nice meeting you. Have a good weekend."

Reed smiled and thanked her, watched her retrieve her purse at the bar and head out. As she left, she turned and waved, smiling at him, making her sudden departure even more frustrating.

Reed frowned at his snifter of Rémy. What the fuck was that? She comes on all friendly and interested, then boom, gone. Reed grimaced and rubbed his chin, trying to clear his head a bit. Was it talking about having a retarded relative? Like it's contagious or something?

Reed took another slug of brandy, wondering why he was so angry. She hadn't done or said anything wrong. What'd you expect? Forget it, he told himself, she's probably late to meet her boyfriend.

But the fast exit bothered him. Why? You thought you had something going there, didn't you? No. No. Telling her about why you went down. About not being sober. Fuck it, he told himself. Keep your mouth shut next time.

Reed swirled the brandy in his snifter, took a half hearted sip. He'd lost his taste for any more alcohol. He felt himself sliding into an angry funk. Yet he still could not shake her image. Sitting across from her at the same height, she looked even more engaging than in the dimly lit dining room. He had been particularly struck by her eyes. They were green. A penetrating green. The eyes had captured him as much because of their vivid color as because of who she was. She had seemed spontaneous, interested, uninhibited . . . then nothing, as if she could turn it off at will.

Reed forced himself to stop thinking about her. He finished his ice water, checked his watch. A little after ten o'clock. Past his bedtime. He left the remains of his brandy on the table and reached over awkwardly to retrieve the wheelchair from where Angela had moved it, glad that she hadn't worried about putting it back, but not happy that the barman stood watching him.

As he wheeled back to his ground floor room, it occurred to Reed that tomorrow he would be seeing his cousin. He also realized how little he'd thought about it. Worried too much about just getting here. And with drinking and mooning over that waitress.

Reed tried to picture his cousin, estimating his age, imagining how he might look four years older. What is he, forty? Forty-one? Reed knew his cousin was younger than he, but couldn't remember if it was by one or two years.

Reed pulled himself into his cramped room. Sitting in his wheelchair, dulled by the alcohol, still smarting from the sudden rejection by the waitress, unable to think clearly about his cousin, he smirked and shook his head. What the fuck are you doing, man? Up here in this godforsaken place. Reed pushed himself up out of the chair, intending to hop the two or three short steps to the bathroom. But he lost his balance. He was just barely able to hop clear of the wheelchair and twist so that he could fall onto the bed.

"Shit."

The temptation to just close his eyes and fall asleep, just give it up until the morning nearly overwhelmed him. But that would just mean sleeping uncomfortably in his clothes, and being awakened with a full bladder in a strange place.

He roused himself into a sitting position. Grabbed his crutches. Set to it. Step by painful step. One step at a time.

NINE

Bill Reed woke at his usual time, 4:00 A.M., feeling achy from too much vodka, wine, and brandy. Not a hint of daylight softened the cold gloom of his room. He rolled over, stretching out from under his blanket to pull aside the drapes that covered his single window.

High-intensity light bathed the parking lot in a yellow glare. Frost glistened on the cars, on the black asphalt lot, and on the fringe of brown lawn within the circle of the glare. Beyond the perimeter of light, pine trees stood motionless, their branches covered with a veneer of frost. Back among the trees, remnants of the first tentative snowfalls remained, but the winter season and deep cold that would keep ice and snow covering the North Country for weeks on end had not yet set in.

Reed fought off the urge to curl up and attempt a return to sleep, refusing to let the cold and isolation and strange, depressing surroundings interfere with his usual routine, knowing that if he gave into it now, he could easily sink lower.

In one ruthless move, he threw back the covers, rolled to the edge of the bed, sat up, and placed his foot on the cold, dank carpet. He perched at the edge of the bed. No heat had come up in the room. Dressed only in T-shirt and shorts, he steeled himself against the cold. He quickly used the bathroom, came back, and lowered himself onto the floor stretching slowly, preparing himself, planning it, figuring out ways he could exercise all his body parts: sit-ups, leg lifts, push-ups, dips between chair back and desktop, arm curls using his weekend bag . . . dozens and dozens of repetitions, working them up into the hundreds, working the muscles, making himself sweat, hardening his body to withstand the constant strain he endured.

The musty carpet, the cold room, the cramped space . . . nothing dissuaded Reed from relentlessly working all the parts of his body that remained after his amputation. He stuck to his workout with the tenacity of a drowning man clinging to his life preserver.

He worked at it for almost two hours, determined to at least try to replicate the effort he expended in the gym. And then he set about the rest of his tasks, figuring out ways to shower, shave, towel down, brush his teeth, use the toilet, dress in the warm clothes he had brought: wool slacks, cashmere polo shirt, tweed jacket, shearling coat . . . all with one crutch or two crutches or no crutches, hopping, standing, grabbing on to anything within reach for support.

At seven o'clock, exercised, dressed, and ready for the day, Reed found himself the only person in the dining room. He ordered his breakfast from the same young woman who had checked him in the night before.

By seven-thirty, Reed found himself driving by the entrance to the Ullmann Institute, having remembered the road that led there, but forgetting exactly where the entrance came in. He passed by a discreet wooden sign hanging by two chains from a tree limb extending out toward the road. It announced: ULLMANN INSTITUTE FOR THE DEVELOPMENTALLY CHALLENGED in black script against a white background. Reed made a U-turn and headed back, turning onto an unpaved road where a second sign said: ULLMANN INSTITUTE, 200 YARDS AHEAD.

He continued past the entrance to the institute, driving along the dirt road that ran along the perimeter of the institute's grounds, using the time to refresh his memory of the place and its surroundings.

Reed tried to peer through the scrub forest passing on his left, hoping to see a clearing that would open a view to the property; he saw nothing but mostly pine and birch trees, brush and bush, the whole area neglected, cluttered with fallen trees and a thick mat of dead leaves that had accumulated for dozens of years. Occasionally, a splotch of trash littered the roadside: fading beer cans, empty plastic bottles, cellophane bags—the kind of things kids on drinking binges pitch out the window of a moving car.

After about ten minutes, when the road narrowed to a point where Reed started worrying that he would not be able to turn the big car around if he chose to return the way he had come, the road suddenly widened and Reed found himself climbing above the treetops on his left. Just before the road turned right around a small outcropping, he spotted an open area where he could pull over. He looked down to his left and discovered that he had circled halfway around to the back side of the property. His parking spot on the shoulder of the road afforded him a view of the clearing where most of the institute's buildings were situated. The sun had come out, glinting occasionally through scudding dark clouds and burning off the night frost, leaving everything moistened, looking as if it had all been hastily hosed down in an attempt to freshen up otherwise dreary surroundings.

Reed could have made his way across the road to the far edge to gain a more encompassing view of the grounds, but he sat where he was, content with being able to see the cluster of buildings at the far left that comprised the two men's and one women's dorms, the dining hall, and the new clinic building behind the dorms. Yellow lights burned in the kitchen attached to the dining hall, telling Reed that the food-service people were at work.

Off to the right, Reed could just make out the rooftop of a single-story building, which he remembered being rather grandiosely referred to as the administration building, and part of the large red barn situated on the east end of the property.

It all came back to him. The Ullmann Institute seemed to be such a selfcontained place, set in the middle of a large plot of land, but with almost all the activity confined to a relatively small section at the south end of the property. Reed had always thought of the place as a strange hybrid. Not a farm, not a school, not a hospital, but something of all three, placed in a remote, rural setting that ensured its privacy. He recalled that he had been impressed at how clean and orderly everything appeared to be. Everything in its place. Everybody in their place. Well run, but as Reed remembered, not a warm, friendly place.

Reed looked away from the view below him and settled back in his seat, checking his watch. He wished he had a newspaper to read while he waited. Instead, he pulled his cousin's message out of the breast pocket of his sport jacket.

He unfolded the page, gazing at the now-familiar blobs of tiny, torn-out numbers and letters and convoluted, tortuous lines that had been pressed onto the paper. He focused on the crudely drawn stick figure buried under the lines, considering once again but not admitting that the figure was meant to represent his cousin. The chaos and pain in the picture stood in stark contrast to the orderly, meticulously neat enclave below.

Reed recalled the day his uncle had told him of his decision to send his son John Boyd to the residence. They had met in Washington, D.C., where both men were working at the time . . . Leonard Reed at a Washington law firm, William Reed at FBI headquarters. They had lunch at the Jockey Club in the Ritz-Carlton hotel.

"Why a place way upstate in New York?" Reed had asked his uncle. "Isn't there anything closer?"

"Not really," his Uncle Leonard told him. "So many of these places are second rate. This one is recommended pretty highly. Their waiting list is five to seven years. There's an opening now. I like their philosophy. I can't afford to wait another seven years."

"What's their philosophy?"

"They believe in the outdoors. They believe in structure. And work. Keeping them busy. John loves being out and about. And he's a little lazy by nature, you know. He'll sit looking out the window while the housekeeper putters around. He could sit there all day. Emily doesn't talk to him. His mother never says very much to him beyond baby talk. He's getting more and more isolated. I can't be with him all the time. At some point, he's going to have to break away. Start his own life, such as it is. I'd like for it to happen while I can be around to help with the transition."

"Lenny, you're not ill or anything, are you?"

"No. But Christ, Bill, I'm sixty-four. I won't be around forever."

"No. Of course not."

"John's almost twenty-six now, and still a baby. A real homebody. It's time," Leonard said.

"How's it work? Who pays for it?"

"It's a private place. Actually, it isn't certified because they started out as a school years ago. The state oversees it, of course, but they're quite a bit less encumbered with regulation, staying private and uncertified. You have to pony up a pretty hefty fee to get in. Then you contribute another pile to their endowment. Then it's John's SSI disability payments, plus eight thousand a year, which I can swing."

"Eight thousand on top of all the rest?"

"Sure. It costs a lot of money to take care of people like John. And it still doesn't cover it. They do a good amount of fund-raising to make up the difference. It's a lot of money, but it's for the rest of his life. He needs a place of his own."

"Sounds good," said Bill Reed, not knowing at all if it was or it was not, trusting his Uncle Len to have found the right solution for his retarded son. Reed could see that time and responsibility weighed heavily on his uncle and he did not want to add to the burden. Out of politeness he didn't ask the amounts of the "hefty fee" and the endowment payments.

They had briefly discussed the plans for John Boyd's support after Reed's uncle passed away, touching only very briefly on it, not wanting to bring attention to the inevitable reality that at some point John Boyd's father would not be around to take care of him. Leonard had explained the trust fund he planned to set up. He was going to work it through his stockbroker, a man he had dealt with for many years. Plan it so that the fund's investments would be able to keep up with the expenses and fees that would certainly increase over time. Knowing full well his nephew's background in accounting and financial matters, Reed's uncle asked for his opinion, but it seemed to Reed that he sought assurance rather than advice, which he tried to give his uncle. Reed also had the feeling that his uncle had been sending out a feeler to see if Reed felt slighted at not being named a trustee of the fund.

Although Reed knew he would be a good choice to manage a trust if called upon to do so, he did not volunteer. He knew about the mental instability of his uncle's wife, and did not relish dealing with her. His Uncle Leonard seemed relieved that Reed didn't ask any questions, and they let it go at that.

Eight thousand a year, thought Reed, fifteen years ago. At least double that now, probably more. He tried to recall the trust fund figure his uncle had mentioned. Whatever the figure, Reed remembered thinking it seemed more than adequate to generate eight thousand a year, and enough to keep up with any increase in expenses at the institute.

Reed gazed back down to the clearing. From one of the dorms, two residents emerged dressed in long denim jackets. Two more straggled out from a second building, and three from the third, all but one of them wearing the denim barn jackets given to the residents. They gathered in a loose circle around a flagpole centered between the three dorms. Reed remembered the jackets. Barn jackets, each bearing the resident's name in script stitched on the chest. John Boyd had been proud of his jacket. It made him feel important.

A tall man came striding out of the middle building, moving with more purpose than any of the residents. He wore a blue windbreaker with the word STAFF written across the back. He smoked a cigarette, his breath fogging the air more than the others. When he arrived at the flagpole, Reed saw the group of residents forming around him. After a few moments of head counting, the group moved across the open area toward the barn.

Barn duty. Morning chores. Reed remembered his cousin talking about it . . . head down, speaking in that way of his, talking through his nose. John Boyd had tried to make his work sound important, talking about the chickens in the barn, describing their size with his hands, obviously proud to be taking care of something alive.

The therapeutic value of being on the other side of dependency had seemed obvious back then. Reed wondered if Johnny still took care of the chickens. As he watched the group shuffle off, Reed thought maybe he had overreacted. Or maybe John Boyd had overreacted, becoming inexplicably upset over something inconsequential. Down below him, the figures seemed to be blithely following the system that had worked for many years.

Six hours of driving, a night in that crummy room, and for what? Reed asked himself. Reed fired up the BMW and carefully turned around on the narrow road. "Well," he told himself, "it's about time I found out."

TEN

Reed unloaded his wheelchair, assembled it, started the long push to the administration building. He didn't notice the building had no wheelchair access until he was about twenty feet from the entrance. Almost all the other buildings at the institute had wheelchair access for their more severely handicapped residents, but not the administration building. A set of three wide steps blocked his way.

"Nice," he muttered.

He brought the chair up close to the bottom step. There were two more steps blocking his progress. He edged forward until the wheels touched, locked the wheelchair, slid forward, and placed his right foot on the first step. He had planned to push himself up into a standing position, turn and grab the back of the chair, balancing, using the chair almost as one would use a walker, then lift and turn and place the chair on the top step in front of the door . . . all in one quick move. Then turn, sit back in the chair, and back the chair through the front door.

His strength and the light weight of the chair made him think he could do it, but he didn't even come close.

By the time he stood up on one foot, he was already so off balance that instead of executing a neat pivot, he basically turned and pitched forward, grabbing the seat of the chair instead of the back. This left him bent over too far with barely enough leverage to lift the chair. Only his extraordinary strength saved him. He pulled, lifted, twisted awkwardly, and slammed the wheelchair down on the top step behind him.

"Shit."

He felt his heart pounding: from the effort, from the fear of falling, and from the inevitable anger the situation engendered. Anger at being crippled, anger at being awkward, at having to take a crazy chance that could have meant falling down on his left side, re-injuring his recently healed broken elbow and arm, and the dislocated shoulder and the hip that still, nearly seven months later, didn't feel completely right. It could have meant tearing skin that had taken so long to heal. And most infuriating, it might very well have meant lying on the ground until someone showed up and helped him.

"Fuck."

He dropped into the chair, took a deep breath, exhaling slowly, willing his heart to stop pounding in his chest. He turned the chair, struggled to open the door from chair height and push his way into the building. The closing glass door banged into his left shoulder, the chair bucking over the door saddles. A pair of large wooden doors blocked his way. He bulled through them, feeling the anger rise in him, plaguing him, wearing him down.

Reed found himself in a lobby area facing a counter. He was just able to peer over the counter and see three desks, a set of filing cabinets, the tangle of a hanging spider plant, a coffeemaker. A three-quarter-full coffeepot sat under the still-dripping spigot, filling the air with the scent of fresh brew. Reed looked around for whoever had made the coffee. To his right and left ran opposite corridors of equal length. Reed saw only empty doorways leading off the two corridors.

He yelled out, "Hello?"

No answer.

He backed away from the counter and turned to head down the corridor to his left. Just then a thin, balding man dressed in khaki slacks, blue shirt, and tie emerged from one of the offices. He seemed quite surprised to see someone coming down the corridor toward him.

"Excuse me," he said, the tone conveying offense rather than apology.

Reed ignored the reproach in the man's voice and said, "Yes, can you help me?"

"With what?"

"I'm here to see my cousin, John Reed."

"And you are?"

"William Reed. Who are you?"

"Mr. Kitridge. Do you have an appointment?"

"No. Where can I find my cousin?"

"Well, I'm sorry, you can't—"

Reed interrupted Kitridge. "Can't what?"

The slight man was taken aback by the question and the challenge.

"Can't what, Mr. Kitridge? I'm sure you're not going to tell me I can't visit my cousin after driving over three hundred miles, are you? Where is he?"

Kitridge stammered, "Well, you, you realize it's the weekend. The staff isn't—"

Reed's voice rose slightly, interrupting again. "Mr. Kitridge, please, don't make any excuses. Please."

Reed said please, but the word sounded threatening.

Kitridge started to respond, stopped, then ducked back into his office saying, "I'll have to check. Just wait a moment, please."

Reed sat back in his chair, deciding he would give Kitridge a chance. He pivoted his chair slightly to observe Kitridge in his office and perhaps hear what he was saying on the phone.

The man kept his head bowed as he spoke, making it harder for Reed to hear his words. Reed stared at the patch of bare skin at the crown of Kitridge's head, growing more impatient.

Kitridge hung up the phone, raised his head, and saw Reed staring at him. It seemed to unnerve him even more.

"Uh, Mr. Ullmann said he would like to talk to you. He'll be in at about ten. Can you come back at that time?"

"No, I can't come back at ten. That's ridiculous," said Reed. "I'm not here to talk to Mr. Ullmann. Why don't you just tell me where my cousin is so I don't have to wheel all over this place looking for him."

"Sir, it's really not up to me. Mr. Ullmann has to speak to you."

"All right," said Reed. "All right. Why don't you get him back on the phone, and he can talk to me now."

"Well, he just said . . ."

Reed pointed a finger at Kitridge. "Look, I've had all the bullshit I'm going to take from you people. I couldn't even get through to anybody to make a damn appointment if I wanted to. Either tell me where my cousin is, or get Ullmann on the damn phone and let me talk to him. Or give me his phone number and I'll call him."

Kitridge put up a hand, as if to stop Reed, and said, "Please do not raise your voice. And cursing at me is not necessary."

"Cursing at you?" Reed sat up straighter in his wheelchair. He almost started shouting, but stopped himself. Speaking slowly, looking directly at Kitridge, he said, "All right, sir, why don't you just tell me what you're going to do. If you don't want to do anything to help, just tell me, and be kind enough to give me a phone number where I can reach Mr. Ullmann."

Kitridge pursed his lips, hesitated, then picked up his phone, making a point to ignore Reed.

The second call took less time than the first. Kitridge replaced the phone and stood up, but remained in his office, behind his desk with the narrow doorway between him and Reed.

"He said he's coming onto campus now. He'll be over in about fifteen minutes. He asked that you wait for him in the dining hall."

"The dining hall is that big brown building?"

"Yes. On the north end. The large building with the brown wood shake siding."

"Can I get in there with my wheelchair?"

Kitridge appeared confused by the question.

"Is there a wheelchair entrance?"

"Oh, of course, in front, but"—Kitridge looked at his watch—"that door doesn't open until nine."

Reed muttered, "That's convenient."

"But actually you can get in through the kitchen door. It's over on the left side of the building. They have a thing built in front of the stairs so they can wheel in provisions and . . . they'll show you the way to the dining hall."

"Thank you."

Matthew Ullmann hung up the wall phone in his kitchen and returned to the circular table in his kitchen breakfast nook. The nook had been added on to the old kitchen in the Victorian house the Ullmanns occupied. They had built a small cupola ceiling over the area and had the walls painted with trompe l'oeil ivy vines reaching to a blue sky that extended into the little dome. Madeleine Ullmann, Matthew's wife, sat at the table under her pretentious breakfast-nook dome, wearing a twenty-seven-hundred-dollar dressing gown she had ordered through a Neiman Marcus catalogue. Madeleine pushed loosely scrambled eggs onto her fork with an English muffin covered in butter and raspberry preserves.

Annoyed at the second interruption on Saturday morning, she asked in a shrill voice, "Who was it this time?" A blob of chewed eggs and muffin spattered her lower lip as she talked.

Matthew Ullmann answered, "Kitridge."

"Again?"

"Yes."

More muffin and egg sprayed as she asked, "Can't that idiot handle anything?"

Matthew sat opposite his wife and sipped from his coffee. "It doesn't seem so, does it, dear?"

Madeleine responded by looking down at her plate and gathering another small pile of scrambled eggs with the edge of her fork. At sixty, Madeleine Ullmann had grown well accustomed to indulging herself, whether it be with food, clothes, or insistent demands that she be heard and heeded. She focused on the things she wanted, such as her Neiman Marcus robe and the absurdly expensive mural decorating her ostentatious breakfast nook, and she ignored the things that displeased her, such as her spreading hips and steadily thickening body. She would admire her smooth skin in her bathroom mirror while she applied exorbitantly priced skin cream, but ignore the pinched features and small ferretlike eyes reflecting back at her.

"What did he say? Is it about Johnny Boy's visitor again?" Madeleine asked.

"Yes."

"What is it, his cousin?"

"Yes."

"Did you know he was coming?"

Madeleine waited for her husband to respond to her question. Sometimes, he simply ignored her questions. This time he answered her.

"Not for certain, but I'm not at all surprised."

Madeleine shoveled in another forkful, a sour expression on her face as if the food tasted bad. She talked as she chewed, the masticated food mixing with the words.

"The nerve. They dump them in our laps, then show up unannounced making demands."

"Oh, please, Madeleine, it's such an old story with these ingrates, why do you even bother upsetting yourself?" Ullmann flicked his wrist. "I'll handle it. He's not going to be seeing his precious cousin. Johnny Boy is not on the list of residents available to one and all."

"Of course not," said Madeleine.

"I've already taken care of it. No one will be visiting him. At least not for long. This cousin will just have to go back where he came from."

Madeline slurped her coffee and asked, "You sure?"

Ullmann flashed his wife a tight, conspiratorial smile. "Maybe I'll give him a quick look at his cousin, if he's nice about it. Just enough to get him off my back. We'll see how persistent he is."

Ullmann's answer did not please his wife. She pointed her fork at him. "Don't be too clever about this, Matthew. We don't need any trouble from a relative at this stage."

This time Ullmann's smile was condescending.

Madeleine responded with a repetition of her husband's name, elongating the second half of the name, whining in such a way as to project a cautionary tone.

Ullmann pretended to ignore her as he sliced a section from his pork sausage patty and shoved it into his mouth. As he chewed, the pork fat and a bit of saliva glistened his full lips, but after a moment, he laid down his knife and fork, stood up, and walked over to the kitchen phone. He dialed a number. When Madeleine heard him talking to Eddie McAndrews, she nodded to herself, finishing her last forkful of egg and piece of muffin, appearing, for the moment, to be satisfied.

ELEVEN

The dining hall sat about two hundred yards north. Bill Reed pushed himself along an asphalt walkway that descended into an open expanse of lawn bordered by the dining hall and dormitories to the north, and the administration building and barn at the south end. As he neared the dining hall the path rose back up. Reed welcomed the chance to exert some physical effort.

Entry into the kitchen area proved easy. When Reed wheeled in, the smells of institutional food greeted him. The only person in the kitchen, a thin, disconsolate man with a beard and ponytail, stood behind a wide steel table cracking eggs into a large bowl. He gave Reed the impression of a burnt-out hippie who had found his way from a New England commune to the kitchen of the Ullmann Institute. Reed's sudden presence in the kitchen did not seem to make the slightest difference to him.

Reed asked, "Which way to the dining hall?"

The kitchen worker wordlessly pointed to his left, his finger glistening from egg whites.

Reed rolled through a set of swinging doors and stopped, slightly taken aback at the expansive room before him. He realized he had never been in the dining hall, or else they had greatly expanded it. The hall reminded him of a ski lodge restaurant. Ten foot high bay windows at the far end flooded the room with morning light while giving a panoramic view of the fields and forests that Reed had driven through earlier. More windows ran around to the right, revealing a long wooden deck surrounding that side of the dining hall. The room held about thirty tables, each ringed by four sturdy chairs, all in a blond wood Reed thought might be oak. A wood slat floor was worn, but clean. A large A-frame ceiling rose overhead. Exposed rafters that ran the width of the hall held a turn-of-the-century dog sled, which had been set up overhead, tipped sideways, displayed like a museum piece. A large stone fireplace dominated the left side of the hall.

Reed rolled over to a table near the windows that faced the deck. He checked his watch. Nearly eight-thirty. Kitridge had said the dining room opened at nine, which explained why none of the residents were present. Just then, through the double doorway opposite him, Reed saw two staff members walk into the dining hall.

They glanced at Reed and headed for the coffee urns set up

at the food serving area. Both of them filled mugs with coffee. They took their cups and sat at a table near the entrance, the taller one facing Reed. Reed watched the shorter, stocky fellow give him a deadpan look, then sit opposite his friend, his back to Reed.

As he looked at them in their cheap white shirts, bedraggled ties, long hair, and jeans, two words formed in Reed's mind: white trash. He took them for janitors, but couldn't understand why they wore ties. He decided that he would like some of that coffee, too, and started wheeling across the dining hall to get to the coffee urns.

As Reed passed nearby their table, both Ray Boggs and Eddie McAndrews took sidelong glances at him.

Boggs asked, "That's the guy?"

"Who the hell else would it be?" answered McAndrews.

"Ullmann know the guy is a fuckin' cripple?"

"I doubt it."

"What are we supposed to do?"

"Just what the man said. Hang around, see what's up. Get a look at him."

Boggs slurped his coffee and dismissed the idea as a waste of time. "Shit."

But McAndrews surreptitiously watched Reed. He kept his head down but his eyes on Reed, taking in his expensive clothing, the high-tech wheelchair. He smiled slightly at the sight of Reed's amputation.

Reed brought his coffee back, settling in at the table, checking his watch. He sipped the coffee and grimaced. It had a cheap, washed-out flavor. Worse than institutional quality. Not even as good as New York Greek diner coffee, much less the exotic pampered blends of the Starbucks and specialty coffee bars that dotted Reed's Upper West Side neighborhood.

Reed pushed the brew away, looking out the windows on his

right, seeing now several groups of residents, most wearing denim barn jackets or woolen pea coats, heading back from the barn area. He wondered if they actually had to get up and do morning chores before breakfast. As unusual as that seemed, the evidence before him appeared to be clear. They did.

Well, nothing wrong with that, thought Reed. That's what you've been doing the past few months, isn't it? he asked himself. Except they don't get screwdrivers and bagels with cream cheese after. They get those eggs dripping off the fingers of that burnout in the kitchen.

The promised fifteen minutes had turned to twenty-five, but Reed sat quietly, musing about what he had seen so far at the Ullmann Institute. Clean buildings. Residents working. A showpiece of a dining hall. The only thing that nagged at Reed was the defensive runaround from Mr. Kitridge. It reminded Reed of the responses he had received when he'd phoned. Well, thought Reed, maybe they're just extra careful about visits to their residents.

Just then, as if in answer to his thoughts about the staff, Reed caught movement in his peripheral vision. He turned to see Matthew Ullmann striding into the dining area.

Ullmann walked fast, looking quickly at everything he passed: the tables and chairs, the floor, the two men in their dingy white shirts drinking coffee, Reed sitting by the window waiting for him. Ullmann wore expensive wool slacks, a blue, button-down Oxford shirt, and a red V-neck cashmere sweater that helped to hide the extra thirty-five pounds he carried. He could have been a dean at a New England university instead of the eponymous head of an isolated residence for the retarded.

Ullmann looked familiar to Reed, who had seen him once or twice in passing on his previous visits. Even if Reed had never seen him, Ullmann's manner and appearance left no doubt in Reed's mind that he wanted to be recognized as the man in charge, the owner.

Ullmann approached Reed, hand out. "Matthew Ullmann. You must be Mr. Reed."

Reed took the outstretched hand. Despite Ullmann's brusque manner, the hand felt soft, the grip not particularly firm.

"Bill Reed."

Before Reed could say another word, Ullmann took a seat, asking, "Didn't I just talk to you on the phone the other day?"

"Yes. Briefly."

"And now all of sudden, you're here. Is there something wrong?"

"The only thing wrong is I can't seem to get through to my cousin. I'm wondering if maybe there's a problem up here or something?"

"Why? Did someone call you? Contact you?"

"Are you kidding?" said Reed. "I had a hell of a time getting through to you folks. Nothing but getting transferred from one person to the next. You put me on hold the other day and the damn line went dead. What's going on up here?"

"You drove all the way up here from New York because you got cut off on the phone?"

Reed's manner hardened.

"I guess so."

Ullmann stared at Reed for a moment.

"Yes, I see that. I don't think it was worth the drive. We have procedures. We follow them. It's that simple." Reed tried to speak, but Ullmann raised a hand and talked over him. "Look, my family has been doing this for a long time. We know what works. That's why we do things the way we do."

"Ignoring calls and messages? Cutting off phone connections? That's your procedure?"

"Oh, stop," said Ullmann. "You know what I'm talking about. You should have gotten his dorm proctor on the line and arranged a phone call, that's all."

Reed stifled an urge to argue, held back pointing out that he was told all calls went to the administration building. Ullmann had somehow taken him off the point.

"Fine. Whatever. I just want to visit my cousin, see how he's doing. When can I do that?"

Ullmann inclined his head, speaking with exaggerated patience. "If you had waited, if you had talked to him or his dorm proctors, you might have saved yourself a trip. It just so happens coincidentally, there *is* a problem." Ullmann raised his hand to stop Reed from asking, talking quickly. "Nothing major. Nothing unusual. Just annoying. Terribly annoying. A stupid thing. It happens. It—"

Finally, Reed interrupted Ullmann. "What? What problem?"

Ullmann pursed his thick lips, adjusted his glasses, conveying frustration.

"Day before yesterday, Johnny Boy came down with a case of scabies."

"Who? What?"

"Your cousin—"

"What did you call him?" Reed asked.

"Johnny Boy?"

"Johnny Boy." Reed's brow furrowed. "What's that from— John Boyd?"

Ullmann shrugged. "I guess so. The staff has been calling him that for a long time."

"It's a child's name," said Reed.

Ullmann made a face as if the point were meaningless. "Whatever."

Again, Reed squelched his annoyance and asked, "You said he came down with scabies? What's that?"

Ullmann answered as if it affected him more than Johnny Boy. "It's a pain in the ass is what it is."

"What do you mean?"

"Look, it's like head lice, only worse. Much worse. Scabies go all over your body and they're terrible, but believe me this happens all the time in institutions. Head lice and scabies, they're the bane of my existence."

"The bane of your existence? How often does it happen?"

"Often enough."

"Well, how bad is it?"

"Nothing permanent. The damn things just drive you crazy with itching. It's a little mite, a nasty little thing that gets under your skin and causes itching. The problem is, scabies are very contagious. Very. Believe me, I've seen enough of it. You get a scabies infestation, forget it. It can spread like wildfire. Thank God, no one else has it so far, but I wouldn't be surprised if we don't get at least a couple of more cases."

"How did he get it?"

Ullmann shrugged. "I assure you I don't know. This is an institution, people living together, it happens. A lot of our residents go off to day programs. Some others come here. Who knows? Believe me, if I had my way, I'd delouse everyone that comes in and out of here, but the families would crucify me."

Ullmann turned toward the table where the two staff members still sat drinking coffee, and motioned that he wanted a cup brought to him as well.

"So what does this mean, exactly?"

Ullmann turned back to Reed.

"It means you drove all the way up here for nothing. You can't see your cousin. He's in quarantine."

Reed's voice rose, "Quarantine?"

"Yes," said Ullmann. "Quarantine."

Reed leaned forward, asking again as if the term were foreign, something from the Middle Ages. "Quarantine?"

"Absolutely."

Reed started to protest, but Eddie McAndrews arrived at the table with Ullmann's coffee. He set the cup down with a packet of artificial sweetener. Ullmann picked up the pack and started shaking the contents down to the bottom.

"Thank you, Eddie."

McAndrews turned away, heading back to his table, smirking at Reed's consternation.

Reed leaned forward, setting his forearms on the table and spoke calmly. "All right, take me through this, will you? When did John get these scabies?"

Ullmann slurped his coffee and asked, "What's today, Saturday? Saturday morning? I don't know when he got 'em, a few days ago, I suppose, but we noticed 'em Thursday night. Day before yesterday." This time Ullmann asked the question before Reed could. "Why didn't somebody tell you? Because it happened after I talked to you. And we have to do a test to make sure. We didn't know for absolute sure until yesterday.

You have to take a scraping and put it under the microscope or the doctor won't prescribe the medicine. He has to see the scraping. We did that late yesterday. Got the prescription filled. Gave him a treatment."

"A scraping?"

"They have to be sure it's scabies. They have to see the thing under a microscope before they prescribe the medicine."

"What medicine?"

"The usual. A special cream. You have to put this stuff on from head to foot. I mean it. Everywhere. You can't miss a spot. Then leave it on for twenty-four hours."

"That's it?"

"That's it. It kills everything. But it doesn't completely stop the itching. And you have to make sure they're all gone. You have to wait."

"How long?"

"From two to four weeks. You're supposed to wait until there are no more welts, no more itching."

"Look, I can't wait that long. I drove all the way up here from New York. I'm not waiting two weeks or two days. I want to see my cousin."

Ullmann seemed completely unmoved. "You want to get scabies?"

"I don't have to touch him. I just want to see him. Talk to him."

"They're extremely contagious."

"I'll keep my distance."

"Do you mind if I ask, what's the big emergency? What happened that all of a sudden you show up here, after years of no contact, and you have to see your cousin? Is something wrong? Is there something I should know about?"

"You keep asking me that. I just want to see my cousin. I haven't seen him for over three years."

"Four, according to my records. And now, you have to see him. Sounds a little strange to me."

Reed sat back in his chair and looked at Ullmann.

"Mr. Ullmann, do you really think I give a damn if that sounds strange?"

Ullmann snapped back, "Do you think I give a damn about you? We're the ones who take care of Johnny Boy Reed, not you. You haven't done anything in four years, and now I and my whole staff are supposed to snap to attention at your orders? Why? Why should we? You keep denying there's any problem or family emergency or any special reason that you *have* to see him. So what if you drove up here. It's not my fault."

Ullmann sat back, arms crossed, almost daring Reed to do something about his intransigence.

Reed could feel the anger welling up, but held himself in check.

Matthew Ullmann leaned forward. "Look, I've got a million things to do. Why don't you give us a call in a couple of weeks, we'll arrange something. Your cousin is fine. You heard it from me face-to-face so your drive up here wasn't a waste of time. That's all I can do for you."

Reed spoke very quietly, his stomach twisting as he forced himself to take on an appealing tone. "There must be some way I can at least see him before I leave. We don't have to be in contact. Please. Be reasonable."

Ullmann looked at Reed, smiling slightly now.

Reed steeled himself once more and said, "I'm asking you please, Mr. Ullmann. I don't want to go back to New York without seeing my cousin."

"Well," said Ullmann, "I understand you want to see him. But the problem with the scabies isn't my fault, you know."

"I didn't say it was, Mr. Ullmann."

Ullmann rubbed his chin, staring at Reed, making him wait for a decision.

"Where are you staying?" he asked.

"The Maple Inn."

"All right," said Ullmann, suddenly sounding conciliatory. "There's a room in his dorm I can set up, but it won't be available until this afternoon. Go back to the inn, have lunch, whatever. I'll set something up for three o'clock?"

Reed stifled a complaint about the long wait.

"Three o'clock."

Ullmann stood up from his chair.

"Where should I go at three?" Reed asked.

"Go to his dormitory. Davis Hall. I have to clear the hallways, get a room set up . . ." Ullmann waved a hand. "Never mind. Go over to Davis at three. Someone will take care of you. You'll have to talk to your cousin through a door with a glass pane."

"Through a door?"

Ullmann's voice hardened, making it clear his offer was take it or leave it. "Yes, through a door."

Reed almost yelled, oh, fuck you and your door and all your bullshit. The hell with you, the hell with this whole thing, but he grimaced a tight smile and said, "Fine."

Ullmann turned to leave, then he turned back and asked quizzically, as if he had just noticed that Reed was sitting in a wheelchair. "So what happened? I don't remember seeing any of his family members in a wheelchair."

Reed backed away from the table so that Ullmann could see his empty pants leg.

"I had an accident. Lost a leg. Hopefully this chair will be an interim thing until I get my prosthetic leg working."

"You don't have an artificial limb?"

"We're still working on it."

"Hmm. Yes. An accident?"

"Yeah."

"Uh, Johnny doesn't know about that, does he?"

"No. We haven't had any contact since, well, long before this." Reed said it without considering Johnny Boy's message, his mind occupied by Ullmann having reminded him it had been four years since he had seen his cousin.

Ullmann nodded. "Uh-huh."

"Why?"

Ullmann didn't answer Reed for a moment. He seemed to be refocusing his thoughts.

Reed repeated, "Why do you ask?"

"What? Oh, well . . . I don't know. It might upset Johnny. Seeing you in a wheelchair."

"I'll do my best to make sure he doesn't get upset."

"That would be good. Well, I've got a million things to do."

Ullmann turned and walked off without bothering to shake Reed's hand or even say good-bye. As he passed by his two employees still drinking their coffee, Ullmann paused to say something to them. They quickly stood up, brought their coffee cups over to the dishwashing window, and headed out behind Ullmann. Reed watched them leave the dining hall. He checked his watch again, wondering what he would do until three o'clock.

TWELVE

Following Matthew Ullmann's order, Eddie McAndrews headed for Johnny Boy's basement room. When he kicked open the door, even he was shocked by the sight. It had been thirty-six hours since the first itching started. Johnny Boy lay rigidly on the bed, his face contorted into a grimace, both hands under his armpits, holding himself tightly. At first, McAndrews thought he might be having a seizure. He had seen many of the residents go through seizures. But Johnny Boy's pajamas were stained with streaks of blood, and when he saw McAndrews, Johnny Boy opened his eyes and started to speak, only he couldn't get the words out clearly. He could only stammer out sounds.

"Eh, eh, eh."

"Ah shit," said McAndrews. Since he wore only the black rubber gloves, McAndrews stood at the doorway, keeping his distance.

"All right, come on, get up. Come on!" he yelled.

Johnny Boy sat up slowly, grimacing, knowing that moving would intensify the itching, but he struggled to his feet, because it seemed that McAndrews had come to do something that would help.

"Take off those fucking pajamas. Come on, strip. Let's go. You look like shit, man. What the fuck did you do to yourself? Come on."

McAndrews, keeping his distance, watched Johnny Boy peel off the pajama top, the cloth sticking to him with dried blood.

McAndrews turned his head away from the sight, disgusted, anxious to be done with this. He turned back to see Johnny Boy standing, waiting.

"Come on, goddammit," McAndrews yelled. "Pants too, let's go, everything."

Johnny Boy pushed down on the waistband of his pajama bottoms, but there was so much dried blood at his waistline that he had to peel the pajama bottoms off in sections. The movement caused the scabies to burrow deeper, causing another excruciating wave of itching. Johnny Boy managed to step out of his pants, but the pain rippled through him so intensely that he gave out low grunts, grimacing, shifting his weight from one foot to the other.

From his back pocket, McAndrews extracted a plastic garbage bag, tossing it across the room to Johnny Boy who stood grimacing, paralyzed by the itching.

"Come on, dammit. Shove that shit in the bag. Go on, get 'em in there."

Johnny Boy stood where he was, fearing any movement would intensify the itching.

McAndrews, furious now, took a step toward Johnny Boy. "Do it, motherfucker," he yelled. "And don't you fucking start crying on me now. God damn you, Johnny Boy, shove those pajamas in the bag or I'll come over there and stick my boot so far up your ass you'll forget about them damn bugs forever."

Johnny Boy fought to stay in control, his fear of McAndrews outweighing his pain, as he slowly squatted down to pick up the garbage bag and stuff in his bloody pajamas.

"Okay, toss it over here."

McAndrews grabbed the bag and tightly knotted the top.

Johnny Boy remained squatting, his pale skin smeared with blood, ugly welts, and raw scratch marks.

McAndrews extracted a large tube of Elimite from his back pocket. Keeping an arm's-length distance he said, "Stand up and put out your hands, boy."

Johnny Boy did so, holding out his hands, crying now, barely able to contain himself, but knowing that McAndrews was ready to help him.

McAndrews reached out and squeezed a large blob of white cream, filling Johnny Boy's right palm. It felt cool. Johnny Boy could smell the sharp medicinal odor.

"Okay, now rub it into your hands, like you're washing your hands. Yeah, that's it, go on, get it in between your fingers. Good."

McAndrews squeezed out more cream, telling Johnny Boy to rub the cream into his scalp, face, neck, underarms, crotch, pubic hair. Johnny Boy grimaced and rubbed vigorously, spreading the cream as quickly as he could. It burned into the open scratch marks and welts, but the burning felt better than the mind-numbing itching.

"All right, turn around. Hold your arms out."

Johnny Boy turned away from McAndrews, but didn't understand the command about his arms. He stood with his arms held just a few inches from his body, shifting his weight from one foot to the other, shivering now with most of his body covered in cream.

McAndrews poked at the back of Johnny Boy's right arm. "Put your arm up, dammit, come on, shithead, I ain't your goddam nurse. Put 'em up."

Johnny Boy raised his arms quickly and McAndrews squirted a blob of cream onto his back and spread it vigorously, starting high up at the nape of his neck, working it down, under Johnny Boy's arms, into his armpits, down his back, almost grinding the cream into Johnny Boy's skin, unconcerned that working it in so roughly would hurt him. McAndrews applied the Elimite as if he would rub it through Johnny Boy's back right down to where the scabies had burrowed.

Johnny Boy braced himself against the pushing, not daring to tell McAndrews to please take it easy.

McAndrews stepped back.

"All right, turn around. Hold out your hands again."

McAndrews squeezed cream onto both Johnny Boy's hands.

"Now reach around and rub that into your ass and between your cheeks. Get your balls and everything back there. Go on, I ain't touching your ass, you do it."

Johnny Boy gingerly reached behind him and began applying the cream to his backside.

McAndrews watched, waiting, growing increasingly angry at Johnny Boy's tentative, careful moves. He yelled, "Come on, get it in there. Do your pubes, again, too."

Johnny Boy continued rubbing, slowly, almost daintily.

"Turn around. Let me see."

He turned. McAndrews watched.

"Come on, what are you afraid of? Get your fucking hands in there. I don't want any flak from anybody if you don't get rid of these things."

McAndrews watched for a few more moments, then suddenly stepped forward and grabbed the back of Johnny Boy's neck, viciously pushing his head down, nearly doubling him over, screaming at him now, "Bend over, and get that stuff all over you and get done with this, dammit."

Johnny Boy lurched forward, a paroxysm of pain ripping through his lower abdomen. He emitted a truncated scream and fell away from McAndrews, grabbing his abdomen, crumpling to the cold cement floor, his faced tightened with pain, making short, breathless grunting sounds, repeating over and over a garbled, "Oh, oh, oh."

Shocked, McAndrews instinctively took a step back. "Jeezus, what the fuck?"

Johnny Boy lay where he was, immobilized by pain, appearing to McAndrews like someone who had been kicked forcefully in the testicles.

"Now, what the fuck?"

Johnny Boy struggled to sit up, still holding his abdomen.

"My stomach," Johnny Boy grunted. "My stomach."

"For chrissake, what's the matter with you?"

Johnny Boy remained doubled over on the floor, unable to explain any further.

McAndrews frowned disgustedly, screwed the top back onto the tube of Elimite, and shoved the medicinal cream into his back pocket. He pulled off the black rubber gloves and stepped out into the hall, picking up a clean pair of threadbare pajamas he had dropped on the floor outside Johnny Boy's room.

He stepped back into the room and tossed the pajamas at the naked figure on the floor. Johnny Boy had pulled himself up against the side of the bed, one hand on the floor, the other still clutching his abdomen. Scratches, welts, incipient scabs, and the medicinal cream streaked his white skin.

McAndrews shook his head disgustedly and said, "You are one sad, sorry, fucked-up retard, ain't you?"

Johnny Boy did not respond. McAndrews looked at him, considering.

"Fuck is going on with you, Johnny Boy?"

McAndrews asked the question more to himself than to Johnny Boy.

The pain in Johnny Boy's abdomen had waned enough so that he let go of his abdomen and leaned all the way back against the bed frame.

McAndrews spoke more quietly now. Most of his anger had waned.

"You finish rubbing that cream where I told you, get those pajamas on, and get your ass up off the floor. You hear me?"

Johnny Boy nodded.

"Get yourself together and I'll let you out of here. Otherwise you can just lie there and rot for all I care. Go on now, do what I told you."

McAndrews stepped out of the room, letting the door slam shut behind him.

———

After Ullmann left, Reed sat fidgeting at his table in the dining hall, getting ready to head back to the inn and kill time until three. Just then, a slim man, neatly dressed in khaki slacks, a denim shirt, and a plaid tie walked briskly into the dining hall. Reed noticed him the moment he entered, figuring him for about sixty years old. He appeared to be quite normal, almost distinguished-looking, except for a slight smile and an intense gaze that made him appear to be preoccupied with something important.

The man strode over to the gate that closed off the serving area and kitchen from the dining room. He knocked lightly on the metal gate and announced in a whispery, conspiratorial voice, "Lisa's going to have a baby."

A voice from the kitchen answered, "Have a seat, Charlie. Five minutes."

Charlie repeated his message exactly as he had the first time. "Lisa's going to have a baby."

This time there was no response from the kitchen, which did not seem to disappoint Charlie in the slightest. He turned and spotted Reed, and with the same half smile and intense gaze, headed for him.

While Charlie zeroed in on Reed, a group of three women entered the dining room. One lady seemed to be in her forties, tall, wearing a long dark skirt with an elastic waistband, and a white blouse. She seemed to look up at the ceiling as she walked, swaying her head slightly, her eyes unfocused as if she were blind. She seemed to be heading toward Reed, too.

Behind her came a very diminutive woman with Down syndrome. She too wore a long skirt with elastic waistband and a blouse, her outfit augmented by a Boston Red Sox baseball cap perched askew on her head. She held the door for a third woman who was more severely impaired. The third woman used an aluminum walker to shuffle into the dining room, her legs, arms, and gnomelike body bent and misshapen. Reed had no idea what disorder had crippled her so and immediately felt impressed at how steadfastly she struggled forward, step by step, using her walker. Her companion, the woman with Down syndrome, walked next to her until the pair arrived at a table a short distance from Reed. He watched as the baseball-cap lady pulled out a chair for her companion, then became distracted by the elderly man, Charlie, who was now standing next to him.

Charlie placed a hand on Reed's shoulder, telling him, "Lisa's going to have a baby."

Reed smiled back and said, "That's nice."

Charlie stroked Reed's shoulder and said, "That's nice. Nice coat. Soft."

"Thanks," said Reed.

"Lisa's going to have a baby."

"Uh-huh. That's wonderful," said Reed.

The first woman, the tall one who had entered behind Charlie, took a seat at the table with the other two women. Turning toward Charlie, her upper body wavering, she announced in a loud angry voice, "And Charlie is going to have a big, ugly monster."

Reed turned toward her and saw her glaring at Charlie. He smiled, realizing now that this must be Lisa, a woman well past childbearing age and certainly in no position to "have a baby."

Charlie, his enigmatic smile and whispery tone of voice unchanged, simply repeated, "Lisa's going to have a baby."

Two more male residents and a female staff member entered. The staff member was a heavyset woman, who may or may not have been in charge of the group.

Charlie persisted in telling Reed, "Lisa's going to have a baby."

"That's enough, Charlie," said the staff member as she walked into the kitchen.

Charlie quickly pivoted away from Reed and started circulating around the dining hall, presumably to spread the news about Lisa's fantastic pregnancy.

More of the residents came into the dining hall, some of them still wearing their denim barn jackets. Reed heard sounds from the kitchen that told him they were about to begin serving breakfast. He caught the attention of every person who came into the dining room. They obviously had so little contact with other people that Reed's presence was an event. He felt that any moment they would all be coming over to his table out of curiosity, or in search of company, or simply because he was somebody new and different. The thought of the Ullmann Institute residents descending on him made Reed feel uncomfortable. Even though Reed knew his reaction was unfair, their slightly vacant stares, awkward mannerisms, labored ways of speaking, abnormal physiques and faces, all disturbed him. He rolled his wheelchair out from behind the table and wheeled toward the kitchen, unable to shake the feeling that he was running away.

A slight, kindly looking fellow with a neatly trimmed mustache, wearing a flannel shirt, baggy jeans, and red watch cap, walked into the dining room and directly into Reed's path, forcing Reed to stop short. The man appeared to be in his thirties, but the flecks of gray hair at his temples and mustache indicated he was older.

"Hello," he said in a very soft voice. "What's your name?"

Reed, slightly annoyed, stopped his chair and answered, "Bill." And then, not wanting to be rude, said, "What's yours?"

The man answered, "Paul," extending his hand.

Reed shook the soft hand, devoid of any grip.

"Where are you from?" Paul asked.

"New York." Then realizing that his answer might not make much sense in upstate New York, Reed said, "New York City."

"Oh, oh. Is that far?"

"Pretty far."

"What do you do?" asked Paul.

Reed paused for a moment and said ruefully, "Well, it didn't take you long to come up with a question I can't answer."

"What?" asked Paul.

Reed smiled. "Actually, I'm on vacation. I'm not doing anything right now."

"Oh, oh. That's nice. Is that interesting?"

Reed thought over the question for a moment and said, "Yes, actually. In a way, it is interesting, not knowing what you're going to do."

"Oh," said Paul.

"Do you know John Reed?"

"John? John Reed?"

"Johnny Boy."

"Oh, Johnny Boy, yes, Johnny Boy. He's not here now."

"Do you know where he is? Have you seen him?"

Paul, never having changed his wan, slightly confused facial expression during the brief conversation, did not answer. Reed waited a moment, then decided there wasn't much point in continuing.

"I have to go now, Paul. I'll see you later."

"Oh, see you later," said Paul, who stood where he was and watched Reed wheel into the kitchen.

Reed tried not to rush, but knew that he was hurrying to be away from the Ullmann Institute residents. He left by way of the kitchen entrance and pushed his chair slowly but steadily up and down the asphalt walkway that crossed the expanse between the dining hall and the visitors' parking lot. He felt uneasy, and asked himself why, going over it in his mind.

Why was he reacting this way to the residents? Wasn't it really just the way he had been dealing with his own cousin, staying away, feeling guilty about it, but doing it anyhow?

Yes, Reed had to admit to himself, but there was more.

Ullmann. That guy Ullmann had infuriated him. Talking over him. Interrupting him. Making Reed grovel before he gave an inch. Reed shoved harder on his oversized wheels, pushing harder to get back to his car and off the grounds quicker.

But something else bothered Reed. It wasn't just the residents and Ullmann. What else was it? An uneasy feeling clung to him, and he couldn't quite figure out why, until he rolled into the parking lot. Those two sitting nearby, drinking coffee, *they* had made him uneasy. And now one of them, the shorter, stocky one, stood smoking a cigarette, leaning against the trunk of Reed's BMW, one foot propped up on the bumper.

Reed edged the wheelchair toward his car. What the hell is this? He rolled closer to Boggs, waiting for him to move away from the BMW. He didn't.

"You mind getting off my car?"

The man simply stared at Reed, his mastifflike head down, his hooded eyes glaring slightly, as if evaluating him. He didn't move.

Reed shifted in his chair, ready to raise his voice, ready to tell this fellow to get the hell off his car, not ask him, but the man pushed himself upright and stood away from the BMW.

"This your car?" he asked.

"Yeah it's my car. You work here, right? I saw you in the dining hall."

"Yeah."

"What's your name?" Reed asked.

"Ray Boggs, what's yours?"

"Reed, Bill Reed. That the only place you can find for a cigarette break, Ray?"

Boggs took a deep drag, checked the butt to see how far down he had smoked it, then flicked it off to his left.

"As a matter of fact, yeah. They don't let us smoke on premises, you know. Got to go have a smoke where it's allowed."

"The parking lot?"

"That's what I said, isn't it?"

Reed decided not to ask why smoking in the parking lot was not considered smoking on premises.

"I see. Step aside will you? I have to get in the trunk."

Boggs took one step to his left, still very much blocking Reed's way.

Reed sat where he was, looking at Boggs, trying to assess the situation. He couldn't quite believe that this man intended to cause him trouble, but why was he just standing there? Why the obvious challenge? Reed continued to stare at Boggs, waiting to see what would transpire.

After a few more moments, Boggs asked, "What's the matter, chief?"

"I said I need to get to the trunk."

"So what's stopping you?"

"I need more room."

Boggs didn't move.

"Is there a problem?" Reed asked.

"What do you need more room for?"

"So I can sit my ass up on the lip of the trunk while I pack up my wheelchair."

Boggs nodded, but still didn't move.

Reed waited. He could feel his heart begin to pound inside his chest. He looked at Boggs, carefully assessing the man. Even though Boggs wore his blue staff jacket, Reed could see that this was a strong man, with thick neck and big hands, and an air of meanness about him, a man without any physical disabilities.

Reed shifted uneasily in his wheelchair, trying to ban the realization that with only one leg, if it came to a confrontation, he would be no match for the man standing in front of him. Maybe not even a match if he had both legs.

Finally, instead of moving, Boggs asked, "Need any help?" asking it in a way that had little to do with offering help.

"No," Reed answered. "I don't."

Boggs shrugged and stepped away from the car, smirking at Reed as he did so.

Reed rolled toward the trunk. Boggs stood watching him from a few paces off. Reed tried to ignore him, but couldn't stand the idea of Boggs observing his efforts to take apart his chair, pack it up, make his way on crutches to the driver's seat.

Midway through the task, Reed looked toward Boggs and asked, "Don't you have anything better to do?"

Boggs shrugged. "Nah."

Reed refused to look at Boggs after that, but by the time he finally got behind the wheel, he was almost ready to aim his front bumper at Boggs and run him down. But by then, Ray Boggs was casually striding across the expanse of lawn back toward the dormitories.

Thirteen

Bill Reed accelerated out of the parking lot, but had an impulse to turn back and find Matthew Ullmann, make a complaint, demand he call in his employee so Reed could confront that guy. But at the same time Reed felt a desire to simply keep driving, to just leave. Leave all the anger and embarrassment and strangeness behind.

A monologue of questions filled his head. What were those two jerks doing in the dining hall? To be around if I got too demanding? What the hell was that guy in the parking lot doing? Had Ullmann told him to keep on eye on me until I left? What the hell is going on here?

Reed made an effort to calm himself and think rationally, to measure if he were being paranoid or delusional. He wondered if the motorcycle accident and John's weird picture-message and his self-imposed isolation and the sense of being disconnected that he felt in Dumphy had all combined to make him lose perspective? What the hell is going on here? Are these people just naturally meaner up here? More combative? Less civilized? Was that it?

Reed shook his head, banishing the questions. No, he told himself, no, dammit, face it, man, that's not the question. The question is why didn't you get up, stand up on your one damn leg, and call that bastard out? Why? You know goddamn well you would have done it before.

And then Reed told himself, no, no . . . why be stupid? Why get down in the gutter with a guy like that? What's he got to lose? A shitty job at a home for the retarded? He probably hates that job. And you, you want to break a knuckle? Get your teeth chipped or loosened or may even knocked out? Your jaw broken? End up in a hospital? No. The hell with that.

Reed tried to tell himself he had done the smart thing. But he didn't try very hard, because it didn't help.

Five hours later, after an unsatisfying lunch at a local diner, killing time in his depressing room, and struggling through the local paper instead of his beloved *New York Times*, Bill Reed found himself driving back onto the grounds of the Ullmann Institute. His mood hadn't improved. He found himself angry at everything—even his cousin—for causing him all this trouble and inconvenience, for bringing him to this godforsaken place filled with assholes.

He turned off the ignition and sat for a moment, gripping the steering wheel.

"Forget it," he told himself, "just forget it. It's not his fault. Just see how he's doing. Don't add to the poor guy's problems. You're here to see John Boyd. Just forget it."

He went through his routine yet again, assembling the wheelchair, pushing his way slowly and steadily from the visitors' parking lot to Johnny Boy's dormitory. As he passed through the grounds, Reed saw much more activity than he had seen earlier. Residents, mostly in twos and threes, walked from the dormitories to the dining hall, from the barn to the dorms, up along a dirt road leading to a wooded area. Only a large group of about ten residents walking into the woods was attended by a staff member . . . another single male, this one wearing a blue Carhartt jacket and hunting cap. A large patch with yellow letters spelling STAFF had been sewn on the back of his jacket.

Reed saw only one woman with Down syndrome. Several of the residents seemed physically normal. One or two walked with jerky, labored motions that signaled some sort of palsy.

Reed continued to observe the residents from afar, grateful that he wasn't attracting their attention, thinking he was too far away to be noticed. But then, a discomfiting thought hit him. It wasn't just the distance. Wheeling along in his chair he somehow fit into the scene. Suddenly, Reed felt akin to them, another person with a disability.

He broke off his gaze, dismissing the thought, bearing down harder with each turn of the wheel.

Reed arrived at the doorway of Davis Hall promptly at three. Kitridge stood waiting for him, dressed in a pea coat to ward off the cold. Reed was surprised to see Kitridge smoking a cigarette. He had the impression that Kitridge had been waiting more than a few minutes.

On seeing Reed, Kitridge side-handed his cigarette behind a bush and said, "This way." He turned and walked up the two steps that led up to the dorm's entrance. A wheelchair ramp to the right of the steps led to the entrance. Reed detoured to his right and pushed himself up to the landing, Kitridge waiting impatiently at the entrance.

They entered a typical institutional building with cream-colored cinder-block walls, fluorescent lights, green linoleum floors polished to a sheen, acoustical tile ceilings. The building had been constructed without any attempt to fit into a rural setting and although clean and well kept, its contemporary style seemed decades old.

They entered a hallway that ran the width of the building. Three long corridors ran perpendicularly from the entrance area. Kitridge walked to the corridor on the far right. Reed refused to acquiesce to Kitridge's cold reception so as he wheeled along he asked, "How is he?"

Without looking back Kitridge responded, "I haven't seen him."

At the far end of the corridor, they arrived at a large wooden door with a long panel of reinforced glass running vertically almost top to bottom on the right side of the door. Kitridge turned.

"This is the dayroom. For your visit we've put him in a small room off this larger one. You'll have to talk to him through the door, but it does have a glass panel like this one here."

Kitridge opened the door to the dayroom with a key on a large ring, no further explanation given. He held the door open for Reed to wheel past him and merely pointed to the corner.

Reed entered the dayroom, remembering it vaguely, expecting the room to be empty, but off to the left sat the man who had brought Ullmann his coffee, the one Ullmann had called Eddie.

He sat in one of the fiberglass scoop chairs, feet propped on a table, reading a wrinkled copy of *Guns and Ammo* magazine. Reed quickly turned his gaze away, choosing to ignore him, and headed for the door in the corner. He frowned at the sight of the door separating him from his cousin. It matched the thick door he had just wheeled through. It offered only a four feet high and about four inches wide strip of reinforced glass through which to establish contact with Johnny Boy.

Having decided he did not want his cousin to see him sitting in his wheelchair, Reed had brought one crutch, tied to the back of his chair. Reed worked his way out of the chair, up onto one foot, bracing himself on the chair, staying out of sight until he could get his crutch under him. Looking at the narrow strip of glass running down the door, Reed knew it wouldn't be hard to keep his empty pants leg out of sight. If John asked about the crutch, he'd tell him he'd sprained an ankle.

Reed stepped toward the door, aware that McAndrews watched him, but determined not to give him the satisfaction of looking in his direction. He approached the thick door, bent over slightly, and peered through the heavy reinforced glass. He saw a small, stocky figure hunched over, sitting in the corner of what looked like a storage room. The figure, dressed in a dingy, terry-cloth robe, stared at the floor, rocking slightly.

Reed hesitated, then knocked on the door. The figure turned. And at that moment, all of Reed's anger, his resentment, impatience, all his emotions disappeared for a second and a rush of concern filled the vacuum. The face staring blankly in his direction didn't belong to the person Reed had seen only four years earlier. It wasn't just the welts and red marks from the scabies. It was a face that had once seemed perpetually youthful and now looked old and haggard.

Reed quickly forced a smile and yelled through the door, "John, it's me, Bill. Cousin Bill."

For a moment, nothing.

Reed yelled again. "Cousin Bill."

Suddenly Johnny Boy's entire visage changed. First, his eyes widened in surprise, then a wide, uncontrollable grin animated his round face.

Reed tapped on the door, nodding, yelling. "Yeah, it's me. It's me, John. Come here."

Johnny Boy rose from his chair, slightly hunched over, and came to Reed, walking with a rolling gate, still smiling, his tongue protruding, looking almost embarrassed to be smiling so broadly.

Reed yelled, "John. How are you, John?"

In answer, Johnny Boy, still grinning, pressed his forehead against the narrow strip of glass as if he could press through it and bury his face in Reed's chest. Reed felt his throat constrict. He instinctively reached for the door handle to pull the door open so he could gather Johnny Boy into his arms, but the door handle would not turn.

With Johnny Boy closer, Reed could more easily make out the welts and scratch marks on his face and neck. He grimaced and pounded once against the wall, standing up straight so Johnny Boy could not see his face if he looked up. Reed had to clear his throat, breathe hard once before he could force a smile, but not at all sure he could smile without breaking down.

Reed bent down toward the glass pane and yelled, "John, John, how are you?" And again he yelled Johnny Boy's name until finally, Johnny Boy looked up, still smiling, but with tears running. His answer to Reed's question was to silently press his cheek to the glass.

Reed looked away for a moment, wiping his hand over his face. He smiled a tight smile and leaned down close to the glass panel, yelling, "It's good to see you, man. How are you?"

Johnny Boy nodded and smiled, unable to say anything, his tears smearing the thick strip of glass between them. Reed felt his eyes stinging, his own tears about to come. He shut his eyes tight, clamping down on his emotions, refusing to give in to the sudden, overwhelming grief he felt. Reed patted the door gently, "Take it easy, John, take it easy. I know it's hard. It's all right. Take it easy."

Reed watched his cousin, looked closer at his face, seeing the lines of age etched into the corner of his crinkled eyes, waiting for Johnny Boy to settle down.

"What happened? They told me you got scabies."

Johnny Boy, his eyes locked on to Reed's face, nodded and touched a welter of bite marks on his neck.

"You look like you got some real nasty bites there. Did they give you medicine for it?"

Johnny Boy nodded more rapidly, his expression changing to one Reed felt meant to communicate that Johnny Boy didn't want *him* to worry.

Reed started talking, unable now to stop the tears. He wiped them away quickly with his thumb and forefinger, keeping his expression happy. He said, "It's all right, John. They have to keep you alone so nobody else gets them. You understand that, John? Do you?"

Johnny Boy stepped back now, far enough so he could place both hands on the door, saying something, no longer smiling. Almost all expression disappeared, and he spoke as if the door were not between them, looking directly at Reed. Reed bent closer, trying to hear through the door, realizing Johnny Boy did not understand he had to speak louder. Reed pressed his ear to the door, finally hearing the soft voice say, "Cuz'n Bill." And then again, once more, "Cuz'n Bill."

"Yeah, it's me. Here I am. I got your . . ." Reed stopped himself, sensing a presence. He turned to see that Eddie had come closer, almost within earshot. Reed turned away, determined not to let this stranger see the emotion on his face or intrude on his time, and snapped, "You mind?"

Eddie stepped back, hands up. "Yeah, sure. Go ahead. Just wondering if you need anything?"

"Some privacy. Just some privacy," said Reed, making an effort to keep his voice even. Reed bent down to the panel again and said, "John, are you all right? Do you need anything?"

"When?" said Johnny Boy.

Reed mostly read his lips to understand the word.

"Now," Reed said. "Do you need anything now?"

Johnny Boy's face scrunched up and said, "Itch. Bad, bad itch."

"Still? It still itches?"

Johnny Boy nodded and smiled.

"I'll talk to the doctor, make sure he gives you something. Whatever he can. Okay?"

Johnny Boy nodded again, Reed not knowing if in reaction to his statement or simply to his presence on the other side of the door.

"All right, you just hang in, John. Just hang in there. I'm going to talk to them, make sure you get better. Okay?"

Johnny Boy nodded again, but this time said, "Okay."

"I'm going to find out exactly how long you have to be there. Do they keep you in this room?"

Eddie answered from behind. "Just for this visit. He's back in his own room now. We got his roommate cleared out. He has to stay in there."

Reed stifled his anger at the staff member's eavesdropping, but realized he had been shouting to be heard through the door, so he let it go.

Speaking more softly, Reed said, "All right, Johnny. I'm going to go now."

Immediately Johnny Boy's smile disappeared and he stepped back toward the door, suddenly agitated.

"No, don't worry. I'm coming back."

"Cuz, Cuz'n Bill." Reed heard the words faintly, but spoken rapidly.

"Don't worry. I'll be back," Reed saying the words loud and slow. "I'll be back."

He saw Johnny Boy mouth, "When? When?"

"Tomorrow. I'll be back tomorrow. You want anything? You want me to bring you some ice cream?" Reed tried to think of other things that Johnny Boy liked, but couldn't remember.

"Yeah, yeah," said Johnny Boy, nodding his head rapidly, reminding Reed how excited he could get.

"Tomorrow. Same time, tomorrow. Or whenever they can arrange it, but tomorrow for sure."

"Tomorrow," said Johnny Boy.

"Right, tomorrow, John. Tomorrow."

Reed could tolerate leaving, but couldn't stand any more of this. He turned and stepped to his immediate left, moving out of Johnny Boy's line of sight, not wanting him to see the crutch, certainly not wanting Johnny Boy to see the empty pants leg swaying beneath his stump.

Reed did not look back at the panel of glass in the thick wooden door. He did not look at Eddie McAndrews. He headed straight for his wheelchair, strapped his crutch on the back, turned his chair around, and sat down, not even thinking about balancing, just doing it, wanting only to get out, to grab the big twenty-six-inch wheel rims and push and push and push out the door, up the hill, down the hill to find Matthew Ullmann.

Fourteen

As Bill Reed approached the troublesome three stairs leading up to the administration building, he paused. As usual, the physical effort expended propelling his wheelchair had burned off some of his emotions. He sat at the foot of the stairs, thinking, calculating. What are you doing? he asked himself. Jumping on this guy, Ullmann? For what? John? That employee in the parking lot? You're in no shape to even get up those stairs much less get into it with that man. You'll turn into a ranting lunatic if you're not careful.

Reed pivoted the wheelchair and headed for his car.

Reed packed up his wheelchair and made it into the driver's seat with much more deliberate and precise movements compared to his previous exit. This time, Reed did not rush off. He sat behind the wheel, parked. Bill Reed could not move, could not start the car. He felt drained, enervated.

Finally, Reed's face twisted in disgust. He banged his fist against the steering wheel.

"What the fuck is going on here?"

He reached down and fired up the BMW, but instead of driving off the grounds, he drove down near the staff houses and parked in a small parking lot fronting the first two houses. He pulled his crutches out after him as he exited the car, and made his way down a gently sloping hill to the barn area.

A split-rail fence surrounded the yard in front of the barn. He propped his stump against the middle rail and settled himself in, supported now mostly by the fence rail and his good leg, hardly any weight on the crutches.

A huge, rolled bale of alfalfa had been dumped in front of the barn and two male residents with pitchforks were pulling clumps off the bale and pitching them into a large wood-slatted cart. One of the workers stood about five feet two, muscular and compact, appearing to be in his thirties. He wore a denim barn jacket, no hat to cover his unruly black hair. A two or three days' stubble darkened every crease in his rubbery face. While the man worked, he displayed what Reed had to admit was an idiotic-looking grin, but the smile gave Reed the impression that pitching hay truly made the man happy.

The other resident seemed quite unhappy, standing in rubber boots, stained corduroy pants, and a red sweatshirt, scowling as he lifted a clump of alfalfa and pushed it onto the cart. After each halfhearted pitch, the man stopped and frowned and fidgeted. His work partner didn't seem to mind in the least.

An older man, a farmer type who wore denim overalls and jacket over a plaid shirt and a sweat-stained John Deere cap, came striding out of the barn. He told the slacker, "Come on, Josh, keep up. We haven't got all day."

Josh pulled off another small clump of alfalfa and pitched it onto the cart, and again stopped to rest.

The farm man spotted Reed standing at the rail fence and headed toward him.

"You looking for somebody?" he asked.

"Nope," said Reed. "Just visiting."

"A resident?"

"Yes. John Reed."

"Oh, Johnny Boy."

"Johnny Boy. That's what you all call him?"

"Yeah. A lot of us around here do."

"His name is John Boyd."

"Sounds a lot like John Boy. Johnny Boy."

"But it's not."

"What's the difference?"

"The other makes him sound like a two-year-old."

The farmer shrugged as if to say, well isn't he?

"You work here?" Reed asked.

"Just part-time." The man pointed behind him with his thumb. "I keep the barn operation supplied. Take care of the animals."

"Last time I was here you had a lot of chickens."

"Oh, yeah. Still do. Nice little herd of pigs, some sheep, two horses. The cows, of course. A couple of goats. Even got a llama last year. Mean son of a bitch. Spits at you if it don't like you."

"No kidding. Whose idea was that?"

"Mr. Ullmann's, I guess. Don't ask me why. Say, do they know you're waiting out here?"

"Does who know?"

"Mr. Ullmann. Or the day administrator. Whoever's on duty now?"

"Kitridge, I think. What difference does it make? You're not allowed to stay a while and breathe the air after a visit?"

"They usually have someone with the visitors. You know, to take care of them."

"Do I look like I need taking care of?"

The man in the John Deere cap shrugged again. He turned and watched the two retarded men working the alfalfa onto the cart, then he looked up at the sky. "Better get that load in. Supposed to snow tonight."

"Snow?"

"Oh, yeah. Probably won't stick, but it'll make a mess of things for a while."

Reed watched the farmer walk back into the barn. To do what? Reed wondered. Clear a place for the alfalfa, or call somebody and tell them there was an unattended visitor hanging around the barn?

Just then, two female residents came out from the back of the barn, both carrying red plastic buckets filled with eggs. Reed recognized one of the women as Lisa from the dining hall. She walked ahead of her partner, grimacing and staring skyward, then looking down to the ground, walking with a steady but overly determined stride, as if she had to concentrate on each step for it to go in the right direction. Behind her, a smaller woman with Down syndrome followed. Both women wore denim coats and long skirts, but the woman with Down syndrome also wore a knit tam-o'-shanter pulled down on her round head in a way that Reed found distinctly charming. When she spotted Reed standing at the fence, her face burst into a wide smile that made Reed smile back. She waved and Reed waved back as if they were old friends, as if Reed had come there to meet her.

She walked toward him, the smile turning into an open-mouthed grin. Reed found himself captivated, unable to stop himself from smiling back at her.

When she came closer, Reed said, "Hello."

"Hello," she said. "What's your name?"

"Bill, what's yours?"

She paused for a moment, looking up at Reed, still smiling. He asked again, "What's your name?"

"Pauline," she said in a sudden burst.

"Have you been gathering eggs?"

She looked down at her bucket. "Eggs," she said.

"That's a lot of them."

"Yes. Heavy," she said.

"Do you live here?" asked Reed.

Pauline nodded.

"How long?" Reed asked.

"Ten years." Again she answered quickly, the words coming out so they almost sounded like one word.

"Do you know my cousin, John Reed?"

She looked down, then back up at Reed, still smiling but seeming to be a little uncomfortable about the question.

"Johnny," said Reed. "Johnny Reed."

"Johnny," Pauline repeated, head still down, but nodding. "He's my boyfren."

"Your boyfriend?" asked Reed.

Pauline looked up now, shyly, but clearly excited to be sharing this information with Reed.

"Boyfren."

"I see. So you like Johnny?"

Pauline nodded several times, actually blushing now. "I like him," she said.

"That's nice," said Reed.

Pauline stood in front of Reed, charming him.

"Do you and Johnny get to spend a lot of time together?" asked Reed.

Pauline just smiled, not answering the question.

Reed asked, "Do you have a nice time together?"

"He's sick."

"I know. He has scabies."

"No. His 'tomach."

Reed looked intently at Pauline, her smile had evaporated and she looked serious now.

"His stomach? What's wrong?"

"Hurts."

"His stomach?"

Pauline nodded.

"Really."

Pauline nodded again, her eyes wide, mouth open, appearing quite serious.

"Well, I guess we'd better . . ."

A voice from behind interrupted.

"Pauline, bring those eggs over to the kitchen."

She looked past Reed and immediately looked down, quickly turning away from Reed, walking off as if she had never talked to him in the first place.

Reed turned to see Matthew Ullmann standing behind him, dressed in a camel-colored stadium coat, a scowl on his face. Reed lifted his stump back off the fence, pulled the crutches up under him, and turned to face Ullmann.

"Mr. Reed, why are you still here?"

Reed stifled the urge to say none of your damn business. Instead he kept his face impassive and said, "Decompressing, I guess. It wasn't such an easy visit."

"I see."

"John doesn't look too happy."

Ullmann didn't respond.

"He doesn't look well at all. Is he all right?"

"Of course he's all right. He's just had a bad couple of days."

Reed asked, "When does the doctor see him again?"

"Next week," said Ullmann.

Reed nodded. "Do you have a doctor on staff?"

"No. He comes in when we need him. But we have a full-time nurse practitioner."

"What's the doctor's name? I'd like to talk to him."

"Why?"

Reed paused, stifling his reaction to Ullmann's challenge. Trying to speak evenly, he answered, "I'd like his opinion on how John is doing."

Ullmann nodded, but didn't say anything. Reed waited, purposely not asking for the doctor's name again. Reed shifted his weight on the crutches and continued waiting, his face neutral, but staring at Ullmann.

"What are your plans, now?" asked Ullmann.

"I'm not really sure. I'd like to come back tomorrow. My cousin seemed a bit upset by all this. It wasn't much of a visit. I figured I'd give him a chance to settle down a bit, then try to spend some time with him before I go. I told him I'd be back tomorrow. Bring him some ice-cream."

"Uh-huh."

"Is that all right?" Reed asked, pushing it, forcing Ullmann to respond.

"Whether or not it's all right, I'm sure you'll be coming back anyhow, won't you?"

"Why wouldn't it be all right?"

"Why? Because at some point, obviously, you're going back home. It's nice that you and Johnny got reacquainted. I'm sensitive to the fact that he has no other relatives in his life, but as I say, eventually you'll be gone, and he'll be pretty much back where he was."

"Back where he was?"

"Here, at the institute. On his own, just like before. You're going to be visiting him on a regular basis. Visiting him on a schedule he can count on."

Reed nodded. "Uh-huh."

"So . . . it leaves us, leaves him in a situation."

"What kind of situation?"

"The more you see him, the more he'll want to see you. And when you stop seeing him, my experience is that it will affect him. Often times, residents go through a depression after these prolonged visits. As I said, the more times you see him, the more he'll want to see you, and the harder it will be after you go."

"Well, what about tomorrow? He's expecting me."

"You ought not to make commitments before you know what the situation is, what the effect will be."

The corners of Reed's mouth twitched. Ullmann stood in front of him, hands thrust in his pockets, a pedantic tone to his voice. Reed said nothing for fear the anger would be audible no matter what words. Finally, Ullmann said, "Okay, well, tomorrow, what time were you planning on?"

"When is convenient?"

Reed waited, expecting Ullmann to make up an inconvenient time. Finally, Ullmann said, "After morning chores. After nine-thirty. We have his room cleared out, now. He'll get another treatment tonight, just to make sure. Promise to keep your distance, you can meet with him in his room. No contact. No hugs and handshakes. I don't want you blaming us if you come down with anything. Or spread it to anybody else."

Reed nodded.

Ullmann raised a finger, friendly now as if they had known each other for a while. "No contact."

"Right," said Reed. "I get anything I'll just sit in my room and cry by myself."

Reed saw that it took Ullmann a fraction of a second too long to catch the full implication of his statement. For just a moment, Ullmann's slight veneer of civility slipped and Reed saw a flash of anger contort Ullmann's face.

"Good-bye," Ullmann said, quickly, dismissively, turning to walk away.

Undeterred at the slight, Reed called out, "Oh, I almost forgot. What's that doctor's name?"

Ullmann turned back, smiling, condescending. "Dr. Prentice," he said. "George Prentice."

Reed noted that Ullmann gave no further information.

"Prentice. Thanks," said Reed. "I'd better be getting along now."

"Yes," said Ullmann over his shoulder. "You'd better."

This time, when Reed made it back to his car, both Eddie McAndrews and Ray Boggs were in the parking lot, Boggs sitting on the opened tailgate of a red '90 Ford F150. McAndrews leaning back on the tailgate, his feet on the ground. They both watched Reed as he headed for his car.

Reed stopped about ten feet from the BMW and turned toward them.

"You guys have it pretty easy around here, don't you?"

"Says who?" answered McAndrews.

"Says me." Reed looked toward Boggs. "What is this? Another cigarette break?"

McAndrews pushed off from the tailgate and said, "In case you hadn't noticed, Mr. Ullmann doesn't like people just wandering around the grounds."

"Is that so? Is that why you're here?"

McAndrews shrugged. Boggs glared.

Reed stood his ground waiting. Then turned and headed for his car, but not before muttering, "Assholes."

Ray Boggs instantly bolted off the tailgate. McAndrews just managed to grab his thick arm and hold him back. Reed heard the scuffle and turned back. McAndrews had managed to get in front of Boggs, but the look on Boggs's face set Reed's heart pounding.

Boggs yelled, "Say it again, motherfucker. Go on, say it again."

The sudden violence and anger stunned Reed into silence.

"Get in the truck, Ray." McAndrews had to say it one more time before Boggs broke away and headed for the passenger side of the truck. Reed stood where he was. He was only a few paces from his car door, but he knew that if McAndrews hadn't stopped him, Boggs would have easily gotten to him before he could have made it to his car.

Reed hoped the fear he felt didn't register on his face.

McAndrews smiled at him. "You got some mouth on you there, mister."

Reed still couldn't muster a response.

"You like insulting people?"

McAndrews watched Reed. For a moment, Reed thought the man was going to come over and confront him. Finally, he said, "What the hell do you want from me?" knowing that he sounded more plaintive than challenging.

McAndrews smiled again and drawled, "How 'bout you get the fuck out of here. You ain't even supposed to be parked here. Asshole."

Reed nodded, trying not to look as if he were backing down, turned, and made his way to the BMW. McAndrews casually shut the tailgate on his truck, leaned back, and watched until Reed got into his car.

Reed slid the key into his ignition and fired up the BMW. Reed couldn't help but notice that his hand shook slightly.

Fifteen

Johnny Boy sat alone in his room, a room stripped of everything but a mattress covered with plastic and a bed frame. The burning, biting itches had subsided. Now all he had to endure were the discomfort of deep scratches and the tight scabs that had begun to form.

Johnny Boy didn't know the time of day, or even the day of the week, so he could not follow the institute schedule. He knew he was sick, so he didn't have to do chores, but he knew that even if you were sick you had to follow the meal schedule and the sleeping schedule. It worried him, not knowing. The memory of the scabies troubled him. But the worry and apprehension that plagued him, the fear and anxiety that always seemed to be part of his life churned almost imperceptibly underneath the excitement he felt at having seen Cuz'n Bill.

Cuz'n Bill had appeared, transforming Johnny Boy's distant memory into something real. Sitting on his bed, still alone and more isolated than ever, the reality of Cuz'n Bill comforted Johnny Boy. Now Johnny Boy could easily remember Cuz'n Bill's brown hair, the way his eyes crinkled when he smiled, his strong neck and nice teeth. Even alone, Johnny Boy could clearly see Cuz'n Bill's face in his mind's eye.

Johnny Boy sat on the edge of his bed, wrapped in his institutional terry-cloth robe, rocking slightly, thinking about the face he had seen on the other side of that glass panel. Somehow, they had made Cuz'n Bill stay on the other side of the door so he couldn't hug him or even shake his hand. But Cuz'n Bill had come. And Cuz'n Bill had said he would come back. Said it with his loud voice. The kind of voice that when he said things like that, you knew he meant it. Not shouting, not that kind of loud, just strong. Sure and strong. Tomorrow, Cuz'n Bill had said. Tomorrow for sure.

Johnny Boy sat smiling, rocking, wondering how long it would seem before tomorrow came.

Reed drove off the grounds and turned right, not thinking about his direction, not caring where he headed, just wanting out of there. Away from that damn place. Away from that son of a bitch in the parking lot.

He pressed the accelerator hard, needing to feel the power of the big engine at his command, needing to be in control of that power, to press his foot down and make something respond to him, to move him. The BMW surged forward, the carburetors kicking in, the tachometer spiking. In seconds, Reed sped down the empty two-lane road, hurtling along at nearly sixty miles per hour, rapidly increasing the distance between him and the Ullmann Institute. But even though the distance increased, the anger and mortification he felt barely diminished. It clung to him as if something deep inside him had ruptured.

"Shit."

He slammed a fist against the steering wheel. A curve loomed up suddenly, and Reed had to brake hard to negotiate the turn. He felt the tires squealing in protest, sliding slightly. He glanced quickly at the speedometer. It read sixty-eight miles per hour. He made it through the curve, punching the brakes, lightly now, reducing his speed to sixty, then fifty-five, concentrating on reining in his emotions.

He breathed deeply, forcing out his breath, clearing his lungs. He banished every thought, every image from his mind. He concentrated on staring at the road, not allowing himself to remember John Boyd's ravaged, tearful face contorted with a brave smile, crushed against that glass panel, banishing the images of Boggs and McAndrews baiting him, hassling him, making him back down.

"Shit!" he cursed. He grimaced, diving into the anger that

stirred inside him, seeking its power to pull him away from the darker, more debilitating emotions.

"Fuck," he yelled. Shifting in his seat, focusing on what to do. What to do. Making his mind work, pulling himself back from the trap of inaction. He forced himself to confront the source of his pain.

"John Boyd Reed." He said the name out loud, facing the reality of what had happened to his cousin, sick, locked up, abandoned in that place; owning up to the crushing guilt he felt because he had abandoned an innocent person who needed his help and attention.

Reed rubbed his face, grimacing.

Goddammit, he's sick. And not just those fucking scabies. Scabies didn't put those lines of pain around his eyes. Christ, he looked so, so drained. And that sweet little woman in that crazy hat had said it so quickly. She knew it. I know it. Ullmann has to know it. But what is it? What the hell is this with his stomach? Reed asked himself. What the hell is going on?

And those assholes in the parking lot. And Ullmann. Is it just me or do they treat everybody like troublemakers? Is it because I haven't been involved with John? Do they just fucking resent me for showing up out of nowhere?

Reed banged his fist on the steering wheel again and told himself, "Fuck it. I don't care what it is, it's bullshit. They can't do this."

Reed picked up his cellular phone and pressed a speed dial number. He waited for the cellular phone to find a signal and put the call through.

The familiar voice of Adele Simpson answered crisply, *"Hello?"*

"Adele, it's me. Sorry to call you at home. I know it's the weekend, but I need a favor."

"Sure, I'm glad you caught me. I was just heading out. How are you?"

She asked the question quickly this time, getting it in. Adele wanted to know.

"Fine, fine. I'm on the move here, this connection might

break, I'm up in the middle of nowhere, but could you put me on hold, get phone information for Dumphy, New York, find out the number and the address for a Dr. George Prentice. In whatever the area code is here. Dumphy."

"Sure, but hang on for a second," answered Adele. *"I'm at my computer. Stay on, if we lose the connection I'll call you back, or you call me on a land line, but let me see if I can find that information on my phone disc. This is a new edition. Dumphy, New York?"*

"Yes."

"Dr. George Prentice you said?"

"Yeah."

Read could hear Adele's computer keys clicking in the background.

"This might save us a few moments. Phone information is so slow these days. Okay, let's see, hold on a sec . . . here, I have it. There's an office and a home phone."

"Give them both to me."

Reed smiled at Adele's efficiency and prowess. He memorized the phone numbers and addresses she gave him. He needed to hear the information only once.

"Do you want me to go on-line and check the whereabouts of the address?"

Reed saw that he was approaching the Mobil station he had passed earlier.

"No, that's okay. I'll find it. Thanks. Thanks, Adele. Sorry to bother you at home."

"You know that's not a problem. I'm here if you need me."

Reed felt reinforced from Adele's tone that delivered the unsaid message: I'm glad you're back in contact with me and I'll hang in here as long as you want me to.

"That's okay, Adele, I should be all right now. Don't stick around."

"All right. I'll have my cell phone with me if you need anything."

"Yeah, fine. I'm surprised my own phone works so well up here."

"I'm not. A lot of those remote areas have good coverage because so many people rely on cell phones. And no obstructions."

"Aha. A pleasant surprise."

"Call me if you need me," said Adele.

"I'll probably be talking to you tomorrow."

Reed cut the cell phone connection and pulled into the gas station, shoved the BMW into park, and dialed the number for Prentice's office. He found out the doctor kept Saturday office hours. When asked if he wanted to make an appointment, Reed declined.

Reed drove as close to the gas station office as he could, glad that this wasn't one of those stations where a single clerk sat behind a Plexiglas barrier punching buttons and making change.

Reed punched his horn lightly and waved to the man inside the office, motioning him over, watching him frown as he approached. A stocky man, graying at the temples, wearing mechanic's overalls, came out. He clearly did not appreciate being summoned by a man sitting in a BMW that cost quite a bit more money than he would earn over the next year. Reed didn't blame him. He quickly apologized, telling the mechanic he was sorry, pointing to the crutches in the backseat. The man peered into the car. His sour expression changed quickly when he saw Reed's stump. He tried to make it up to Reed by giving very thorough directions to the doctor's office.

Twenty minutes later, Reed drove into a small strip mall. He had no problem spotting the doctor's office occupying the corner of the mall that also housed a Chinese restaurant, a liquor store, a hardware store, and a drugstore. The doctor's office occupied the corner of the mall, taking up a space almost as large as the three businesses next to it. Reed drove close enough to the entrance to see the names of three doctors on the door. All were MDs. One doctor was an ophthalmologist. One an internist. After George Prentice's name were the initials FACS. Reed thought for a moment. A surgeon. Fellows of American College of Surgery.

Reed checked his watch. A little after four. Hopefully this guy's seen most of his patients today.

Reed grabbed his crutches, stepped out of the BMW, quickly getting up on one foot, and made his way to the door. He shouldered it open and swing-stepped his way over to the reception counter where a middle-aged woman sat talking on the phone. She wore a green cardigan sweater over a white blouse primly buttoned to the throat. Reed listened to hear if it was a personal call or a business call. It was business.

While he waited for the woman to finish her quiet discussion about appointment dates, Reed looked around the office . . . typical cheap, efficient construction: sheet-rock walls, Formica counter, fluorescent lights, acoustic ceiling tile. All except for a floor-to-ceiling section of file cabinets that covered the entire wall behind the receptionist. Reed wondered how many of the file drawers were filled with patients' records. Only one patient sat in the waiting area, an elderly lady, still wearing her dark wool coat.

Reed quickly counted the empty chairs, scanning one row, then multiplying, eight times three, twenty-four, the number coming into his head instantly.

Lot of empty seats. Maybe because it's the end of the day, Saturday.

The receptionist finished her call. She looked up at Reed, smiling pleasantly. "You here for Dr. Anthony?"

Reed said, "No. Dr. Prentice."

"Oh," she said.

"Why Dr. Anthony? The crutches?"

"Yes. But . . . I'm sorry, do you have an appointment?"

"No. I just need a couple of minutes. It's not a medical call. Does he have a few minutes?"

"Does he know what it's about?"

"It's about my cousin, John Reed, over at the Ullmann Institute. My name is Bill Reed."

"Oh, I see." She looked down to her appointment book. She scanned the page. "It looks like he . . . let me call him."

She punched in a number. Reed heard the busy signal pulse softly in the earpiece.

"Have a seat, Mr. Reed. He's on the phone. I'll try again in a minute."

None of the chairs in the waiting area had armrests, which made sitting down and standing up hard on Reed's remaining knee, so instead of sitting, Reed stepped over to the window overlooking the parking lot. He looked out at the gray clouds scudding fast across the darkening sky. The temperature had dropped. Just by looking at it, Reed could almost feel the moisture in the air announcing the coming snowstorm.

Dr. George Prentice sat at his desk with a furrowed brow, one hand holding the phone to his ear, the other holding his head.

"Well what specifically does he want, Matthew?"

"He wants reassurance, that's all," Ullmann answered. *"Just reassure him. And call me when he leaves. I want to know what transpires."*

"Why don't I just tell him I have patients?"

"Because I want to take care of the man's concerns and send him on his way satisfied that his cousin is being well taken care of. You've done this a million times, George. Just reassure him."

"Fine. All right."

Prentice, a trim, meticulous man, prematurely gray in his early fifties, replaced the phone in its cradle, only to have it ring almost immediately. Prentice frowned. He stared at the phone, letting it ring, then, with an air of resignation, picked it up, listened, and told the receptionist to send in Mr. Reed.

When he heard the knock on his office door, Prentice said, "Come in," then watched Reed enter. He saw a handsome man who looked rugged enough to be working in the local lumberyard or the hardware store next door, except for his clothes: cashmere polo shirt, wool slacks, shearling coat. And the crutches. But even the crutches, at first, added to the rugged image, as if Reed had broken a leg or sprained an ankle doing hard labor.

But then, as Reed made his way toward the doctor's desk, the swaying empty pant leg told a different story.

"Have a seat," said the doctor. Reed's crutches and amputated leg prompted Prentice into assuming the role of doctor, even though Reed was not his patient. He pointed to a seat placed next to the desk, adding to the doctor/patient feeling.

Reed sat, smiling, holding his crutches in his left hand while he extended his right.

"Hello, Doctor, my name is Bill Reed. I hope I'm not imposing too much."

Prentice shook the outstretched hand, feeling the strength in Reed's grip, even though Reed made a point to only meet the pressure of the smaller man's handshake, nothing more.

"That's all right. What can I do for you?"

"It's about my cousin, John Reed."

"What about him?"

"I understand he's your patient?"

"Well, yes, he's assigned to me. I'm one of several physicians on call at the institute. I follow a few of their residents. My practice is mostly surgical. Although we all do a bit of everything up here."

"You're a surgeon?"

"Yes. General surgery. But again, we don't have a lot of specialists up here. I do many different procedures."

"Well, how does it work? How many doctors are on call?"

"For the institute?"

"Yeah."

"I think there are four of us. I'm really not sure of that."

"Each of the residents gets assigned to a doctor?"

"Yes. But they have a nurse practitioner who does most of the care. And if they need an MD, they call me or one of the other doctors."

"Who's the nurse practitioner?"

"Didn't you know?"

"No."

"Madeleine Ullmann. She's very competent."

Reed nodded. "No, I didn't know that. The boss's wife?"

"Well, yes, she's Mr. Ullmann's wife, but . . ."

"What?"

"They're lucky to have her there full-time."

Reed nodded, trying to be agreeable.

"Right. But if John needs a doctor, he's assigned to you."

"Yes. I haven't, uh, I haven't been taking on any new patients there, so it's mostly the long-term residents I follow. Johnny, John is one of my patients. I mean, if I'm needed."

"You sound like you aren't too involved."

"I am when I'm needed. It's just that I don't do as much work at the institute as I used to. And the number of patients has dwindled over time."

"Why's that?"

"The population there has declined. You know the state is phasing out those places."

"What places?"

"Residences that house more than a handful. Institutions. The state has made a big push to deinstitutionalize over the years."

"So how come the Ullmann Institute is still around?"

"Well, frankly, I think it's because they have a number of patients, residents, that can't get placed anywhere else. Very low functioning. Some of them are also, well, bordering on the . . . I wouldn't say violent, but fairly difficult to handle."

"Really?" said Reed.

"Yes. And, also, they aren't certified by the state. They started out as a school. So they didn't go that route. Of course, they're overseen by the state, at least the residents are . . . it's a bit complicated. Mr. Reed, how familiar are you with the situation? I would think as a relative you'd be informed on these issues."

"I'm not."

Prentice blinked at Reed's abrupt answer.

"Well, that's of course, well, that's not why you're here, is it? To get a history of New York State policy for housing the retarded. I take it your concern is with Johnny? Is it this situation with the scabies?"

"Yes. But it's not just the scabies thing. I saw him just now, and he doesn't look well at all. I'm worried it might be something other than the scabies."

"Like what?"

"I don't know. That's why I came to see you."

"Well, I haven't seen Johnny for a few months. As I said, I usually only see them if there's a problem. Otherwise, just for a yearly physical. What do they say at the institute?"

"They said you're supposed to see him next week."

Reed watched Prentice's reaction. He seemed both surprised and annoyed, but quickly tried to hide it.

"Really? Well, maybe they've made an appointment for him. You can check with the receptionist."

"When was the last time you saw John?"

"Probably July. I'd have to look at his chart. It's July and January when I do my annuals."

"You didn't see him about these scabies?"

"No. I wouldn't normally see him for that. Mrs. Ullmann is fully qualified to handle that. What's worrying you, Mr. Reed?"

Reed watched Prentice's eyes carefully, kept his own expression blank, and then said quietly, "He's complaining about stomach pains. Does that ring any bells? Have you run into anything like that with him?"

"No," said the doctor.

Reed's expression never wavered, but behind his blank stare the calculations flared . . . that answer was too quick, too short, his eyes shifting and blinking twice. He's lying.

"No one has said anything about other problems? Nothing at all?" asked Reed to press the lie.

"Not that I remember. I'd have to pull his chart. I won't be able to review it today, but if you'd like to call me tomorrow, no wait, tomorrow's Sunday. I'll be in Monday. Why don't you call me sometime in the afternoon?"

Now he's equivocating, talking too much, giving me too much information, thought Reed.

"Monday," said Reed.

"Yes."

"Monday afternoon?"

"Yes. You know I'm not really supposed to give out medical information, without a release."

"What?" said Reed. "A release? From whom?"

"Well, I understand. In this situation. I'm sorry, I don't remember your cousin's situation. Any other family members involved?"

"No."

"Well . . . I see."

"This stomach thing . . . it doesn't ring a bell with you, stomach problems?"

"No. It doesn't. But listen, if you're concerned about your cousin, by all means, bring him in to see me. Or we can schedule something with Dr. Porter, he's an internist. We'll try to get to the bottom of this stomach problem you're talking about. You know, my experience, although limited, is that Down syndrome people often suffer from digestive problems. It could be something ordinary. A change in diet. It could be a little more complicated. I suggest you schedule an appointment for him with Mrs. Lee out at reception."

"Uh-huh. But with those damn scabies and all, when would you be able to see him? They tell me he's in quarantine."

"Yes, but once he's gotten a treatment it shouldn't be a problem. If we have to see him, we'll see him. You know, there are procedures. Protective garments. Is he complaining a lot, or . . ."

Then, without a preamble, Reed said, "Ullmann told me a doctor had to see a scraping or something before he could get a prescription. Did you do that?"

"No. As I said, Madeleine would do that. And she's licensed to write a prescription for the medicine he would need. It's a cream."

"Oh," said Reed. "Maybe I misunderstood what he said."

"Understandable. No, I didn't look at the scraping, but I'm sure Madeleine did. She's seen that kind of thing ten times more than me."

"Ah," said Reed. Then Reed just sat and watched the doctor, offering nothing more, just staring at Prentice. Prentice began to sound as if he were talking to himself. "When was it he came down with those? Monday or Tuesday? What's today,

Saturday? I can't quite remember. He should really be clear of everything in another week. We might wait two weeks just to be sure. But I assure you, everything will be fine. Really. He's in good hands. The people at the institute know how to take care of things like scabies. It's really not something for a surgeon. You know, Mrs. Ullmann is very experienced."

"Mrs. Ullmann."

"Yes. She's very much on top of things at the clinic."

Reed watched Prentice for a few moments longer, then abruptly said, "So they never called you at all about this."

"No. They may have called the office . . . I don't know. I don't think so."

Now he's hedging, thought Reed. He looked at the doctor for a few more moments, then abruptly grabbed his crutches that had been propped against his right knee and said, "Right. Well, thanks so much for your time, Doctor. I'll be visiting John again before I leave. I'll see how he feels and if necessary I'll make that appointment."

The doctor stood up, obviously glad that the meeting was over.

"Good. If you have any concerns, just bring him in. We'll make sure everything is all right."

Prentice remained standing while Reed maneuvered up on his crutches.

"When did you undergo the amputation?"

"Just about seven months ago."

"You seem to be doing well."

Reed played along, allowing the subject to change.

"Yeah, the stump is still giving me hell. Not working too well with my prosthesis."

"It takes time. It can be complicated. A year isn't unusual for things to resolve."

"That's what they tell me."

The doctor came out from behind the desk and patted Reed on the back as he walked him to the door.

"Good luck," said Prentice. "Take care."

"Right," said Reed. "Thanks."

Sixteen

Ralph Malone, county sheriff, stepped out of his Mercury Grand Marquis police cruiser, left the engine running and police radio on, windows rolled down so he could hear any broadcast that might come over.

He had parked at the apex of Matthew Ullmann's long crescent driveway, right at the foot of the front porch that bordered three sides of Ullmann's Victorian lakeside manor. Malone walked up the four wide stairs and spotted Ullmann sitting in his favorite Shaker rocking chair at the far corner of the porch. He wore the same camel-colored, wool stadiumcoat he had on at the institute, as if he had come home and had yet to enter the house. Ullmann sat staring at the small lake that filled the northern section of his property.

In about fifteen minutes, the sun would drop below the tree line. The high-altitude cirrostratus clouds had already begun darkening, adding a gloomy cast to the end of the day as well as signaling the snowstorm that had been predicted.

Ullmann heard the footsteps behind him and without turning around motioned toward the rocking chair on his right.

"Ralph," said Ullmann, "have a seat."

Malone took off his Smokey Bear hat and sat down in the rocker, the gray, form-fitting sheriff's shirt under his blue unzipped sheriff's jacket pulled slightly at his paunch. He shifted the nine-millimeter Beretta handgun in the holster at his hip so he could sit back in the chair, but he sat back as if it were expected, not as if he really wanted to, planting both feet equidistantly in front of him, his no-nonsense black work boots flat on the porch.

Sitting back in the rocking chair didn't mean Ralph Malone

relaxed. Not while on duty. That didn't fit the image Malone had of himself. Five-eight, square-shaped, crew-cut, Ralph Malone had the body of a middleweight boxer beginning to balloon. He fought hard against his slowly expanding waistline, working out three times a week, keeping himself firm underneath the extra pounds that seemed to come on him against his will. Ralph Malone would not allow himself to be the stereotypical fat, redneck, country-boy lawman. He was the duly elected County Sheriff in charge of twelve deputies, a lawman good enough to serve on any police force, state or city.

"How's the missus?" Malone politely asked.

"Oh, you know Madeleine," said Ullmann, "always busy, busy."

"That's good. So what can I do for you, Matthew?" Getting right to the point, also in keeping with his image.

"Are you on your way home, Ralph?"

"Yes. This is my last stop."

"I wonder if you could go over to the Maple Inn. There's someone staying there I'd like you to check out."

"What's the name?"

"Reed. Bill Reed. Maybe registered as William Reed."

"Is he a problem?"

"Might turn out to be a pain in the ass. Might not. But I just have a feeling. Don't ask me why."

"Uh-huh," said Malone, waiting for something more. When Ullmann didn't offer anything, Malone asked, "Who is he?"

"Johnny Boy Reed's cousin. Seems to be the only living relative around. For some reason, he's shown up here after about four years without any contact."

"What got him interested?"

"Don't know, Ralph. Curious, isn't it?"

"I guess."

"One thing I do know is that Johnny Boy is one of our assets. I don't want any distant relative being stupid or demanding."

"What do you want to know about this fella?"

For the first time since Ralph Malone had sat down, Ullmann turned to face him, flashing his usual grimace that passed for a smile. "I want to know how big a pain in my ass he's going to be." Ullmann's forced smile disappeared. "No. Just the usual. I want to know who he is. What he does. The usual. I just don't know anything about him."

Malone stirred in his chair, turning his hat in his hand. "Well, Mr. Ullmann, these things take time you know."

"I know," said Ullmann. "I know. And I know how valuable your time is, Ralph."

"Time is time," said Malone. He turned his hat in his hand, again waiting for anything more that Ullmann might say. When he didn't, Malone asked, "You think he might need a little push in the right direction?"

"Maybe," said Ullmann. "Maybe. Did you have plans for tonight?"

"Not really."

"Something besides hanging out at the gun club with your cronies."

Malone ignored the gibe and asked, "What does he drive?"

Ullmann smiled again, this time a genuine smile knowing what he was about to say would annoy Malone.

"He drives a big silver BMW. A Seven-Forty. Nice car. New York plates. I'll bet there aren't two of them parked at the Maple Inn. What do you think?"

Malone stood up as if sitting in a comfortable chair were bad for him. He took a step toward the railing that circled the wooden porch and gazed out at the lake.

"Say New York plates? Whereabouts in New York? Do you know?

"New York, New York. Manhattan."

"Uh-huh. Well, okay then."

Malone turned and adjusted the rocking chair, putting it in the exact spot it had been before he sat in it. He placed his sheriff's hat on his head, squaring it, ready to leave, keeping to his image of a man who did not engage in small talk. But before he stepped away, Ullmann raised a hand.

"Ralph."

"Yes, sir."

"In case you want to know . . ."

"Yes?"

"He's only got one leg. Gets around on crutches and a wheelchair. Doesn't have a fake leg or anything."

"That so."

"Yes."

Ullmann smiled again.

"What?" asked the sheriff, seeing the smile.

"Just thinking," said Ullmann.

"Yes?"

"Kind of hard to kick anybody's ass when you've only got one leg."

Malone didn't smirk or smile back. He seemed to take the comment seriously, asking, "Why? He seem like the ass-kicking type?"

"He seems like he'd want to be. Maybe he used to be."

"Uh-huh. Big BMW-driving, New York City ass kicker, huh?"

"Could be."

"That's fine with me. We'll see about it."

"Thank you, Ralph."

Seventeen

As Bill Reed pulled into the Maple Inn parking lot, he checked his watch. Almost five-thirty. He wondered if that corner bar was open. He hadn't been through so much in one day for a long time. He needed a drink.

The unpacking and assembling the wheelchair routine was becoming familiar, but certainly not less tedious. As was the trip up the ramp to the side entrance of the inn. Just as he was about to turn into the doorway, Angela Quist came striding out. Reed had to grab the wheels to stop from running into her.

"Oops," she said. "Sorry."

"Sorry."

Reed practically had her pinned against the door. He pivoted, she stepped in the same direction; he reversed, she matched his move.

"Hold it," she said. "I haven't done this dance with anyone in a wheelchair. You're too fast for me."

"Right, right," said Reed. "Let me get out of your way."

He began backing up, looking behind him so he wouldn't end up on the ramp. When he turned forward, Angela Quist hadn't moved.

"You're pretty good in that thing."

"Thanks."

Reed stopped, looking at her now. She wore the same tan leather coat, but blue jeans and a sweater instead of her waitress uniform.

"You working?"

"No. Saturday is my night off. I come in and help with the prep." She shrugged. "That's how I get out of the busy night. And I work Sunday dinner."

Reed nodded.

"How was your day?" she asked.

Reed smiled. "Surprisingly bad."

"Oh?"

"Yeah."

"You saw your cousin?"

"Yeah."

"How was he?"

"Terrible."

Angela dropped her leather shoulder bag on the ramp rail and leaned back against the rail.

"How was the Ullmann Institute?"

Reed saw now that she intended to talk to him instead of rush off. In the harsher light from the parking lot and the fixture above the service entrance, he could see that she ap-

peared to be older than he had first thought in the more flattering light of the inn's restaurant and bar, but no less striking.
She was a beautiful woman. One that Reed would sit and talk
to as long as she wanted him to, even though he was preparing
himself for one of her abrupt exits.

"Not very pleasant. I wouldn't recommend the place."

Angela nodded, saying nothing.

"Is that little corner bar open?"

She checked her watch. "No. Not until six-thirty."

"What's the matter, you people don't believe in happy
hour?"

"I guess not." She smiled. Seemingly uneasy about something. "Listen," she said. "About last night. My rather abrupt
exit. It wasn't too polite."

Reed cocked his head, waving off the comment.

"No," she said, "I just . . . I don't know. I just didn't want
you to get the wrong impression."

"What impression?"

Angela straightened up off the ramp rail. "I don't know. It
just wasn't very polite."

Reed wondered if Angela thought she might have given
him the impression she hadn't wanted to be around a guy with
one leg.

"Hey, don't worry about it. You were tired, done with work,
whatever."

"Right."

"So what's good tonight?"

For a moment Angela looked at Reed quizzically. "Oh,
here? You mean the food?"

"Yeah."

"Nothing. No specials."

"No fresh fish?"

"They've got salmon, but that's nothing very special."

"So where's a good place to eat around here? Something
not too far away so I won't get lost."

"Well, the Homestead in Edgemont is the best place around
here. Not too far. A little pricey for North Country folks, but
you look like your budget can manage it."

"Why don't you join me?"

Reed asked the question fast, without planning, without being sure exactly why he had asked, except maybe because he really wanted to know if his amputation made her uncomfortable.

"No," she said. "No thanks. But that was pretty slick."

"What?"

"Setting me up like that."

"It wasn't a setup. Honest. And it would be much easier going with someone who knows their way around here. You'd be doing me a favor. Come on, I can tell you don't have any other plans."

Reed could see now that she was considering it.

"Come on. It'll make up for your fast exit last night."

Angela lifted her chin at Reed, looking a little defiant.

"Oh, I see. Trying to make me feel guilty."

"If it works, sure. Just say yes."

And then she decided, all at once.

"All right. Yes. Pick me up at eight."

Angela dug a notepad from her large bag and quickly sketched a precise map with carefully printed directions.

"If you don't make any wrong turns, you can get to my house in about fifteen minutes from here."

With that, she stepped around the wheelchair and strode down the handicapped ramp. Reed resisted the urge to turn around and see what she looked like from the rear.

Angela Quist spent most of the time until Reed was to arrive tidying up her house. But she had showered and done her hair, conceding somewhat reluctantly that she was going out on some sort of a date.

She checked the image in her bathroom mirror and quickly applied lipstick as if it were a chore rather than a pleasure. She stepped back from the mirror to check her outfit . . . black jeans and a white blouse. Too much like her waitress uniform. She made a face at herself and walked into her bedroom, pulling the blouse out from her waistband, unbuttoning it, and laying it on her bed. She went to her dresser drawer where she kept her sweaters neatly folded and stacked, thought about putting on a dark sweater artfully flecked with nearly imperceptible flecks of violet, but that would mean changing her white bra. She pulled out a gray sweater, but decided it was too tight. It would emphasize her full breasts a little too much for a date with a stranger.

"Fuck," she said, but it sounded more like fock.

She unhooked her white bra, slid it off, folded it neatly, placed it in her dresser drawer with the rest of her lingerie. She pulled out a black lace bra, slipped into it, thinking—he'll never know you've got this sexy thing on so don't worry about it. Then she lifted the dark sweater out of the second drawer of her dresser and pulled it on.

She looked at herself in the mirror over her dresser and said, "Very colorful."

Opening her jewelry box that sat on the back corner of the top drawer, she picked out a pair of cone-shaped earrings made from a thin piece of metal colored and burnished with earthy shades of brown, yellow, and red. She slipped them into her pierced earlobes, checking the mirror once again. Better. She adjusted her hair, which she had shampooed and blow-dried into the shape she wanted. It fell in soft waves to just above her shoulders.

She turned away from the mirror and looked at the white blouse she had rejected lying on her bed. She walked out of the bedroom leaving it there, sure that no one would be visiting her bedroom that night.

She thought about a drink while she waited. A drink and a cigarette. Why? Because you're nervous? No. Not nervous. Anxious? No. Annoyed? Is that it?

She made a face, dismissing the question. She walked into her living room, avoiding the kitchen where she kept her bottles of liquor in a cabinet under the silverware drawer, looking for her leather jacket that she had hung over the back of a chair.

Why are you so annoyed? Because it's a pain in the ass, this going out. Dressing, doing your hair and makeup. You don't need a free meal this bad, do you? You know you're going to spend the night talking about Lizzie and that cousin of his. That's why you avoided a conversation last night, isn't it? So why are you doing this?

She thought about Reed. Damn good looking guy. Sort of cool, the way he says things with that sly half smile. So why not? The leg thing? Were you afraid he'd think his stump creeped you out, so you said yes? Angela thought about that. No, not really. But she had to admit, if the guy had both legs she probably wouldn't even be thinking about it. You'd go out with him. Even if he does have a relative in the institute. Wouldn't you?

Angela shook her head, consciously putting it out of her mind. She was committed, right? So the hell with it. She headed for the front of the house, carrying her jacket, digging into the pocket for her cigarettes. Skip the drink and have a cigarette, she told herself.

Bill Reed sat in his car, engine running, parked in the Maple Inn lot, comparing the map that Angela Quist had drawn to a road map of the county he had picked up at the inn's reception desk. He had laid down for a quick nap that had lasted longer than he expected. Now he had just about fifteen minutes to find Angela's house. No time for wrong turns.

Angela's map had been so accurately drawn and the directions printed so clearly in precise capital letters, that the county map seemed unnecessary. But Reed persisted, comparing the hand-drawn map and the printed map until he had a clear sense of the distance. Satisfied, Reed finally drove out of the Maple Inn parking lot, heading in the right direction, but watching carefully for the first turn onto County Road 11.

He set the odometer on the BMW and tried to relax. Reed figured he had about three miles before he had to look for his first turn on White Birch Road.

Reed pushed a hand through his thick brown hair, still wet from his quick shower.

"Well, well, your first date as a gimp. How's it feel?" he

said out loud. Better than eating alone in that dining room filled with old ladies and retired tourists, he thought.

He made the first turn, and every one after that, making no mistakes, except for driving past the big white rock that Angela had told him marked the entrance to her driveway.

Reed backed up and turned into the entrance, driving a surprisingly long distance along a gravel driveway bordered on both sides by pine forest. After about a tenth of a mile he emerged into a clearing, the site for what looked to him more like a hunting lodge than a house. Angela had told him to beep his horn and she'd come out, but Reed hauled out the crutches and made his way up the set of wide stone steps to the front door, which opened just before he reached out to knock.

Angela stood there, surprised to see him at the door, as he was her.

"Oh," she said. "I saw your lights."

Reed looked back toward his car. There were no other lights on the property other than a single bulb burning in the fixture near the front door. He realized his headlights must have lit up the outside noticeably.

He turned back to Angela. "Right. Well, I know you told me to beep, but I thought it more polite to come up and knock."

"Ah," said Angela, "politeness counts."

Reed smiled. She wore her tan leather jacket, black jeans, and a sweater that made her look arty and chic. And she had done her hair. It looked fuller, more groomed. Even in the dim glow of the entrance light, Reed could see she had made an effort to look as if she were going out. He felt flattered.

"Well, would you like to come in for a moment?"

"No, no. Thanks, that's all right. We can move along."

Reed had no intention of trying to make his way around Angela's house on his crutches. What if he had to walk up a flight of stairs? Or down? No thanks. He turned and started to ease his way down the stairs leading up to Angela's front door. She kept pace with Reed's slower steps, making Reed a bit uneasy, but he took it as a kindness on her part.

"Did you find the place, okay?" she asked.

"Not one wrong turn."

"Congratulations. I'm kind of out here in the boonies."

"That's a huge house."

"I know. The gentleman who built it couldn't seem to make up his mind what he wanted. I guess he kept adding to it over the years."

"It looks almost as big as the Maple Inn."

"Hmm, I'd say about two-thirds the size, but there's more grounds. He bought up about twenty acres around the place. Not very scenic, but private."

"So you rent from the guy who built it?"

"No. He's dead. The new owner is renting it to me until he figures out what to do with it. Which is why the rent is so cheap. I have to get out on short notice. How do you like the Maple Inn?"

"It's all right. I stayed there once before a long time ago. Had a better room than this time. This time they put me in a little room on the ground floor. I guess that's the *wheelchair-access* room. There's no elevator in that place is there?"

"Nope. A lot of the older guests complain about the stairs."

Reed nodded, not wanting to dwell on the fact that he had joined that category.

Angela stepped ahead of Reed, heading for the car's passenger-side door, making it obvious she did not want Reed to trouble himself opening it for her.

Reed quickly stepped to his side of the car and dropped into the driver's seat. He had been accustomed to placing the crutches in the front passenger seat and struggled to stow them in the back. Angela had to lean out of the way.

"Sorry."

She said, "No problem."

They settled into their seats.

"Nice car," said Angela.

"Thanks. How far to the restaurant?"

"About half an hour."

"Oh."

"A half hour up here is like around the corner."

"I guess."

For a while, they made small talk about the roads and the

weather, Reed driving carefully but occasionally glancing over at Angela simply because he enjoyed looking at her. Angela held up her side of the conversation, but she kept her gaze forward toward the dark road ahead.

And then Reed asked, playing up the line a bit, "So what's a nice girl like you doing in a place like this?"

At this, Angela turned toward him for the first time. "You mean up here in the middle of nowhere?"

This time Reed kept his eyes forward, making it easier to say what he wanted. "Yeah. By your last comment, about a half hour seeming like around the corner made it sound like you've lived in places not so isolated."

"Oh?"

"And you don't exactly look like you fit in up here."

"What does that mean?"

"Oh, I don't know. The average woman up here seems to have about twenty years and a hundred pounds on you."

Angela smiled.

"Not to mention, you've got a real style and presence. I dig your tattoo. You seem very with it, educated . . . I don't know, you just don't look like a waitress in an isolated inn up in the North Country."

"I like the flattery, but what's wrong with being a waitress?"

"Nothing. Not a damn thing. But I'd bet that's not all you do."

"Okay, you're right. I grew up in Boston. Graduated from the Rhode Island School of Design. Lived in London for a while. And New York. But now I'm up here."

"What brought you here?"

"Space. Work. Cheap rent. I build and design furniture and cabinetry. I need a woodworking space, a studio. Couldn't possibly afford it in New York. Also there is cabinet work up here, some carpentry, not a lot, but they're building more and more up here. And it's really a beautiful part of the East. Plus, there's the waitress thing."

"Uh-huh."

"And my sister lives here. At the Ullmann Institute."

"Oh."

She mimicked Reed's "Oh?" turning it into a question. "I know, I sort of slipped that in, didn't I?"

"Yes."

"Everything else is true, but she is the main reason I'm here. Okay. So now you know. Last night, when I heard about you and your cousin, I didn't say anything about my sister living there too simply because I didn't want to get into a long discussion. You know, relatives and their—"

"I understand," said Reed.

"So maybe you were right, I was feeling guilty."

"I was only kidding about that, but if it ended up with you agreeing to dinner, I'll take it. But there's absolutely nothing to be guilty about, you know that, right?"

"Yeah. I know." Angela pointed ahead and said, "Slow down, the restaurant is around that bend. See if you can squeeze into a space out front. The parking lot in the back is a hassle."

Reed just managed to get the last space in front of a slightly ramshackle one-story building set right on the highway. They were close enough to the entrance that Reed easily made it into the restaurant on his crutches. The modest exterior belied the warm, nicely finished interior. They walked into a packed bar area. Reed could see that most of the tables in the dining room were filled.

"Christ," said Reed. "This place is popular. Did we need a reservation?"

"I made it," said Angela. "Barely. Luckily, I know the owner."

"Wow. Nice work. I hadn't even thought of it."

The hostess seated them quickly at a table for two near a window that gave them a pleasant view of a small, derelict barn behind the restaurant. The old barn was dramatically lit by one floodlight set close to the wall and angled upward, artfully illuminating the weather-beaten texture of the barn's side.

Reed eased into his chair, but bumped his stump on the hard wooden seat, setting off a jolt of phantom pain that ripped up from his nonexistent ankle and shin. It burned as intensely as if someone had whipped his leg with a wet leather belt. Reed tried to turn the grimace of pain into a smile. But his expression immediately made Angela ask, "What? What's the matter?"

"Nothing, nothing." Reed's eyes had almost shut with pain. "It's a cramp. Nothing, it'll pass."

"Where?" asked Angela.

Reed waved the question off, as if he couldn't answer it until the pain had passed. Angela couldn't hide her concern.

"It's okay." Finally, Reed relaxed his expression, letting it just hurt, knowing that the worst of it had passed, ignoring the intense desire to reach down and rub a shinbone that was no longer there.

"What happened?"

Reed shook his head as if to say, never mind. "It's complicated. I'll explain it to you later."

"Is it your leg?"

"Yeah, the one that's not there."

Reed's tone told Angela he did not feel inclined to pursue the subject. They busied themselves with ordering drinks and checking the menus. Reed asked a few questions about the food, mostly to change the subject.

The restaurant was inviting. The decor felt natural, genuine country inn as opposed to the artificial aura at the Maple Inn. They ordered drinks, Reed's vodka and Angela's bourbon.

After they clinked glasses, Angela said, "Okay, so what about you?"

"Fire away."

"Married?"

"Divorced. Four years. Very sweet woman. Julia. But we were ridiculously incompatible."

"Why'd you marry her?"

"She was beautiful. Mild-mannered. Cultured. Sensitive. I guess I thought she might have a civilizing influence on me."

"Get you off your motorcycle?"

"Something like that."

"Didn't work?"

"Nope. Good lady. Bad choice. What about you?"

"Never married. Lived with a couple of guys over the years. That was close enough."

"Kids?"

"Nope. You?"

"Nope. Seeing anyone?"

"Not at the moment. You?"

"No."

"Wow. That was a very definite no."

"Definitely."

"Why so adamant about it?"

Reed scrunched up his face.

"You don't have to tell me."

Reed took a long sip of the cold vodka, feeling the cold liquor warm in his empty stomach. Letting it relax him. He looked at Angela. The warm light, her touches of makeup, the conversation, all made her appear more relaxed and sensual, and yet . . . as she returned his gaze her green eyes seemed more penetrating than ever.

"Well," said Reed, "what's that expression, when the going gets tough, the tough get going? Well, the woman I was living with when this happened turned out to be real tough. All I can tell you is that before I even got home from the hospital, she was gone. Out. See ya. Said something about not wanting to be in my way. I guess she figured I might trip over her or something. What was her name again, Margaret? Yeah, Margaret. Just a wonderful person."

Angela shrugged. "I guess that's one way to find out."

"I guess," said Reed.

"So you don't have any overwhelming desire to get back up on the old trapeze."

"No desire. And not a hell of a lot of opportunity."

Angela veered from the obviously sensitive subject.

"So what do you do? For a living."

"Not much of anything right now."

"Because of your accident?"

"I guess."

"Well, what did you do? Aren't you going to get back to it?"

"We'll see. I'm a forensic accountant."

The answer obviously surprised Angela.

"What's the matter?" asked Reed. "I don't look like a pencil pusher? A numbers guy?"

"No."

"Well I am."

"What exactly is a forensic accountant?"

"I'd rather not see your eyes glaze over when I explain it to you."

"Make it simple."

"Well, let's see. They steal the money. I figure out how. They hide the money. I figure out where. And then I usually end up in a court somewhere trying to explain it to a jury."

"Okay."

"But it can get complicated."

"I can imagine."

"Can you?"

"Probably not. How'd you get into that?"

"College. MBA Law school. FBI."

"Oh. I see. FBI. That's a little more glamorous."

"I suppose. But there's quite a bit of boring bureaucracy involved."

"So you left."

"Yes. It wasn't a big deal. I was with the Bureau for about eight years. I was spending too much time working so that I could work. I figured it would be easier to eliminate the bullshit and go out on my own. The last ten years, I've built up my own firm. We do a range of private investigations."

"So you're like a private eye?"

"I suppose. I've got a PI license. I don't need that license, but it helps. Being from the law enforcement end, a good deal of my stuff has to do with crime. The money side. A lot of it is just finding assets and things. You see, your eyes are glazing over."

Angela batted her eyes at Reed. "No they're not."

The dinner came. The food wasn't great, but better than the Maple Inn. The wine was much better, a bottle of Washington State pinot noir, however, Angela had only one glass. Reed kept his consumption to two glasses so she wouldn't worry about his driving.

Finally, over a shared dessert of Bavarian chocolate cake, Angela dropped her fork on the plate and said, "All right, Bill, you've been very polite and considerate not talking about the Ullmann place, but it's bothering me knowing it's coming. So let's get it over with."

"We don't have to talk about it."

"Yes we do. It's like . . . don't think about pink elephants. What's the first thing you think about? I told you I don't like talking about my sister and the situation at Ullmann's, but we should."

Reed leaned back in his chair, took another sip of wine.

"Well, look, your situation with your sister is your business, family business. We certainly don't have to discuss that. But maybe you can tell me why everybody I met at that place acts like such an asshole. Starting with Ullmann."

"Matthew Ullmann considers that place his little fiefdom. Although compared to other businesses up here, it's not so little. And the institute isn't the only business he owns. He employs a lot of people in this county. He does what he wants. Doesn't take any shit from anybody. Power and all that."

"What about his employees? They ranged from offended to offensive."

"What do you mean?"

"The guy on weekend duty or whatever, Kitridge, he acted like even talking to me was a huge bother."

"Kitridge? He's just a scared little man. Scared of Ullmann mostly."

"What about those guys in the white shirts and ties."

"The proctors?"

"I guess. Is that what they are?"

"Yeah. White shirts and ties. That's what the proctors wear. Some of them are decent guys. Some of them are kind of local rough boys."

"I think I ran into two of the rough boys. They just about threatened to kick my ass unless I left the premises."

"What'd they look like?"

"One guy, sort of your big redneck type, tall and rangy, ponytail. Kind of a constant smirk on his face. The other one short, stocky, looked a little muscle-bound and stupid. Looked like he was a pit bull in his past life."

"The tall one would be Eddie McAndrews. The other one his pal, Raymond Boggs. Eddie is basically your local asshole tough guy. Ray's worse. I think he's done some prison time. If they got offensive I wouldn't worry about it. I think Ray was born pissed-off."

"What are guys like that doing working a residence for the retarded?"

"Well, the pool of possible employees isn't all that broad and deep up here. Not a lot of well-trained people. Face it, not a lot of people even want to do that work. And I'm sure Ullmann doesn't pay much. Also keep in mind that the population isn't just retarded people there. Some of the residents have physical as well as mental disabilities. At one time, I think the population had quite a few people with neurological problems that made them a little difficult, maybe even violent. Some had seizures. There was a need for strong male proctors. Which doesn't excuse those guys, but helps explain why they're there. I think Eddie and his buddies are a bit hardcore, a little too territorial."

"So it's just testosterone I ran into."

"Probably. The proctors think they run the place."

"I got the feeling Ullmann runs that place."

"Oh, he does. Eddie and his pals won't go too far, that's for sure."

"So how do you get along with Ullmann?"

"Pretty well. I flatter him. And flirt. The usual female tactics to get what I want."

"So you get to see your sister whenever you want?"

"Pretty much. You can't walk around there like you have free rein. You have to check in, make appointments, all that bullshit. Did you get a little too demanding maybe?"

"Hell, I didn't get anywhere. I barely saw my cousin. He's in quarantine. He's got scabies."

"Scabies?"

"Yeah. You know what that is?"

"Yeah, my sister told me about one of the residents who got a case of it. Sounded horrible."

"Your sister ever get it?"

"No."

"How long has she been there?"

"Five years. Your cousin has been there longer. I know him. He's a sweetheart. I'm sorry he got an infection. Is he all right?"

Reed shrugged. "They say he's being treated. He looks terrible."

"I can imagine. Didn't you know he had them when you came up?"

"No."

"What prompted the visit. I don't remember ever seeing you there before."

"We're not that close." Reed hesitated, deciding not to go into it. "I'm basically his only living relative, so I thought I should do more. To see him."

"Well. It sounds like you had a lousy visit."

"It was. I had to talk to him through a door."

"A door?"

"There was a strip of glass in it, but it was ridiculous. And I had to practically beg to do that. The poor guy looked like hell. I think he's sick. More than the scabies."

"What does Ullmann say?"

"Says he's fine except for the scabies. I talked to his doctor. He doesn't know anything about other problems."

"His doctor?"

"George Prentice."

Angela shook her head. "I don't know him. Ullmann's wife does most of the medical stuff up there."

"His wife?"

"The charming Madeleine. You think Ullmann is bad, wait'll you meet her. She's a nurse practitioner. She thinks she's a doctor, among other things. I'm surprised they even let you talk to somebody else. I'm surprised he even sees a doctor outside there."

"Prentice said all the residents are assigned to doctors in the area."

"I suppose they are. On paper. I'm not familiar with how they sort that out." Angela rapped her knuckles on the table. "Knock wood my sister hasn't had many physical problems. Your cousin is Down syndrome, right?"

"Yeah."

"I understand they have more physical problems."

Reed nodded. "Well, okay. Enough of that, huh?" He checked his watch. "You've been a wonderful dinner partner. And very kind to deal with my angst. So what do you want to do now?"

Angela looked at her watch. "Well, I hate to be a party pooper, but we North Country girls need our rest."

"Come on, it's Saturday night. Your big night off. What do you usually do?"

"Not a whole lot. I do sort of force myself out the door, just to keep from being a hermit."

"Okay, so where do you go?"

"I usually go hang out at this semi-shit-kicker bar near my house and listen to music. Drink a beer. Get up and . . ."

She stopped herself.

"Get up and what?"

"Well . . ."

"Drink beer, listen to music . . . get up and dance?" asked Reed.

"If I feel like it."

"With who? Am I taking you away from someone?"

"Didn't we cover that over the entrées? I usually end up just jumping around by myself."

"Right."

"Sometimes I'll let some guy have a chance, if he doesn't dance like a geek."

"I see."

"Unfortunately, you let a guy dance with you they seem to think the next step is sleeping together."

Reed smiled. "I guess that depends on how well the guy can dance."

Angela smiled back.

"Hey, you know," said Reed, "if he's a really good dancer . . ."

She raised her eyebrows. "I don't know anybody that good."

Reed clapped his hands together, rubbing them in anticipation. "So let's go. I can definitely do the drinking beer and listening to music part."

"I wouldn't be surprised if you could do the dancing part, too."

"One leg on crutches?"

"You wouldn't be the first."

Reed cocked his head and with a sly smile said, "Yeah, but what if it turns out I could *really* dance?"

Angela flashed him an exaggerated look of skepticism.

"Yeah, what-if . . . Okay, look, Sunday is my day in my studio. I don't want to blow the day. So we'll stop by. It's on the way back to my house. One drink, a nightcap, then I'm out of there."

"Perfect," said Reed. "Perfect."

EIGHTEEN

"He's a fag," said Ray Boggs.

"Who?" asked Ronnie Barrett.

"Yeah, who?" asked Ronnie's brother Lyle.

Eddie McAndrews answered, "The asshole who came to see Johnny Boy Reed. Another retard relative."

"Why's he a fag, Ray?" asked Ronnie.

" 'Cuz I fucking said so, that's why."

The four of them, all Ullmann Institute proctors, sat in the Davis Hall proctor's office finishing off a six pack of twenty-four ounce cans of Labatt's ale. Sitting with McAndrews and

Boggs were Ronnie and Lyle Barrett, both thin and wiry, weasely, with greasy hair and underslung chins. Lyle was a year older and five inches taller than Ronnie, but other than that, not much differentiated the brothers. Together they seemed to add up to one of Ray Boggs or Eddie McAndrews. Neither protested when McAndrews and Boggs commandeered two cans of ale to one each for them.

McAndrews said, "Ray wanted to rip his head off, din't you, buddy?"

"Fucker called me an asshole."

Lyle Barrett asked, "So whyn't you kick his ass, man?"

Ray Boggs turned his massive head toward Ronnie Barrett. "Eddie pulled me off him."

"Why'd you do that, Eddie?"

"The guy's a cripple. I always give cripples a break. At least the first time."

"A cripple?"

McAndrews drained his can and said, "Got his leg cut off."

Lyle Barrett smiled idiotically and said, "That's right. You got to cut some slack for cripples. And retards, too."

"Just the first time," said McAndrews. "Except for you and Ronnie. We been cutting you two retards slack forever."

"Fuck you, Eddie," said Lyle.

McAndrews smiled at the retort. Ronnie laughed. Lyle turned and punched him on the shoulder and yelled, "What the fuck you laughin' at?"

Ronnie stopped laughing and rubbed his shoulder. "You. Asshole."

"Fuck you. Shut up."

McAndrews slammed his can down on the desk. "Both a you all shut the fuck up. Cripple or not, that guy gives me any more shit, I'll bust his ass right off, I God damn guarantee you that. No rich assholes gonna come up here acting like they own the place." McAndrews let out a belch and sprang up out of his chair. "Come on. Let's get the fuck out of here before Rita shows up. She'll get all pissy and make us clean up the empties."

Bill Reed pulled into the Lincoln Tavern parking lot. Angela Quist led the way into the bar, Reed following behind her, fantasizing about walking next to her, holding her hand, walking her up to the door of the tavern. He imagined himself on two legs, able to keep up with her, with his hands free so he could push the door open and gently guide her inside, his hand resting lightly against the small of her back. He decided at that moment that if she left him at a table staring into a drink while she went out on the dance floor, he would be annoyed, but he would still enjoy watching her dance.

Reed stepped into the tavern. To his right, a long bar ran along the far wall. On his left stood a pool table, and beyond the pool table was a small dance floor fronting a compact stage elevated a couple of feet above the floor. The stage was covered in a dark, stained carpet. A drum set, two microphone stands, speakers, and amps just about filled the small stage, but no musicians.

And then, a few paces in front of him, the crowd parted a bit and Reed saw a thick-armed, big-bellied biker type, long hair pulled back in a ponytail, black leather vest over a black T-shirt and well-worn blue jeans, talking to Angela. His forearms, both covered in dense blue ink, were crossed in front of his chest. Reed recognized a bouncer when he saw one. Angela turned to see him standing by the doorway and motioned Reed to approach. Three swing-steps on his crutches and he stood with them.

"Joey," said Angela, "meet my friend, Bill Reed."

Joey stuck out a meaty hand. Reed squeezed his right crutch under his armpit and extended his hand, making sure to return a tight grip. The bouncer said nothing, taking a moment to look over Reed, who immediately sensed that his shearling coat, cashmere polo shirt, and wool slacks made him way too overdressed for both the bar and the bouncer.

Angela pointed a thumb toward Reed's empty pants leg and said, "Motorcycle."

Joey frowned slightly, still holding on to Reed's hand, nodded up and down twice, conveying a complete understanding of what that one word and Reed's empty pants leg meant.

"Sorry," he said.

"Thanks," said Reed, suddenly feeling accepted and also grateful to Angela for how deftly she had handled the introduction.

Joey let go of Reed's hand and turned toward the bar. Reed gripped his crutch. Every stool at the bar was occupied, as were all the tables that lined the wall opposite the bar.

The bouncer said, "Hang on a sec."

He walked over to a table occupied by two local guys who appeared to be in their early twenties. Joey dropped a friendly hand on the shoulder of the one nearest and said a few words. Both stood up, their mugs of beer in hand, and ambled over to the bar.

Joey turned and motioned for Reed and Angela to come over to the table.

"Well, I guess it's good for something."

"What? Joey, or your missing leg?" said Angela, heading quickly for the table.

"Both, I guess."

"You bet."

Country music blared on the jukebox, but Reed heard Angela tell the bouncer, "You're a sweetheart."

Joey smiled in a way that said, don't mention it. As Reed passed him on the way to the table he thanked him.

"No problem, man," said Joey.

Reed took his seat, but Angela remained standing.

"What're you drinking?" she asked. "I'm buying."

"I'll have a shot of Old Grand-Dad, and a short beer back."

"Right."

She turned for the bar and Reed grabbed her wrist lightly, the one with the tattoo. She turned.

"Let's buy those guys who gave us their seats a drink."

Angela winked at Reed and nodded, saying, "Good idea," making Reed feel pleased that he had thought of it.

Reed watched Angela make her way to the bar, as did most

of the other men. She edged her way easily in between the drinkers, signaling the bartender. Reed folded his arms and watched her waiting at the bar for the drinks, admiring her long legs and shapely backside, enjoying how she stood with a hand on one hip, confident, not at all intimidated by the crush of mostly men drinking at the bar.

She returned with his shot of bourbon and beer in one hand and her drink, bourbon on the rocks, in her other hand. She set the drinks down before she sat, instantly reminding Reed that she worked as a waitress, and making him feel special when she sat down, as if he had his own personal waitress. What's more she seemed happy to be serving him.

She pulled her cigarettes out of her jacket and said, "What do you think of the place?"

"I like it. You know the band?"

She raised her drink. He clinked his shot glass against her dripping glass. "Cheers," she said.

They both took a sip.

"It's some country band. Fiddles and banjos and stuff, but supposed to be pretty good."

"I like fiddles and banjos," Reed said.

"Yeah, it's like a real *Deliverance* scene in here, huh?"

"It's not that backwater around here, is it?"

"Close."

She sipped again and unwrapped her pack of cigarettes. She offered him the opened pack.

"Smoke?"

"Yeah, okay." Reed slid out a cigarette and she lit it for him, reinforcing the pleasant feeling that he was being served.

She lit her own cigarette on the same match, exhaled, settling into her seat.

"So, you still thinking about your cousin?"

The question surprised Reed. "No. I don't know. Maybe. Do I looked distracted or something?"

"A little."

"Sorry," said Reed, realizing now that his attention had been elsewhere. He looked at Angela, focused on her for a moment, smiled, nodded, noticing now the music on the jukebox, a female country artist with a bit more twang in her voice than fashionable. "I find myself trying not to think about him."

"Why?"

"I don't know. Guilt." He shrugged. "A feeling I can't do much about it one way or the other."

"You can do whatever you want."

"Oh?"

"Look, the situation sucks. Your cousin. My sister. They're retarded."

Reed grimaced.

"What? That word sound harsh to you? It's the only word for it. It's the word everybody who lives with or deals with retarded people uses. There's no shame in that word. We're the ones who put that into it."

Reed thought about what she said, nodding.

"Hell, you ought to know that by now," she said.

Reed nodded again.

"You're dealing with it. You'll deal with this, too."

"Right," said Reed. "Right. The hell with it. Maybe I should just stay around until he's out of quarantine. Make sure everything is all right."

"If you can. Why not?"

"Mostly because Ullmann said it would be at least two weeks. I don't get the feeling they'd want me showing up every day for two weeks."

Angela shrugged. "Maybe you can get around that."

"How?"

"Suck up to him. That's what I do." Angela gave a fake smile and batted her eyelashes.

"He's not my type."

"What? You think he's mine?"

Reed smiled, reached out, and dropped his hand on Angela's forearm. "Hey, thanks. It helps, you know. Everything. The company. The advice."

Angela smiled back. Reed felt a closeness, and a sense of belonging. And then, every good feeling in Reed evaporated. Behind Angela, he saw McAndrews, Boggs, and two others walk in.

Reed muttered a curse. Angela followed his gaze, turned around, and saw the group. She turned back to Reed.

"Ah yes, our charming local boys from the Ullmann Institute."

"All of them?"

"Yep. Eddie McAndrews, Ray Boggs, and the lovely Barrett brothers, Ronnie and Lyle. They all work there. You see one you often see the others."

"What's their story?"

"Between them they have about half a brain. They kind of toady after Ray and Eddie, along with some of the other dolts that work there."

"Is it all male proctors up there?"

"No. There are a bunch of women that work there, too. But the men have first call on jobs and the good shifts. The women usually work at night."

Reed gazed behind Angela and checked out the group. McAndrews and Boggs stood talking to Joey the bouncer, while Ronnie and Lyle slouched behind them.

"Nice bunch," said Reed. He turned his attention back to Angela. She took another sip of her drink, and Reed did, too, but he couldn't help looking up over her shoulder to see McAndrews giving Joey a buddy shake and slapping him on the back like an old friend. It made Reed feel like an outsider. As if to drive the point home, McAndrews turned and saw Reed staring at him. He squinted at Reed, making sure it was him, then gave Reed a disgusted look as if to say, what the hell are you doing in here?

McAndrews turned to Joey, pointing a thumb in Reed's direction, he said loud enough for most of it to be heard by Reed, "Why'd you let that city-boy fancy-ass in here, hoss?"

Joey glanced briefly at Reed. "He came in with Angela."

"Angela? What's the deal? Some sort of be-kind-to-cripples thing?"

Joey shrugged.

McAndrews shook his head. "Fucking a." He turned his

back on Reed and headed toward the opposite end of the tavern, Boggs and the Barrett brothers following him.

Over Angela's shoulder, Reed watched the group as they commandeered a table off to the left of the stage, as if they alone had the right to it. When McAndrews sat, he faced Reed, staring at him from afar. Reed returned the stare, as if to say, I'm here . . . what are you going to do about it?

Angela glanced quickly over her shoulder and saw Eddie McAndrews staring in their direction. She turned back to Reed, tapped a knuckle against the back of his hand, saying, "Hey, Mr. FBI, what are you doing?"

Reed broke off the staring contest and looked at Angela. He tossed down the rest of his bourbon and chased it with a swig of beer.

"What?"

"You looking to start something, those guys will accommodate you. Come on, forget about them."

Reed frowned. "You're right, sorry. No problem. You ready for another drink?"

"No. We're just in here for a nightcap. I'm going home."

Reed said, "You mind if I get one more shot?"

"Why? To prove to them you're staying as long as you want?"

"Maybe."

Reed got up on one crutch. Angela sat silently, watching Reed head for the bar, managing with one crutch, holding his empty shot glass in his free hand. Reed brought his shot back to the table, sitting down heavily, having lost his balance a little bit at the end of his last trip.

Angela looked at her watch, lit another cigarette, finished her drink, and sat back in her chair.

"You know it's stupid," she said.

"What?"

"Playing this little game."

"What game?"

"Trading hard looks with those idiots."

"Hard looks? Is that what I'm doing?"

Angela motioned her head backward. "You're looking at those guys back there as if you want to call them out. You really want to get into this macho you-lookin'-at-me nonsense?"

Reed leaned forward, looking straight at Angela now, asking, "What exactly is their problem with me? You heard what he said just now to your bouncer friend."

"Listen, Bill, there are two bars in this area. One of 'em caters to the people who own things in this county. The other one caters to the people who work for the people who own things. Which bar do you figure you're in?"

"The latter."

"Yes. And the people in this bar have a fairly prickly attitude when it comes to issues like self-respect. In case you didn't notice, you probably wouldn't have gotten in here if you weren't with me."

"Really?"

"Yeah, really."

"You mean that bouncer would have actually told me I couldn't come in?"

"Not in so many words."

"So how would he have kept me out?"

Reed knew he was pushing Angela, but it didn't stop him. She, however, wouldn't be pushed. She sat back, looking at him, making a decision.

"Forget it. Do what you want to do."

Reed saw her harden. He could read her thoughts by the look on her face . . . men, they're all the same.

Reed touched her hand with his forefinger to get her to look back at him.

"Angela, I'm sorry. I'm not trying to be an asshole."

"What, it just comes naturally?"

"Maybe, it's just that I don't like it when people try to intimidate me."

"So you're still bugged about that parking lot thing?"

"I'm just not accustomed to taking a lot of shit, that's all."

Angela jerked her thumb back toward her chest, indicating the group on the other side of the bar.

"Those idiots are very accustomed to doling out shit. They're assholes. Who cares what they do? You're not in any position to pick a fight, anyhow."

"Right. Being disabled and all."

"I didn't say that. I don't care how many legs you have and neither do they. You can have one leg or two or none, it doesn't matter to them. All four of those guys won't hesitate to drag you out of here and beat the crap out of you. And nobody here is going to rush to your aid."

"Well, if you say so."

Angela shook her head. "Man, you have a skewed sense of where these people are at. How many BMWs did you see parked outside? How many people in here do you think are going to stick up for you? Particularly if they think you're wrong."

"Wrong about what?" Reed felt his voice and his anger rising, but he didn't try to stop himself. "Wrong about what? I came up here to visit a sick, handicapped relative. And all I've caught from everybody at that Ullmann Institute is bullshit and bad attitudes." He pointed toward the proctors, not caring now who saw it. "Including those two white-trash assholes over there in that corner. But I'm supposed to keep my head down and swallow their shit? Fuck that." Still pointing, Reed motioned with his chin toward the proctors, raising his voice even louder. "And fuck them, too."

Reed's raised voice caught even Robbie's and Lyle's attention. They joined McAndrews and Boggs in looking at Reed. Even Joey, the big biker bouncer, had clearly heard Reed and now looked over at him, too.

Angela realized she had started something in Reed and reached out, grabbing his wrist, worried now, anxious to stifle it.

"All right. All right. I understand. I'm just trying to—"

"To what?"

She purposefully lowered her voice. "Take it easy, will you?"

Over at the proctors' table Boggs said to McAndrews, "You hear what that prick just said?"

McAndrews continued watching Reed, now talking quietly to Angela. "I heard him, Raymond. I fucking heard him."

"Motherfucker," said Ronnie Barrett.

"Just hold your water, boys. We got all night for that fella."

Angela continued trying to talk Reed down. "I'm just saying you should be careful. You really want to get down in the gutter with those guys? Is it worth it? For God's sake there are four of them. You don't know this area or the people in it."

Reed asked evenly, "What else is there to know?"

"Just know you're an outsider, okay. If it comes down to anything, it's their word against yours. Now just shut the fuck up, okay."

Angela's vehemence stopped Reed cold. He blinked, but kept his mouth shut.

"Look, I'm finished. How about just taking me home?"

Angela turned and pulled her leather coat off the back of her chair.

Reed scratched his cheek watching her get ready to leave. Done, over, good night. Just like that. Reed extended his hand toward Angela who was standing now.

"Hey, why don't you just sit down and take it easy."

"No. Forget it," she shot back, shrugging into her coat. "Small town, macho bullshit."

She gathered her pack of cigarettes and matches off the table and shoved them into her pocket. She looked at Reed, waiting for him to move. He returned her gaze, but kept his mouth shut. He pulled his coat on, then reached for his crutches. Angela stood at the table, buttoning her coat, waiting for Reed to get up. Her standing there watching and waiting impatiently annoyed Reed. He struggled too quickly to stand up on one foot and pull his crutches under his armpits, feeling awkward.

Once Reed had the crutches under him, Angela turned and headed for the door. More people had come into the tavern so it took a bit of maneuvering to get through the crowd. Reed followed behind Angela, aware that she did not turn to see how he fared making his way through the bar crowd. Most people moved aside for him. Several stared at him, some for the way he was dressed, others because of his crutches and empty pants leg, but all of them looked upon Reed as an outsider.

Reed tried to spot Angela ahead of him and saw that she had stopped to talk to a man who looked like he had just come off a work shift. He wore jeans, a Woolrich coat with holes in the elbows, and a beat-up DeWalt Power Tools cap tipped back on his head. He had a bushy mustache, and when he smiled at Angela he revealed a set of feeble-looking teeth that seemed misplaced in his robust face.

Reed caught up to her, but stood a few paces away waiting while she finished her conversation. Standing and waiting were not what he wanted to do. Nor was leaving now just as the band began stepping on stage something he wanted to do. It felt as if he were running away.

Reed stood behind Angela, resisting the urge to look at the table where the proctors sat. He wasn't sure if he could endure seeing one of them smirking at his departure.

But McAndrews kept watching Reed. From the moment Reed had raised his voice, all four of the proctors had watched him.

"Fucker's got a big mouth, don't he?" said Boggs.

"Take it easy, Raymond," McAndrews told him.

Lyle Barrett asked, "What's that crippled fag doin' with Angela Quist anyhow?"

"I don't know," said McAndrews. "Anyways, it looks like she's got enough sense to get him the hell out of here."

"She s'pose to be with him?"

"Fuck if I know," said McAndrews.

"And maybe she ain't," said Boggs.

"Yeah, I'm pretty sure you're right."

"I'm pretty sure I want to fuck that guy up," said Boggs.

McAndrews finally looked away from Reed, smiling at Boggs. "No shit, Ray? You could hardly tell at all." Boggs scowled at McAndrews. "Well hell, boy what're you sitting there for? Let's go." With that, all four stood up and headed for a side door exit.

Reed shifted his grip on the crutches, still waiting for Angela. It wasn't comfortable for him to stand on the crutches, but he could do it for quite a while if necessary. He decided he didn't want to.

Fuck this, she wants a ride, she can follow me. She wants to stay here, she can get a ride from Mr. Mustache.

Reed turned, gripped his crutches, and swung his leg forward, heading for the door. When he reached the door, he spun around, pressed his back into the door to push it open, He was annoyed at Angela, but when he finally muscled the door open and turned to the outside, Reed wished he hadn't even come. Wet snow filled the air, blowing hard, whipping into his face. Much of the snow had melted on contact, but it came down so fast that the gravel parking lot already had a thin white coating.

The wind blew the door shut behind him. Reed began to make his way to the parking lot. Unable to shield his face from the blowing snow, he looked down, steeling himself against the cold and wet, moving carefully, worried now about losing his footing.

"Shit."

He walked slowly, but was still surprised when Angela suddenly appeared next to him.

"They forecast this, but it wasn't suppose to blow in until the morning."

Reed responded with a grunt. He moved carefully on his crutches, testing to feel how slippery the snow had made the surface.

"Sorry about making you wait in there. That guy was telling me about a job he might have for me."

Angela's apology and explanation assuaged Reed's anger. "That's okay," he said.

Angela put a hand up to shield her eyes from the flurry and maneuvered in front of Reed as if to block some of the driving snow.

"My house is five minutes away. I'll have you back at the inn before this gets too hairy."

Sheriff Ralph Malone watched Reed and Angela step their way through the Lincoln Tavern parking lot to the silver 740iL. He sat in his police cruiser, parked far back in a driveway across from the tavern. He sipped coffee from a metal thermos, comfortable yet alert, the Mercury's engine running, providing power for the radio, the heater, and the windshield wipers set to intermittent.

The white exhaust from the car whipped away in the cold wind and quickly mixed with the flurry of snow that also helped to conceal the sheriff's white car with red lettering.

Malone had followed Reed from the time he had left the Maple Inn, waiting patiently at each stop, calling in occasionally to his dispatcher for updates, talking to the deputies on night patrol . . . letting them know the boss was out there keeping tabs. And now, when Reed pulled out of the Lincoln Tavern lot, Malone made no move to follow the BMW. He knew where Reed was headed. No rush. Give 'em a couple minutes head start, then check it out. Malone wondered if Angela Quist would invite the big city fella in. That might be interesting.

NINETEEN

Bill Reed leaned forward in the driver's seat, peering out at the blur of fast falling snow. His headlights turned the fat flakes bright white. So much of it blew directly at the windshield that Reed had difficulty seeing. He slowed down, driving carefully, but not overly concerned. He could see far enough ahead to make his way and he could clearly see two black lines of tire tracks running out ahead of him, cutting through the still thin coat of white.

He glanced over at Angela. She, too, stared straight ahead, saying nothing, concentrating on the road and giving directions, but also using the storm as an excuse to avoid talking to Reed. He regretted making her angry, particularly when he silently glanced at her profile highlighted by the dim glow of his instrument lights. Just a silhouette of her was enough to remind Reed that Angela Quist was a striking woman. Reed had been admiring her the whole night . . . her strong yet refined features, her figure, the way she moved with a natural grace. Suddenly Bill Reed was acutely aware of how long it had been since he had held a woman or felt a woman's body next to his.

Reed turned away from his stolen glance at Angela. You won't be feeling any part of that body, pal. Not even a damn handshake. So what? You think you even had a chance? Do you even *want* a chance?

Angela interrupted Reed's thoughts when she pointed ahead.

"Slow down, it's the next right, that road up there."

Reed remembered turning onto the road from the opposite direction. He slowed down and steered the car to the right, feeling the wheels of the BMW slip for a moment, then grip the slushy, icy surface. He recalled that the road curved to the right, then straightened out and led to Angela's driveway about a half mile ahead. But just after the curve, Reed slammed his foot on the brake pedal. The BMW's antilock braking mechanism kicked in. Reed just managed to pull over onto the narrow shoulder before slamming head-on into a red pickup truck parked across the road.

"Goddammit," Reed cursed.

Just as they jerked to a halt, Reed and Angela heard the rumbling engine of another truck coming out of the woods. It pulled in behind them. They were trapped.

Reed's heart was already beating hard from the near crash. Now, seeing that he was trapped on a dark road, fear and tension flooded into him.

"What the hell is this?"

"Dammit. Those idiots from the bar."

"What?"

Reed felt his mouth going dry now, his heart pounding hard enough so that he could feel it in his throat. He peered out into the swirling darkness. He thought he saw dark figures coming toward him from the direction of the red truck, but the swirling white snow obscured any clear sight of them. He powered open his window, peering out into the dark. Snow and cold air blew into the car and suddenly Eddie McAndrews appeared at the driver's side.

Reed yelled, "Are you crazy? You trying to get someone killed?"

McAndrews pointed at Reed. "Hey, Big Mouth, get the fuck out of the car. We want to talk to you."

Reed felt the rage burst inside him. And this time, he just let it come, let it propel him to a point from which there would be no backing down. Not this time.

He yelled, snarling at McAndrews, "Get your goddamn truck off the road."

Reed shoved the BMW's gearshift into reverse and backed up, trying to make a Y-turn so he could drive around the red truck. His bumper banged into the truck behind him. Fuck it, he told himself, giving in to the crazy rage. He shoved the shift into drive, punched the gas, and rammed the BMW into the side of the red truck in front of him.

McAndrews yelled, "Hey!"

Reed shoved the gear into reverse, slammed into the truck behind. He shoved the gearshift into drive, but before his foot could leave the brake, the barrel of a rifle poked into the side of his head.

McAndrews stood at the open window, pressing the muzzle into Reed's temple.

"Don't fucking do it, asshole."

Reed kept his foot on the brake, waiting for the rifle to blow open his head.

"I told you to git out here. Now git the fuck out here."

Angela leaned over and yelled, "Eddie, what are you doing?"

McAndrews scraped the muzzle of the rifle across Reed's head, pointed it at Angela.

"Shut up, Angela. This is none of your business. We're gonna teach Mr. Big Mouth here some manners."

Reed slowly lifted his hands off the steering wheel, feeling his focus and composure coming back, the rifle quickly bringing everything into perspective.

Reed reached down and pushed the gearshift into park.

Reed yelled into the night, "All right. Take it easy. You don't need that rifle."

"Get out, asshole."

Reed yelled back, "All right, all right. Just put the rifle away and I'll get out."

"That ain't all you're gonna do. You're gonna pay for fucking up my truck, too, smart-ass."

McAndrews's comment about the truck gave Reed a small slice of time, a moment to will himself calm, to prepare to face what he knew was coming.

"All right," said Reed, "just put the rifle away and I'll come out."

"Shut down your car."

Reed leaned forward and did as instructed. "Okay."

McAndrews handed the rifle to a figure standing beside him

and said, "Go put that in the truck, Ronnie." Then he turned back to Reed and snarled, "Git out."

The second Reed popped the latch, McAndrews stepped forward, wrenched the door open, and grabbed a handful of Reed's sweater and shirt.

And then Reed exploded. He gripped the back of McAndrews's hand, twisted it clockwise, and viciously bent McAndrews's hand back toward his wrist bone. McAndrews dropped to one knee. Reed, still bending McAndrews's hand back, leaned to his left, brought his leg out from under the dash, and rammed his foot right into the side of McAndrews's head. McAndrews grunted. Reed reared back and kicked again, but McAndrews ducked under the kick and lunged forward, grabbing the back of Reed's left hand, pushing Reed back, then pulling him out the door, their hands sandwiched one between the other, two strong men wrestling for leverage, each matching the other's twists and turns.

Reed heard fists pounding on his car now and voices yelling.

"Get him the fuck out here, Eddie."

"Come on, motherfucker."

McAndrews suddenly let go of Reed's hand and threw a punch at Reed's face.

Reed took the blow on the top of his head, but roared back with both hands now, levering McAndrews down to his knees again. McAndrews immediately grabbed Reed's hand again, to stop Reed from breaking his wrist.

Reed heard someone fumbling with Angela's door handle. Then he heard a fist punching into the passenger-side window.

Reed's grip and arms were stronger than McAndrews's, but McAndrews managed to brace a foot against the bottom of the door frame to pull Reed out. Reed felt the extra leverage McAndrews's leg gave him so he released his grip and McAndrews fell back onto the wet snowy ground, landing hard, grunting, cursing, but he quickly scrambled to his feet.

Reed snarled, "You want me out, back off. I'll get out. Go on, get the fuck out of my way. I'll fucking get out."

McAndrews yelled back, waving Reed toward him.

"C'mon then, tough guy."

The Barrett brothers stood behind Eddie hunched over like jackals ready to leap into the fray. McAndrews motioned them back, giving Reed more room. He yelled to Boggs who was just about to kick open Angela's window, "That's okay, Ray. Leave it. He's coming out."

Reed reached into the backseat and grabbed one crutch.

"Are you crazy?" Angela yelled, gripping Reed's arm. "Don't go out there."

Reed pulled his arm free, wrenched his car phone from its cradle, and handed it to Angela. "You want them to go through you to get me? Close the windows. Lock the doors and call the cops. Now."

Reed stepped out of the car, quickly moving away from the open door, slamming it before any of them could rush him and shove the door back on him. Reed shoved his crutch under his left armpit and held on to the car roof with his right hand, hopping to the front fender, backed up against the car.

McAndrews stood about five feet away, watching, blocking the Barretts' way with his long, muscular arms, waiting just inside the circle of light created by Reed's headlights. He wore only a red, sleeveless insulated vest over his white shirt, no hat, no gloves. Both the Barrett brothers wore cheap winter jackets, jeans, and boots. None of them seemed bothered at all by the cold wind and blowing snow. Reed looked quickly to his right and left to spot Boggs, but couldn't see him. He squinted against the blowing snow, staring at the three in front standing motionless in the white swirl.

Reed slightly lifted his stump so that he half sat on the fender and hood, his right foot planted on the ground, his crutch braced directly in front of him. McAndrews continued watching, smiling at his victim, waiting, amused at Reed's preparation.

"You ready for your ass-whipping, boy?"

Reed nearly surprised himself by spitting back, "Yeah, I'm ready," and actually meaning it. He asked, "Who's first?"

McAndrews looked at him, an exaggerated question on his face.

"First? Shit, we're *all* first."

And with that they rushed him . . . Lyle Barrett coming in low and fast on Reed's right, Ronnie Barrett on Reed's left, and McAndrews straight at him.

Lyle was ahead of the other two in front, sneaking in low, thinking Reed would be focused on the two coming in standing. But Reed was too fast. He grabbed his crutch in both hands and rammed the crescent end of the crutch straight into Lyle Barrett's face, shoving Lyle Barrett's eye back in the socket, splitting the skin over his cheekbone and the bridge of his nose. His head snapped back, his feet flew out from under him. He gave out a garbled grunt, thudded to the ground, his blood staining the snow under him red.

Reed immediately levered the crutch clockwise, just in time to catch Ronnie in the ribs, then twisted the crutch counter-clockwise to block a looping overhand punch coming at him from McAndrews.

But the crutch couldn't keep them off. McAndrews and Ronnie piled into Reed. Ronnie threw a looping punch at Reed's chest. McAndrews slammed into Reed, knocking him back onto the car hood.

Still holding the crutch, Reed planted his knee and foot in McAndrews's chest, then levered forward, his powerful stomach muscles and arms pushing the weight of both men off him, pushing and shoving with his leg and the crutch.

McAndrews fell back, grabbing for the crutch, ripping it out of Reed's hands as he fell down taking Ronnie Barrett with him. Just then Ray Boggs scrambled over the hood and slammed into Reed from behind.

Reed grunted. It felt like someone had hit him with a bag of concrete. He just managed to twist to his left and grab Boggs around his neck and head as Boggs pushed Reed forward off the hood. Desperately, Reed locked his right hand around his left wrist, gripping Boggs in a crushing headlock, twisting his body, pulling Boggs around off the car. Boggs went down hard with Reed crashing on top of him. As they hit the ground,

Reed heard Boggs grunt under the impact of his weight landing on him.

Reed tried to ram a punch into Boggs's face, but too much of his head was covered by Reed's forearm and body, so the punch landed mostly on the top of Boggs's skull, nearly cracking Reed's knuckles.

Boggs slammed his right fist into Reed's upper back and then hit again, landing a painful blow to Reed's left ear. Reed responded by viciously twisting Boggs's head and trying to ram his right thumb into Boggs's exposed right eye. Reed felt his thumb bang into Boggs's forehead, then into the bulbous eye. Boggs snarled as Reed reared back to jab again, just as someone winged the crutch at Reed's head with a roundhouse baseball bat swing.

Reed managed to duck, the crutch cracked into the side of the BMW. Boggs dug his feet into the ground and drove Reed back against the car. Somehow, Reed managed to hold on to Boggs, but not for long as McAndrews dropped down and grabbed Reed's left arm, bracing his booted foot on Reed's chest, pulling the arm to break the grip around Boggs's neck and head. But Reed gripped his left wrist, held tight and twisted and lifted, trying to break Boggs's neck. It took McAndrews three jerking pulls, but finally he ripped Reed's arm away and Boggs broke free.

Boggs scrambled back, clearing the way for McAndrews to stomp his boot into Reed's chest. Reed bounced off the car and kicked out with his right foot, aiming for the side of McAndrews's left knee, trying to shatter the knee joint. McAndrews pulled his leg away from the kick, catching most of it in his calf, but the kick stung him enough so that he danced back on one foot, unable to stomp on Reed again.

Boggs, on his feet now, touched his face near his eye, feeling for blood. When he tried to open the eye, the pain hit.

"You fuck," he yelled at Reed. The enraged Boggs tried to crash a knee into Reed's face, getting in the way of Ronnie Barrett trying to tomahawk the crutch into Reed's head. Reed just managed to block Boggs's knee with his arms, but the force of it and Boggs's weight shoved Reed's head into the side of the car. Somebody landed a punch on the top of Reed's forehead. Then a steel-toed boot kicked his shoulder.

They were too close now. Even though their punches had to be directed downward, Reed knew the fists and knees and feet would be coming in too fast to do any fighting back so he brought his hands up around his head, twisting sideways to cover his left side, balling up into a curled position, but still lashing out with his right foot, trying to hit whatever body part came within range.

It was the sound of Reed's head banging into the car that brought Angela out. She saw now that they had him surrounded, all except for Lyle Barrett who was just managing to get onto his knees, the left side of his face covered in blood.

Angela bolted out of the car screaming, "Stop it. Stop it." She ran around toward the front of the car screaming for them to stop.

McAndrews, hunched over, breathing hard, spread his big arms out and held back Barrett and Boggs. Reed pushed himself into a more upright position, leaning back on the car, as McAndrews yelled, "Hold it. Hold it."

Boggs and Barrett stayed behind McAndrews who looked over at Angela.

"Who the fuck you tellin' to stop, you dumb bitch?"

"It's enough."

"Shit, it ain't nearly enough. You like cripples? Come over here and watch . . . we're going to take care of this guy's other leg. He ain't gonna be kickin' anybody with that one either when I get through with him."

Reed worked his right leg underneath him, turning back toward the BMW, he grabbed the top of the front tire to push himself up.

McAndrews watched Reed trying to get back up.

"Feisty bastard, ain't he. Ronnie, gimme that crutch. Let him get up. It'll be fun knocking him down again."

Reed turned away from them, using the fender to pull himself up, finally getting his leg under him. He turned to face them, again bracing himself against the car. Reed's breath fogged out in quick bursts. He felt the cold snow blowing against his face dripping with sweat. Steam rose from his head and neck. He sat back against the fender, trying to steady himself with both hands against the car, head down, eyes on his attackers.

Angela stood her ground. "Eddie, this is crazy. You've done enough."

"No I ain't."

McAndrews gripped the crutch. Reed leaned forward, focused, all fear burned out of him, determined to block the blow and grab the crutch, to pull McAndrews into him, to get his hands on him or Boggs or the other one, to gouge out an eye or crush a throat or rip apart a mouth. Just one of them. Whoever came at him first. Get at least one before he went down again.

McAndrews raised the crutch, ready to bring it down at Reed hard enough to break any arm trying to block it.

And then without warning, approaching with surreal slowness out of the snow-blown darkness, two quick whoops of his siren and his red and blue lights flashing, Ralph Malone's cruiser appeared on the far side of the truck behind Reed's BMW. Malone's high beams and searchlight suddenly illuminated the scene, seeming to paralyze everybody where they stood, eyes blinking at the sudden glare, faces highlighted by the roof-rack Visibar flashing red and blue.

Sheriff Ralph Malone, his blue winter sheriff's coat zipped up tight to his throat, walked out of the darkness and into the circle of light.

McAndrews quickly lowered the crutch, shifted his grip on it, making it appear that he was simply holding it instead of brandishing it. He assumed a relaxed posture. Boggs took two steps back, slinking halfway into the darkness.

"What the hell's goin' on here, boys?"

McAndrews pointed to Reed. "Hell, Sheriff, good thing you showed up. This guy run us off the road. Banged into my truck there. Ronnie's, too. He's drunk as a skunk. Just look at him."

Angela started to protest, "Sheriff, they tried to . . ."

Malone pointed a finger at Angela, raising his voice, but speaking precisely, "Get back in that car. Now."

Angela hesitated. "Sheriff, you can't—"

"I'll listen to you when I'm ready. Get back in the car, now, miss."

Angela stared at Malone for just a second, then turned and made her way back into the BMW, slamming the door behind her. Reed stood where he was, hands on the left front fender, bent over, recovering.

Malone turned toward McAndrews and Boggs. Pointing at them, he said, "You two, get that truck out of here. Go on. You're blocking the road. Move it. Now." Turning to Ronnie Barrett, Malone said, "Ronnie, go help your brother and get your truck out of here, too. Now."

Reed raised a hand. "Hey. Those guys—"

Malone turned to Reed. "You hold on." Malone stepped toward McAndrews, taking the crutch from him.

McAndrews and Boggs turned toward the red Ford 1-50.

"Sheriff," Reed said.

Malone held up his hand and came toward Reed, bringing him his crutch.

"I know where to find them. I want these trucks off this road before we have another accident."

"Accident? This was no accident!"

Malone handed the crutch to Reed.

"I want you back in your car. And I want you to dig out your registration and license for me."

Reed started to protest, but Malone interrupted him. "Sir, you do this my way. From what I saw when I pulled up, there's gonna be two stories conflicting here. I ain't standing out in this wet snowstorm sortin' it out. Get in your car."

Reed watched Malone rest his hand on the butt of the nine-millimeter Beretta holstered at his hip. The trucks in front and behind him were firing up, pulling out.

Reed looked carefully at the man in front of him. Small-town sheriff acting tough, midnight, nobody else on the road.

Reed nodded once, his eyes on the sheriff. Using his crutch, steadying himself against the BMW, he slowly made his way to the driver's door, testing his leg, waiting for any sharp pain to signal something broken, feeling now the cold, clammy wetness coming through his pants from rolling around on the snow-covered ground.

Reed made his way into the driver's seat. Angela had turned on the engine to power up the window. The warm, dry air cut the penetrating chill that had gripped Reed now that the adrenaline had burned off. But his anger simmered, unable to put out of his mind McAndrews's threat about ruining his good leg.

Angela sat motionless in her seat, staring straight forward, the horror of what she had just witnessed etching lines into her face. She spoke quietly, without turning toward Reed, hardly moving her lips, "Do what he says."

The way she said it, not looking at him, as if she didn't want the sheriff to see her talking, made Reed refrain from asking her any questions. He kept his window up and reached for his wallet. He could see the sheriff standing next to the car, waiting out in the cold, blowing snow.

With his head turned away from the sheriff, Reed quietly asked, "What's the matter with that guy? Didn't you call him?"

Still staring straight ahead, Angela said, "No. I just got through, then the idiot who answered put me on hold. I heard your head banging against the car. That was it. I couldn't just sit here while they killed you. I didn't wait for the 911 person to come back on."

"He just happened by?"

"I don't know."

Reed pulled his wallet out of his back pocket and extracted his license and registration. Malone stood motionless outside his window as if the snow and wind meant nothing to him.

Reed powered the window down just far enough to hand out the license and registration. Malone flashed a light on the cards, then turned to walk back to his cruiser as the two 4x4 trucks rumbled down the road, disappearing into the night. Reed powered up the window.

Finally, Angela turned to Reed.

"He doesn't take a lot of shit from people. The less you say, the better."

Reed did not respond. He rubbed his hands slowly to warm them, flexing his fingers to test if any bones had been broken. He checked the knuckles of his right hand, noticing the skin had scraped off the first two knuckles. He felt the side of his head and face where punches had landed. No skin had broken. No blood anywhere. He slowly rolled his head, checking his neck, then he lifted his left shoulder and felt a dull pain in his back on the left side where Boggs had slammed into him. Nothing too bad he told himself. There'll be bruises, but nothing cracked or broken. Lifting his shoulders caused no pain.

A rap on the window startled him. He looked out and the sheriff motioned for him to open the window again. Reed complied and the wind blew cold and snow into his face.

Malone handed the license and registration back to Reed. Bending down to the window level, he raised his voice to be heard. "I can't cite you for driving violations because I didn't see any. But the scene here shows signs you've been driving under the influence."

"What?"

"I think you heard me, sir."

"What signs?"

Malone bristled at being questioned.

"Skid marks. Driving off the road. Damaged vehicles. Lack of focus in your eyes."

"That's because that trash had this road blocked with their trucks. You saw it. They blocked me in here, pulled a rifle on me, dragged me out of my car, and tried to beat the shit out of me."

"That type of language is not necessary, sir. And I saw no rifle on the scene."

Reed looked at Malone's deadpan expression, trying to gauge the man, to see if he in any way believed what he was saying.

"What the hell is going on here, Sheriff? You know what happened."

"I suspect I do. Some dispute that started in that tavern back there. That's where you all came from, isn't it?"

"So what?"

"Isn't it, sir?"

Reed did not respond.

"Like I said, I'm not standing out here listening to who said what or did what." Malone lifted a small device into sight and said, "This is a Breathalyzer. It will test you for alcohol content in your blood. If you refuse to take this test, you'll be arrested and detained for driving under the influence. Your car will be impounded—"

"I know the drill," said Reed, once again interrupting Malone. "I know what that is and I know my rights, even in your county court out here. I also know I have the right to demand a blood test instead of that machine, which I'm inclined to do right now since I'd rather have you escort me to your station than drive around in the dark so those bastards can run me off the road with their damn trucks. And I know how to calculate the blood alcohol level based on my weight and what I drank so I also know I'll pass your damn test. I don't exactly get what your game is, Sheriff, but you picked the wrong person to play with."

Malone looked at Reed for a moment.

"What are you, some big-city lawyer? Am I supposed to be impressed?"

"You can be whatever you want."

"I asked you a question. Are you a lawyer?"

"I don't practice law."

"So how come you think you know so much?"

"They teach that information at the FBI Academy."

"You FBI?"

"Retired."

"Is that so?"

"Yes."

"Are you armed?"

Reed squinted, lifting his hand to shade his eyes from the

flashlight. "If I were armed, Sheriff, I guarantee you there'd be more blood out there on that snow."

Malone nodded at Reed, thinking it over. He lifted his flashlight and shined the beam at Angela. She turned into the light, squinting.

"Ma'am, are you comfortable with this individual behind the wheel?"

"Yes, of course," she said. "I'd like to go home."

"You're right up there past Pine Hill Road, right?"

"Yes." She added "sir," after a pause.

Malone nodded, flicked off the flashlight, and told Reed, "My feet are getting cold out here. I'd rather not deal with you and your lip on a night like this. Consider yourself lucky. Get the young lady home safe. I'll be following behind you for a ways, just to make sure you're driving right. You want to file a complaint against those boys, you come to my office in the morning."

TWENTY

Rita Glover saw the headlights before she heard the truck engine. She had just sat down after making the rounds, checking the hallways and bathrooms. Rita hefted her two-hundred-sixty-pound bulk out of the old wooden desk chair and made her way over to the window.

She shaded her eyes to see into the dark, snow-filled night, just as the red Ford 1-50 pulled up and parked behind the dormitory. She watched Eddie McAndrews exit the cab of the truck. He turned to say something to the other person inside. Rita knew that would be Raymond Boggs without needing to see him in the dim light of the truck's interior light. She frowned. There was no good reason for Eddie McAndrews to come to Davis Hall after midnight in the middle of an early winter storm.

Rita Glover had survived a chronically depressed mother, an alcoholic father, abandonment at seventeen, a bad marriage at eighteen, three children, including a middle child with diabetes, and a husband who had died two days after she turned thirty. She had worked every job in the county from waitress to shortorder cook to house cleaner to cafeteria cook at the Ullmann Institute. And from that job she had worked her way up to night proctor. Rita Glover was not afraid to face trouble when it came, but that didn't mean she looked forward to it. And by the look on Eddie McAndrews's face, trouble had arrived.

She wore a baggy blue sweatshirt over black stretch pants and a pair of Payless penny loafers whose sides had split open under the stress of her swollen feet and considerable weight. She hitched the right side of her pants up and walked into the main hallway, getting herself ready, thinking, Let's try being nice. See what that gets me.

The front doors popped open and McAndrews strode in.

"Eddie,"—she smiled—"what're you doin' here? You bring me coffee?"

"No I din't bring you no coffee. What good is coffee without the half a dozen damn donuts you eat with it?" he yelled back at her as he turned down the east corridor.

Rita's smile turned to a frown. She put her head down and again hitched up the elastic waistband of her stretch pants as she set out after Eddie.

"Boy's as mean as a stepped-on snake," she muttered to herself, moving down the hallway as fast as she could, trying to catch up to Eddie McAndrews.

McAndrews reached Johnny Boy's room just as Rita turned into the corridor, well behind him. Without hesitating, he shoved open the door and flipped on the light. He stood at the doorway. Rita slowed down, knowing there was no reason to rush now. McAndrews stepped out and turned toward her.

"Where the hell is he?"

Rita yelled from up the corridor.

"What are you going in there for, Eddie? You know he's in quarantine."

"Fuck that. There's nothing left alive on him. Where the fuck is he?"

Rita came toward him, holding up her hand to signal she was out of breath.

"He's in the clinic."

"Since when?"

"Just tonight. I sent him over there about a half hour ago."

"Why?"

"He said his stomach was hurtin' him."

"You just said he's supposed to be in quarantine."

Rita put her hands on her hips, "They can keep him separate over there, you know that."

"Don't get smart with me, Rita. Why the fuck you calling up the clinic every time one of these retards whines about something?"

"You're not supposed to use that language, Eddie."

McAndrews leaned into Rita. She could smell the alcohol and cigarettes on his breath, yelling at her now, "Well, they're fuckin' retarded, ain't they? Everybody so goddamn politically correct all a sudden."

"What do you want with him the middle of the night?"

"None of your damn business, Rita."

"Oh, really?"

He turned away from her, dismissing her with a wave.

"Don't bust my balls."

Rita knew that the worst of the anger had gone out of McAndrews, so she persisted, smacking him in the shoulder as he walked by.

"What do you want with him, Eddie?"

McAndrews turned and grinned at her, amused that she would actually get physical with him.

"You're really somethin', ain't you, Rita? Feisty as hell, ain't you?"

"Feisty enough to kick your sorry butt."

"I'll bet you are. You fuckin' outweigh me by about a hunnert pounds."

"Don't be a smart-ass, Eddie. You ain't goin' over to the clinic are you? You know that's off-limits. Mrs. Ullmann finds out you're in there she won't like it. You know that, don't you?"

McAndrews smirked at Rita.

"Fuck that clinic. I wouldn't set foot in there. Catch some deadly shit in that place."

He slouched back up the corridor, obviously ready to leave now.

"Ain't nothing that can't wait. I'll find out what I need to tomorrow. Go back and finish your macaroni and cheese or whatever else you snuck out of the kitchen."

Rita watched him walk away, that slouch-shouldered, loping gait of his, shaking her head, wondering what Eddie McAndrews would do to that poor fellow Johnny Boy tomorrow. When he turned out of the corridor, she stepped into Johnny Boy's room and switched out the light and pulled the door shut. She walked slowly back to the office, her stretched out penny loafers sliding quietly on the polished linoleum floor. God knows what goes on here during the day, she told herself, once again shaking her head.

By the time Bill Reed pulled up to Angela Quist's front door, the temperature had fallen and the hard driving snow had begun to rapidly accumulate. The only words spoken during the short drive were when Angela told him to turn left into her driveway road.

Reed shoved the gearshift into park and waited for Angela to open the door and get out. She turned to him and asked, "Are you all right?"

"All right enough."

"You know the way?"

"Yeah."

"You've got a bad scrape on your forehead."

Reed reached up and felt around.

"Over on the left."

When he touched the left side of his forehead he felt a sting thinking he might've been hit with the crutch there.

"I wouldn't worry about it."

Angela sat looking at him, trying to decide what to do.

"What?" Reed asked.

"I don't know what to say."

"Neither do I," said Reed.

"Do you think you should see a doctor?"

"Not unless there's one living in your house. I'm not driving fifty miles to a hospital in this mess."

Angela shook her head, annoyed. "It's about fifteen, not fifty. I could drive you."

"No. I'm all right. Look, I appreciate you stepping in back there. I'm just, I don't know, just ready to kill someone and I'm not someone you want to be around right now."

"You're not serious."

Reed turned to look directly at Angela.

"You think I'd let that white trash cripple me if I could stop them. You think I wouldn't have shot them if I'd had a gun?"

Angela didn't respond to his question.

Reed pushed it.

"Next time someone puts a rifle to my head I'm going to kill him."

"Please. All right. Enough. I told you in the bar those idiots are dangerous. You wouldn't listen. I'm not surprised they jumped you. You're lucky the sheriff showed up."

"Lucky?"

"They weren't letting up. And neither were you."

"Why didn't that sheriff do anything about it?"

Angela turned and faced Reed. "He did. He stopped them."

"He should've arrested them."

"You're an outsider. I keep telling you that. He's not going to take your side against theirs. Look, if you don't mind, I've had it for one night. And you'd better get back before this snow gets worse."

Reed paused for a moment, then simply said, "Yeah. Listen, thanks for everything you did. I'm sorry about all this. Hell of a way to end a night."

"No kidding."

Angela popped open her door, but Reed lightly touched her arm and said, "Thanks again."

Angela's full lips compressed into a thin line as she shook her head and said simply, "Good night."

She pushed open the door and rushed out, head down against the wind. Reed watched her nimbly ascend the stone steps to her front landing and move quickly to her door. He watched until Angela stepped into her house, then put the car in gear and drove off.

By the time he arrived at the Maple Inn, the BMW had to push its way through four inches of slushy snow in the parking lot. Reed scowled at the only empty spot near the entrance, the one for handicapped parking. He'd never gotten the handicapped plates. He'd never wanted the plates.

He pulled into a space about fifty feet from the inn's front door. He turned off the engine and sat in the car looking at the slushy mess in the parking area and the snow-covered steps leading up to the front porch.

He looked over at the wheelchair ramp leading to the side entrance. It was covered over with undisturbed wet snow. Reed knew he'd never get up the ramp in his wheelchair, yet sitting in the car, he could almost feel the crutches slipping out from under him if he tried to make it across the icy, snow-filled parking lot. He felt trapped.

"Christ."

He wondered if it would be easier with his prosthetic leg or harder. *Should have thrown the fucking thing in the trunk with me. Got to be easier, even with the pain.*

He turned and reached for his crutches.

Fuck it. Worse comes to worse, you'll crawl to the entrance.

The first step out of the car filled his shoe with wet snow. Simply getting his crutches under him and moving away from the car door felt precarious. He slammed the door and leaned back against the car, steeling himself, steadying himself. He buttoned up his shearling coat, wishing he had gloves and a hat. He felt the cold, wet snow covering his head.

For a moment, he thought the hell with it, drive the car up to the goddamn front porch. But decided, no, he just wouldn't do that, cause trouble like that. They'd probably come pounding on his door asking him to move his car anyhow. He could make it, he thought, it's just going to mean getting wet and cold and pissed off.

He pushed away from the car, transferring his weight to the crutches. They sank down into the snowy mess. For a moment, he could hardly envision stepping out, putting all his weight on the crutches, then pulling them forward through the snow. He took a small step, the tension building immediately, just waiting for the crutches to slip when he transferred his weight onto them. He planted his foot, trying to ignore the icy snow numbing his ankle and foot. Then slowly, he moved the crutches one by one, not daring to transfer all his weight off his one good foot or step until both crutches were set firmly into the mess. He could almost bear falling, but not sliding, not a sudden uncontrollable fall.

Slowly, he moved toward the inn, step by small cautious step, twisting one crutch out into place, then the other, the tension in him cranking up, feeling the rubber tips of the crutches ready to slip out any second. He tried to keep his foot close to the ground, shoving the slush out of his way, feeling it packed into his shoe, freezing his ankle. It took him over seven minutes to get from the car to the entrance. It felt like a frozen eternity.

Finally, finally Reed made it to the porch steps. He dropped down on his knee, feeling the cold and wet immediately coming through his slacks. He lay the crutches on the porch in front of him, placed his bare hands on the snow and crawled up the four steps and across the porch, pushing his crutches ahead of him. At the door, he propped one crutch against the wall and managed to get up, using the doorknob and the other crutch. As he reached for the handle, he told himself, If that fucking door is locked I'm breaking the glass.

The knob turned. The door opened. Reed stepped in, exhausted, wet, drained. He stood for a moment, grinding the bottom of his shoe into the floor mat, twisting the rubber tips of his crutches into the mat, trying to dry the bottom of everything that touched the floor so he would not end up slipping in the foyer, falling, hurting his already battered body, possibly damaging his stump.

Reed entered his room, his face a mask, his chin jutting slightly, his eyes narrowed with focus and determination. He dropped onto the bed, stripped off his wet shoe, sock, pants, shivering slightly until he pulled the quilt cover off the bed and wrapped himself in it.

He grimaced as he leaned over and pulled the telephone off the night table near the head of the bed. He tried to estimate what would hurt the most in the morning. Probably that one kick to his shoulder. It had felt like being hit with a stone. Or the sharp stomping kicks McAndrews had landed on his chest. He flexed. Maybe his back. Remembering how it had felt when Boggs had come over the hood, banging into him with that huge head.

Running the inventory of pain, adding it up, calculating it, did not interfere with Reed dialing Adele Simpson's home phone. He checked his watch. A little after one. Sorry, Adele.

Reed spoke her name loudly so he would penetrate her just-awakened state.

"Adele."

A husky voice answered, *"Mr. Reed."*

Reed smiled. Even half asleep Adele Simpson had her wits about her.

"Yeah, it's me. Sorry to wake you, but it's important."

Adele cleared her throat.

"Yes. Go ahead."

"Is Irwin in town? I'm sorry to bother you, but if he's off somewhere I can't waste time trying to find him."

"No, he's around. You want me to get a hold of him?"

"As long as you're up."

"No problem. I might have to make a few calls."

"I need him to do something tonight. Right now."

"I understand."

"Have him call me at this number."

"Okay."

Reed recited his telephone number at the Maple Inn and hung up. No apology, no repeating himself. Sorry, Adele.

While he waited, Reed made his way to his toilet kit in the bathroom, finding his pain medication. He smiled at the weird idea that it might be refreshing to feel some pain other than the phantom pain. Feel some real pain.

He downed three Naproxens and made his way back to the bed just as his phone rang.

"Yeah?"

"Bill! What's up? How are you?"

The gravelly voice of Irwin Barker reached him through the background noise of Irwin's favorite Upper West Side bar. Reed pictured his colleague sitting at the bar in one of his rumpled suits, tie undone, hulking over a rocks glass of straight Irish whiskey, smoking an unfiltered Pall Mall.

"Great, Irwin. How are you?"

Irwin heard the sarcasm in Reed's voice.

"That good, huh?"

"Yeah."

"You must be—calling me this time of night. What's up?"

"I'd like you to take care of something for me."

"Name it."

"Go to my apartment. You have a set of my keys, right?"

"Yeah. They're back at my place, but that's five minutes away. I'll get them."

"Good, get the keys and go over to my place. Now, Irwin. I need you to get over there, tonight."

"Right."

"You're going to have to put together a little shipment for me."

"Go ahead."

"Pack up my laptop. It's on my desk. The case is there, too. My portable printer. It's in the hallway closet. Pack up the Colt nine, the Commander. It's in the wall safe in my bedroom closet, just turn the dial clockwise to fifty, it'll open. Also the .25-caliber Beretta and a box of ammunition and an extra magazine for both guns. There's a couple of trigger locks in there. Lock the guns before you pack them up. There's a hip holster for the Colt and an ankle holster for the Beretta. Include those. Also a cleaning kit in a black leather case. All that stuff is in the safe."

"Got it. What else?"

"There's money in the safe. Packets of a thousand. Toss in two. No, make it three."

"Okay."

"What else? The calculator on my desk. Make sure the power cords and phone cords are in with the laptop. Throw in some disks and a couple of rolls of paper for the printer. Put together about a week's worth of clothes. Whatever is clean, you know seven of everything. Underwear is in the top drawer of my dresser. You got all that?"

"Yeah."

"Call a private courier. Earlybird goes twenty-four hours, right?"

"You want I should bring the stuff up myself? You need a little backup?"

"Not right now. I might need you down there to do some things for me."

"Okay."

"Get a courier. Adele knows the ones we use. I'm sure she'll be up waiting for my call. Have her arrange it. But you be there to hand the stuff to the guy. Make sure he's carrying only my stuff. I don't want the guns bouncing around on the truck with a bunch of other shipments. One guy, one car or truck, on its way up here tonight. Send everything to me in care of the Maple Inn, Dumphy, New York. Adele has the address and directions. It's about a six-hour drive. I want the stuff here tomorrow morning." Reed checked his watch. "I mean *this* morning. Sorry I'm doing this so late. If you hustle you should get it here by nine or ten. No later."

"Anything else?"

Reed hesitated. "Yeah. In the front closet off the living room."

"What?"

"In the closet you'll see a cane and my leg, my prosthesis. Put that in with everything else. There's a trunk in the back of that closet that will hold everything."

"Got it."

"About the leg, don't think it's supposed to look like a real leg. It's basically a socket and tubes with a mechanical foot on the end."

"Okay. I'll have everything to you by ten, at the latest."

"Good. Thanks, Irwin."

Then, just before he broke the connection, Reed remembered.

"Irwin."

"What?"

"A shoe. I need a left shoe. I don't have any left shoes with me. There's a pair of running shoes that work with the Flex-Foot. Pack those up, too. And there's a pair of plain brown tie shoes. Put those in, too."

"Got it. Call me if you need anything else. My phone's on now."

"Thanks, I will. After Adele sets up the courier tell her to go back to sleep. I don't want her sitting by the phone drinking tea all night."

"Okay, will do."

"Thanks."

"Hey, boss."

"What?"

"Nice to have you back."

"Yeah, well, there's going to be a few people who might not feel that way."

"Fuck 'em."

TWENTY-ONE

The clinic nurse, Patricia Stern, had called Madeleine Ullmann shortly after Rita Glover brought Johnny Boy Reed into the clinic.

Patricia, a pale blond girl of just twenty, rather wan and nervous, was not a registered nurse, but rather a practical nurse who had graduated second to last in her class of twelve. Patricia knew how to take care of practical things like cleaning up after accidents in bed and calling Mrs. Ullmann when anything serious happened.

Johnny Boy Reed looked serious to Patricia. When Patricia first saw him, she winced so sharply that the skin on her neck tightened enough to show the tendons. Johnny Boy's scabs had turned ugly. He seemed frighteningly pale. He held his stomach, grunting quietly in pain, tears seeping out of his eyes, telling Patricia it hurt.

She gave him Pepto-Bismol and was kind enough to slip on a latex glove and stroke his back as he lay doubled over in bed. The Pepto seemed to help a little bit.

Almost two hours later, Madeleine Ullmann strode into the clinic, moving quickly despite her generous hips and heavy legs, her short brown hair unkempt at the early hour, but her ferretlike eyes darted alertly, taking in everything with a look that told Patricia she expected to see only trouble.

"Where is he?" she announced in her shrill, accusing voice, as if the timid, worried Patricia Stern were responsible for making her come out this time of night in the nasty early snowstorm.

It was perfectly obvious where Johnny Boy was—doubled over in the hospital bed closest to the far wall, curtained off in a corner separated from the other four beds in the clinic, only one of which was occupied by a thirty-eight-year-old profoundly retarded woman who had contracted another of her innumerable bladder infections. The clinic had put her on intravenous antibiotics, a procedure most often done in a hospital, but a procedure that the extremely well-equipped, if not well-staffed, Ullmann Institute clinic could render.

Madeleine Ullmann grabbed a pair of latex gloves from a dispenser and strode over to Johnny Boy. She wrenched the curtains aside and pulled his arms away from his stomach and put a hand on his abdomen, feeling around and down.

She was not a doctor, but Madeleine Ullmann already knew what was wrong with Johnny Boy Reed. He winced. Madeleine continued feeling his stomach and abdomen just to confirm her conclusions.

She turned away from Johnny Boy and yelled at Patricia in her loud, accusatory voice, "Don't just stand around. Come over here."

Madeleine Ullmann made Patricia administer the enema. Not an efficient, contained Fleet Enema, but a full enema using the large bag. Mrs. Ullmann stood on the other side of the bed, her gloved hand on Johnny's shoulder, not to comfort him, but to shake him if his attention waned, yelling at him, "Hold it, hold it, I said. Hold it in until I tell you to let it go," as if Johnny Boy's bowels were under her command, as if she had every right to make Johnny Boy suffer until she decided when to let him stop suffering.

When it was over, while Patricia cleaned up the bloody, watery mess of stool, Madeleine Ullmann sat calmly at the desk in the clinic office, writing in the chart as if she were a nurse or a doctor, calmly writing matter-of-fact words: *patient complained of stomach pain . . . interview elicited that patient had not moved bowels in three days.* She wrote words that looked perfectly reasonable on the page, even professional: *administered enema, patient evacuated.* But any medical professional reading the words would have wondered why the need for an enema? Why is the patient constipated in the first place? Madeleine Ullmann wrote nothing in the chart as to why.

She knew why. And she knew why only an enema using nearly a gallon of water would be effective enough to soften and loosen Johnny Boy's stool to the point where it could move around the growing constriction in his colon. And Madeleine Ullmann knew that soon Johnny Boy Reed would not be able to move his bowels at all. Not even with laxatives and a stool softener and an enema. She knew that he was also anemic. The bloody stool told her that the tumor was seeping now, tearing slightly at the wall of the colon as it continued to grow. For a moment, she thought about giving Johnny Boy a transfusion, but dismissed the idea. Too much bother.

She made her careful entry into the medical record knowing that Johnny Boy Reed did not have much time at all. Soon, when the tumor blocked his colon completely, he would be in excruciating pain that would be relieved only by major surgery. Surgery performed by George Prentice at the local hospital.

They would open up Johnny Boy Reed and remove the tumor and a small section of his bowel, keeping both for close examination. They would run tests to see how far the cancer had spread, almost certainly to his liver and most probably throughout most of his intestines. Prentice would sew Johnny Boy back up, and declare him terminal. They would order the morphine drip. Her husband would sign orders not to intervene further, and Johnny Boy Reed would die.

Probably a month, six weeks at the outside, thought Madeleine Ullmann. But what she wrote in the chart, a satisfied smile on her lips, simply said: *patient resting calmly. Will be discharged from clinic in the a.m., advised to eat soft foods.*

Reed woke as his normal hour, 4:00 A.M., but turned over and resolutely forced himself to sleep until six-thirty, whereupon he slowly, carefully got out of bed and made his way to the small shower stall in the cramped bathroom.

Even after standing as long as he could in a steamy hot shower, taking more painkillers, and easing himself back into bed, Reed wasn't even close to being able to do his morning exercise routine. He lay in bed and spent about a half hour stretching, flexing against the various painful areas on his body, trying to gently force his body to function against the pain.

After the thirty minutes of stretching and flexing, he sat on the edge of his bed, dressed only in his shorts, inventorying the damage done to his body. A vague lingering headache reminded him that he had been hit in the head with a crutch and a fist. The first two knuckles on his right hand were sore and swollen enough from hitting Boggs's head that he had difficulty making a fist. The finger joints in both hands were swollen and sore from hitting, blocking kicks and punches, grabbing. Both forearms had bruises, also from blocking kicks and punches. His back on the left side ached from ribs bruised when Boggs had slammed into him. That damage, and his battered hands, made it almost impossible to walk on his crutches.

He rolled his head, stretching carefully, checking where else it hurt. He looked down at his stump and began massaging it, as if he could form it and prepare it for what was to come. There's no choice now, pal, he told himself.

Just as Reed finished dressing, his phone rang. The receptionist told him a man was in the lobby with a delivery. Reed told the receptionist to send the man to his room. The courier, as per Irwin's instructions, would not deliver the trunk to anybody in the inn but Reed.

When he arrived at the room, he asked for identification and Reed's signature, before he wheeled the trunk in. With the guns and ammunition being part of the shipment, Reed approved. The courier apologized for not arriving sooner, telling him the snow slowed him down a little on the local highway.

Reed thanked him and pressed a fifty-dollar bill in the man's hand, telling him he had done a good job.

He opened the lid of the trunk. Everything had been packed neatly . . . the prosthesis and computer equipment on top of the clothes, the guns, ammunition, holsters, cleaning kit on the bottom, and three packets of bills placed into a large manila envelope.

Reed lifted the prosthesis out of the trunk. Although the device had cost over twenty-one thousand dollars, the sight of it did nothing to comfort Reed. It represented more pain and discomfort . . . a cold, mechanical device, a plastic socket, a complex knee joint, titanium tubes, a mechanical foot that flexed and responded to his weight and gait . . . Reed looked upon it as something that should be on a robot, not a human.

The prosthetist had assured Reed that he had a state-of-the-art device. Reed had asked him, "How do I get a state-of-the-art stump?"

The prosthetist had taken the question seriously, answering, "That's mostly up to you. We'll get the limb right, one way or another. But you might have to go through a bit of hell before that happens. Some people, everything clicks fairly easy. Others, it's hard. You had a traumatic limb loss. That's not the best way to lose a leg. But I've definitely seen people walk on much, much worse. You got the muscle padding, good skin flaps, great muscle strength in your thigh and buttocks. You're healthy, fit. It's all there. You just have to work through the discomfort and hassles. And we'll keep adjusting the socket until the fit is perfect."

Reed had believed him, but when the prosthetist had attached the first version of his artificial limb, Reed was stunned at how awkward it felt. It seemed to require an inordinate effort to pull the device forward with each step, plus more effort to make the knee bend. The foot, on the other hand, flexed so easily that it felt very unstable, as if it would spring Reed forward against his will.

They made adjustments. The limb got better. Reed became more adept. But the more he tried wearing it, the worse the stump pain became.

He stared at the limb, remembering all the reasons he did not want to wear it, but knowing full well that now he had no choice. "All right," Reed said to himself as he picked up the limb, "fuck it."

He set the limb down on the bed next to him, slipped off the pressure sock that held his stump tightly, helping to shape and protect it. He rolled on the suction sock with the small attachment on the tip that would click into the socket of his stump. He looked around the trunk for the socket lubricant. He hadn't remembered to ask Irwin to pack it, but it didn't bother Reed. It didn't seem to help much anyway.

Just sliding the stump into the socket made Reed uncomfortable. It brought to mind memories of pain, blisters on the back of his thigh, instability, and facing the reality of his limb loss. Attaching the prosthesis allowed him to stand upright and walk, after a fashion, but underneath that effect lurked the constant reminder of what walking had been like before the loss. Reed had not yet lived nearly long enough without his left leg to forget what it was like to live with it.

Once the limb was attached, he dug out the blue jeans Irwin had packed and the running shoes. The left running shoe had been augmented so that it would slide onto the Flex-Foot.

Finally, Reed stood, feeling for the first time in too long the pressure on his left hip and stump as he carefully shifted the weight from his right leg. He shifted the weight back to the right leg, lifting his left leg, sending the artificial limb forward, simulating a step. He reviewed the physical therapist's tips on the proper gait. He tested himself and the limb, walking back and forth in the small room. He gained confidence. He walked to the window and pulled up the shade, checking the depth of the slushy snow outside. The parking lot had been plowed, the black asphalt bordered now with a glistening snowbank.

The slush that had turned to ice in the cold night air had begun to melt into slush again under the glare of the early morning sun. He doubted if he could really make it through the remains of the storm on his artificial limb, but for now, it would replace the crutches. He'd use the wheelchair for long distances. The prosthesis and cane for short. Either way, wearing the prosthesis would hide the limb loss from Johnny Boy.

He strode over to the desk chair where he had hooked his cane over the back. And just as he reached for the cane, Reed thoughtlessly shifted most of his weight forward. Without warning a sharp jolt of pain shot through his stump, not phantom pain, pain at the site where the socket had set off a nerve. He quickly backed off, almost losing his balance. He grabbed the back of the chair, trying to take some of the weight off, waiting for the pain to resolve.

Bill Reed gritted his teeth, snarling, muttering a curse. He resisted the impulse to pull off the limb that tortured him. He lifted his artificial leg, placing it squarely down on the carpeted floor, distributing his weight evenly, ignoring the residual discomfort from his misstep. He gripped the cane, ignoring his swollen knuckles, stepped over to the closet, then to the dresser, gathering his clothes, wary with each movement that the shocking pain might hit him again.

"Fuck it. Fuck it," he said, determined to dress and eat and make his way to the car, and drive to the Quik Mart at the edge of Dumphy, and step through the snow from the car to wherever they kept the ice cream in the Quik-Mart, then back to the counter, walking up straight and tall, cane in one hand, the pint of Ben & Jerry's ice cream for John in the other hand.

No one, nothing, was going to stop him from standing, walking, driving, wheeling in his chair, whatever it took to visit John Boyd. Nothing.

Having just finished her double shift, eight to eight, Rita Glover exited the front door of Davis Hall eager to get home and have the rest of Sunday afternoon to herself. She'd catch a few hours sleep, get up in time for five o'clock mass, then come home and make dinner for the kids. But when she saw Bill Reed rolling up the walkway in his wheelchair toward Johnny Boy's dorm, she stopped and waited.

She knew this must be Johnny Boy's cousin. She, like most of the staff, had heard about him, but Rita hadn't expected to see him on campus just as she was leaving. Nor had she expected him to be so handsome. Dressed in jeans, running shoes, a plaid shirt, sweater, and shearling coat, Reed's clothes fit in with the North Country surroundings. They just happened to be more expensive versions of anyone else's clothes.

As Reed wheeled toward the entrance, Rita asked, "You looking for Johnny Boy?"

Reed stopped and looked at the large woman standing in front of him. She wore a well-worn corduroy jacket, unbuttoned. Her features were somewhat obscured by fat, her dark hair was thin and plain, and her smile revealed a missing eye tooth on the right side. But her smile was open and sincere and very engaging. And her skin was flawless, so much so as to seem like porcelain, giving the large woman a feminine, even delicate quality. This was the first person who had ever smiled at him at the Ullmann Institute.

"Yes," he answered. "How did you know?"

"I heard a relative was visiting him. Someone in a wheelchair. So who else would that be but you?"

Reed nodded. "Right. Right. Well, is he around? Where can I find him?"

"He's not in his room."

"Isn't he supposed to be?"

Rita saw Reed's expression turn, as if he was expecting bad news.

"Where is he?" Reed asked.

"We had to take him to the clinic last night."

"Why? What happened?"

"Oh, nothing too serious. The poor guy got a wicked awful stomachache so I sent him over to the clinic. I called the nurse a while ago. Said they had to give him an enema. He's okay, now."

Reed shook his head in dismay. "What happened? Why did he need—"

Rita waved a hand as if to signal how ordinary the situation. "Oh, listen, a lot of them get irregular. Some of them have had bowel problems since they was babies. What with those rotten scabies and all, I'm sure they threw him off his regular schedule. You know how that can be. But the nurse, Patricia at the clinic, she said he's fine now."

"Where's the clinic?"

Rita hesitated. "Say, you're supposed to check in with the day administrator and all."

"Yeah, I know." Reed smiled at her. "I often don't do what I'm supposed to do. Are you going to get in trouble if you tell me where to find him?"

Rita smiled. It had been a long time since any man had worried about whether or not she would be getting into trouble.

"Who's gonna tell anybody I told you?"

"Exactly," Reed responded.

"Tell you what you do." Rita pointed behind her. "You go into the dorm here. That way it'll seem like you were looking for him on your own. Just wheel right on through and go out the back door at the far end. Outside there, you'll see on your right the roof of a new building down in the hollow behind the dorms. That's the clinic. You can't miss it."

"Thanks," said Reed. "I appreciate it."

Rita checked her watch and immediately turned and made her way down the steps, her rather hefty legs carrying her bulk quickly in the direction of the parking lot.

"Don't mention it," she shouted back over her shoulder. "Ask for Patricia. She's the nurse over there."

Reed didn't ask for Patricia when he arrived at the clinic. He entered the clinic, saw Johnny Boy off by himself in the corner bed, sleeping. Reed rolled right over to the bedside. For a moment, he just sat and looked at Johnny Boy's face in repose. Even sleeping, Johnny Boy looked troubled, a V of worry etched between his eyes. The slowly resolving red welts and scabs along his hairline, chin, and neck didn't help appearances either.

Reed reached out and placed his palm over Johnny Boy's shoulder, gently shaking the smaller man.

Speaking softly, he said, "Hey, John Boyd. Hey, buddy, wake up."

Suddenly Johnny Boy's eyes opened wide, staring blankly into space. He seemed slightly shocked, blank, as if his mind hadn't caught up to his open eyes.

"John, it's me, Bill."

Johnny Boy lifted himself up onto his elbows and turned to face Reed, looking down at him sitting in the wheelchair, still uncomprehending, eyes open, but nothing registering.

Reed leaned closer and repeated, "John, it's me, Bill. Wake up."

And then Johnny Boy smiled. A slow tentative smile that at first made Reed feel as if Johnny Boy didn't recognize him. And then the words Reed had spoken and his image seemed to finally register and Johnny Boy's smile broadened and his eyes seemed to almost glaze over with a look of relief and joy that made Bill Reed feel as if he had accomplished something truly wonderful by just showing up at Johnny Boy's bedside. Johnny Boy pushed himself upright and leaned back on his pillows and said, "Cuz'n Bill."

Reed instinctively reached out for Johnny Boy's hand, but he saw the angry welts and scabs between Johnny Boy's fingers and held back.

"Oh, man," he said. "Look at you."

And then Reed spotted a box of latex gloves sitting on the table next to Johnny Boy's bed. He reached over and pulled out two of the floppy gloves and slipped the translucent latex over his hands.

"All right," said Reed, "this is good."

Reed grabbed the side rail of Johnny Boy's bed and pulled himself out of his wheelchair into a standing position next to the bed, balancing himself on his prosthesis. He reached out and patted the side of Johnny Boy's face and head.

"Hey, how're you doin', partner?"

At first Johnny Boy seemed to twitch under Reed's touch, but then he smiled again and reached up and held the back of Reed's hand.

Gently, softly, Reed asked, "How are you, John? Are you okay? Those bugs stop biting you?"

Johnny Boy sat up straighter and nodded, saying, "Yeah. Yeah. I'm okay."

"How's your stomach?" Reed asked.

"Okay, okay," said Johnny Boy. But even as he repeated the word *okay,* Johnny Boy rubbed his stomach and abdomen. And Reed could not help but see the anxiety etched into Johnny Boy's face.

"How long has it been bothering you, John? Your stomach. How long?"

Johnny Boy shook his head back and forth in tight, rapid movements.

Reed pointed to Johnny Boy's stomach.

"Your stomach, your tummy, it hurts?"

Reed nodded, trying to elicit an answer. Johnny Boy nodded back, but it felt like he was mostly mimicking Reed's nod.

"How long, John? How long has it hurt?"

Johnny Boy just nodded again, frustrating Reed, making him feel inept. Reed started to formulate another way to ask, but stopped himself. He could see the topic made Johnny Boy uneasy.

Reed nodded. "Well," he said, more to himself than to Johnny Boy. "Talking about all that isn't the first thing we should do, is it?" Reed forced himself to smile and said, "Hey, John, you still like ice cream?"

Johnny Boy made a face at Reed and said, "Hell, yeah."

Reed laughed. "Hell, yeah? Guess you know that answer don't you?"

"Hell, yeah."

Reed punched Johnny Boy lightly on the shoulder and said, "There you go. You want some?"

"You got ice cream?"

"Hell, yeah," said Reed. He reached over to the carryall bag attached to his wheelchair and pulled out a pint of Ben & Jerry's mint vanilla. "Here, have some, but not too much. I don't want it to hurt your stomach."

When Patricia Stern came to check on Johnny Boy, she found Reed sitting quietly in his wheelchair next to Johnny Boy's bed; Johnny Boy sitting up, smiling, eating directly from his pint of Ben & Jerry's mint vanilla ice cream with a white plastic spoon.

Patricia was so concerned about the ice cream that instead of asking Reed who he was and how he had gotten there, she blurted out, "Oh, my, what's that he's eating?"

Reed turned to her, surprised by the question, and when he saw the confused look on Patricia Stern's face, he thought she might actually be one of the residents come to visit Johnny Boy.

"It's ice cream," he said.

"Well, I know, but he's not supposed to. I think. I don't know if that's all right."

Reed nodded, understanding the question now.

"Are you the nurse?"

"Yes."

"It's just ice cream. Not a lot. Just a couple more spoonfuls. That's all right, isn't it?"

"Well, Mrs. Ullmann said only soft foods, so I guess it's all right. He's supposed to go back to the dorm for lunch you know."

"Is he out of quarantine?"

"No. It's okay over here, because we're careful about contact. But he's supposed to go back to his room before the kitchen closes. Who are you?"

"I'm his cousin. It's all right. I have permission to be here. You don't have to call anyone."

"Well, I . . ."

"No, it's fine. Really. I won't be long."

Reed raised his hand and nodded at her reassuringly.

"It's okay, really."

Now that Johnny Boy seemed to be settled down and content, Reed wanted to return to gently questioning him. He smiled one more time at Patricia and turned back to Johnny Boy. The nurse lingered a moment, not sure what to do, then wandered off, still worried.

"So, John, you got sick, huh?"

"Last night."

"Last night. Your stomach hurt last night?"

Johnny Boy nodded, obviously more interested in the ice cream, however, than in thinking about his stomach pain.

"John." Reed reached over and shook Johnny Boy's knee to get his attention. "Give me the ice cream, John. Don't eat too much."

Johnny Boy handed him the pint container without hesitation or protest. That surprised Reed and disturbed him. Someone had taught his cousin to take orders and take them quickly.

Reed spoke slowly. "John, when did your stomach start hurting?"

"Last night."

"What about before last night? Did it hurt before last night, too?"

Johnny Boy nodded.

"How long? How long has it been hurting?"

Johnny Boy smiled, but just for a moment. He nodded more to himself than to Reed. He seemed eager to answer his cousin Bill's question, although the topic obviously deeply disturbed him.

"Long," he said. He looked up at the ceiling grimacing slightly, perhaps at the memory of it. "Long," Johnny Boy repeated.

Reed nodded. "How long? A week, month, year?"

Johnny Boy nodded again and said, "Long. Long time."

Bill Reed patted Johnny Boy's knee again, trying to smile reassuringly at him. After a pause, he asked, "So how are your scabies? Your bug bites."

Johnny Boy made a face as if he had tasted something bad and shook his head with rapid little side-to-side movements. Reed nodded, trying to show that he understood. An awkward silence passed, neither one knowing what to say. It was Johnny Boy who broke the silence.

"Hey, why are you in a wheelchair, Cuz'n Bill?"

Reed waved a hand as to make nothing of it. "I hurt my leg."

"Bad?"

"It *was* hurt bad. Not now though. Now it doesn't hurt."

"And your head?"

"My head?" Reed remembered the scrape on his forehead and touched it lightly, shrugging it off. "Oh, yeah, my head. Yeah, I hurt my head, too. Not at the same time, but yes, I hurt my head, too. It's okay."

"Sure?"

"Yeah, sure. Sure." Reed smiled reassuringly, then asked, "John?"

"What?"

"Do you like it here? Here at this place?"

If Johnny Boy had been five years old, an age more in line with his mental capacity, he probably would have started to cry when he shook his head, no. But he was forty-one. A man who had lived through adult problems. But he had lived through them without the mental abilities of an adult and that had taken its toll. The constant apprehension and worries had given Johnny Boy Reed an awareness beyond his IQ. His round face twisted into a grimace that somehow reminded Reed of the strangely disturbing page that Johnny Boy had sent him.

"No," Johnny Boy said. Just the one simple word, but the single word struck something deep inside Bill Reed stirring the dark emotions that seemed to be always lurking under the surface.

Reed started to ask, "Why, what . . . ?" but he stopped himself. Did it matter why? And what was he going to do about it? Why keep pushing at it?

"Would you like more ice cream, John?"

Johnny Boy smiled and nodded, his oversized tongue sticking out of his mouth.

Reed handed the container to his cousin.

"All right, take it easy, John. Don't eat too fast."

Reed pivoted his wheelchair and saw Patricia Stern standing behind him at a respectful distance. Reed wheeled toward her.

Somewhat harshly Reed asked, "What's wrong with him? He looks terrible."

The question, so direct, flustered the young woman. She

patted her blonde hair and smoothed the white apron she wore over her blue skirt.

"Oh, I don't know any of the medical stuff. I'm just a practical nurse. The regular staff is here on the weekdays. Or on call."

"Who's that?"

"Who's what?"

"The regular staff. Who makes up the regular staff? Mrs. Ullmann?"

"Yes. And Mrs. Dellgoff works here, too. She's a nurse. And me. And some of the women proctors help out if we need them." And then she added, as if not wanting to make a mistake, "But Mrs. Ullmann is in charge. Mrs. Ullmann supervises. She's a nurse practitioner. She's in charge."

"Mrs. Ullmann?"

"Yes." She nodded at Reed as if trying to elicit his agreement.

Reed didn't nod back. He glanced around the clinic. It seemed more like a small hospital wing than a clinic. There were four more beds in addition to his cousin's, all well equipped. Across from the beds, glass partitions revealed an office, an examining room, and a larger area that looked like a mini-operating room.

Reed looked back at Patricia Stern.

"This place looks very new. Very well equipped."

"Oh, it's very up-to-date."

Reed motioned with his head toward Johnny Boy.

"Does he have his clothes here?"

The nurse looked over at Johnny Boy as if to remind herself. "No, no. Mrs. Glover brought him over in his robe, wrapped in a blanket. She walked him over herself. He was all hunched up. I gave him Pepto-Bismol."

"I see. Do you think I could walk him back? Bundle him up in another blanket and take him back to his room?"

"Oh, no. *You* can't do that. I have to wait for the day proctor to come in and get him."

"The day proctor."

"Yes. Mr. McAndrews."

Reed felt a kick of emotion. "I see. When is he coming?"

She checked her watch again.

"Any minute, I guess. Any minute."

Reed nodded. "Good. I'll wait."

Reed wheeled back to Johnny Boy's bed, but this time he positioned the wheelchair so he could see the entrance. Reed hadn't expected to encounter Eddie McAndrews so soon, but if he was coming, then so be it. Reed shifted in his wheelchair, feeling the Colt Commander holstered under his coat, behind his right hip, pressing against the back of his wheelchair.

"The nurse said you're going back to your room soon, John."

"Oh, oh, okay."

"The proctor is coming to get you."

Reed watched Johnny Boy's expression closely.

"Eddie?" asked Johnny Boy.

"Yeah. Eddie."

Johnny Boy's face went blank.

"What's the matter, don't you like Eddie?"

Johnny Boy quickly shook his head, no, looking around as he did to make sure no one saw him.

"You don't like him."

"Don't like him," said Johnny Boy, blurting out the words.

"Why? Did he ever hurt you, John?"

Johnny Boy looked around again. He even made sure to check how closely Patricia Stern stood. He looked back at Reed and nodded two quick, but very definite nods.

Reed slowly nodded back, shifting, lifting his stump, watching the knee on his prosthesis respond to the movement as if testing it.

"How, John? How did he hurt you?"

To this, Johnny Boy looked down, shook his head rapidly in a movement that Reed began interpreting as his way of saying no and dismissing a topic at the same time.

Reed, leaning closer to the head of the bed now, reached out and patted Johnny Boy's shoulder. He gently called to him, "John. John," until Johnny Boy looked up in his direction.

"Nobody is going to be hurting you anymore, John. You understand me. Nobody."

Reed watched Johnny Boy, wanting to see if he understood what Reed had said, wanting to see if Johnny Boy believed him, and if it had reassured him. It didn't. Johnny Boy's expression remained just as apprehensive and guarded as before Reed spoke.

Reed leaned forward to say it again, to make Johnny Boy believe that Eddie McAndrews would never hurt him again, but a voice interrupted, a loud, arrogant voice tinged with an irritating, exaggerated, country-boy twang.

"There you are, Johnny Boy."

Johnny Boy flinched at the loud voice of Eddie McAndrews, shouted at him from the doorway of the clinic. Reed turned and watched McAndrews stride over to the far side of the bed, carrying a set of folded clothes with latex-gloved hands. McAndrews dropped the clothes on Johnny Boy's lap, not even acknowledging that Reed sat staring at him.

"C'mon, partner. Time to get your lazy ass up and out of here. You only got about twenty minutes before lunch is over. C'mon, I brought your clothes. Git dressed."

Johnny Boy quickly pushed aside the blanket and sheet, and pivoted away from Reed, toward McAndrews. He sat at the edge of the bed, concentrating on unbuttoning his pajama top.

Now that it was clear which of them had Johnny Boy's attention, McAndrews turned to Reed and asked quietly, "What're you doin' here, shithead. Come back for some more?"

"McAndrews, right? Eddie McAndrews."

"What's it to you?"

"I see you're back at work. You live here, Eddie? You live right here at the institute? As I remember it, all the staff people had to live in one of those crummy houses off beyond the barn."

"No, not all the staff. Not anymore."

"But you live in one of them, don't you? Ullmann probably

stuck your ass in the worst of his shit boxes, a piece of white trash like you."

McAndrews handed Johnny Boy his plaid shirt off the pile of clothes, then turned to look at Reed, a sly smile covering his anger.

"Ain't you something, now? Still got a mouth on you, ain't you?"

"So I'm right about where you live."

"You ain't right about shit, you nosy prick. What's this, you askin' me where I live? I'll be here anytime you want to find me. I ain't goin' anywhere."

Reed nodded, speaking quietly. "You don't have to tell me where you live. You can hide anywhere you want and I'll still find you."

Johnny Boy continued dressing, but with his head down he surreptitiously shifted glances between his Cuz'n Bill and Eddie. He could tell by the way Cuz'n Bill looked at Eddie and the sound of Cuz'n Bill's strong voice that he was standing up to Eddie McAndrews. It made Johnny Boy nervous, frightened enough to feel funny in his stomach, but he kept looking, wanting to see what would happen. Nobody he knew had ever stood up to Eddie. At least not for very long.

McAndrews smirked. "You won't need to come lookin' for me, asshole. You stay in this part of the world, I'll be comin' to see you real soon."

"Uh-huh," said Reed. "You going to bring all your friends when you come looking for me?"

"Hell no. Too many assholes gettin' in the way makes it hard to get your licks in. Hell, from now on I'll tend to you myself." McAndrews poked Johnny Boy's knee with a knuckle. "Him, too. Hurry up, Boy. I ain't got all day."

Reed leaned forward and raised his voice, "Hey."

"Hey what?" McAndrews asked.

"Next time I find out you touched him, hurt him in any way . . . you'd better get your rifle out again because I'll find you and I'll beat you so bad you'll never be the same. I'll break your fucking arms."

McAndrews answered with a sneer. "Shit. You?" Eddie looked over at Johnny Boy, then back at Reed sitting in his wheelchair, the hospital bed between them. "How the fuck you gonna watch out for him?"

Johnny Boy stopped dressing, bracing himself, feeling the meanness welling up in Eddie. Feeling the waves of anger, the dark spirit coming off Eddie like heat.

McAndrews balled his left hand into a fist, cocking his arm.

Johnny Boy seemed to contract into himself, hunching his head into his shoulders, steeling himself for the fist backhand across the side of his head. Quickly, fearing it might prompt Eddie to lash out, but unable to stop himself, Johnny Boy glanced at Cuz'n Bill. He saw him, leaning forward in his wheelchair seat, his left hand braced on the seat of the chair, his right hand back toward his hip.

"Don't," said Reed. "Don't do it."

A shrill voice came from their left. "Don't what?"

McAndrews, Reed, Johnny Boy, all looked in that direction. Madeleine Ullmann stood at the clinic doorway, her hands on her broad hips, scowling at the scene in front of her.

"Don't what?" she insisted, asking Reed, making it sound like a reprimand.

Reed did not answer her, looking back at McAndrews instead. He was in no mood to be ordered to answer a question by anybody. As McAndrews relaxed his fist and let his arm drop, Reed sat back, bringing his right hand away from the gun. He gripped the wheels of his chair, rolling it back clear of the bed, turning it toward Madeleine Ullmann who remained near the doorway.

Reed asked her, "Who are you?"

"I'm Madeleine Ullmann. I just work here. Who are you? Johnny Boy's cousin? The one causing all the fuss around here?"

"What kind of fuss would that be?"

She ignored Reed's question and walked into the clinic, heading for Johnny Boy's bed. She stopped at the foot of the bed and told Eddie McAndrews, "Standing around doesn't help, Eddie. Get him dressed and over to lunch. Just eggs. And some prunes if they have them. No coffee, either. Water if he wants it."

Eddie took Johnny Boy by the arm and lifted him off the bed onto his feet with just enough extra force and abruptness to make a point. Reed knew at that moment, without any doubt, that sometime, one way or another, Eddie McAndrews would hurt his cousin.

Johnny Boy stood on the far side of the hospital bed from where Reed sat in his wheelchair and stepped into his pants. At the foot of the bed, Madeleine Ullmann turned to Reed and said, "You're not allowed in here."

"Why is that?"

"This is a clinic. Visits are confined to the dayrooms. Or on the grounds somewhere. And usually family members are courteous enough to stop in the administration building and let us know they're here."

"I did that yesterday. And I told your husband I'd be back today. Isn't that enough?"

"Apparently you think so."

Reed had no interest in sparring with Madeline Ullmann. He looked over at his cousin who stood concentrating on pulling his belt buckle tight and fingering the buckle prong into the hole. He called out, "John."

Johnny Boy did not turn toward Reed until he had secured his belt.

Reed said, "John, take it easy. I'll be around. We'll talk later."

Johnny Boy said nothing. But he smiled and bobbed his head once. McAndrews grabbed his arm; Johnny Boy looked down and let himself be led out of the clinic.

Reed, making sure to make the point again, called out, "John, I'll see you later."

As soon as Johnny Boy was out of earshot, Reed turned to

Madeleine Ullmann and asked pointedly, "What's wrong with my cousin?"

"Constipated. We had to give him an enema. Not pleasant for any of us, but we're accustomed to things like that here. Many of our patients have digestive problems. It's just one of the things we deal with."

"But he's all right now?"

"He's all right. I wouldn't be sending him back if he wasn't. I understand my husband spoke to you yesterday about your visits here."

"What do you mean?"

"Are you dissatisfied with how we operate? Is that why you keep showing up here unannounced?"

"Why are you asking me that?"

Her voice rose and she snapped back, "Because I want to know."

"Is there some reason I should be dissatisfied?"

"Don't spar with me, sir. If you have problems with your cousin's situation here, I suggest you find another place for him. We are under constant pressure by the state to reduce our enrollment. And, at the same time, we have a very long waiting list. So if you have a desire to find other accommodations for your cousin, just let us know. Do you have plans for housing your cousin?"

"Are you serious?" Reed asked.

"If he's leaving, I'd like to know. Are you telling me you're going to be taking him out? If you are, I want to know. Now."

Reed snapped back, his voice rising. "I'm not telling you anything."

Madeleine Ullmann's anger and tone immediately matched his.

"Well, sir, I'll tell *you* something. I don't appreciate you coming in here upsetting everybody, upsetting our routine, making accusations, making demands on everybody."

Reed raised his hand. "Hey, wait a minute. Upsetting everybody? Who am I upsetting? What demands?"

She stepped toward Reed and nearly shouted, "Don't interrupt me."

"What!"

"And I'll thank you not to raise your voice to me."

Reed bolted up out of his wheelchair, surprising even himself at how quickly he had gotten to a standing position. He grabbed the side rail of the bed. Balancing on his artificial leg, he shouted at her, "Raise my voice? Raise my voice? You don't want to hear me raise my voice? Who the hell do you think you are? What kind of game are you playing here? Threatening me. Demanding answers from me. Telling me I'm making accusations. You want to see me upset somebody? You wait." Reed pointed at Madeleine. "You just watch how upset you're going to be. You and these goddamn thugs you have working here."

They stood no more than four feet apart, glaring at each other. Madeleine Ullmann balled her fist and banged the bed rail next to her.

"How dare you threaten me? How dare you? You have no idea what it takes to run this institution. You have no idea what we deal with every day. I want you off this property immediately. Get out. Now."

Reed watched her face contort in rage. As Madeleine Ullmann's anger seethed, Reed felt his own anger ebb.

Reed stood up straighter now, looming over Madeleine Ullmann, and calmly, quietly asked, "Or what? What are you going to do, Mrs. Ullmann? Are you going to call that rent-a-sheriff who runs things around here? You going to yell for those white-trash thugs that work for you? Go on, call them. Please, call them in here to throw me out and see what happens."

For a moment, Reed actually thought Madeleine Ullmann was about to step toward him and take a swing at him, but just then Matthew Ullmann entered the clinic.

Matthew Ullmann spoke sharply, "Madeleine." She turned toward him. Ullmann held up a hand and simply said, "Don't." Then he looked at Reed and spoke with the confidence of a man who considered himself totally in charge.

"The sheriff has already been called, Mr. Reed."

"Good," said Reed. "I'm anxious to talk to him."

"Fine. I'm sure he'll accommodate you."

Reed sneered, "What's he going to do when he gets here? Arrest me?"

"We can arrange that if you'd like," said Ullmann. "Or you can be sensible and leave now. Or you can stay and we'll ask him to escort you off the property. If you resist, then he can arrest you."

Reed looked at Ullmann, and nodded. He slowly settled himself back in his wheelchair and casually crossed his arms in front of his chest.

"Well, Mr. Ullmann, I'll tell you what. Let's play it your way. I think things are getting a little out of control around here. In fact, I don't feel safe around you and your employees and your wife. I'd like to wait for the sheriff. Have him escort me off the property." Reed pulled out his cellular phone. "You said you've already called the sheriff?"

"He's on his way."

"Let's see if we can get some additional law enforcement over here. Something beyond a two-bit county sheriff for hire. I'm going to call my lawyer, make sure I have representation. And I'm going to stay on the line while he notifies the state police. I wouldn't mind getting a state trooper over here. They must have a barracks somewhere in the vicinity." Reed started punching in numbers on his cellular phone. "I'm just going to sit here in my wheelchair, being disabled and all, and hope for all our sakes that I don't get assaulted or threatened any further."

Reed watched Ullmann and his wife watch him. He waited for the call to go through. It answered on the third ring.

"Hello, Charles, I'm sorry to disturb you at home on a Sunday, but it's urgent." Reed held the phone to his ear, never breaking his gaze at Ullmann. "I've got a problem here, and I need your help. Can you get on your other line there and contact the New York State Police, find out which barracks has jurisdiction over a place called Dumphy, New York. Yes, the northwest part of the state."

Ullmann stepped closer toward the hospital bed where Madeleine stood and Reed sat in his wheelchair to better hear

Reed's side of the conversation. Reed kept his eyes on Ullmann, occasionally shifting his gaze to the wife.

"Right. Yes, Charles, I understand. Tell them one of your clients has been threatened and assaulted. Yes, let them know I'm a recent amputee in a wheelchair. Right. Right. Uh huh. Yes, I'll hold on."

Ullmann finally spoke up. "That's not necessary."

Reed paused, looking up from his call. "What?"

"I said that's not necessary."

Reed turned back to his phone, "Hang on a second, Charles. Don't hang up. Give me a minute, but while you're waiting, is there any way you can come up with the name of a criminal attorney in this area, today, or will it have to wait for Monday?" After a pause, Reed said, "Okay, hang on a second." He lowered the phone and said to Ullmann, "Why isn't it necessary?"

"This is getting out of hand. We both know it. If you'll just agree to leave, I'll tell the sheriff there isn't a problem. Let's all cool off a little bit. Then you and I can sit down later, today if you wish, and resolve whatever concerns you have. My wife is upset. I'd like to speak with her. Then you and I can talk. None of this is necessary."

Reed stared at Ullmann for a few minutes, deciding. Finally, he lifted the phone to his ear and said, "Charles, I'll have to talk to you later. In the meantime, I'd like you to find that lawyer for me, and also the district attorney for this county. I'm considering bringing charges against a couple of people up here. Why don't you also talk to the state police commander if you can get a hold of him on a Sunday. Right. Just get me that information so I can proceed with the right people in charge up here. It's a little complicated. Sorry to bother you, Charles, but it's important. I'll call you back in an hour. If I don't speak to you in an hour, have a lawyer contact the county sheriff's office up here and inquire about me. I might be in custody. Okay. Thanks. Talk to you in an hour."

Reed turned off his cellular phone, having left a long message on the answering machine in his New York apartment.

"All right, Mr. Ullmann. I'm going to leave now. Where are you going to be later?"

"Home."

"What's the number there?"

"I'm in the book," said Ullmann.

Ullmann stepped to his left a few paces, guiding his wife in the same direction, opening the way for Reed to wheel toward the door. Reed watched their faces as he rolled past them. Madeleine Ullmann could not successfully hide all of her rage. Matthew Ullmann's face revealed nothing. At that moment, Reed wasn't at all sure which of them was the more dangerous.

TWENTY-TWO

Sundays were Angela Quist's quiet day, the day she kept all to herself, starting with a leisurely breakfast in her studio. She'd curl up in a big, battered club chair set back in the corner of her woodworking studio enjoying spoonfuls of yogurt mixed with granola, sips of steaming coffee, and the Sunday paper. Every once in a while she'd look up and stare at the cabinet or piece of furniture she was building. Eventually, she would get out of the club chair and start working on the piece, usually keeping at it straight through until she had to leave for the Maple Inn to work the dinner service.

This Sunday morning, she had no stomach for food or sitting in her chair reading the paper. She paced the studio sipping coffee from a sixteen-ounce Dunkin' Donuts travel mug. She had barely slept the night before. It had taken hours to calm down after witnessing the attack on Reed. She kept seeing the twisted faces of Eddie McAndrews and Raymond Boggs and the Barrett brothers, hearing their curses and grunts as they punched and kicked at Reed. She kept hearing the sickening cracking, slapping sound of fists and boots against flesh, and the thudding, the horrible thudding sound of Bill Reed's head against the side of his car.

Angela couldn't rid herself of the sounds and images. They plagued her, making her stomach queasy.

And now, pacing in her studio, she couldn't shake the concern for Reed that nagged at her. She pictured him driving back alone through that storm, passing out in his car, or waking up in the middle of the night convulsing from a head injury or some other terrible aftereffect of the fight. She wanted to call the inn, assure herself that he was all right. But at the same time, she didn't want to have anything more to do with Bill Reed. She still was angry that he had provoked McAndrews and the other proctors. So bullheaded. So stubborn. Why hadn't he listened to her and just dropped it? And that horrible fight. So stupid.

She set her coffee down. She felt torn between wanting never to see or hear from Bill Reed again, and wanting to know he was all right.

She had almost decided to just make the damn phone call to the inn when she heard tires crunching along her driveway. She peered out the window and saw Reed's BMW pulling up to her house. Her first reaction was to be annoyed. Now what? What the hell is he doing back here? But she couldn't deny the stronger feeling of relief that flooded through her. He must be all right, she thought. He must be okay.

She put down her mug of coffee and headed to the front of the house to open the door for him.

As she approached her front door, she heard the knock.

"Bill?"

"Yeah, it's me," said Reed.

She opened the door and her look of concern turned to one of surprise when she saw Reed standing in front of her.

"Oh," she said.

"What?"

"You . . . you're not on your crutches. What happened to your crutches?"

Reed held up his cane. "I'm down to this. Got the fake leg on. Just for short distances."

"Good. Yeah. It's a real improvement. You look . . ."

Reed filled in, "Normal?"

"Something like that, I guess. You're okay, huh?"

"Pretty much."

Angela stood at the door, hesitating.

Reed had to ask, "Do you mind if I come in?"

Angela moved aside and opened the door wider.

"All right."

Reed stepped into the foyer. Straight ahead, a stairway led upstairs. On his right was a large living room and to his left an archway opening onto a surprisingly formal dining area with a large chandelier and ornately patterned wood floor.

"I didn't expect to see you."

"No. I guess not."

"I was worried you might be in the hospital or something."

"No." Reed shifted, leaning on his cane. "Look, I'm sorry, I wasn't sure if I should come. I don't expect you're too happy with me."

Angela shook her head. "I don't know. I guess not. I think last night was pretty stupid and ugly. But I'm glad you're okay."

"Thank you. I'd like to talk to you for a few minutes if you don't mind."

"About what?"

Reed shifted again, not wanting to get into it while standing in Angela's foyer.

"Well, do you mind if we sit down?"

"I guess not," she said. "Come in. You want some coffee or something?"

"Coffee is fine."

She led the way toward the back of the house. Reed followed her down a hallway into a large, well-equipped country kitchen . . . open shelves, cabinets, and ample counter space flanked a double-size sink; a formidable commercial stove took up most of one wall; a three-by-six-foot butcher-block counter dominated the middle of the kitchen. Everywhere Reed looked he saw items relating to food preparation: cookbooks, utensils, a rack of knives, copper pans hanging from a ceiling rack over the butcher-block counter. The same slate as in the foyer covered the kitchen floor.

Reed found himself wondering why Angela rented such a luxurious house.

"You do a lot of cooking?" Reed asked.

"Sometimes. I didn't build this kitchen, but it's great, isn't it?"

"It is."

"How do you take your coffee?" she asked.

"Black."

Reed stepped over to the butcher-block island and pulled out one of three stools, sat with his good foot on the ground. He pulled up on the prosthesis, bending the mechanical knee, setting the Flex-Foot on the lower rung. He propped his cane against the butcher-block counter.

He watched Angela glide across the slate floor to a coffee machine near the sink. She wore no shoes, just thick woolen socks, black jeans, a tight-fitting white turtleneck under a heavy, plaid Woolrich shirt left unbuttoned. The tight turtleneck emphasized her figure while the wool shirt covered it. She had piled her shoulder-length brown hair on the top of her head and secured it with a large, red plastic clip, just as when he had first seen her at the Maple Inn. Reed couldn't resist watching her. She moved so gracefully. Being with her, in her house, on a Sunday morning, lent a feeling of intimacy to their meeting that Reed tried to ignore.

Angela poured Reed's coffee. Turning with it, she noticed him staring at her. She frowned slightly, perhaps uncomfortable about being observed so closely, but she didn't comment. Angela held the mug and said, "You don't look very comfortable there. C'mon, we'll sit in the living room."

She led the way back toward the front of the house into the living room, a large room with a double-height ceiling and four expansive windows running along the wall that faced the front of the house. The room felt bright and airy, but somewhat empty. Only the area in front of a large stone fireplace had been furnished. Angela had placed a comfortable old velour couch there, two wing-backed chairs, and a coffee table made out of a four-inch slab of maple wood, varnished, set into a triangle of legs made out of stout branches, but otherwise just as it had come out of the lumber mill, bark and all.

Angela sat in the corner of the couch, pulling her long legs underneath her. Reed sat in the wing-backed chair closest to her, turning it just a bit so he faced her more head-on. He sat back, grateful to take the weight off his stump.

"That scrape on your head looks a little nasty."

Reed cocked his head, dismissive, not wanting to dwell on it. "It could have been worse. How are you?"

"I'm all right. Just can't get that thing out of my head."

"The fight?"

"Yeah."

Reed nodded. "Most people don't see things like that. You're sensitive."

"I guess. I don't think I've ever seen a fight. A real fight. It's sickening."

Reed nodded his head slowly. "It could have been a lot worse. A lot worse. They were going to cripple me."

Angela held up a hand. "Please. I know that's what he said, I know, but . . . I don't want to think about it. I just don't think any of that had to happen."

"How do you know?"

"I just don't think anything would have happened if you hadn't . . ."

"Hadn't what?"

"Mouthed off like that. Gotten them so riled up."

Reed set his coffee down. His face hardening.

"I think it would have happened eventually. Some sort of run in."

"Why?"

"I found out a few things this morning about my cousin. There would have been a confrontation."

"What are you talking about?"

"That guy, Eddie McAndrews, maybe some of the others, he's hurt my cousin."

"Hurt him?"

"Yes."

"Like how? I know those guys are pretty rough sometimes. It's almost part of the style of that place."

"Style? What do you mean?"

Angela looked away, then back at Reed.

"It's hard to explain. Discipline is a big thing at the institute. They make the residents toe the line. Get up, get out. Do their chores. I don't know. I never saw anybody abusing a resident. Nothing more than a yell and a push."

"Nothing more? You're telling me that after seeing those guys last night?"

Angela frowned but didn't answer. Reed could see his anger was making him push too hard. He softened. "Look, I appreciate that you've probably had it with me. If you want me to leave, I will. But you're the only person I know who has any experience with that place. Who knows the people around here. I have to ask you."

"What? Ask me what exactly?"

Reed shifted in the chair. His cane had been resting on his right thigh. He grabbed the stick, a black piece of hardened oak with a silver handle on top, and cupped his hands over the top of the handle. Sitting forward he said, "I have a lot of questions. Help me with them."

"What?"

"For starters, what do you make of that sheriff showing up like that? In the middle of everything. You said your call never went through."

Angela frowned, hesitating. She looked at Reed, just sitting in front of her, waiting, not pushing, letting her decide. After a moment, she said, "You're right. It was weird."

Reed's eyebrows raised just slightly as if to say, yes, go ahead.

Angela continued, "I mean, the way he showed up like that out of nowhere. The way he pulled up. So slowly."

"Uh-huh."

"With his lights and siren on. All of a sudden like that. As soon as we heard him, he was there. It didn't seem like he had time to come around that curve and turn everything on."

"You're right," said Reed. "There wasn't enough time. It felt to me like he'd been sitting there watching for a while before he hit the lights and siren."

Angela nodded. "Yeah. Afterward, I was thinking about it. That's the way it felt."

"Maybe he was sitting there enjoying the show for a while," said Reed.

Angela didn't answer, but the thought of Sheriff Malone watching such a brutal beating and doing nothing obviously disturbed her.

"You realize how that sounds?" Reed said.

"I don't know," she answered. "How does it sound?"

"It sounds like he didn't mind it happening. You know more about these people than I do. How do you explain it?"

"I don't know."

"You don't?"

Angela shrugged.

Reed pushed. "Showing up like that. Maybe waiting until they got a few whacks in. Then letting those guys go afterward."

"You're an outsider. He's going to give the locals the benefit of the doubt."

"You said that before. Do you really believe it?"

She hesitated, then answered, "I don't know."

Reed sat back in the wing-backed chair. He shifted the cane into his right hand. Bouncing the rubber-tipped bottom off the hardwood floor.

"Fact is, I think that sheriff was following us most of the night."

"What makes you think that?"

"Like you said, he was there. He was there when the whole thing started. Or shortly after. I saw headlights in my rearview mirror more than once while we were driving around. I didn't say anything last night, but I remember thinking it was a little strange, seeing other headlights on those empty roads."

"Why would the sheriff follow you?"

"You tell me. What gives around here? I can't believe law enforcement checks out every visitor? Follows them around to see what they're doing."

Angela did not answer, thinking over the question, testing the possibility of it being true. "I don't know," she said. "Maybe the sheriff just doesn't have anything better to do. Ralph Malone likes to stick his nose in everything around here. The guy gives me the creeps. He's always around, always showing up when you don't expect him."

Reed waited, but nothing more came. Then he said, "Ralph Malone, that's the sheriff's name?"

"Yes."

"What's his relationship with Ullmann?"

"Why?"

"What's his relationship with Ullmann?"

Angela looked away from Reed, staring out the big front windows of the house. Reed had the impression that any moment she might stop answering his questions.

"Is that a difficult question?" Reed asked.

"I don't know. Maybe. Why are you asking me all these questions?"

"Because last night four local men thought they could beat me, cripple me, and get away with it. Because the sheriff watched them do it, then let them go. Because this morning when I visited my cousin I found out he's been sick for a long time. I found out that he's afraid of Eddie McAndrews. That Eddie McAndrews has hurt him. And maybe those other guys have hurt him, too."

"Hurt him? You keep saying that. What do you mean? How exactly?"

"I don't know, *exactly*, Angela. It's a little difficult to get details from an obviously frightened, retarded man. Then Ullmann's wife came in there and starts giving me shit. Threatening to throw John out, demanding I leave. Then her husband comes in and tells me he'll have me arrested. Is it really that fucking difficult to understand why I'm asking you questions about what the hell is going on up here?"

Angela turned away from the windows, shaking her head. She looked back at Reed, meeting his gaze.

"No," she said quietly, resigned to it. "No. It's not hard to understand. It might be hard to explain, but it's not hard to understand why you're asking all these questions."

Reed spoke quietly, sincerely. "Would you please explain it to me. Please."

Angela answered tiredly, "I'm not sure I can."

TWENTY-THREE

Despite the fact that it was Sunday and no other staff people were in the administration building, Matthew Ullmann had made sure to close the door to his corner office.

Madeleine and Ralph Malone occupied opposite corners of the office couch. A coffee table separated them from the chair McAndrews slouched in. Ullmann sat behind his desk.

Ralph Malone, sitting forward on the edge of the couch, a stenographer's notepad in his hand, finished his report on the information he had uncovered about Bill Reed.

"That's it so far," he said. "Monday morning I'll most likely get more details."

Matthew Ullmann said, "Thank you very much, Ralph. Very enlightening. I appreciate your coming here so quickly. And I recognize the effort you put in on a weekend to get us that information. I don't want to keep you any longer."

"Right," said Malone. He flipped shut his notepad and stood up, his holster and leather belt creaking as he made his way around the coffee table. The others sat and watched him leave. But just as he reached the door to the office he stopped and turned back toward the others.

"I don't usually offer opinions on these things, but this time I will. Last night was a mistake with that man. I saw a crippled man hold off four others. I saw him ready to go the distance with me. We'll talk some other time about just exactly what's at stake. But my advice . . . either deal with this fella quickly and for sure. Or put on a good face and say whatever you got to say to get him home and away from here happy. If that's possible."

Matthew Ullmann nodded slowly, making sure to convey that he had heard what Malone had said.

"Thank you, Ralph. Your advice is always appreciated."

When the door shut, Ullmann dropped the pen he had been chewing on and said to McAndrews, "Are you a complete idiot?"

McAndrews arched forward in his chair, protesting, "Hey—"

Ullmann cut him off, snarling. "Shut up. An ex–FBI agent? Are you insane?"

"How was I supposed to know?"

"Matthew, don't upset yourself."

Ullmann turned to his wife, addressing her icily, eyebrows raised, his voice at first quiet but gradually taking on a cutting edge to it.

"Upset myself? Upset myself about an ex–FBI agent who runs his own investigative accounting firm? Why should I upset myself over that?"

Madeleine responded, "I heard, Matthew, I heard."

"He's still an asshole," drawled McAndrews.

Ullmann turned to McAndrews, pointing his finger, "And *you* are still a moron. Your heavy-handed nonsense has put us all at risk. What the hell were you thinking?"

McAndrews sat up in his chair. "What was I thinking? Who the hell came over and said to us that the fella wasn't wanted around here? Who? Was that my imagination?"

"So what? Do you think you have the brains to do anything unless I tell you? Unless I tell you specifically?"

"All right, so we went a little overboard. But I'll tell you as sure as shit, what happened last night didn't have nothing to do with you, Mr. Ullmann. That guy was a prick. I don't take that kind of shit from anybody."

For the first time, Ullmann's voice rose in volume. Slowly, emphasizing each word, he said, "Everything about everything around here has to do with me. Do you understand that? Do you?"

McAndrews answered glumly, "Yessir."

"Thank you."

Madeleine broke in, "All right, Eddie, why don't you let Mr. Ullmann and I discuss this. We'll call you."

McAndrews shrugged. "Sure. Whatever."

McAndrews slid off his chair and loped out of the room. As soon as the door shut, Matthew Ullmann sighed, "Idiots. Goddamn idiots. I'm surrounded by them. Macho idiots."

Madeleine Ullmann tried to sound confident. "All right, Matthew, what's done is done. It really does sound to me that if this man Reed said the things he said in that bar to anybody around here, he would have had trouble. We can very reasonably make believe it has nothing to do with us."

"Oh, really?" Matthew responded derisively.

"Well then, Matthew, what do you propose we do about Mr. Reed. I don't want him meddling."

"Hmm, let me see. Maybe we should have Ralph take him out in the forest and shoot him? Eddie and his pals beat him to death? Is that what you had in mind, dear?"

She didn't answer.

"Madeleine, have you lost your sense along with everybody else? Did you or did you not hear him ask his lawyer to contact the state police? And the county district attorney?"

"He was bluffing."

"You're sure of that?"

"I'm sure. Talk about idiots, what is that idiot district attorney Carl Daly going to do about anything? He couldn't prosecute a crime if it happened to him. And Ralph can handle any state police inquiries. But we both know there won't be any."

"You think so."

"Yes. Either way it only proves my point. He has to be dealt with."

Matthew Ullmann tiredly repeated Madeleine's words. "Dealt with."

"Yes. He's a loose cannon. I don't want him meddling over Johnny Boy. Not after all the effort we put into him. He should not be allowed to continue coming around here unannounced, wandering around, meddling in our affairs. Action must be taken."

"You're being repetitious, Madeleine."

"What are you going to do if he insists on taking Johnny Boy to his own doctor?"

"That can't happen. Don't you think I know letting Johnny Boy out of our hands now would be a ridiculous waste at this point? And I certainly don't want a forensic accountant poking around in our affairs after he dies. It's just intolerable. Totally unacceptable. Not now."

Madeleine stared at her husband, waiting for him to say it, waiting for him to admit what had to be done. Matthew returned her gaze, defiantly. She grew tired of waiting.

"So? What do we do?"

Ullmann did not answer.

"What do we do, Matthew?"

Still Ullmann didn't answer.

"Why don't we do what you said. Have Ralph take care of him, or Eddie."

"Take care of him?"

"All right, I'll say it if you won't. Kill him. There. I said it. You won't say it. I will." She spoke very slowly, "Kill him, Matthew. Eliminate him."

"Oh, please, Madeleine, that's insane. An ex–FBI agent who's already been in touch with his attorney."

"I've already told you what I think that adds up to. Nothing. And I'm sure ex–FBI agents die every day. A car accident. Ice on the road. Eddie will do it. You know he will. Ralph can arrange things. Then he'll investigate it and make sure it's covered over nicely. It's really not such a problem. Ralph knows where his bread is buttered. Every damn time you ask him to do something he hits you for more money. Give him money. Give him as much as he wants. He'll do it. Gladly. We don't even have to make it all that serious. The man is already in a wheelchair for God's sake. We don't have to kill him. Just put him in the hospital for a month or so. Get him out of our hair. A month and it will be too late for him to do anything. And he certainly couldn't care less about any of our other residents."

Ullmann shifted in his high-backed executive desk chair. "We can't lose Johnny Boy. Not now."

"Exactly. So you'd better lose the cousin."

"Perhaps we should get Johnny Boy off to the hospital."

"Oh, please, that will just encourage him to keep hanging around. You don't know what Johnny Boy will end up telling him. That's why you put him in quarantine in the first place. He's retarded, Matthew, in case you forgot. He has no judgment, no control. You don't know what will pop out of his mouth. You know how they are."

"Johnny Boy has no idea what's going on."

"He doesn't have to know, Matthew. All he has to do is mention something, describe something, and that cousin of his will never stop meddling. Putting Johnny Boy in the hospital will give Mr. Reed another reason to stay and more chance to talk to Johnny Boy. And if he's here when Johnny Boy dies, he'll cause even more trouble. Listen to me, Matthew," she said, her voice rising, becoming shrill and insistent in the same demanding voice she used when ordering around the people who worked for them. "This is Johnny Boy's only relative. We take care of him, we end any chance for something that can hurt us. Do what you have to do, Matthew, or I'll do it for you."

Ullmann had been staring out the window, but now turned slowly toward his wife, his eyes narrowing, his face showing her that she had gone too far with him.

The quiet, icy edge returned to Ullmann's voice.

"Excuse me, what did you say? You'll do it for me?" Acid anger and ridicule constricted his face. "Don't insult me, Madeleine. Don't insult me and don't order me around like some nigger slave."

Madeleine Ullmann's lips pursed, twitching with anger, the tension she felt suppressing the emotions made her nostrils flare slightly. Her husband watched her closely, waiting.

She stood up, smoothing her skirt, placing her hands on her wide hips.

"I think you know very well what's needed here, Matthew. That's all I'll say."

TWENTY-FOUR

Silence descended upon Bill Reed and Angela Quist.

Reed waited, giving Angela time, but she seemed unable to begin telling him whatever she had to tell, so he asked, "Where do we start?"

Angela shifted on the couch, pulling her legs farther under her as if to prepare.

"I guess I should start with myself. Myself and Ullmann."

"Ullmann?"

"It's nothing terribly sinister. I think I even alluded to it earlier." Angela turned toward Reed, looking at him square on, as if facing up to her admission. "I have a lot of reasons to make Matthew Ullmann, I guess I'll say . . . react favorably to me. More reason than just my sister."

Reed nodded. "So you draw the line at what, flirtation?"

"I suppose."

"So what does that have to do with—"

"With you wanting to know the situation up here? I don't know. I just think you should know where I stand."

"Okay. You said you had a lot of reasons to make Ullmann think favorably toward you. Such as?"

"Oh, let's see, such as this house and my job."

This time Reed didn't try to hide his reaction.

"Don't looked so surprised. Matthew Ullmann is a very big fish in this little pond up here. He employs most of the people in this county, owns most of the businesses, and owns a great deal of property. He owns this house. Why? Because when old

Mr. Donohue died and his heirs put it on the market, nobody else would bid against him for it. What's Ullmann going to do with it? Maybe he'll turn it into another inn, or a game lodge, or who knows what. But until he decides, I weaseled my way into renting it at a low price. Ridiculously low. We're pretending the low rent is because I've agreed to move out within thirty days. But I'm not stupid. I'm just waiting for the day he tells me to forget about the rent and pay by other means."

"And then what?"

Angela's voice hardened. "Then I move."

Reed nodded. "A girl's got to do what a girl's got to do."

"Is that an endorsement or a criticism?"

"I'm not sure," said Reed. "I'm pretty sure I'm not one to judge. About the job . . . we're talking about the waitress job?"

"Ullmann owns the Maple Inn, too. The job isn't so unusual. Most of the people in the area work for him."

"I see." Reed nodded. "Okay, I appreciate your honesty about the situation, but what does that have to do with what we're talking about?"

Angela pulled her legs out from under her and leaned toward Reed.

"Listen to what I've just told you. Isn't it obvious that Ullmann figures he's King Shit up here."

"Okay."

"He does whatever the hell he wants. You walk into his precious Ullmann Institute, you do it his way. Did you have an appointment?"

"How the hell do you get one?"

"Call and ask."

"I did."

"For an appointment?"

"No, to speak to my cousin. But all I got was the runaround."

"So you just showed up. Unannounced. You raised a stink, didn't you?" She didn't wait for him to answer. "You're a hard ass, Reed, look at you."

"What do you mean?"

"Did you ever look in the mirror? You have this built-in thing."

"Thing? What thing?"

"A look. The way you stare at people."

"A look?"

"Yes. This doesn't at all sound familiar?"

"I don't know."

"For chrissake, look in a mirror. You took on four of those proctors last night. With one leg and your damn crutch. I saw you. They held back when I came out of the car, but partly because they knew at least one of them was going to take a beating from you."

Reed didn't answer for a moment, sitting motionless with no expression on his face. He thought about Angela's statement. He thought about the nine-millimeter Colt on his hip, a semiautomatic weapon with fifteen bullets in a clip and one in the barrel. And then he slowly nodded, just a series of almost imperceptible head movements, but still remained silent.

"So what do you think Ullmann's reaction is to somebody like you who barges into his little empire? He's not going to take any shit from you."

"So he sics his proctors on me. Tells the sheriff to make sure I'm not welcome?"

"It doesn't seem too far-fetched to me. Maybe he gives them the word that he thinks you're a troublemaker and they take the rest upon themselves. Or like I said, maybe you just rubbed those guys the wrong way and it got out of hand. Or some combination of both."

"Okay, what about my cousin?"

"What about him?"

"They're not being honest about him."

"How so?"

"He's got more medical problems than just those scabies. There's something wrong with his stomach."

"What? What's wrong?"

"I don't know."

"And you think they aren't treating him for whatever it is? All I can tell you is that my sister has been fine. The few times she's had a cold or flu or something, she's been taken care of. They spent a lot of money on that clinic, mostly because of Madeleine Ullmann from what I can tell. She may not have any bedside manner, but she's damned efficient."

Reed thought over what Angela said, then rejected it.

"No, something doesn't add up. I talked to his doctor. He was bullshitting me, I know it."

"I'm sure Ullmann heard about that, too."

Reed didn't respond.

"Did you push him around?"

"No. Actually, I was very cordial. But he still lied to me."

"He lied? You're sure about that?"

"Yes. I am."

"Well, I don't know the man. But I don't know many doctors who are exactly forthcoming. They're all afraid of getting sued."

Reed considered it. Maybe she had a point.

"I don't know what to tell you about your cousin's stomach problems. I don't see him that often. I don't know."

Reed nodded, holding his tongue.

Finally, Angela asked, "What are you thinking?"

"Something about a big fish in a little pond."

"What?"

Reed cocked his head. "Wondering how he got to be so big."

Reed's answer surprised Angela.

"What does that mean? What difference does that make? He's been up here forever. He probably just acquired things over the years."

"Maybe."

"So what difference does it make? What's the point of any of this? If he put those proctors on you and told the sheriff to give you a hard time . . . so what? You came up here to visit your cousin, right? You don't like what you see. You think he's being mistreated or not taken care of. Okay, that's it. What-

ever else is going on with the sheriff, those asshole proctors . . . the point is, you don't think your cousin is being
taken care of the way you want."

"Yes?"

"So what are you going to do? Are you going to take him
out of there? Isn't that the bottom line? Is that the important
issue?"

Reed tapped his cane on the floor, nodding, but more to
himself than as an answer to Angela's question.

"Interesting," he said. "Very interesting."

"What?"

He looked up at Angela Quist.

"That's their ultimate threat. Their leverage. You don't like
it, leave. Take your relative and get the fuck out. That's what
Madeleine Ullmann threatened me with. They know damn
well that most people aren't prepared to do that. Can't do it.
So in the end, they win. That's how they stay in control. Actually, I admire you. Sounds like you get a hell of a lot more out
of them than most. Somehow, you've found an edge."

"Is that a compliment?"

"Yes." Reed paused. "And it occurs to me that I may have
screwed up your deal here."

Angela suddenly appeared to be restless. She stood up off
her couch and walked over to the fireplace. "No shit."

"That wasn't my intention."

"When people give in to their anger and bullshit, they don't
have much intention."

Reed's mouth turned into a hard line.

"Is that what I did?"

Angela didn't answer. She looked down and toed scraps of
firewood and bark that had fallen from a pile of logs stacked
next to the fireplace.

"I'm sorry," Reed said. "That's the last thing I wanted to do,
make things difficult for you. And your sister. You put yourself
on the line for me last night. If you want to disassociate yourself from me, I'll understand."

Angela turned to Reed. "You will, huh?"

"Yes."

Angela gave Reed a condescending smirk. "Well, nice of you to give me permission."

"It wasn't permission. I just meant . . . I'm trying to tell you I appreciate what you did last night and I'm sorry if I've put you in a bad light with these people up here. That's all."

Angela stopped fooling with the firewood and turned to Reed. "I didn't do anything last night I didn't want to do."

Reed returned Angela's direct gaze, but remained silent.

After a few more moments of silence, when Angela saw Reed wasn't going to pursue that statement she asked, "Okay, so, whatever . . . where is all this taking you? What are you going to do?"

"About you or my cousin?"

"About your cousin. I can figure out my side for myself."

"Why do you ask?"

"Because I want to know just how much trouble you intend to cause up here."

Reed felt the anger welling up in him.

"You're saying I'm the one causing trouble?"

"Why don't you just answer me? What are you going to do?"

Reed paused, trying to think it over, trying to make sure he gave Angela an honest answer. Finally, he said, "I don't know."

Angela repeated his answer. "You don't know."

"No. Not until I look into things. Find out the answers to a few questions I have."

"What questions?"

"Don't worry. No one will know what I'm doing. The way I work, it won't be noticed. I won't cause any more trouble."

"You could have fooled me so far."

Angela shook her head.

"What?" asked Reed. "What's that look for?"

Angela walked back to the fireplace. A pack of cigarettes sat on the mantel. She took one out and lit it. She turned back to Reed.

"Pardon me if this all makes me a little upset. You come in here asking for information. And I give it to you, honestly, even though it's pretty damn certain telling you the things I did isn't going to do me much good. Or maybe even my sister. And then, you make these kind of snide statements about not making trouble."

"Snide?"

"Yeah."

"What was snide?"

"The way you said it, sounding so superior, so above it."

"I'm not being snide. It's easier for me to be objective."

Angela's anger began to match Reed's.

"Objective? You? Spare me. You've got a chip on your shoulder a mile wide. What gives you the right to say everybody up here is going along with some nefarious plan or something. What gives you the right to fuck up everybody's situation? Sure the guy may be a pompous asshole, and the sheriff kowtows to him because Ullmann controls the votes that get him his job, and his proctors walk around like they own the town, but is that really different from any other small-town situation? Whoever he is, whatever he is, the man built something here. That residence takes care of a lot of people who need taking care of. I don't know about your cousin, but I know my sister is happy there."

"You know that?"

"Yes, I know that."

"For sure. Even though your sister probably isn't able to communicate everything she thinks and feels, like my cousin can't."

"My sister has a life because of that place. And I have a chance to have a relationship with her. You come up here to see your cousin out of the blue, how long has it been? A couple of years? And all of a sudden, you're the judge as to what's right and wrong up here."

Reed stood up, his voice rising as he pulled himself up to his full height.

"That's right, Angela. That's right. I'm the fucking judge of what's right and wrong. Me. Bill Reed . . . long-lost relative. And you want to know why? You want to know why?"

Angela shot back, "Yeah. I want to know why. What gives you the right?"

Reed leaned forward and spoke very quietly now, looking directly at Angela.

"Because I'm the only one around here who isn't profiting off the backs of retarded people, that's why."

The shock and disgust on Angela's face were immediate.

"What?!"

"Yeah, go ahead. Stand there like that notion is completely ridiculous. But you think about it, Angela, one way or another, you ask yourself, how did Ullmann get what he has? I've spent a lot of years learning how to ask that question and answer it. And I'll tell you right now, unless I find out that Ullmann's family or his wife's family had a lot of money, I'll bet you more than this house and your job that Ullmann's bankroll, his money, came out of that residence. I don't know how your sister got in there, but I know it cost my uncle a lot of money. One way or another, directly or indirectly, Ullmann's money is coming out of the hides of retarded people. You don't want to hear that? I understand. You don't want to believe that? I understand that, too. But that doesn't mean I'm wrong."

Angela did not back down an inch.

"I think you should get the hell out of my house."

Reed almost answered, it's not your house, but he stopped himself. Instead, he said, "Yes. I think I should, too. I'm sorry I upset you. I hope I don't cause you any more trouble."

Angela stood with her back against the fireplace, inhaling her cigarette, watching Reed make his way to her front door. As he reached for the door, she said to his back, "I hope so, too, but somehow I fucking doubt it."

Reed paused, opened the door, and stepped out.

TWENTY-FIVE

As Bill Reed drove back to the inn, he grimaced, angry with himself for his behavior, wishing he had kept his mouth shut. What good did it do to rub her nose in it? Well, he thought, now she'll keep her distance. Probably better that way. Stay away from her. Better for her, better for you, Reed told himself.

And then Reed asked himself, Isn't it a little late for that? You know you're going to go at these people. You know it's going to involve her. Is that fair? If you have a problem with the place, suck it up, make a decision and find someplace else for John. But Reed wondered, Do I have that right? Is it my responsibility?

Reed took a deep breath and exhaled, clearing his head, trying to sift out the emotions.

"Just take it easy," he told himself out loud. "Just fucking take it easy. You've done this before." Take it step by step. Don't decide anything yet. Even if you decide to do something, you don't go up against somebody blind. You know that. Didn't you learn anything at the Bureau. First, the facts ... information, background, numbers, reality. That comes first. What to do with the information, what to do about the problem ... that comes second.

What do they own? Where do they live? What are their names? Is that the real name? Where is their bank? Their money? How much? How long? Where? Why? How did they get it? When did they get it? What did they do to get it? What did they do? What did they do?

The questions without answers, the questions with answers hidden far away in unseen computer files, scratched on pages in hidden notebooks, held unspoken inside heads ... the questions without answers did not discourage Reed. He knew how to find them, how to uncover the numbers. If you're going to do this, he told himself, do it right.

Almost as if he might need reminding, Reed drove past the spot where the proctors had trapped him. Just remembering it now, seeing that spot on the road set off his fight-or-flight reaction. Reed felt the adrenaline, felt his heart rate kicked up, remembered the feeling when he had first stepped out of the car.

It isn't over, Reed told himself. Like it or not, it isn't over. He knew he already had one answer . . . they aren't going to let this lie. And neither are you.

Madeleine Ullmann storming out of his office rankled Matthew Ullmann. Sometimes he wondered if she was truly worth all the aggravation she caused. Most of the time, it proved very useful. Ullmann enjoyed unleashing her on people he wanted pushed and prodded. Something about a demanding harridan like Madeleine was so effective. Men wanted to hit her, but couldn't. Women were usually shocked into tears. All ended up avoiding her, but no one ever defied her. She usually made Ullmann smile. But this last little tirade he'd found less than amusing. Quite annoying actually. Probably because most of what she said had been correct.

As if to confirm what she had described, Ullmann turned on his computer, waiting for the interminable boot up, typing in his password with a rapid four-finger technique, slapping angrily at the keyboard.

Ullmann had spent countless hours at his computer, constructing his database files, then his spreadsheets, logging onto his on-line brokerage accounts, sucking up data, downloading it onto his spreadsheets, watching the instant calculations of dollar amounts and percentages.

Ullmann was a modern-day miser, a hoarder of wealth, but instead of endlessly counting bills and coins, he watched numbers on a computer screen, stock quotes, account totals, spreadsheet calculations and graphs, watching, monitoring, checking to see if the numbers grew, sometimes two or three times a day, every day, week after week, year after year. With the Internet access and his spreadsheet software, the totals appeared almost instantly. And Ullmann became obsessed with making them grow.

And grown they had. The money, the dollar amounts, had grown to the point where even a fraction of a percent change in value meant tens of thousands of dollars. Ullmann hated it when the hoard decreased, and hated it almost as much when it increased, because it never grew fast enough or dramatically enough.

But Matthew Ullmann was patient. The big payoffs were coming. They were locked in now, he knew it. All he had to do was protect his assets, play it out, be patient, watch closely, then cash in. One year at the earliest, two at the most. Maybe, if prudence required, he would wait three. Maybe. But only if he had to. Then everything would be in place. One or two years, maybe at the outside three years, then Matthew Ullmann would be able to harvest his rewards . . . enough so that he could live anywhere in the world in any house he desired. Yes, depending on what he deemed to spend, any house. He would have not just millions, he would have tens of millions. Enough millions so that the earnings would coddle him and care for him for the rest of his life. Enough so that he would never again see the vacant stares or watch the tongues loll or smell the messes of retarded people, palsied people, brain-damaged, helpless people.

Never, ever again, thought Ullmann. Let the damn state take these messes away like they want to. Let me get out of this frozen, godforsaken part of the world. Let me cash in, sell it all, carefully stash it where no one will ever find it . . . in the Caymans or the Isle of Man, or even in a staid, stuffy, expensive bank in Switzerland.

Ullmann scanned the numbers on Johnny Boy's spreadsheet. This one and two more, thought Ullmann. He narrowed his eyes at the screen and pursed his thick lips, adjusting his wire-framed glasses. Not bad at all. Worse comes to worse, we could just about make it work with this last one.

Suddenly, the thought of Bill Reed ruining his life's work made Matthew Ullmann furious. He wondered just what kind of stupid, random, insidious bad luck had brought that man into the picture . . . the worst possible kind, an ex–law enforcement type who felt entitled to ask questions, a man accustomed to making demands, to asking questions.

"Idiot," muttered Ullmann. "The goddamned fucking nerve of that bastard. The fucking nerve."

Ullmann had to consciously calm himself down. He found himself breathing hard, his face in an ugly grimace.

Ullmann dragged his mouse and began to slowly, methodically close down his open files, shutting down the various programs, making sure all the encrypted files closed in an orderly fashion so his data would be right where it should be. For a moment, Ullmann let himself think that McAndrews and the others had convinced Bill Reed he should finish up his visits with Johnny Boy and be on his way.

No, Ullmann told himself. You know better than that. They made it worse. Ullmann could have sworn he saw the outline of a gun butt behind Reed's coat when he leaned forward in that ridiculous looking wheelchair of his.

No, don't be a fool, he told himself. He won't be letting this go. Not him. Hope for the best, but prepare for the worst. Madeleine is right.

He swiveled around in his desk chair and grabbed the phone, punching in a number from memory. The answer came after the second ring.

"Dr. Prentice," the soft voice said.

Ullmann sneered at the pretense of answering a phone with your title and said pleasantly, "Hello, George, Matthew Ullmann here."

"Yes, Matthew, how are you?"

"Fine, fine. George, do you have some time this evening, say around seven? I need to talk to you."

There was a moment of silence on the other end. Ullmann knew full well that the last thing George Prentice wanted to do on a Sunday evening was see him, but after the slight pause, Prentice responded, "Sure, sure. Around seven?"

Ullmann checked his watch. "Yes."

"Would you like to eat?"

Ullmann smiled. Prentice had remembered his manners.

"I don't want to put you to any trouble, George."

"I don't mind. Cooking for two is as easy as for one. Oh, what about Madeleine? Is she coming?"

"No, George, we'll be bachelors tonight."

"Right. Good."

Don't be so transparently happy about that, thought Ullmann.

"Fine, George, looking forward to it. See you at seven."

Ullmann dropped the phone onto the receiver, smiling. They so hate Madeleine. The notion provided him a perverse pleasure. But he had to admit, it would go easier without her. He had no desire for her to be monitoring his every word. Even better, she couldn't complain about being left out. After all, she'd said take care of it.

Ullmann swiveled back to his computer.

And so I shall. Starting with a little note to Madeleine about Johnny Boy Reed's dinner tonight.

TWENTY-SIX

Bill Reed had never envisioned how difficult it would be to crawl around with one leg. Or more accurately, with one knee.

He had to lie on his side, using his right leg and arm, forearm and elbow to make his way over the musty carpet and under the desk, looking for the phone and electric outlets.

Serves you right, Reed told himself. Instead of his superfast desktop, Reed had to make do with a notebook computer and a regular 56K modem instead of his fast T1 connection, and a slow, finicky, portable bubble jet printer instead of his high-speed laser printer.

Rummaging through the trunk Irwin had packed, Reed had been grateful to see that Irwin had included a full-size keyboard and mouse. That helped some.

It took forty minutes to get everything up and running, all the equipment jammed onto the small desk in his cramped room at the inn; the laptop resting on the two local phone books, elevated, so Reed could slip the regular-size keyboard underneath. All the power cords and cables and the phone line bunched up at the back of the desk; everything plugged into the same power strip/surge protector.

Reed endured it all with equanimity, solving each problem one by one, steadily, methodically, keeping his cool even when he found out the closest ISP connection meant a long-distance call to Buffalo. He tried to ignore the hourly cost of going on-line, but automatically calculated the figure in his head, multiplying calling card rates with the estimated number of minutes, plus a fee for the hotel connection. He knew, in the end, it would mean hundreds of dollars just in phone time, not including the fees he would run up at the proprietary databases he would be searching, but the cost of the effort actually gave him a sense of power. It helped allay his frustration and feelings of helplessness. His ability to unleash a nearly unfathomable resource of information gave him almost as much power and security as the Colt Commander on his hip.

Reed listened to the notebook's small speaker emit the muffled, echo-y noise of the modem connection to his ISP. As he waited for his home page to come up, he rolled his head, listening to the muscles and tendons creak. He slowly rocked his head side to side, rolled his shoulders, checking the insistent painful spots: back, chest, forearms. The tender area on the left side of his back hurt the worst. Reed clenched and unclenched his hands, feeling now how the fingers had swollen up even more than they had overnight.

He checked his watch, nearly four o'clock. The pain medication he had taken that morning had long ago worn off. He wished he had taken more before he sat down. But he had already slipped off the prosthesis. Struggling onto his crutches, making his way to the bathroom . . . to hell with it. The pain would keep him focused.

Reed scanned the customized information on his home page, ignoring most of it except the list of stock quotes he tracked. He remembered how he had begun to rely more and more on those stocks, keeping a running calculation in his head of how long his holdings would last if he had to dip into them, cashing in chunks to keep going. He realized that he had never completely confronted the concept that he might never work again. He'd simply avoided both the work and the considerations that not working should have engendered.

Suddenly, Reed smiled. Even if he sold the business, it wouldn't bring him much. Except for the equipment and the lease on his office, there wasn't much to sell except Bill Reed. He was the business. And even if he wanted to work, how many buyers were in the market for an angry, one-legged forensic accountant too down on life to do much of anything but lift weights, brood, and drink vodka?

What was his life span? Thirty, forty more years. He'd been a fool to think he could walk away from the obligation to earn a living.

"Fuck it," said Reed out loud. "Looks like you're working now, doesn't it?"

He slid the mouse to the list of bookmarked Internet sites and highlighted the site he wanted to check first—Choice-point—a huge proprietary database that Reed expected to hold the first wave of information he sought: the social security numbers for both Ullmanns, their addresses, properties owned, and more.

Reed expected their social security numbers would be easy to find because their names were unusual enough so that he wouldn't have to sort through long lists of matches and, best of all, their location was out of the ordinary. Reed felt the beginning rush of anticipation as he typed in his billing code to gain access. He quickly stepped through the various screens, setting up the search parameters, carefully filling in the data, the simple letters and numbers and back slashes that would unleash the first wave of information on Matthew Ullmann.

Reed tapped the enter key and waited. And waited. The slower modem connection was going to bother him he knew. The screen blinked.

"Don't you fucking no match me, dammit."

And then, in an electronic blink, the screen filled.

Reed leaned forward, gazing at the crisp images on the active matrix screen.

"Bingo."

There it was, the key to the kingdom . . . Matthew Laurence Ullmann's social security number and the first raft of information.

Reed scanned the screen, noting addresses, property listings, line after line of information he did not want to strain his eyes reading.

He clicked on the print icon and at the same time mentally ran through the next database he would dive into, Lexis. There, he would double-check property holdings and assets, as well as search for corporations owned by Ullmann. For the most part, he'd be replicating his Choicepoint search on Lexis, checking their information against Choicepoint's, paying particular attention to corporate filings, liens, civil actions, and bankruptcies, all of which he would in turn check through Casestream, which would also give him a chance to find out if Ullmann had been involved in any criminal court cases. And knowing that Casestream would mostly provide cases on the federal instead of the state level, Reed would also quickly check Reuters and Dow Jones to search news articles for frauds or criminal cases connected with Ullmann.

Then he'd double back and check the New York Department of State Web site for its information on any New York State corporations he uncovered.

Each search would be compared with all the others, all the information compared and sifted, analyzed and compiled to fill in layer after layer of facts, all the while following any lead that one database might provide that the others didn't.

Reed's fingers moved in quick bursts as if he were playing a jazz riff on a piano instead of rapidly typing questions through his computer keyboard. As information appeared, new lines of inquiry opened. As he started building a sense of Ullman's corporate holdings, Reed decided to check Dun & Bradstreet to find out what information Ullmann submitted for public consumption, which when compared with the proprietary information would shed further light on the way Ullmann conducted its affairs.

Reed checked his watch. He might run through Autotrack, too, just to be as thorough as possible, even though Choicepoint should have whatever was available there.

Although no two searches were ever the same, Reed followed a general system. After he had the rough outlines of Ullmann's holdings, he'd check Experion and Equifax for credit ratings, credit accounts, credit reports. And then he would begin the hunt for bank and brokerage accounts, a hunt that no database could help him with, but one that Reed had several ways of accomplishing.

And still there would be more. Reed thought about safety-deposit boxes in banks and deposit boxes in private depositories outside the banking industry. He thought about out-of-state bank accounts and foreign accounts.

The speed of Reed's queries picked up, his mind spinning out plans and moves at least two steps ahead of his printer and modem connection.

Reed knew the sequence. First, find what Ullmann has. And as difficult as that might be, it would be followed by a distinctly tougher task . . . find out *how* Ullmann had acquired it.

The first part could be attacked in several ways. The second, fewer. But in the end, Reed knew that, given enough time, he would find out everything.

When Angela Quist saw Matthew Ullmann walk into the kitchen at the Maple Inn, she was not surprised, but she still felt a rush of tension and fear flooding through her so quickly and forcefully that she actually shuddered.

Angela stood at a long steel table, prepping string beans for the chef, Peter Hastings, a big man with a neat beard whose stomach showed the effects of constantly sampling his cuisine.

Ullmann had entered the kitchen, not bothering to take off his stadium coat, as if he would be staying for just a few minutes. He stood talking to the chef. Angela couldn't make out the conversation, but she didn't try. She knew Ullmann hadn't come to see the chef. He had come to see her. He was just putting up a front. Or, more like him, he was dawdling, taking his time so that she would dread the moment more.

And then, when she had almost lost herself again in her work, the soft, unctuous voice sounded in her right ear.

"Angela."

She turned. Ullmann stood at her right side, smiling slightly, looking relaxed, casual, as if he were just saying hello.

"Hello, Matthew."

"How are you, Angela?"

"Fine."

"I see Peter has you pitching in."

"Yes. The dining room shouldn't be filling for a while yet, so—"

"How's the dinner crowd been lately?"

"Not too bad. About normal."

"Uh-huh. There's one dinner guest who isn't normal."

"Oh?"

"Oh?" mimicked Ullmann.

Angela winced at her feeble effort to feign ignorance about Bill Reed.

Abruptly, Ullmann seemed to change the topic. Speaking a little louder now so that the others in the kitchen could hear him, Ullmann said, "Angela, I need some wine. Would you come help me carry it up?"

"Sure," she answered, a little too quickly.

Angela led the way to the wine cellar. She could feel Ullmann walking close behind her, his presence making her slightly hunch her shoulders.

Once down in the cool cellar, Ullmann dropped his air of politeness.

"Here," he said as he walked toward a rack of French red burgundies, pointing to an empty wine box. "Get that box."

Angela retrieved the empty cardboard box, glad to have something to do.

Ullmann walked quickly to the rack and began removing bottles, glancing at their labels, handing them one by one to Angela.

"So what exactly do you think you're doing?"

Angela had to instantly decide how to play it.

"What are you angry about, Matthew?"

"Don't ask me questions and don't act stupid. You're not stupid. At least not as stupid as some."

"What do I think I'm doing? You mean going out with that guy Reed?"

"Yes."

Angela had set the carton on the floor of the cellar, slipping bottles in between the cardboard sleeves as Ullmann handed them to her.

Smiling, she said, "Why, Matthew, are you jealous?"

Ullmann handed her the last bottle and turned to her.

"I asked you not to be stupid. And don't act like you think I'm stupid."

Angela's expression went blank. She held the bottle of burgundy and looked at Ullmann directly.

"I don't think you're stupid, Matthew. I never have."

"Well you must," he hissed, "acting the way you do."

"What way is that?"

"Acting like you can flaunt yourself at me, play the tease, then take advantage of my generosity."

"I don't think that."

Ullmann looked bored. "Yes, yes, of course."

"I don't."

His voice suddenly hardened. "Stop it."

Angela spoke slowly, trying to dispel the fear and dread she couldn't quite shake.

"What is it you want, Matthew?"

"Don't worry. I'll tell you."

"Go ahead. Is this some kind of loyalty test coming up? What do you want? Tell me."

"Are you challenging me?" Ullmann glared at her waiting for a response. Angela hesitated, not sure she should push it. "I'd advise against it." Ullmann paused, waiting, then continued, his voice losing some of its edge. "I suppose I ought to appreciate the fact that you might be willing to call my bluff."

"That's not it. I just know where I stand."

"You do?"

"Yes."

"Good. Because it's time to use your feminine charms where they might actually do me some good instead of cause me problems."

"What do you mean?"

Ullmann smiled at Angela, a smile that told her she clearly knew what he meant.

"Matthew, let's not have any misunderstandings. What do you mean? What do you want me to do?"

"I'll make it very clear. I have a problem with our guest, Mr. Bill Reed. He's under the impression that he can come up here and make demands, push people around, insult my wife."

"He insulted Madeleine? Is that why you had McAndrews and his pals beat him up?"

"No. What in God's name were you doing with him, Angela?"

"For goodness' sake, Matthew, I ran into him on the way out of here yesterday. He started asking me about restaurants in the area because he knew I was a waitress. I recommended a place. And then he asked me if I wanted to join him. Christ, I was just looking to get a free meal at the best restaurant up here. So I'm sorry."

"You were with him at that wretched tavern you go to."

"Spontaneous thing. A nightcap on the way home. Believe me, I didn't know Eddie and his pals would be there."

"Neither did I. I did not approve of what they did. Now they have this Reed fellow on the warpath."

"So what do you want me to do, Matthew?"

"Keep an eye on him. I hear he likes to drink. Let him do his drinking here. You're working tonight, make sure his glass is full. He obviously likes your company, so join him for an after-dinner drink if you have to. I don't want him wandering around out there getting into any more trouble. I don't want him feeling the need to go out anywhere else."

"That's it?"

"For now. If he leaves the inn, which he'd better not, I want to know."

"What are you getting at here, Matthew? How far am I supposed to go with this?"

Ullmann's face went blank as he turned to face Angela. He stood no more than two feet from her in the dim, cool, quiet basement of the Maple Inn. Slowly, he reached out and cupped her left breast in his right hand, his thumb resting on top, fingers underneath. He had never touched her before. Angela had to force herself not to pull away.

"Don't bait me," Ullmann said.

"I'm not."

"Don't lie."

"I'm not, Matthew."

Without warning Ullmann brought his thumb and forefinger together, squeezing Angela's nipple, just enough to make it uncomfortable, but not painful. Not enough to make her pull away, but enough to establish the threat of pain.

"What is it, Angela? Do you want my permission to whore yourself for me?"

The question shocked her too much for her to muster an answer.

"You already are a whore. A whore who hasn't delivered yet on her side of the bargain."

"That's not—"

"Shut up, Angela."

Ullmann squeezed harder. Angela flinched, but tried to hold her composure, determined not to let him see her fear and pain.

"You're hurting me."

"I know. You're hurting me. In more ways that your stupid little brain can imagine."

Angela reached out and grasped Ullmann's wrist.

"Stop."

Ullmann kept his grip, squeezing hard enough for Angela to know that she couldn't push his hand off her without hurting herself.

"I may or may not want to see you naked someday. Up until now I've gotten some sort of perverse pleasure in knowing that you're demeaning yourself for me already."

"Matthew—"

"Shhh. Quiet," he spoke softly, caressing the nipple now. "Why do you think the men in the county haven't gone after you? Why do you think someone like Eddie McAndrews or Ray Boggs hasn't harassed you, maybe even raped you by now? Huh? Why?"

Angela grimaced slightly. "I really hadn't thought about it until now. But I suppose because you've made it known that I'm your property."

Ullmann smiled. "That's the first honest thing you've said since you've opened your mouth today."

"Thank you."

Ullmann flicked his hand away from Angela's breast, inflicting a sharp little jolt of pain.

"It's time you earned your keep around here, Angela. So you keep your pants on and your eyes and ears focused on Mr. Reed. You keep him drunk and staring at your tits and ass until he goes to sleep tonight. Is that understood?"

It took a moment, but Angela steeled herself and said, "Yes."

"All right. Then everything will be just fine." Ullmann looked down at the case of wine and said, "Take that out to my car for me, will you?"

Angela watched Ullmann walk out of the cellar, then a wave of hate and anger and humiliation hit her so fiercely that she doubled over and dropped to one knee, feeling as if she might throw up. She took a deep breath, squeezed her eyes shut, and grabbed the case of wine. She wasn't sure she could lift it, or ascend the stairs, but she focused, grabbed the case, lifted, took a step . . . then another and another, breathing hard, ascending the stairs, the tears now rolling down her face.

TWENTY-SEVEN

At precisely seven o'clock, Matthew Ullmann turned off County Highway 23 and drove his all-wheel drive Audi 6 station wagon up the short driveway leading to Dr. George Prentice's house.

Like most North Country homes, the doctor's house had been built close to the road so as to minimize the plowing needed after the regular snowstorms that blanketed the area in winter. The compact, wood-shake shingled house, laid out parallel to the road, sat at the top of a small rise. To the left, about a hundred feet from the house, a small red barn occupied about a quarter acre. Behind the house three more acres of lawn rose up, meeting a wooded area. From the road, the house and grounds seemed no more than adequate, belying the elaborately refurbished and expensively decorated interior of the house, and the fact that Prentice owned a little over fifty acres of land that surrounded his house.

Ullmann knocked on the front door, waiting impatiently. He pictured Prentice coming out from his kitchen in the back of the house, wiping his hands on a dish towel, removing the apron he wore while cooking.

Ullmann toyed with the idea of asking Prentice about his apron. He knew it would be tantamount to asking him about his homosexuality, which Ullmann had never gotten around to doing. Ullmann was quite aware that George Prentice preferred to remain resolutely in the closet, which meant Ullmann would at some time be able to exact an advantage of some sort. But that would have to wait.

The door swung open.

"Matthew, come in. Good to see you."

"Yes."

Ullmann stepped into an immaculately clean foyer tastefully decorated with a mahogany-framed antique mirror, side table, and a small, exquisite landscape painting from the Hudson Valley School. The beige walls accented by green chair-rail trim and molding blended nicely with the colors in the landscape painting, making the entranceway feel warm and inviting.

Ullmann handed Prentice the bottle of red burgundy without comment.

The small foyer opened onto a large, tastefully furnished living room, dominated by a flagstone fireplace at the far wall. The room boasted a high A-frame ceiling, lush sofas surrounding the fireplace, an oriental rug over a hardwood cherry floor, and walls decorated with nineteenth-century paintings done by itinerant naïf American painters. Ullmann knew the least expensive work cost Prentice eleven thousand dollars at auction, five years prior.

Prentice wore khaki slacks and a blue oxford button-down shirt, no apron. He fussed over Ullmann's coat, hanging it carefully in the foyer closet. He led Ullmann into the living room and sat him by the fireplace, asking Ullmann what he wanted to drink.

Ullmann said, "Scotch would be fine."

"On the rocks, as I recall."

"Yes. Just one or two."

"Right."

Prentice hurried off to get Ullmann his drink.

For the next two hours, Prentice generally fawned over Ullmann, serving him a meal of tossed salad, baked potato, broiled Angus strip steaks accompanied by Ullmann's bottle of burgundy.

Prentice had played a Best of Miles Davis CD during the dinner and had generally expended so much effort to make the evening a pleasant one that Ullmann could hardly wait to ruin it for him.

By the time they sat back on facing sofas near the fireplace, the logs having turned to mostly embers, brandy snifters in hand, Ullmann decided to hold off a few more minutes, to indulge in small talk just for a while longer, just to see Prentice grow increasingly restless.

Prentice had tried to discuss Bill Reed's visit to his office the day before, but Ullmann had abruptly changed the topic. Now, Prentice crossed and recrossed his legs for the fifth time, having grown thoroughly tired of talking about the stock market, the weather, the various residents of the county, Ullmann's house, his lumber business, and even about his wife, Madeleine, and her heavy-handed attempts at cooking. The last bit, having to make believe that Madeleine's overcooked, overspiced dishes were admirable, just about sent George Prentice over the edge.

Prentice was actually considering calling it a night, when Ullmann finally broached the topic he had come to discuss.

"So you met with Mr. Reed."

Prentice leaned forward, his brandy snifter in both hands.

"Yes. I thought it went pretty well. I set it up so that—"

Ullmann interrupted him. "No. It didn't."

"Oh," said Prentice. "I thought he—"

"No. I don't know what you told him, but it didn't help. He showed up this morning. Barged into the clinic. Sat with his cousin for I don't know how long until one of my people got over there."

"He wasn't alone with Johnny Boy was he?"

"It amounted to the same thing. That moron practical nurse was the only one in the clinic on Sunday morning."

"Did Johnny Boy say anything? Was there any—?"

Ullmann snapped, "How the hell should I know?"

"Well, what did that fellow Reed say?"

"Plenty. He got into a rather heated altercation with Madeleine."

"With Madeleine?"

"Yes."

Prentice took a large sip from his brandy snifter.

Ullmann continued, "Something has to be done about the situation."

Prentice did not say anything.

"Did you hear me, George?"

"Yes. Yes, of course."

"Well?"

"Well what? What do you want done?"

"I thought you might have a suggestion."

Prentice drained his brandy and stood up, holding out his snifter.

"How are you fixed? You want another splash?"

Ullmann had hardly touched his brandy.

"No."

Prentice went to the dry-sink cabinet on the wall near the kitchen entrance and poured a generous amount into his snifter. By the time he had returned to his seat on the sofa opposite Ullmann, he seemed to have regained his composure.

"You asked what's to be done. Obviously we, or rather you, have to restrict the cousin's visits. What about this quarantine thing? Isn't he buying that?"

"Does it sound like he's buying it?"

"How can he not?"

Ullmann put his snifter down on the end table to his left and sat back on the sofa. He began picking a bit of grit at the corner of his eye, speaking casually about the unspeakable.

"All right, George, here's what has to be done. Johnny Boy's tumor is getting to the point where the man is just about unable to shit. It's becoming tedious." Ullmann brushed his fingertip once more at the corner of his eye and focused on Prentice. "Madeleine tells me it's only a week or so, maybe less, before he's completely plugged up. So . . . it's almost time. Anyhow, with this meddlesome cousin of his constantly butting in, showing up unannounced, I say we just cut to the chase and finish off Johnny Boy now. No pun intended."

Prentice tried to make believe Ullmann's comments were reasonable, to be taken in stride, as if he could ward off the evil he felt creeping into him.

"Hmmm. When did you have in mind? After the cousin leaves?"

"George, don't be dense. The cousin isn't leaving. He's on some sort of crusade. He actually threatened us this afternoon with the state police."

"What? Why?"

"Because I threatened to have him arrested. Did you know he's an ex–FBI agent?"

"What?"

"And he runs an accounting firm, or some kind of business that has to do with forensic accounting, which according to my dictionary means he's involved in legal cases, investigating and testifying on people's assets and things."

"Good Lord," said Prentice.

"It's time to wrap this up. We eliminate Johnny Boy; we eliminate the reason for Mr. Reed to be poking around in our business."

Prentice shook his head at the onslaught of bad news. "When did all this happen? I mean, how did this start? I thought you'd picked Johnny Boy carefully."

"Of course I did."

Prentice exhaled, resigning himself to the situation, trying to act almost blasé about it.

"I'm sure you did. Of course. Of course." Prentice grimaced slightly, then asked, "So what is the schedule for this?"

"Tonight."

Prentice jolted forward nearly sloshing the brandy out of his snifter.

"What?"

"You heard me, George, tonight. Late. Say around midnight, one o'clock. Johnny Boy is going to have a blockage. You're going to have to perform emergency surgery. And he isn't going to survive it."

"A blockage? What do you mean? I thought you just said

Madeleine estimated a week or two before the tumor blocks his colon."

"We fed him enough rice and vegetables at dinner to block a normal colon. Before morning he'll be blocked, don't worry."

Ullmann watched Prentice fight for his composure. He thought he saw a gleam of sweat forming on his upper lip.

"Wait a minute, wait a minute. Matthew, these things are more complicated than you obviously think they are. What are you proposing here?"

"He goes into the operating room alive. He comes out dead. How hard is that?"

"You can't just kill a man on the operating table."

"Why not?"

"There are other people involved while you're doing major surgery."

"Who? In that Podunk hospital? Clearbrook? How big a staff do you have?"

"There's the anesthesiologist for one. A surgical nurse. If I'm lucky, I might get a resident to assist. Believe it or not, it takes a lot of work to remove a tumor and do a colon resection."

"Spare me. Make a mistake or something. Slice an artery. Screw it up. Just make sure he dies."

"Christ," muttered Prentice, "nothing like a bit of warning."

Ullmann casually glanced at his watch. "It's only nine. You have hours. I'm sure you'll think of something. Time enough to burn off some of that wine and brandy. Or time enough to drink more. Going in drunk might be best."

Prentice looked at his nearly empty snifter.

"Being drunk would not be wise."

"I suppose not."

Prentice rubbed his face, trying to clear his head.

"Have you notified—?"

"Everything is in order, George. You just do your part. It's your time now. Time to earn your keep."

Prentice raised a cautionary hand.

"Now, Matthew, don't think I'm second-guessing you. Just a precaution. I bring it up simply as a check . . . but might it not be better to just put Johnny Boy out of commission? I could take out only the tumor. Just temporary relief. I won't even do a colostomy. Just reattach the colon. Close him up. Make note of the spread. I would imagine it's extensive by now. Close him up, call the cancer inoperable, in a month or a week, who knows—"

"Tell you what, George . . . why not let *me* do the thinking? Do you really think that's a solution? Do you *think* sticking Johnny Boy in the hospital is going to keep the cousin away from him?"

"Well, I . . ."

"It'll just be more reason for him to hang around. And I'll have less control."

"Well, don't you think he'll be hanging around for the funeral?"

"So what? Let him. He won't be having any more discussions with his cousin, that's for sure. We'll finish our business, have our little memorial service, and it's done with."

Prentice brushed the back of his hand across his mouth, swallowing, clearing his throat.

"This all hangs on me, of course. I don't like people dying on my operating table."

"Tough. There are a lot of things I don't like. People die. It's time. Do your job. No more discussion."

Ullmann stood and stepped away from his chair, heading for the front door.

"My coat," Ullmann said.

Prentice had to scramble quickly to the closet so Ullmann wouldn't be waiting too long in the foyer. He helped Ullmann on with his coat. At the open door Ullmann turned and said, "Keep all the parts in order, or whatever the usual is."

Prentice nodded. "Yes, don't worry."

For the first time during the entire evening, Ullmann smiled.

"Worry? Why should I worry?"

Eddie McAndrews fumed. Sometimes he wondered if Madeleine Ullmann knew who she was fucking with. While Matthew Ullmann and George Prentice were sitting down to dinner, she had called McAndrews into the dining room kitchen. He and Boggs had been eating at the proctors' table. Sundays twelve to twelve were usually a great shift. Nobody did much on Sundays. Basically a day off.

But now, as McAndrews walked back to the kitchen, responding to Madeleine's shrill summons, he thought to himself, Fucking Madeleine, has to show up here busting my balls.

When he entered the kitchen, McAndrews saw Madeleine Ullmann standing at the prep table dropping a dinner plate filled with food onto a tray. She pushed the tray toward McAndrews. "Take this meal to Johnny. Mr. Ullmann and I are very concerned that he eats it. Do you understand? Make sure he cleans his plate."

McAndrews looked at the plate, not noticing the food, just reacting to having been placed in the role of a porter bringing Johnny Boy Reed his supper.

"Make sure he eats it all," she said.

McAndrews stood glumly looking at Madeleine.

She whined at him, "Did you hear me?"

"Yes."

"Good. All of it."

McAndrews left the kitchen with the tray, fuming. It wasn't until he walked almost all the way to Johnny Boy's dorm room that he looked at the food Madeleine had set on the tray: rice, oatmeal, beans, broccoli, cauliflower, about a cup of mixed nuts. He wondered, what the fuck is this, some sort of natural food vegetarian thing?

He opened Johnny Boy's door without knocking. McAndrews never knocked. Johnny Boy sat at the head of his bed, his knees drawn up to his chest, his face blank. He had been gently touching the scabs on his neck.

"Heads up, Brainiac. It's dinnertime."

Johnny Boy watched McAndrews, but did little more than move his eyes.

"You hungry, Boy?"

Johnny Boy did not respond. McAndrews lifted the heavy plate off the tray and placed it on the night table near Johnny Boy. He shoved the fork into the pile of food.

"Eat, motherfucker."

Johnny Boy looked at the food, but did not move. McAndrews gazed down on him.

"What the fuck do you do all day, sittin' in here?" McAndrews watched Johnny Boy for a response. "Nothin', that's what you fuckin' do." He kicked the bed frame. "Go on, goddammit, I ain't got all day. Eat that food, and make it fast. I want to get back to my own supper."

Slowly, Johnny Boy turned toward the food, picking up the bowl.

"Eat!"

Johnny Boy hunched over the bowl, his lower lip pushed out. He looked at the food with an air of distaste.

"Go on," McAndrews yelled.

Johnny Boy pushed the fork into a piece of broccoli and bent toward the food, pushing it into his mouth. He poked at the food in a desultory manner while he chewed slowly.

McAndrews watched him for a moment and stepped toward him. "Listen, goddammit, I ain't your fucking servant and I ain't your nurse. They got me running my ass all over the place 'cuz of you. Now I'm telling you once, you get that fucking food down your throat pronto, or I swear I'll beat the shit out of you right here and now."

Johnny Boy frowned, but began eating faster now. But even as he ate, McAndrews could see a hardening in Johnny Boy's attitude. He didn't say anything, or even look directly at McAndrews, but it seemed to McAndrews as if Johnny Boy were dismissing him, ignoring him.

McAndrews continued to stare at Johnny Boy, saying nothing, but just nodding to himself. You little shit. You little fucking asshole, sitting there like I ain't even here. Like you don't have to listen to me, don't even have to look at me. And why? 'Cuz you think that crippled fuck cousin of yours is going to protect you. Think he's gonna kick my ass if you tell him to.

"You are one stupid motherfucker, you know that, Johnny Boy."

Johnny Boy had finished a good portion of the food, slowing down now, but still chewing, still not deigning to look at McAndrews.

McAndrews stepped toward him, his right hand clenched into a fist. McAndrews squatted down, bringing himself level with Johnny Boy.

He spoke now in a soft voice infused with threat. "Hey, Johnny Boy, I got sumpin' to tell you."

Slowly, Johnny Boy turned. McAndrews, now face-to-face with Johnny Boy, angled his head slowly as if he were closely examining Johnny Boy.

"You all of a sudden getting to be some kind of uppity motherfucker? Huh? Think you can stand up to me? Why? 'Cuz that cousin of yours says he's gonna kick my ass? You know what I'm gonna do to him? Oh, and not just me, Ray, too. He wants in on it, too. That sum'bitch cousin of yours threatens to break my arms again? I'm gonna kill him." McAndrews nodded slowly, wide-eyed, his face inches from Johnny Boy's. "Yeah. I'm gonna kill the motherfucker." McAndrews brought his big knobby fist up in front of Johnny Boy's face and slowly extended his index finger, pointing it at the center of Johnny Boy's forehead. He poked the finger into Johnny Boy's head and said, "Gonna beat his ass into the ground. Bust up his leg. Then put a bullet right there." He poked Johnny Boy again. "Nice big thirty-thirty right the fuck there, Johnny Boy."

Suddenly Johnny Boy jerked his head away and sputtered, "No, no. He's gonna kill *you,* Eddie. He's gonna kill *you.* You hit me and I'm gonna tell him, and he's gonna kill *you.*"

A fleck of food spattered McAndrews's face. He jerked his head away and stood up, wiping the food from his face. "You dumb fuck."

Johnny Boy yelled back, "No, *you* dumb fuck. *You* dumb fuck."

Without warning, McAndrews's fist snapped out and he punched Johnny Boy squarely in the forehead, not a full strength punch, just enough to stun Johnny Boy, to hurt him.

Johnny Boy's head snapped back, but he jerked himself forward. He didn't touch the spot where he had been hit. Nor did he let out a sound or cry. He stared at McAndrews, glaring, looking right at him.

"All right, you happy now? Go tell your fucking cousin I hit you. Go tell him so I can fuck his ass up, too."

And then something in Johnny Boy Reed snapped, something deep and primal cracked the bonds of fear and confusion and suddenly nothing would stop him. He launched himself off the bed, hands extended like claws, suddenly flying at Eddie McAndrews. It was beyond punching back, beyond hitting. He threw his whole body at McAndrews, scabby hands clutching for him, contorted face twisted beyond reason or thinking, beyond intelligence or retardation or anything but an instinctual defense of himself and his cousin.

For a split second, the attack so surprised McAndrews that he did not move. And then his reaction kicked in. Instinctively he stepped back, lifting his boot just in time. Johnny Boy slammed into the work boot, chest high, then McAndrews shoved him away. Johnny Boy went down hard, but still tried to grab at McAndrews's leg. Surprise, anger, a grudging approval all flashed through McAndrews. And then the sudden realization of what Johnny Boy was trying to do.

McAndrews quickly pulled his leg from Johnny Boy's clutching hands.

Johnny Boy lay on the floor, struggling for breath, the kick having knocked the wind out of him, but still clutching after McAndrews's legs.

McAndrews stepped back, looking down at the nearly helpless Johnny Boy.

"Ain't you somethin'. What? You think you gonna get those scabies on me, Boy?"

Johnny Boy didn't answer, struggling to sit up. McAndrews saw that he was about to come at him again. He quickly picked up a chair and held it in front of him.

"Don't be stupid, Johnny Boy. Stay the fuck where you are."

McAndrews held the chair out. Johnny Boy got up on one knee, waiting, watching.

McAndrews stared back at Johnny Boy, nodding, observing.

"Well, you dumb shit, at least you finally got some balls. Too bad it don't fucking matter."

McAndrews casually tossed the chair at Johnny Boy, turned, and walked out of the room, yelling over his shoulder in a lazy drawl, "Finish the damn food or I'll come back and shove that chair up your ass."

TWENTY-EIGHT

Ullmann's lumberyard occupied a fifteen acre plot about a mile outside Dumphy. In the northeast corner of the lot sat a large warehouse constructed out of corrugated steel siding. When Ullmann entered the warehouse, he could see the dim glow of a single light burning in the back office. He wondered where Malone had parked his patrol car. He hadn't seen it out near the loading dock. Just as well, he thought. No need for anyone to see our cars parked together at nine-thirty on a Sunday night.

Even as he walked into the office, seeing Malone sitting at the rolltop desk, his thermos bottle and police radio set on the desk next to him, Ullmann hadn't yet decided on how exactly to handle Ralph Malone.

"Hello, Ralph."

Malone sat in the unheated office with his coat and hat still on. He tipped his forefinger against his Smokey Bear hat brim.

"Mr. Ullmann."

Ullmann looked around the dimly lit office for a chair. A metal folding chair and a beat-up old wooden desk chair were pushed against a worktable to Ullmann's left. He pulled the folding chair over near Malone and sat, unbuttoning his stadium coat, crossing his legs, trying to get comfortable on the hard chair.

Malone waited, hands folded across his small paunch, both feet planted on the cement floor. Occasionally, static-filled phrases came over the police radio.

Ullmann blinked once behind his glasses and started talking, knowing now how he would put it.

"So . . . there were a few things I didn't tell you this morning about our friend Mr. Bill Reed."

Ullmann watched for a sign of curiosity, but Malone kept his expression deadpan. "Things that are not positive."

"Mmm-mm."

Ullmann flicked an imaginary speck off his knee. "Unfortunately, Mr. Reed thinks he can threaten us."

"Threaten?"

"Yes."

"How so?"

"Well, in several ways. You know, Ralph, when someone threatens you, they think you're weak. Don't you agree?"

Malone nodded.

"You swallow a threat, they'll swallow you."

"Me or you?"

"What?" asked Ullmann.

"You first said he threatened *us*. Now you're saying *you*."

Ullmann spread his hands, palms up. "Well, isn't it the same thing? If I go, you go, Ralph."

"I don't know, Mr. Ullmann. If you go, I go. But if I go . . . what's going to happen to you?"

"On the contrary. It would in no way be good for me if that happened. Our interests are intertwined. I want you to be sheriff of this county. And I want you to do well here."

Malone nodded, then asked, "What kind of threats?"

"From Mr. Reed?"

"Yes."

Ullmann sat back, making a face, a slight shrug, a small frown. "He threatened to call in the state police."

"The state police."

"And to notify the county district attorney."

"Why? For what?" asked Malone.

"Well, I don't exactly know. He was complaining to Madeleine about something, and of course Madeleine, she blew up at him and told him to leave. He got very insulting. I showed up in the middle of it and said I'd call you and have you escort him off. He said something about you being a two-bit sheriff for hire, said he thought he should call in more law enforcement, the state police . . . you know."

Malone shifted. He made a quick sucking sound as if he were trying to get a piece of meat from between his teeth.

"Infuriating, isn't it, Ralph?"

"All right, Mr. Ullmann, I get the picture."

"Oh, I know you get the picture, Ralph. I know you do. And believe me, what I've described is the picture. It isn't a pretty one, and it's not going to get any prettier."

"So why not just leave the guy alone until he leaves? What the hell are the state police and DA gonna do anyhow? What's the big deal?"

"He's not leaving."

"Why not?"

"Because his cousin is sick. And he's not going to get better. And our friend Mr. Reed isn't the type who's going to just up and leave. Particularly after those idiots Eddie and Ray and their friends tried to beat him up and you let them go."

Malone nodded.

"So what exactly do you want me to do, Mr. Ullmann?"

Ullmann flashed a quick, vicious little smile and said, "I want you to put that son of a bitch at the bottom of a ravine somewhere."

The words popped out of Ullmann as if they had been bottled up for too long.

Malone cleared his throat.

"You know I'm not employing hyperbole here, Ralph."

"Hyperbole?"

"I'm not exaggerating."

"Well," said Malone, "it sounds like you're real sure of this."

"I am."

"You really think that's necessary?"

"Yes. I *know* it's necessary. I want that man to have a serious accident. I want him out of the picture."

"It might take some figuring."

"No," said Ullmann. "Not at all. I've already figured it out. While I've been sitting here. I see it all very clearly. Picture it with me . . . that road out of Dumphy running along Cobbleskill Creek, weaving along there for about three miles until it curves around to Route Twenty-eight."

"Yeah."

"I have an image of that annoying man in his expensive car hitting that curve, just before the bridge, and never making it. You know, right there to the left where the riverbank drops down about forty feet. How many drunks miss that turn every year?"

Malone nodded. "I know the spot. I guess we average about one a year."

"This is Mr. Reed's year. I see it happening tonight."

"Tonight?"

Ullmann's voice picked up enthusiasm as if he were trying to engender belief in a skeptic.

"Yes, Ralph, tonight. This very night."

"What would bring the man out on the roads tonight?"

Ullmann feigned surprise. "Oh, didn't you hear? His cousin Johnny Boy is going to the hospital tonight. Yes, yes, terrible thing. An emergency. Mr. Reed will be getting a call later, say around eleven, eleven-thirty." Ullmann fluttered his hands in front of him. "He'll be told he has to *rush* to the hospital. He'll probably be barreling along at a very brisk speed."

"Uh-huh."

"I hear he likes to drink, too. You've heard that, haven't you?"

"I know he likes to hang out in bars."

"Yes. I'm pretty sure he'll be drinking tonight, with dinner and all, so you see how this can work out, don't you?"

Ullmann paused, allowing Malone to go over the plan in his mind, watching him figure it.

Malone finally said, "This is risky business."

Without hesitation, as if he wanted to prevent Malone from saying it, Ullmann said, "Risk brings rewards. I'll make it worth your while, Ralph. I know compensation is important to you."

"Only what's fair, Mr. Ullmann."

"Yes, of course. No one wants to be taken advantage of, least of all you, Ralph." Ullmann waited a moment, then asked, "Do you think you'll need any help?"

"Yes."

"Call Eddie."

"Might use Ray, too."

"Be my guest."

"How much do I tell Eddie and Ray?"

"What do you mean?"

"About compensation."

Ullmann let out a short laugh. "About now I expect they'd do it for free." He stood and buttoned his coat, taking a few moments to consider the figure.

"Give them each a thousand. Ten for you, Ralph. Ten if it goes right. I don't want to see that man again. I really don't care if he dies or ends up in a hospital for a month or more. Let him break his neck, lose that other leg, I don't care. I just want him gone, out of the picture. For a long time."

"Right," said Malone.

Ullmann turned to leave, but then turned back. "Report in when you're done. After you're done, we'll call up the volunteer ambulance guys and you'll escort them over to Clear-brook Hospital with Johnny Boy."

"Okay."

"I guess we've got a long night ahead, hey, Ralph."

"It appears so."

Ullmann smiled another fake smile. "No rest for the weary, hey?"

Malone said, "I always thought that saying was, No rest for the wicked."

"Really?" Ullmann seemed to think it over. "Interesting. Well, I've got one more stop to make. I'll talk to you later."

TWENTY-NINE

Bill Reed sat back, squeezed his eyes shut, and gently rubbed them trying to relieve the stinging fatigue. He had been at the computer for nearly three hours. He checked his watch . . . almost seven o'clock.

He gathered up the curled pages of oily thermal paper that had eked out of his portable printer. Then he sat forward and slid his mouse, pointing and clicking and punching keys until he had successfully consolidated twelve files he had down-loaded, translated them into a Word file, then E-mailed them to Irwin Barker.

Finally, he logged off the Internet, picked up his phone, and punched in Irwin Barker's number.

While he waited for the call to go through, Reed turned away from his desk, leaned forward, elbows resting on his thighs, and gently flexed and stretched his lower back, trying to loosen up the muscles that had stiffened up while he had worked so intensely. He massaged his stump, lifting it a few inches off the chair, trying to get the blood flowing a bit so he wouldn't generate any pain when he stood.

The phone connected.

"Yeah."

"Irwin, Bill, where are you?"

"Watchin' the Knicks game at Delta."

"How are they doing?"

"They're blowin' a fourth quarter lead. 'At's all right. Another five minutes Miami beats the spread and I win."

"Good. I won't take you away from the game, but tomorrow, first thing, I'm going to need you to do something for me."

"Name it. What's goin' on? You get that stuff this morning?"

"Yeah, thanks."

"So what's next?"

"It's about my cousin and this place he's been living at."

"Yeah?"

"The guy who owns the place is turning out to be a bad guy."

"Yeah?"

"Name is Ullmann. Matthew Ullmann. And his wife Madeleine. I E-mailed you a bunch of stuff on them. Take a look at it, but don't get too bogged down in it. There's a lot of property listings and corporations, almost half of them involved in some sort of litigation . . . this guy pays himself and lets everybody else sue him."

"One of those, huh?"

"Yeah. And worse. Much worse. It's complicated. But the bottom line is, he's the guy who's running the institution where my cousin lives. He's stealing, I'm sure of it."

"Who from?"

"I don't know for sure yet, but as far as I can see, everything he's gotten has come since he took over the place. Ultimately he has to be stealing from the residents."

"What're you, kiddin' me? The guy's stealing from retarded people?"

"Nice, huh?"

"How? Those people got money?"

"Hell yeah. This isn't Willowbrook up here. It's a private

institution. My uncle dropped a lot of cash to get my cousin in. I imagine a lot of the other families have money, too."

"So ain't the families the ones handling their money?"

"Usually, they strip the retarded family member of any assets and set up family trusts so they can qualify for federal and state money. I assume the families run the trusts, but a lot of these people have outlived their families. My cousin has. I don't know who's watching over his trust."

"I hear you. So you think this guy might be raiding your cousin's trust fund?"

"Maybe. That's one source. There are other possibilities. Maybe this guy is ripping off Medicaid and SSI, Social Security, double billing, inflating bills."

"I know that drill."

"He also has a lot of service companies that he owns that do business with his residence."

"Paying himself twice what costs? Shit like that?"

"Yeah. But the way it's looking to me now, it doesn't seem like that would be enough. This fucking guy has somehow managed to own half this county. I haven't figured this out yet, but first I want to make sure my cousin's funds are safe."

"Obviously."

"That's what I want you to get on."

"Okay. If this fuck is raiding your cousin's trust, we'll find out."

"He's an asshole, Irwin. And he's got this area locked up tight. Got a bunch of thugs working for him and he runs the sheriff. It's his own little world up here."

"Sounds like you better watch your ass, boss. You want me up there?"

"Not yet. Take care of this inquiry first. Tomorrow morning, first thing, call up Charles Whitcomb at our law firm. Have him contact my uncle's old law firm in Virginia. Falls Church, just outside of DC. Bank, Keenan, Greene and Davey. I'm sure they drew up the will and did the estate planning and family trust. I remember my uncle telling me the trust had been set up with a broker working out of New Jersey. The broker was the trustee. But I can't remember or he never mentioned the firm or the guy's name. Tell Charles we need the law firm to give us the name of that brokerage and the trustees."

"Got it."

"Charles will know how to finesse the information out of them. Let Adele know what you're doing with Charles so she can follow up on it if I need you here."

"Okay."

"Once Charles finds out the brokerage firm, I want you to get in touch with them and find out who's overseeing the trust now."

"I understand."

"Now these guys will probably clam up. Especially if any nefarious shit has gone on. If they do, you get your ass over to Jersey and lean on whoever you have to."

"I hear ya."

"Keep Charles out of that part."

"I hear you. Not a problem."

"Don't get heavy-handed unless you have to. Tell them the situation straight up and see what happens."

"Hey, like you say, if they're stealing and I show up, we'll know. You're not worried it might come back around to this Ullmann character?"

Reed's voice rose. "I don't give a shit what comes around. I'm ready to go to war with this fuck."

Irwin Barker smiled at the other end. *"Hey, sounds like fun. I'm in. Just watch your ass. You got your shit, right, so stay strapped. I don't like hearing this guy has the local sheriff under his control."*

"I know. I know."

"Bill, what about your cousin? You gonna leave him in this guy's hands?"

Reed paused, imagining for a moment what his life would be like if he took full responsibility for his cousin. Reed expunged the images and questions.

"I don't know," he told Irwin. "Right now I don't have much choice. He's not too well physically. I don't know what's wrong with him. I'll have Adele start looking into how to medevac him out of here if I have to."

"All right. Well, it sounds like you have your hands full up there."

"Yeah." Reed thought about how Irwin would react if he told him he'd been waylaid in the woods and beaten by McAndrews and his buddies. "Yeah," said Reed, "I know."

"I'll get on the trust thing with Charles first thing. I'll call you tomorrow. Soon as I have anything."

"Thanks. Oh, by the way," Reed asked. "Where's Doctor Doom these days?"

"Doom? He's gone legit. Or almost anyhow."

"You're kidding me. What's he doing?"

"He's running seminars for big companies, tellin' em how to protect their networks and such."

"Still calling himself Doctor Doom?"

"Apparently. His customers like it."

"That's a little like inviting the fox into the chicken coop."

"What the fuck, he's already in the coop. You know what his sales pitch is?"

"What?"

"He goes in to his prospects and guarantees them he can hack into their system within five hours."

"Five hours?"

"He always does it in less than two. Scares the shit out of them. It really gets their attention."

"So he's busy."

"Real busy."

"What about SR?"

"Silicon Rat?"

"Yeah."

"Christ, that bug is hard to find. Particularly when he's off his medication."

"If we can't use Doom, find SR. I'm going to need someone willing to skirt legalities."

"Hell, SR is your man. It's like his sworn mission in life to fuck around with rules and regulations."

"Find SR, get some sleep, Irwin, and be around in case I need you."

"Will do."

Reed dropped the phone, yawned, and stretched.

He struggled up on his one leg and grabbed a crutch, slowly making his way across the room, monitoring his stump, guarding against the blood flowing down triggering a phantom pain reaction. He needed a drink; he needed food; he needed more pain medication. But thinking about eating in the Maple Inn dining room, Reed wasn't at all sure he needed to see Angela Quist.

Reed had considered going out for dinner, but quickly rejected the idea. He was too tired and had no desire to be driving around looking for another place to eat. When he wheeled his way into the dining room, it seemed that the Maple Inn was one of the only places serving dinner on Sunday night. There were more people than he had seen the first night. The same blonde hostess who had worked Friday night greeted him and ushered him to the same table. He was a regular now.

Reed looked around for Angela, but did not see her in the dining room. He picked up the menu, glancing at the printed descriptions, but his thoughts were on his cousin. A doctor, that was the next thing he had to figure out. He'd get Adele to find someone within driving distance. And then it occurred to Reed he had no idea what legal problems might exist in taking over Johnny Boy's care. Reed wondered who had the right to decide on medical care for Johnny Boy. He thought about his Aunt Phyllis, Johnny Boy's mother, wondering how hard it would be to track her down if he needed her. His lawyer, Charles Whitcomb, would have to advise him.

A delicately tattooed wrist setting down an Absolut martini on the rocks with a twist interrupted his thoughts.

He looked up to see Angela standing at the table. She appeared to be distracted, or somewhat harassed. Was his presence upsetting her?

"I assume you want that," she said.

"Yeah. Definitely."

Reed tried to assess Angela's mood, but suddenly felt distracted himself. All he could muster was a mumbled, "Thanks."

He sat up straighter, trying to come up with something more to say. Angela waited a moment, then said, "I'll be back. It's just what's on the menu tonight."

"Okay."

Reed watched her hurry off, getting the distinct impression she wanted to have little to do with him. Bringing the drink like that had seemed like a peace offering of sorts, but rushing off had dispelled that notion. Or maybe it was simply because the dining room seemed so busy. Or maybe she just can't stand the sight of you, Reed told himself. The hell with it. It's better if she doesn't want to be around me. But it didn't feel better.

Angela brought him his second martini and his salad without saying a word. Reed decided to keep his head down, be polite, finish his food and drink, and return to his room. The hell with Angela Quist. He'd take a long shower, try to loosen up some of the stiff soreness he still felt. Then get in bed and read his printouts until he fell asleep. Let his subconscious mull it over, go at it again tomorrow.

Reed had arrived at a familiar state. A head packed with names and numbers, a sense of it, but not yet a grasp of the whole picture. A piece here and a piece there, information gathered as one fact connected with another, retrieved bit by bit, piling up. Reed forgot almost none of it. Even at this first run, he could match an address with a property with a purchase amount with an outstanding tax lien with a mortgage with an insurance policy. All the pieces and connections were inside his head. He would keep accruing information, connecting it all until he had a clear picture of Matthew Ullmann and his North Country empire.

He'd have it all soon enough, he thought. But then what?

Midway through his salad, Angela suddenly appeared at Reed's table, nodding at his second martini.

"How're you doing with that?"

Reed looked at the glass. He had barely touched it.

"Fine."

"You thinking about a wine, tonight?"

"I don't know. Yeah, I guess."

"You're not planning on going out are you?"

The question struck Reed as unusual, particularly after her previous distant treatment.

"Tonight?"

"Yes," said Angela.

"Where would I be going tonight? You thinking of going out for a nightcap?"

"No, no," she answered quickly.

Reed looked at her for a moment, wondering what she was getting at. Annoyed that she was now speaking to him, annoyed that he had immediately tried to take it as an opportunity to connect with her again.

"Is there—?" he asked.

Angela shook her head, waving off the issue.

"Nothing. Nothing. Just forget it. I don't know," she said. "I'll be back."

She turned and walked away. Reed watched her walk off. He had suddenly lost his taste for the martini.

The rest of the meal passed with no more than a few words exchanged between them. Thanks. Here you go. Enjoy. How was it? No more inquiries about whether or not Reed might be ready for another martini. He had to ask Angela for a glass of red wine, which she brought promptly, but she didn't ask if he needed another when he finished it.

Reed found himself alternating between thinking about Johnny Boy and Ullmann, and wondering about Angela's shifting moods. Nevertheless, Reed kept trying to assemble the pieces of information he had gathered into a whole that told him something.

Throughout the late afternoon and evening, the list of holdings and assets had slowly, inexorably added up to a substantial sum. There was real estate, both developed and not developed. There were businesses, the value of which Reed could only estimate because he had not found any bank accounts yet. But piecing together the different entities, Reed could sense an order underlying all of Ullmann's holdings. It seemed clear that the businesses were tied in with each other. A few quick phone calls confirmed that the lumberyard Ullmann owned was sold to a construction company he also owned, which in turn did construction and repairs at the institute and the inn and probably built whatever Ullmann wanted to create on his other properties.

The same with a food-service business and a trucking company that leased trucks to the lumberyard, hauled food in for the institute and the Maple Inn and a couple of local restaurants. Reed had not seen any balance sheets or tax returns for the businesses, but he could almost imagine them. Virtually all the commerce took place in a relatively closed system, a small consortium that fed on itself. The businesses billed and paid each other, except for the few outside vendors they used. And by the liens and civil actions it was clear that those suppliers were consistently shortchanged.

The trouble, Reed knew, was that he hadn't found out where the initial funding came from. Somebody had to pay the companies for their services, even if it amounted to Ullmann paying himself. That money obviously came from the institute's budget, but was it enough to pay inflated bills? And where exactly did that money come from? The normal channels? He hadn't cracked that part of it yet. And where had the money come from to acquire the businesses so Ullmann could create this loop where the vast majority of dollars that came into the institute flowed out into one of his pockets? Where had he gotten the capital to create his closed system in the first place?

Had he really raided a number of trust accounts to get his capital?

How long could he get away with something like that? It seemed very risky.

Had he borrowed the money? Reed hadn't found any outstanding loans other than normal mortgages. Perhaps he had colluded with a local bank to kite mortgages back in the eighties when the savings and loans banks were playing fast and loose. The acquisition dates for some of the properties dated back to then. Maybe that was it, thought Reed.

Reed had been lost in his thoughts for so long that he hadn't realized his empty dinner plates had been sitting for quite a while. The dining room had emptied considerably. A sudden peacefulness had seeped into the room.

He refocused his attention, thinking now about dessert and coffee, and maybe a brandy before bed, but still Angela didn't appear at his table. When she finally showed, she had his check in hand, as if she were sending him out of the dining room. What's this, Reed thought, the bum's rush? But now Angela appeared to be friendly, be more like herself, asking him, "Was everything all right?"

"Yeah," said Reed. "It was all right. How are you? Busy tonight."

"Yes. About usual for a Sunday."

She stood there, not saying anything, but not leaving. Again, Reed tried to gauge her mood. It seemed she wanted to say something to him, but felt reluctant.

"Listen," he said. "About this afternoon, you know, I was out of line. Your situation, anybody else's up here, it's really none of my business."

Angela quickly contradicted him. "No, it is your business," she said. "It's your business what goes on up here. Your cousin lives there. You care about him. You're right. There are people up here who think just because they own a lot of stuff they own you. Think they can tell you what to do."

"Me or you?" asked Reed.

"Both," said Angela. "But definitely me and most of the others around here. We're all involved."

Reed nodded, handing her the signed check and the pen. She smiled a tight smile, pushing the pen behind her ear, holding the check.

"Okay," she said. "Just, you know, follow your instincts about this place. Okay?"

She rushed off again. Before Reed could respond, she was gone.

By the time he opened the door to his room, Reed was more than ready to call it a day. The door closed behind him and he rolled his wheelchair across the room, heading for the bathroom. He grabbed the sides of the doorjamb, anxious to empty his bladder after the long dinner, and just then his phone rang.

Reed muttered a curse and dropped back into the chair. He wheeled over to the phone, wondering who it might be, Irwin? Angela?

"Yeah?"

Ullmann's voice was definitely not one of the voices he expected to hear.

"Mr. Reed, Matthew Ullmann here."

"Ullmann?"

"Yes. Sorry to bother you so late, but we're having a problem with John."

"With John? What's the matter?"

"He's having some severe stomach pains. I've already called for the ambulance service. You know, he had that problem last night, and now tonight. It's probably nothing, but I don't want to take any chances. I'm sending him over to Clearbrook Hospital. I want them to make sure it's nothing serious. I just thought you should know."

"You're sending him to the hospital?"

"Yes. Actually, I thought you might want to go over there. It's late and all. I didn't wake you did I?"

"No."

"I know you're concerned about him."

"What do you think is wrong with him?"

"I don't know. That's why I'm sending him over to the hospital."

"How far is it from here?"

"From where you are, it's about ten, twelve miles. From the inn there, take Main Street, turn left out of Dumphy for about a mile, then you hit Crossville Road to Route Twenty-eight,

*which takes you to the hospital. They can give you exact direc-
tions at the inn. It's not complicated."*

"How soon will he be there?"

*"Oh, he's on his way now. He just left. I'd say about ten or
fifteen minutes. I'm sure he'll be fine, I just—"*

"When did this happen?" Reed demanded.

*"It started about an hour ago. Listen, I'm leaving now. I'll
see you at the hospital. We can talk this over there. You'd better get going."*

The line went dead. Reed dropped the phone on the hook,
feeling slightly disoriented, rushed, the tension coming over
him. Severe stomach pain. He pictured John Boyd, his face
twisted, unable to describe anything, just hurting. The frustration of it, the distance, the helplessness, all roiled Reed. John
Boyd's inability to explain anything. The hassles with Ullmann and his proctors and wife. And now this.

Reed quickly used the bathroom, hopping back to the bed
unbuckling his belt. He dropped his pants away from his
stump and sat down on the bed. He picked up his prosthesis
from where he had laid it on the floor, just under the bed. The
last thing he wanted to do was put the damn thing on, but he
rolled on the suction sock, shoving his stump into the socket
until the pin clicked, adjusting the suction.

He checked his watch. Almost eleven. He picked his left
running shoe up off the floor, adjusting the insert that fit over
the Flex-Foot. As he pulled up his pants, the empty gun holster flapped around on his belt. He hadn't taken his Colt into
the dining room. Should he take it into the hospital? They
might not appreciate that. He glanced out his window, staring
into the dark beyond the parking lot lights. He heard the gruff
words of Irwin Barker, *Stay strapped.* It occurred to him that
he might run into the sheriff at the hospital. Or maybe even
one of Ullmann's proctors. He grabbed the Colt from his
dresser drawer and shoved it into the holster.

He fit the left shoe on over the Flex-Foot, grabbed his cane,
his coat. He stopped at the lobby, wanting to rush out, to get
going, but he listened carefully to the young man giving him

directions. Even as he listened he worried that John Boyd would arrive at the hospital so far ahead of him he might not be able to even see him before the doctors whisked him away somewhere.

"Take the right to Main Street, then left and straight out of town, go for about a mile, then turn right onto Crossville. That runs for about four, five miles along the Cobbleskill River. It's real obvious. Then you'll come up on a bridge that crosses the river and hooks right into Route Twenty-eight. Turn right and straight into Greenport. The hospital's on Route Twenty-eight. On the left. You can't miss it."

"Greenport," repeated Reed.

"Yeah."

"How far from the turn?"

"After the bridge?"

"Yes."

"I'd say six miles or so after you turn onto Twenty-eight."

"Okay, thanks," said Reed. Noticing now that the young man wore a nameplate on his shirt pocket that said Brian in capital letters. "Thanks, Brian."

"No problem. Hope everything works out."

"Yeah," said Reed, turning toward the door, moving quickly now, even with the prosthesis and cane. But when he opened the door, a blast of such bitter cold wind hit him so suddenly and with such force that he turned back into the lobby.

"Shit."

Reed felt in his pockets for his hat and gloves. His gloves were in the pocket, but not his cap. For a moment, he thought about going back to the room for it, but cursed again and turned back bareheaded into the bitterly cold wind, thinking the temperature must have fallen thirty degrees since he had come into the inn.

Reed walked toward his car, face into the wind, feeling the cold black night descend around him.

Suddenly, not knowing why, not knowing if it was the dark night, the sound of Ullmann's voice, Angela's strange mood, his fatigue, the frustration, not knowing why but convinced of it, Reed suddenly felt a terrible sense of foreboding come over him about John Boyd. It seemed to hit him with the same force as the cold arctic air that swirled around him.

Suddenly Reed had the seemingly irrational notion, no the conviction, that this night held disaster for his cousin. Such a strong sense of foreboding about John being in the hospital came over him that Reed had an irrational urge to get into his car, drive as fast as he could through the dark roads, take his gun and just go into that place and bring John out. Point the Colt Commander at anyone who tried to stop him and get into the BMW and drive to New York. Now, this night.

The notion seemed so extreme that Reed asked himself out loud, "What the fuck has come over you." What would that be? thought Reed. Kidnapping? Abduction? Would he even make it out of the county before that sheriff got him? What about the guards at the hospital?

Reed bent into the wind, struggling over to his car, and asked himself, What the fuck is the matter with you? Are you losing it?

THIRTY

Ralph Malone, as was his usual habit, sat waiting in his patrol car. He had parked in the back edge of the lot next to the gas station/video/convenience store across from the Maple Inn. He had just hit the end button on his cellular phone after listening to Matthew Ullmann tell him that the New York man had just been notified.

Malone checked his watch: eleven-fifteen.

He thumbed the transmit button on his two-way radio.

"Unit One, come on. Unit One."

He waited for the crackling response.

"Yeah, go ahead."

"You in position?"

"Yeah."

"All right. He should be on the road in the next few minutes. There's no other way over there, unless he gets lost or makes a wrong turn, but I'll be behind him making sure. If he goes off a wrong way, I'll let you know."

"Got it."

"Out. Unit Two, come on."

"I'm here."

"You catch that?"

"Yeah."

"Stay in position and stay on."

Eddie McAndrews shoved the two-way radio between the dashboard and windshield of his truck, then reached for the volume knob on the police radio and turned it up a bit. He sat in his ten-year-old Ford F-150, 4x4, engine running, heater on, lights off.

McAndrews rolled down his window and flicked his cigarette into the cold, windy night. He rolled up the window and strapped on his seat belt, pulling down sharply on the chest strap, making sure it grabbed. He gripped the steering wheel and wedged himself back in the driver's seat.

This ought to be pretty fucking cool, he thought.

Reed barked out another curse as he approached the BMW. The wind felt like it was blowing a frozen ice pick into the side of his head. Everything that had been wet or melting during the day had frozen rock hard.

Reed stepped in between his car and the one next to it, edging his way forward to get to the front door, stepping carefully, feeling the ice underfoot. Suddenly he felt his good foot slide, the Flex-Foot slipping, too. Fortunately, his car and the car next to it were so close that he fell against the cars. He steadied himself on the two roofs.

"Shit," he cursed again.

He turned sideways and tried to plant the prosthetic foot and slide his good foot toward the driver's door, but he had too little control and felt the Flex-Foot sliding sideways out from under him.

"God damn it to hell."

He gave it up and slammed his cane down on the roof of his car, then laid his forearms on the two car roofs and swung forward, using the cars like giant crutches. By the time he got his cane back down and struggled into the driver's seat, he found himself slightly out of breath, overheated, more anxious than ever to get going.

Malone picked up his two-way radio.

"Heads up, One and Two . . . our guy is in his car. Be ready, but by the look of him trying to get behind the wheel, I'd say he had plenty to drink with his dinner."

Reed fired up the BMW, strapped on his seat belt, and waited for a moment, trying to calm down, settle down from all the rushing. He let out a deep breath of air.

"Take it easy," he said out loud. "These roads are going to be shit."

He flipped on his headlights. Foot on the brake, he slid the gearshift out of park into reverse, turning around to back up, but Reed did not take his foot off the brake.

It hit him all at once. A phone call in the middle of the night? From Ullmann? Why? Angela's cryptic words at dinner ran through his head: *You're right about these people. Follow your instincts.* Why would that son of a bitch Ullmann do him the favor of calling him? Reed remembered his words: *I know you're concerned.* So what? thought Reed. You knew I was concerned when I called from New York, and you wouldn't give me the time of day.

Reed slid the gearshift back into park. Suddenly his foreboding made perfect sense to him. He looked around, unable to see anything outside the single high-intensity light illuminating the parking lot.

No, he thought. This isn't right. No way.

He reached behind him and slowly pulled the Colt out of his hip holster. He pulled back the slide, chambering a round, setting the hammer back. He carefully checked the safety, making sure it was set, then slid the barrel under his shorter left thigh, muzzle pointing toward the car door, the gun handle right between his legs, ready now so that all he had to do was grab it with one hand, thumb off the safety, and pull the trigger.

Malone watched Reed pass him, waited for a few moments, then slowly pulled out of his hiding spot, headlights off, moving slowly.

He lagged behind Reed for a half mile until he was sure Reed was heading in the right direction. Only then did Malone turn on his lights and increase his speed, turning right onto a local road that cut up and over the small mountain ridge that Reed would be circling around. The road had been plowed and sanded, but Malone drove carefully, focusing his brights and his searchlight out ahead of him, wary of any patches of ice that could send him slipping off onto the narrow shoulder. The plan could work without him reaching his position first, but if he made it, the chance of anyone getting in their way would be eliminated.

The sheriff thumbed his handheld radio.

"One and Two, heads up. He's on the way. Get ready, I'd say six or seven minutes he'll be coming by. Take your time. Get out into position. Give him time to get close before you make your move. I'll be on the other side blocking."

Malone heard the static-filled voices of McAndrews and Boggs reply.

Reed pulled out of the lot slowly, testing the road for ice. He remembered his uncle once talking about black ice in the North Country, ice the color of asphalt that is virtually invisible on paved roads. Certainly invisible at night.

But no, he thought, as he headed north out of Dumphy, it's too early in the season. That's after weeks of cold. Or is it? he wondered.

The road seemed clear and dry and Reed increased his speed to just under fifty, holding back, even though he felt like blasting along at seventy-five to reach the hospital as quickly as possible. He checked his rearview mirror for any headlights behind him. He saw nothing but black. There were no tail-lights out in front of him, but a nearly full moon overhead illuminated the countryside with an eerie glow. As Reed passed by fields still covered in the previous night's snow, melted then frozen again to an icy sheen, the moonlight reflected off the surface, bathing the road and the surroundings in an ethereal glowing gray.

Reed tried to relax. The road seemed fine. No traffic. No problems. He edged up to fifty-five, checking the odometer again. About five more miles to the turnoff. The kid at the inn, Brian, had said he couldn't miss it.

Reed had traveled this way before. He thought he knew where the turnoff onto Crossville Road came in. When he saw a familiar yellow sign indicating an intersection, he slowed. There it was, Crossville. He turned right and within thirty seconds he came abreast of a river that ran along the road, about ten, fifteen feet below to his right, confirming his route.

He glanced at the river running below him, catching glimpses between the trees of a moonlit stream about thirty feet wide. The water boiled along, flowing between the rocks and outcroppings that lined the riverbed. On the far side of the river, a narrow bank butted against a rocky mountainside that ran up about five hundred feet. On his side, a narrow shoulder and interspersing trees and rock rubble separated him from the embankment. On his left, the road ran past mostly forest with an occasional open patch of rocky, rolling fields.

As he continued on, the river slowly descended, cutting deeper into the land until it flowed along about thirty feet below the road. All Reed could see below him now were black patches of wet, sometimes completely disappearing as the width of the riverbank on his side increased. Occasionally, a steel guardrail ran alongside where the road curved, but otherwise only a narrow gravel shoulder and jagged mounds of frozen snow separated the two-lane road from the steep, rocky drop-off that bordered the river.

Reed was just about to slow down a bit, wary of traveling alongside the drop-off at a high speed, when a blast of light suddenly appeared behind him. Reed instinctively lifted his left arm to block the glare from his rearview mirror and just as reflexively he accelerated.

Reed looked back quickly and saw truck headlights coming up behind him, full bore, the truck's brights and a rack of spotlights mounted on the roof flooding the interior of his car.

Reed cursed, squinting, ducking away from the glare. He accelerated, even though with so much light flooding into the BMW, Reed could barely see the road out in front of him. For a moment, the truck fell back, but then quickly closed the gap.

Reed felt his heart pounding. He concentrated on the road in front of him, glare once again flooding the interior of his car. Who is that? What the hell is going on? It's those guys again. Those fucking proctors. No. The truck roared up behind him, nearly touching his bumper. Yes, who else would do that? Christ.

Reed accelerated away from the oncoming truck. What the hell is he trying to do? Run me off the road? Stay ahead of him.

But Reed knew that on the dark road, running so close to the drop-off, racing along at this speed was insane. A curve, ice, anything could happen any second to make him lose control. Desperate, he searched for a road, a place to turn off. Anything to get away from the riverbank. Reed could almost feel himself being sucked to the side and over the drop-off.

Almost involuntarily, Reed lifted his foot from the accelerator, just a bit, just enough to feel slightly more in control as he careened down the dark road in the middle of the cold night. And suddenly, the truck slammed into his rear bumper with a thunderous crack, the force of it snapping Reed's head back into the headrest, the big BMW lurched forward, careening over to the right.

Reed felt the right front wheel plow into a snowbank, the car sliding, rising up ominously on the icy packed mound of snow. Reed braked hard and wrenched the steering wheel back left. Somehow, with only one wheel on the road, the car swerved back left, sliding off the snowbank, away from the terrifying drop, but too far now, swinging into the left lane. Reed accelerated trying to pull back into the right lane, even though he knew that would put him in front of the truck again. He fought for control, fishtailing between lanes, checking the mirror, squinting from the lights glaring, cringing down out of the glare, looking out ahead for oncoming traffic.

He heard, more than saw, the truck rushing at him again from behind. Reed swerved left, despite his fear of oncoming traffic, anything to avoid being shoved off the road and over that drop-off.

The truck missed him, surging ahead, coming parallel to Reed, revealing Ray Boggs behind the wheel, but also revealing just how slim Reed's chances of survival were. Reed saw now that Eddie McAndrews's red Ford had been following behind Boggs. It swerved over into Reed's lane and roared up behind him, joining the attack, trapping Reed in the left lane, forcing Reed to maintain his speed, staying where he was racing toward any oncoming vehicle that might appear at any moment.

The three vehicles roared down the highway inches from each other, Reed keeping up his speed so McAndrews could not ram him from behind; Boggs staying with him but slowly coming closer and closer on Reed's right. The black truck suddenly bounced into the BMW. Reed fought for control.

Reed's mind raced along with the trucks, trying to figure what they were doing, trying to figure a way out of it. He glanced quickly to his left considering the option of driving off the road, but a formidable ditch ran next to the shoulder, and beyond the shoulder it was almost solid trees now.

Boggs jogged his wheel just a tiny jerk to the left, banging into Reed, toying with him. Reed reacted by turning hard right, slamming into Boggs, hearing the sheet metal tear and scrape, but knowing now he could never move the heavier truck out of his way.

Reed floored the BMW, surging out ahead, but he had to brake almost immediately to keep control. Boggs disappeared, but roared back next to him, and McAndrews came up tight behind him.

"Fuck!" Reed cursed. They were either going to run him off the road or into oncoming traffic. No. No! Worse. Suddenly Reed saw their terrifying plan. As they roared forward, all three vehicles locked into position, about a third of a mile ahead, Reed saw the road curving slightly toward a one-lane bridge that spanned the river. About five hundred yards past the bridge, a sheriff's cruiser blocked the road, blue and white strobes flashing, a set of flares glowing red a hundred yards out on the far side of the cruiser, blocking the possibility of oncoming traffic.

Reed could see it now. He would never make it to the bridge. They never intended to knock him down the embankment on the right. They wanted to keep him jammed over to the left so that he would be forced wide of the one-lane bridge. As the river curved left under the bridge, the embankment dropped off to over fifty feet. Only the right lane ran onto the bridge, Boggs would simply hold him where he was, preventing him from making it into the bridge lane. Boggs would hit the bridge. McAndrews would stay tight behind Reed and shove him off the embankment on the left. Even if he braked, the heavy F-150 could easily push him over, sending him down a fifty-foot drop into the icy water.

"No," Reed screamed. "No."

Reed lifted his foot off the accelerator, immediately slowing down. McAndrews's truck banged into his rear bumper, but not hard enough to knock him off the road, just enough to keep him heading toward the fifty-foot plunge.

Reed mashed his thumb down on the button to open the passenger-side window. Icy air blasted around him, making him squint against the grit and cold. The roar of the surrounding truck engines mixed with the icy wind.

Reed could see the highway running out ahead of him closing fast on the one-lane bridge.

Reed slammed on his brakes and immediately felt a shuddering impact from behind as McAndrews crashed into him. Reed had gripped the steering wheel prepared for the impact, but he still lurched forward, his seat belt grabbing him painfully, wrenching all his bruises and aches.

Reed's sudden deceleration meant that Boggs's truck shot forward. Boggs braked, the tires squealing and sliding, the truck coming back toward Reed. Reed fought for control as McAndrews's truck pushed him forward. Reed kept his brake pedal jammed down, forcing the truck to push the heavy BMW forward.

Engines roaring, tires squealing and sliding, Reed grabbed the Colt from between his legs. Boggs's truck slid closer. Reed raised the Colt and fired out the passenger side window, extending his arm, aiming at Boggs's rear left tire, pulling the trigger as fast as he could, as if he were pounding the truck, shot after shot, the gun bucking in his hand, exploding, hot spent cartridges cracking into the windshield, bouncing off the car's interior, the car filling with gun smoke as quickly as the wind whipped it away.

The fourth booming shot hit the mark. Boggs's rear left tire exploded. The black truck lurched sideways and slewed across the road. In an instant, Boggs lost control. The momentum flipped the truck. The mass of metal bounced and flipped again. Plastic, glass, hubcaps, pieces of a truck tire—all flew past Reed as he steered left, fishtailing around the truck. He steered back hard right to stay on the road, to get out from in front of McAndrews, fighting for control, steering for the right lane, aiming for the bridge just as McAndrews made it past the tumbling truck behind them, coming up fast. Reed fought for control, steering, braking, and McAndrews slammed into the left rear corner of the BMW.

Reed grabbed his steering wheel with a death grip, ramming his foot into his brake pedal. Reed spun clockwise. McAndrews shot past him. Reed crushed his brake pedal. His antilock brake mechanism kicking his foot, pulsing, pulsing. Reed's front wheels hit a snowbank on the right shoulder with a shuddering crash, the bank hard, frozen, almost like a wall. The force of the crash shuddered through the car frame right into Reed's body. The BMW burst through the wall of ice and snow, flying up, then nosing down with a stomach-churning dive as the road disappeared and Reed felt himself pointing downward into darkness.

For one long, frozen moment, Reed felt himself suspended in air, rising off the seat, pitching forward, the seat belt the only thing that kept his head from banging into the ceiling of the car. And then an unimaginable, sickening jolt as the car banged down onto the rocky incline, heading down, running out of control, now at the mercy of gravity.

The first jolt slammed Reed down into the seat so violently that he felt his spine, his ribs, his whole torso contract. The impact forced the air out of his lungs. He cracked his forehead on the steering wheel. Another sickening jolt. And another. A rock slammed into the car's under carriage with such force that Reed felt the impact through the floor all the way up into the seat.

Reed kept his foot jammed on the brake pedal, but it did nothing to stop the car from jolting down, slamming down the rocky embankment with teeth-shuddering impact, sliding, banging, lurching down and down a terrifying thirty-foot drop. The car banging into rock and ledge and ground, an axle cracking, the right front tire bursting, then the left and the right rear, rims banging, the car frame cracking, and then a sudden horrifying stop as the nose of the big sedan walloped into the river, popping the air bag.

Eddie McAndrews braked hard, wrenching his wheel, just managing to slide onto the one-lane bridge, the back end of his truck banged off the guardrail on the left side of the bridge with a shuddering crack, the impact sending him careening off the right side, fighting for control. He punched the brake pedal, straightened out, slowed down, regaining control.

Out ahead on the other side of the bridge, he saw Malone standing off to the side of his cruiser, a shotgun braced against his hip. McAndrews's truck rumbled off the bridge on the other side, and he screeched to a stop ten feet from Malone.

McAndrews almost had to pry his fingers off his steering wheel.

Malone's headlights blinded McAndrews, but McAndrews didn't bother to pull off the road. He fumbled with his seat belt, cursing, angry at being so shaken.

"Fuck! Fuck, fuck, fuck!"

The sheriff came walking toward the driver's side window, still carrying the shotgun, and pulled open McAndrews's door.

"What the hell happened?" Malone said. "You ran him off the wrong side."

"I'm fucking lucky I ran him off any side," McAndrews yelled. "Did you see what happened to Ray?"

"I couldn't tell. What? He lost control. What made him flip like that?"

McAndrews screamed at him, "The motherfucker had a gun, goddammit. He got behind Ray's truck and shot the piss out of it. Jeezus!"

"Those were muzzle flashes."

"Hell yeah. Fuck the wrong side. I'm lucky I smacked him in time to get into that lane or I woulda been the one dropping fifty feet on the left of the damn bridge. That fucker better be dead."

"I don't know," said Malone. "It's not nearly as much of an incline on that side."

"Fuck the incline," said McAndrews.

Malone indicated with his head. "All right. Get down out of there and get in my car. I'm going to pull your truck off the road here and then we'll see. Go on. Just get in and sit down."

McAndrews walked to the police car, but found himself needing to steady himself on the hood as he made his way over to the passenger side. When Malone piled in next to him, McAndrews realized he had lost awareness of anything until Malone slammed the door and shoved the car into gear, accelerating quickly toward the bridge, his tires spewing gravel as he pulled onto the asphalt.

McAndrews looked over at Malone. There seemed to be an intensity about him, but no sign of rushing or anxiety. As they came off the bridge, McAndrews finally focused on the sight of Ray Boggs's overturned truck. Mostly all he could see of it was the exposed underside facing them, the truck lying perpendicular, almost centered across the two-lane road.

McAndrews flashed on what he had seen . . . the truck swinging clockwise, the rear end sliding sideways perpendicular to the road, the sudden flip as if the truck were some toy. McAndrews remembered how suddenly the truck had flipped, how hard it had slammed down on the pavement, making a horrible noise, bouncing up, turning in the air behind him as McAndrews aimed for the BMW, intent on running it off the road.

Malone slowly drove around to the other side of the wreck. He positioned the police cruiser, aiming the headlights into the back window of the pickup. Both men got out and walked over to the truck, McAndrews hunched over against the cold and the wind, Malone walking straight, head up. McAndrews noticed that the sheriff did not rush, as if he already knew there was nothing he could do for Raymond Boggs.

The headlights from the sheriff's cruiser backlit the interior of the truck cab. Both men leaned around and peered through the windshield that had fragmented into a spiderweb of cracks. Even with the light coming in from behind and through a cracked windshield, they could see that Raymond Boggs was dead. Suspended in the driver's seat by his seat belt, with the truck lying on its side, Boggs sagged toward the ground, his head looking slightly detached. Blood dripped from a gash in the right side of his head.

Malone straightened up and stepped back.

"Looks like his neck broke."

"Shit."

Malone made a circular motion with his forefinger.

"Truck flipping like that, sideways, going so fast . . . smashed his head on one side, then whipped it back the other way. Snap."

"Damn."

McAndrews lit a cigarette, shivering slightly in the cold as he took one deep drag after another.

"Fuck, man. That's Ray in there. What the fuck are we gonna do now?"

"Nothing," said Malone. "We do nothing. It's a car accident. You weren't here. I wasn't here. We leave everything as is until someone comes by and calls it in. Let's go see what happened to the other guy."

"Better be dead."

McAndrews tossed his cigarette into the wind and followed Malone toward the bridge.

Reed had never lost consciousness. He had felt every out-of-control, crashing, banging, terrifying jolt of the journey down toward the river.

Even as the BMW had smashed into the river at the bottom of the embankment, Reed felt the impact of the air bag and the sudden pull of the seat belt and chest strap holding him in place.

For a moment, the fear and trauma paralyzed him, and then he suddenly realized the steering wheel air bag was stuck to the right side of his head. He clawed at the bag with his left hand, pulling it down from his face. Reed found himself gasping. He hadn't taken a breath during the fall down to the river. He had been paralyzed with fear and terror. His body was still rigid, his chest constricted. He could only take short, rapid breaths.

He still held the steering wheel in a vise grip with his right hand. He looked at his left hand, still crimped, clawlike. He slowly forced his left hand open, then his right, barely able to break his grip on the wheel.

Still, he could not breathe easily. He found himself gasping, grunting slightly, grabbing one short breath after another, his chest too constricted by fear to expand. Everything in him seemed paralyzed, paralyzed by the shock and panic burned into him during the plunge down the embankment.

He continued struggling to breathe, then realized that he was facing down, his chest and stomach painfully pushing against his seat belt and harness. Gravity kept him pressed forward. He tried to push himself back from the steering wheel and the first shock of pain hit him . . . his neck had been wrenched so violently that it felt as if someone had stuck an ice pick at the base of his skull. He gasped another breath of air and another, the pain and oxygen bringing everything more into focus.

Slowly, his senses returned. He saw the glow of his headlights in the river water, smelled the burning brakes and oil and hot fluids spewed from the torn engine, and suddenly he felt the icy cold water surrounding his right foot.

Reed lifted his right foot out of the water, automatically bracing the unfeeling, mechanical left foot against the watery floorboard. He remembered something about turning off the car to lessen the chances of a fire after a crash. He reached for the keys and switched off the ignition. The headlights burning underwater darkened. He felt around for his seat belt, pushing the release, freeing himself only to pitch forward awkwardly against the steering wheel for a moment before he pushed himself back with his left arm and prosthetic leg.

"Fuck," he muttered, trying to turn himself so he could lean against the steering wheel. He reached for the door handle to open it, but just then he saw the lights from Malone's patrol car coming over the bridge from the far side.

Reed involuntarily ducked down, his mind racing. He turned back toward the steering wheel, looking out the windshield, gauging whether or not the car seemed to be stable, fighting the urge to shove open the door and get out. They had tried to kill him. If they saw him moving, getting out, what would they do? Reed pictured them taking out rifles and shooting him.

Feeling panicky, Reed frantically looked for the Colt, barely able to see anything in the dim moonlight. Would they climb down to check him? He needed his gun.

Reed felt around on the passenger seat next to him. Nothing. He pushed himself out from behind the steering wheel, and holding the steering wheel with his left hand, plunged his right hand into the cold water around the accelerator and brake pedal, nothing. He reached over and felt the floor on the other side of the transmission hump, his right hand rapidly growing numb. In the far corner, underwater, his freezing fingers felt the reassuring solid mass of the gun.

Reed pulled the Colt out of the water, fighting gravity, pulling himself back behind the steering wheel. He shoved his right foot against the dashboard and stuck the Colt and his hand under his left armpit, wiping off the gun and warming his hand, then he shoved the gun in the crease of the passenger seat next to him. Still bracing himself with his right foot on the dashboard and his prosthetic foot in the water on the floorboard, he struggled into his seat belt.

He looked over his left shoulder, then his right, trying to spot what was happening back up on the road above him. He could see the glow of headlights near the truck that had flipped over. They were checking out their buddy. Next will be me, thought Reed. He braced his hands against the steering wheel and pulled his right foot from the dashboard, propping his heel on the transmission hump, trying to keep his foot out of the water as he carefully lowered himself against the steering wheel. He reached over to adjust the rearview mirror so he could see behind him, then picked up the Colt, resting it on the steering column in front of him.

McAndrews walked around the truck, trying not to think about Ray Boggs, following Malone back toward the bridge where Reed's car had slammed through the snowbank and dropped out of sight.

They stepped carefully to the edge of the embankment and peered down. They could see the wrecked BMW, twenty-five feet below at the bottom of the steep, snow-covered, rocky embankment, front jammed into the river, smashed rear end angled up slightly.

"You see 'im?" asked McAndrews.

Malone peered down at the moonlit scene below.

"Doors are closed. I don't see anything around the car." He aimed his powerful flashlight beam at the rear window, edging closer to the drop-off to get a better angle. "I think he's still in the driver's seat." Malone handed the flashlight to McAndrews and said, "Hang on," as he headed back toward his car, walking briskly, but not rushing.

McAndrews shined the light, squinting, trying to see into the car, but too much of the light's beam reflected back off the rear window. Malone returned holding a pair of binoculars. He motioned over to his right and told McAndrews, "Stand over there and shine the light in at an angle so it doesn't reflect back at us so much."

McAndrews did as told, and Malone peered down through the binoculars.

"All right," he said. "He's in there. Looks like he's just hanging over the steering wheel."

"Is he dead?" asked McAndrews.

"I don't know," said Malone. "Maybe. Maybe not. He's got to be at least busted up some and with that water running in there, him half sittin' in it . . . at this temperature he'll probably freeze to death pretty quick."

"You don't want to go down and check him out?"

Malone dropped the binoculars away from his eyes and turned to McAndrews.

"All that snow and ice on those rocks, I doubt you'd get down there in one piece. Much less get back up. You want to try?"

McAndrews peered down at the BMW.

"Hell no. Maybe we should peg a couple of shots into him."

"No. Why complicate it? Let him freeze down there. C'mon. It's better we don't mess around here, Eddie. Not too many travel by here this time of night, but I'd rather not be seen."

"What if he gets lucky and somebody comes by sooner?"

"Doesn't matter," said Malone. He looked at his watch. "Even if someone happens by in the next five minutes, by the time they call it in, get someone out here . . . he'll be an ice cube. Hell, nobody is gonna get down there and get him out in time. Let's go. I'll drive you back to your truck, and we'll get the hell out of here."

McAndrews asked again, "Think he's alive?"

"I told you, I don't know."

McAndrews flicked the butt of his cigarette at the BMW below.

"Fuck 'em. He ain't dead, he still ain't gettin' up here with only one leg. Hope he broke the other one, too, mother-fucker."

Malone checked his watch.

"Let's go, Eddie."

They returned to the cruiser. McAndrews climbed in quickly and slammed the door shut behind him, more than anxious to get in out of the cold. He rubbed his hands and shivered once to dispel the chill. Malone pulled his cellular phone from his breast pocket and punched in a call.

THIRTY-ONE

Matthew Ullmann dozed, his feet resting on his desk, his executive chair tipped back. The sharp electronic beep of his desk phone roused him. Ullmann opened his eyes, scrunched his face to clear his head, and picked up the phone.

Without waiting to hear who was on the other line he spoke. "Done?"

"Pretty much," Ralph Malone answered laconically.

Ullmann tipped forward in his chair, his feet dropping off the desk.

"What do you mean, pretty much?"

"You lost one of yours," Malone said. "It got a little complicated. I'll tell you more when I get there."

Ullmann's face twitched with annoyance. "All right. Hurry up."

Ullmann hung up, angry at the complications, angry at Malone's cryptic comments, angry with Johnny Boy for not being sick on time, angry at being kept up late.

He stood, wandering out of his office over to the small refrigerator near his secretary's desk. He needed something to eat. Gladys always kept something in there. A donut. A piece of pastry or cake. Ullmann needed something sweet. Something filling.

By the time Reed heard the police cruiser drive off, the adrenaline rush had burned off. Now a wave of pain and discomfort enfolded him. He seemed to hurt everywhere, all at once. His chest, back, shoulder. His right knee. Now all the muscles and joints that were wrenched so violently began to ache. His neck suddenly felt as if moving his head might break something inside.

He pushed himself back off the steering wheel, groaning in pain, shoving the Colt into his waistband, unable to maneuver around and put it into the holster under his coat.

Out, out, he had to get out before he froze to death.

He released the seat belt harness. Bracing himself against the steering wheel, he struggled out of the belt, turning sideways, left shoulder leaning against the steering wheel pad. He slid back and unlatched the driver's side door, shoving against it with his back, once, twice until it popped open. He struggled out of the car into two feet of icy river water.

He began shivering violently. He reached back into the car and grabbed his cane. He straightened up, braced himself against the car, and stepped carefully on the rocky river bottom toward the bank. He almost fell twice before he made it out of the water. He struggled around to the back of the car where he finally sat back on the crumpled trunk, pulling his shearling coat closed, trying to button it with freezing hands, shouting now against the cold, cursing, blowing on his hands to warm them.

He sat up straighter on the trunk and reached inside his coat for the Colt, pulling it out, releasing the slide, and setting the hammer carefully back, hoping he wouldn't drop it with his numb fingers. He set the safety and shoved the Colt back into his hip holster. He dug into his coat pockets and pulled out his gloves, struggling into them, grateful for the protection, flexing his hands to get the feeling back in his fingers.

He levered himself back and forth while propped on the trunk to generate body warmth. He grabbed his freezing head and ears.

"Fuck."

Reed looked at the moonlit cliff that loomed in front of him. The embankment appeared to be very steep running straight up to the highway.

"What the fuck do you do now?" he asked himself. Reed reached into his pocket and pulled out his cellular phone. He turned it on, checking the battery strength. It had run down to its last third. He couldn't dial 911. If the sheriff heard his call, he'd come back to finish him off. If he stayed down here, he would freeze to death.

Reed felt his right foot, soaked through his running shoe and sock all the way to the ankle, growing numb as if he had lost both feet instead of one. Angela. Reed pulled off his right glove and dug into his pocket, feeling around for the map that she had drawn him. Her phone number was on it. She'd have to come. Bring a rope or something. Tie it to her car, pull him up out of here. What if she was still at the Maple Inn? He tried to recall the number, fairly sure he had it right.

Reed looked at the phone's screen. The signal strength was at the lowest setting.

"Shit."

He dialed the number. Hit the talk button. Nothing. He couldn't get a signal at the bottom of this riverbank.

Reed turned off the phone to save the battery.

"You got to get moving," he told himself. "You can't wait. You'll freeze." And then a terrible thought struck him. What about John Boyd? If they tried doing this to me, what in God's name are they doing to him?

Reed pushed himself off the trunk, stepping forward. He took a shaky step toward the embankment. He had no choice. He had to make the climb.

The sheriff and Matthew Ullmann sat in Ullmann's dimly lit office.

"So you just left them both out there?"

"As is. Looks like a nice tragic accident. It'll be easy to wrap it up. Even with a death involved."

"Death?" said Ullmann. "I hope you mean deaths."

"More'n likely," said Malone. "I wasn't about to hang around making sure. If Reed ain't dead from that crash, or if he don't freeze to death lying in that river water, he sure as hell won't be bothering anybody for a long time. That's what you wanted, isn't it?"

"Yes. I suppose you're right." Ullmann paused, then almost as if remembering his manners, he said, "Too bad about Ray."

Malone had been sitting on Ullmann's couch, his winter coat unzipped, turning his Smokey Bear hat in his hands, staring down at the hat. Now he looked up at Ullmann.

"Why?"

Ullmann swiveled his desk chair around to face Malone.

"What do you mean?"

"Why is it too bad about Ray?"

"I don't know. He was useful."

"For what? Useful for what?"

"Around here. With the residents."

Malone snorted.

"Ray was a thug. I never quite understood why you needed the likes of him around here. McAndrews and some of those others aren't much better, but Boggs was the worst of the lot. A loose cannon, too." Malone shook his head disgustedly. "Wouldn't listen. I told him to wait 'til just before the guy reached the bridge. Would've been easy to come up real fast, right there, just run him off. Idiot made a demolition derby out of it. Thing should have gone a lot smoother. Now I got to worry about his dead body out there and the other guy."

"What are you complaining about?" asked Ullmann. "It's a goddamn car accident. Simple."

"Simple? With bullet holes in one car and the other guy with a gun? With one car on the road a hundred feet this side of the bridge and the other going off the road a hundred feet away? How do I explain that?"

"Who are you going to explain it to?"

"What if some state trooper happens by there tonight?"

"So what? None of it is your fault. You don't have to explain why Bill Reed shot Ray Boggs. You don't know anything, right?"

"I suppose."

"Don't worry."

"It's more than I bargained for."

"So what are you saying? Ten K isn't enough."

"I don't know if anything is enough to put up with all this mess."

"How about fifteen? Is that enough?"

Suddenly Malone hardened. He stared at Ullmann, expressionless, but clearly insulted.

"Yeah, Mr. Ullmann, that's enough. Enough all the way around."

"Fine. Then we'll stop talking about it."

"Right."

"Besides, we have more jobs to finish tonight." Ullmann stood up abruptly. "Starting with getting our patient over to Clearbrook Hospital."

"You call the ambulance?"

"Not yet. Let me go over there and see how he's doing. Either way, I'll call from the dorm."

Reed made his way to the base of the embankment. He leaned against his cane, looking up at the rocky incline, trying to discern a way up. The embankment appeared to be mostly solid slabs of rock running upward, chunks and masses of it shoved together, piled one on top of another, cracked and splintered all the way up to the shoulder of the road. Most of the separations and lines ran vertically, but there were plenty of jagged surfaces and protrusions. Snow and ice covered the horizontal sections of the embankment, but the vertical surfaces appeared to be mostly clear.

With two legs, Reed would have worried about the height, but he would have tried the climb. With one leg and a prosthesis that still did not fit right, still felt like a foreign attachment . . . Reed looked down, not wanting to even think about doing it.

A gust of wind blew around him, the fierce cold making his bare head ache and his ears sting. He wished he had his hat.

He looked back at the wall in front of him. The moon was nearly full, reflecting off the snow that seemed to cling to every horizontal surface on the embankment.

What are you going to do? he asked himself. Wait for someone to come along? When is that going to be? Ten minutes?
An hour? Two? And then what? No way some passerby can
pull you out. They'll still have to go for help. Then what?

Reed turned away from the embankment and tossed his
cane back toward the wrecked car. He jammed his fingers
deep into his leather gloves, stepped forward, planted his
good foot on the lowest rock, brought his artificial leg up onto
the rock, balancing. He leaned forward, reached up with his
left hand, and grabbed hold of a nub on the stone face. His
gloved hand slipped. He brushed off the snow, feeling around
for a spot free of ice, and grabbed again. Then he reached up
with his right hand, again trying to feel something solid, balancing, steadying himself.

He felt awkward. Unsteady. The cold wind gusted. He
cursed. He leaned farther into the rock face, laying his body
against the incline, letting gravity push him against the surface instead of straight down. He felt more secure, even as the
cold from the snow and freezing rock seeped through his coat
and pants.

He thought to himself, Just lie against the side, take it easy,
step by step. Don't rush.

First, he made sure both hands had a grip on something,
brushing more snow away, testing to make sure the rock above
him wasn't covered in ice. Once he felt his hands secure, he
slowly brought up his right leg, feeling the weight transfer to
his prosthesis, feeling the pressure on his stump as it sank into
the prosthetic socket. He tried to hold as much of his weight
as possible with his hands and arms.

He felt around with his right foot, testing, placing it, digging his foot into the snow to find the solid rock underneath,
then he planted the foot. Slowly shifting his weight, he
stepped up, pulled himself up, thankfully taking the weight
off the prosthetic limb, pulling his stump and the prosthetic
limb up after him.

But as soon as he stepped up, he realized that his hands
were now just below shoulder height, making it very difficult

to hold his weight. Almost everything rested on his right foot. He quickly brought up his artificial limb, trying to find a spot to plant his Flex-Foot. He thought he saw a place where he could wedge it between the wall of the embankment and a small outcropping of rock. But he couldn't feel with the artificial foot. He could only estimate how solid the spot was, pushing down, trying to get a sense of it through the running shoe, the Flex-Foot, up the shaft of the prosthesis, the socket and into his stump, all the while balancing on one foot.

He shoved the Flex-Foot down. Lifted it. Stomped down. It felt solid. But taking the step raised him still higher. His hands were now at just above chest level. Reed had to lean backward to keep his grip. He could feel himself being pulled off the wall. Clamping down on his panic, he looked up and saw a place for his right hand, but when he let go to raise his grip, he nearly lost his balance. He pitched himself forward, luckily felt something solid under his hand, grabbed, and held on.

He leaned into the wall, steadying himself. He waited until his breathing steadied, tried to calm down, relax, but almost immediately started shivering . . . the cold embankment pressing into him in front, the chill wind blowing against him from behind. Christ, all that for one fucking step.

"Come on," he yelled to himself. "Come on. Do it. If you fall, you fall. Better than lying out in the damn cold doing nothing."

Reed pushed out a hard breath of air, then filled his lungs and breathed out hard again. He reached up for a handhold, but this time he did not lift his hand from the face of the embankment. He slid it up along the face of the wall, maintaining contact until he found another spot he could grab on to. He followed with his left. Keeping his hands on the wall made him feel more secure and confident.

The next two steps up were shorter, but went easier. He began to have a sense of control with his stump, as if the attached prosthesis were a tool that he could direct and place, lift and plant. For a moment, Reed thought he might pry off the running shoe from the Flex-Foot so that he would have a more precise instrument to dig into the snow or wedge into the side of the embankment, but the thought of trying to get the shoe off while clinging to the embankment made his jaw tighten and his heart pound faster.

He reached up again, grabbed, held on, took another step with his right foot, bringing the prosthesis up next to it.

After another two steps, hanging on to his position, Reed cautiously looked down behind him. It seemed like a long way, but comparing the distance to his six-foot one-inch frame, Reed figured he had only come about ten feet from the riverbank. Maybe a little more than a third of the way up. He felt secure on the wall, strong. The sense of freezing cold and shivering had passed. He felt warmed up and ready.

He saw a spot for his right foot, a little high up, but almost a ledge. He'd have to plant the foot awkwardly, parallel to the wall, but it looked doable. He shifted his weight, lifting his right foot up, keeping his knee and thigh against the wall, he found the little ledge, twisted his foot onto it, digging in with the ball of his foot, getting under the crusty snow, feeling for ice. It felt solid. Ready for the step up.

He shifted his weight, pulled up with his arms, stepped up to his right foot. His muscles bulged and burned across his upper back, his right thigh quivering with the effort, and then he realized, midway in the step, he had gone too high. He had stepped up to a part of the incline that was too steep. The higher up he pulled himself, the farther he had to lean back away from the wall.

He stopped halfway, holding his position, exerting an enormous effort to hold on to the wall. He remained halfway up, his right knee flexed, burning, holding his position. His forearm muscles began to cramp. His triceps and back muscles burning. Quickly, desperately, he pulled up his prosthetic foot, scrabbling against the side of the wall to find a purchase, a spot, anywhere to take some of the weight, and then his right foot slipped off the sliver of a ledge, his chest and face slammed into the wall. But still he held on, just with his hands, trying to get his right foot back on the wall, somewhere, anywhere. And then his right hand lost its grip, and immediately the left, Reed felt each part of him give way and the sickening, inexorable force of gravity overtaking him. He slid, scraping down the embankment, turning sideways so his face wouldn't be smashed as he slid down the wall, flailing with his arms, trying to slow his slide.

Reed had slid down the rocky embankment mostly sideways. The first thing to hit the ground was his prosthesis. The impact of it ran through Reed's stump into his hip, almost as if the riverbank had decided to ram his stump home into the socket. He pitched sideways away from the embankment and landed with a thud.

Reed waited a moment, too stunned by the suddenness of the fall to move. He rolled over and looked back at where he had fallen. Luckily, he had come down along a sheer part of the incline where there were few outcroppings to bang into.

Reed slowly pushed himself up off the ground, got to his knees, stood up, amazed and grateful that he hadn't been badly hurt. He could see now that the embankment leveled out a bit near the bottom, saving him from a worse landing. Ten feet lost in two seconds. Reed gazed up the incline. If he pulled that fall at twenty or twenty-five feet, he doubted if he'd get up again.

Winded, drained, his heart still beating hard, Reed stepped toward the embankment. He leaned forward, laid his two hands against the wall and pressed his forehead into the cold rock, feeling the deep chill penetrate through his sweat.

"Christ."

This is crazy. Just get in the car. The backseat is out of the water. Lie down. Get out of the wind and cold. Wait for someone to come by up there. They can't miss that wrecked truck. They'll have to look down and see me. Really? Why? What guarantees they'll look any farther than that truck? And even if they do, then what? Are they going to climb down here and carry me out?

No one is going to save your ass, Reed thought. And if by some miracle they do, what're you going to say? That someone tried to run you off the road so you shot at his truck. What if one of those bullets hit that guy? "They'll arrest you and charge you with murder," Reed told himself.

And then he thought about John Boyd. John Boyd, John Boyd, what the hell are they going to do to you in that hospital?

And suddenly an image came into Reed's mind, a clear, vivid image of Matthew Ullmann looking smug with that insufferable air of privilege and superiority. He set me up. That phone call. This is his work.

"No," he shouted. "No fucking way. No way."

He pushed himself back off the wall, hocked up a wad of phlegm and spat it out, narrowing his eyes, focusing, forcing himself to be stronger, smarter, better. He planted his right foot, starting again. But this time, Reed changed his method. Instead of going up as straight as he could, Reed tacked along the face of the wall, moving sideways in the direction of the bridge that lay off to his right. He would go as much sideways as up—figuring to take longer, but fight gravity less.

He stepped to his right, keeping his good foot and artificial foot on the same level until he could step up comfortably, always keeping his hands on the wall, always leaning into it, not worrying so much about going up, but just moving slowly, steadily sideways and up, up in small, careful increments, feeling more secure, but hoping his strength would hold up.

He remembered the words of the social worker Sarah Carpenter, also an amputee: *You can do it all, it just all takes longer.*

"Yeah," said Reed. "Let's see another one-legged bastard do this."

THIRTY-TWO

Matthew Ullmann and Sheriff Ralph Malone walked down
the main hall in the Davis dorm, heading for the corridor
that branched off toward Johnny Boy's room. Malone hung
back, as if this part of it were outside his duties, but when he
heard the far-off but distinct screams he increased his pace.
The screams were garbled, mixed with grunts and a constricted cry for help. Malone had never heard anything quite
like it.

They turned the corner toward Johnny Boy's room, which
was about thirty feet down the hall. Four of the dorm residents
stood near their doorways, middle-aged retarded men, di-
sheveled, wearing their night clothes . . . sweatpants, T-shirts,
mismatched pajama tops and bottoms. They stood just outside
their doors, blinking in the harsh light of the hallway, confused by the disruption.

Seeing that Johnny Boy's door was open, Ullmann stopped.
Malone came up next to him and also stopped. The sounds of
anguish were clear and chilling. Rita Glover came out of the
room, obviously distressed, rushing toward the proctor's office. She knew the protocol: first call the Ullmanns, then the
volunteer ambulance service, then the hospital.

She had her head down, moving her stout body as fast as
she could. Ullmann waited for her. Seeing Ullmann and Malone standing there added to her confusion, but she didn't
bother to ask why they had come.

"Johnny Boy," she said. "This one's bad."

Ullmann held up a hand to cut her off, nodded, smiling to
reassure her, but simply appearing smug. "It's all taken care
of, Rita. We've called the ambulance. Why don't you just go
back there and hold his hand or something."

Rita looked at Ullmann, trying to figure out how he knew to call an ambulance. The screaming had started not more than five minutes ago. She started to ask, but stopped herself, saying simply, "It's the worst I've ever seen him."

"That's twice you've told me. Now just go stay with him."

Rita nodded, turned around, and headed for Johnny Boy's room, shooing the other residents back into their rooms as she hurried down the hallway.

Ullmann turned away, squinting, annoyed at the helpless, piercing sounds of pain coming from down the hallway.

"I'll call them from the proctor's office," said Ullmann.

Malone nodded, distracted by Johnny Boy's grunting, crying screams. He said, "Just tell them to get the hell over here fast. I don't think I want to hear that for much longer."

Ullmann shook his head, waving off the comment. "You think I do?"

There was one other time when Bill Reed thought he might die. That time the paralyzing sensation had lasted only twenty-eight seconds, the short but seemingly interminable duration it took for him to exchange gunshots with a bank robber in Leesburg, Virginia.

This time, the feeling that he might actually die had plagued him for almost an hour. With each painful, relentless push and pull up the side of the wall, the possibility of falling to his death had become greater. With each move upward, each foot of height he had painfully extracted from the side of the wall, ten feet up, fifteen, now nearly twenty-five feet above the rocky riverbank, the terror had grown. Now, hanging on to the embankment, Reed refused to look down, fearful that the sight might paralyze him.

Twenty-five feet. Craning his head back slightly to see what lay above him, careful not to tip his weight back too far, it seemed to Reed he had about four feet to go. But now, he wasn't at all sure he could make it to the top.

His hands had cramped into claws. Exhaustion had seeped so deeply into his arms, forearms, back, leg, even his stump and left hip . . . that one more pulling, pushing step could only be done after he'd rested for a minute to gather his waning strength.

Reed held on, fighting the panic that looking up had engendered. He had reached a part of the embankment where the angle of incline was not as steep as before, but an outcropping loomed above him. It bulged out much too far to climb over. He craned his head to the right, trying to see around it, trying to find a way up past the last four feet. He could see nothing.

His fingers were almost cramped to the point where he could not open them. He had to move. He could not stay in this position. He had only one option . . . sliding along farther to his right, toward the bridge, in the hope there might be a way around the outcropping. It would mean expending energy and effort to merely move sideways, not up. And even if he made it clear of the overhang, there was no guarantee that there would be enough space between the outcropping and the concrete wall that supported the base of the bridge on his side. If there wasn't a way up over there, Reed would be trapped. He knew he would not have enough strength to return all the way to his left and then continue on for who knew how long to find a new way up.

Reed forced down the panic and despair. This was it. At worst, he would get close to the bridge. If he found himself stuck, maybe he could wedge himself between the rocks and the bridge and hold on until somebody came. He could certainly be more easily pulled up onto the road from this height. But could he hang on?

He edged over, fingers crimped into a crease of stone overhead, stepping with his right foot, sliding his left, his stump aching now in the socket, sore from all the grinding pressure.

He continued, two more sliding sideways steps, fighting the urge to peer around to see the far side of the outcropping, determined to do nothing that would alter his balance.

His breath came in short gasps now. Almost drained, another step, another, his clawed hands hanging on, he had almost reached the sheer concrete wall on his right. But Reed felt no sense of relief. He could already tell that outcropping above him extended very close to the base of the bridge, certainly too close to wedge his body between the rock and the bridge base.

Another step and Reed's right shoulder pressed against the base of the bridge. He looked up. The bulge in the rock face butted right up against the sheer concrete wall that formed the base. It was as if they had used the rock itself as a form when they poured the concrete.

Reed turned his head away from the bridge, lying the side of his face against the cold rock. He closed his eyes, emptying his mind, refusing to think about anything, refusing to let anything into his consciousness. No anger, no despair, no desperate prayer to a God he had stopped believing in decades ago. Nothing. He would not let it end this way, clinging to the side of a cliff until he either dropped off or someone happened by to pull him up the last four lousy feet that separated him from level ground.

Reed ran his tongue around his dry mouth and looked up. He sensed that the ground above the outcropping leveled off sharply. So goddamn close, he told himself.

Reed adjusted the grip of his left hand and felt his little finger and ring finger slip into a crack. He had been so intent on looking and moving to his right that he had missed something. Lifting his head from the rock, gingerly leaning back slightly, he squinted at what appeared to be nothing more than a wide vertical crack in the outcropping. Moving ever so carefully, Reed stepped left and peered more closely. The crack started at just about knee level and ran all the way up the outcropping. The snow that had filled in the crack had made it appear more narrow than it was. He stuck his left hand into the space, scraping out the snow and ice that had formed on the walls of the crack. It seemed to be about four inches wide, a seam that ran right up the rock, about two feet to the left of the bridge.

Reed envisioned it . . . maybe if he carefully made his way over to his left, got his right foot into the crevice . . . ?

He slowly shifted his weight, feeling his sore stump press into the prosthetic socket, slid to his left, getting his right foot in front of the crevice. His weight now on the prosthesis, he stepped up with his right foot and tried to work it into the opening. He couldn't get much more than the tip of the running shoe into the crack. He turned his foot, forcing it farther in, almost the whole shoe, but he knew it wouldn't do him any good. He couldn't shove himself upward with his right foot sideways in the rock.

He gingerly eased the foot out and stepped back sideways to his right. Looking to his right, he saw there was a small space between the bridge base and the embankment, maybe an inch. Enough for a finger grip.

He felt himself weakening, his breath ragged now, the burning, cramping muscle aches tearing through him.

Carefully, carefully, Reed slid his feet closer together, making his perch on the rock extremely precarious. Using up his last reserve of strength, his fingers barely holding in the crack and crevice, he wedged the back of his left running shoe under his right heel and pushed it off the back of his Flex-Foot. Wincing at the danger of it, standing precipitously on the thin ledge, he carefully pulled the Flex-Foot out of the left shoe. It immediately fell off into space behind him. It seemed to take a long time before he heard the shoe slap against the rocky riverbank. Reed did not look down after it.

Desperate now, knowing he might have only seconds before his hands gave out, Reed lifted the prosthesis and shoved the Flex-Foot into the crack. The flat metal piece, about four inches wide and three-quarters of an inch thick, formed and bent gracefully to simulate a foot, slid snugly into the crevice. Reed pushed down, trying to keep the Flex-Foot level so it would fit evenly, take some of the weight off his hands. It held. He pushed down harder. It wedged in tightly, immediately taking some of the weight off his cramping hands. His heart pounded, his breathing constricted from fear, Reed refused to even consider that the prosthesis might remain stuck in the crevice.

He fought to gather his strength, knowing now he would expend whatever he had on this final effort, he reached as high as he could with his left hand, shoved it into the crack, working it back and forth until the snow and ice were clear, then balled his hand into a fist, wedging the hand tightly in the crack.

He slid his right foot over and braced the rubber-soled flat of the running shoe against the rough vertical slab of concrete that made the bridge base and felt for a finger grip with his right hand.

For the first time since he'd started the climb, Reed felt secure. All four of his limbs were set. A deep breath, his heart pounding, he pulled up with his left arm, stepping up on the prosthesis, grabbing with the right hand, pushing against the bridge with his right foot. He rose almost two feet up the face of the outcropping. Bent back now, straining to hold on, to gather himself for one more step up to bring him over the bulge that blocked his way.

First, he had to free the Flex-Foot. He had felt it slip maybe an inch or two when he put most of his weight on it. Had it wedged in the crack too tightly? And could he hold on with just his hands and his foot against the bridge while he tried to free it?

Gasping for air, his strength waning rapidly, he stuttered his right foot up the side of the bridge base a half step, pushing himself against the outcropping. He slid his right-hand finger grip a bit higher, holding on, ignoring the cramping burn in his right forearm, he quickly unballed his left hand and slid it higher in the crack, once, twice, risking a third time until his left hand was high up in the crevice, balled up, wedged in tight.

This was it. The end. One way or another, it would end now.

He concentrated all his strength, all his reserve to hold on so he could free the Flex-Foot for the final step up. One more.

He pulled up from the hip. Stuck. Stuck!

Gasping for air, a piercing cramp ran up his right thigh into his hip. Fighting the terror and the exhaustion, his right hand cramped, muscles burning, Reed pulled up again, feeling his stump almost come out of the socket. No. No. If he lost the prosthesis now, it would be all over. He needed it for one more goddamn step.

Desperately, but with his last sliver of control, Reed pivoted his stump counterclockwise, pulling up, twisting to exert sideways pressure on the Flex-Foot to work it out of the crack. He felt movement. He levered his stump right, then left, then right again. Another twist, a pull upward, another, his strength almost gone, hanging on with steel will, once more, he pulled up, heard the metal scrape against the rock as the Flex-Foot came free.

But the sudden loss of support almost broke his grip. Now, without thinking, without calculating, now as if the limb were a part of him, as if his sense and estimation and visual memory of its shape and size and components were ingrained, Reed quickly lifted the Flex-Foot higher and still higher, bending, lifting the stump as high as he could without pushing himself too far back off the rock face, turning the Flex-Foot flat, jamming it down into the crevice, regaining his purchase on the rock, positioning it for one more step up, one more step as high as he could to bring him over the outcropping . . . stepping up, pushing the Flex-Foot into the crevice, hearing the sides scrape against the rock, stepping up, his stump pressing deep into the socket, once more, hands pulling, his left thigh and hip burning, one final step up, up and over the hump of the outcropping. Reed fell forward over the top onto nearly level ground.

His stomach and chest hit hard, gravel stung the right side of his face, exhausted, spent, prostrate, out of breath, out of strength, his Flex-Foot still jammed in the crevice, his left hand still wedged in the crease, he had done it. Reed had made it.

THIRTY-THREE

Angela Quist stood at the large steel sink in the Maple Inn kitchen, washing her hands, soaping them over and over. She felt dirty. Violated. Not just because of what Matthew Ullmann had done to her in the basement, but because she had actually started following his orders . . . bringing that first drink to Reed. Asking about his next. She felt as if she had violated herself as much as Ullmann had.

She turned off the hot water, shaking her hands, asking herself, How far have you sold yourself, girl? What are you doing?

She shook her head, grabbed a dish towel, and dried her hands, still shaking her head as if to dispel the mindset she had let Ullmann instill in her. And then she walked out of the kitchen looking for Bill Reed.

She looked for him in the bar, already knowing he wasn't there, but checked anyhow, determined that if he wasn't there she would go to his room, knock on his door, wake him if she had to. Tell him what Ullmann had told her to do. Why? she asked herself. To confess? To be absolved? Redeemed?

She didn't know why. She just knew she had to.

Angela passed through the lobby. Brian, the night man, was on duty. She decided to ask if he'd seen Reed, calculate from his answer if Reed was still awake.

"Brian."

"Yeah, Angela."

"Have you seen Mr. Reed?"

"You mean that guy in the wheelchair?"

"Yes. Mr. Reed," Angela said.

"Angela, that guy surprised the shit out of me."

"How? What did he do?"

"He walked out of here about an hour ago like he was up on two feet, you know. Like he had grown a leg or something. I guess he's got a fake leg."

"He left?"

"Yeah, he hustled out of here. Some kind of emergency."

Angela's face twisted with concern and disbelief. "He went out?"

"He asked me for directions to Clearbrook Hospital."

"The hospital?"

"Yeah."

"When?"

"I'd say about an hour ago."

She felt confused, anxious, but stood in the lobby for only a few seconds before she nearly ran to the kitchen for her coat and car keys. And it wasn't until Angela made the turn onto Crossville Road that she considered how little she had hesitated before setting out after Reed.

By the time she had fired up her old Isuzu Trooper and headed out into the cold night, Angela had decided Reed's departure must have something to do with his cousin. She knew if the cousin had been sent to the hospital, it had to be something serious, something they couldn't take care of at the Ullmann clinic.

But now, as she peered out at the dark road ahead of her, lips pursed in concentration, she began to feel worried about Reed, out alone on these dark roads. None of it felt right.

As if to confirm her fear, a dark mass suddenly loomed into her headlights, blocking the road up ahead. She hit the brakes a little too hard, sending the Trooper into a skid.

She saw just slim glints of taillights, one above the other. And, for some reason, the reflection of her own headlights. She didn't understand, and then as she approached, Angela realized she was looking at a truck flipped over on its side, lying across the road.

The fear hit her viscerally, a cold, jarring sensation in her chest, spreading to the base of her throat making her jaw clench. She knew the moment she saw the truck that someone had died. As she slowly approached the wreck, her car heater pulled in the disconcerting smell of gasoline fumes.

She steered around the flipped-over truck, her left wheels crunched into gravel on the shoulder. She knew it was Raymond Boggs's truck. She didn't look inside. They had come after him again. She had no doubt that Reed had done this. But what had they done to him?

And then she saw the figure on the ground, up near the bridge, lying far enough back on the shoulder so that the body looked as if it would slide down the embankment any moment. She pressed the accelerator. As the form came under the glare of her headlights, she recognized Reed's shearling coat. It was him. Dead? Alive?

"Oh, God," she muttered.

And then the head moved. Alive! But how alive? How badly hurt? What had they done to him?

Only when the glare of the headlights roused him did Bill Reed become aware that he had succumbed to his exhaustion. He had no idea how long he had lain on the rocky ground, but when the headlights roused him, he felt amazingly alert and refreshed, as if making it to the top of the embankment had released an untapped reserve of strength. And now, almost miraculously, a vehicle had appeared. He looked up, clearing his throat to speak, but a woman's voice calling his name stopped him. Angela's voice.

"Bill. Bill!"

He was too stunned to respond. She called out again, "Bill!"

"Yeah," he croaked.

Angela dropped down on her backside and took two tentative, sliding steps toward him, pushing gravel in front of her. A piece of it tumbled into Reed's face. He turned away, yelling, "Hold it. Hold it."

Angela stopped, her hands and heels firmly dug into the dropping shoulder of the road.

"Are you all right? Are you hurt?"

"I'm all right."

"What are you doing lying there? What happened?"

"They ran me off the road. What the hell are *you* doing here?"

Angela peered down at the riverbank. Seeing the BMW nosed into the roiling water below, she yelled, "My God, you went over? How did you get up here?"

"Christ, what does it look like? I climbed, dammit. Back off a second. You're making me nervous."

She offered her right hand. "Well come up the rest of the way. What're you doing just lying there?"

Reed looked at the extended hand, thinking it seemed like a very big hand attached to that delicately tattooed wrist. For a moment, he wondered if Angela were actually strong enough to drag him up to the road.

"Hold on a second, my foot is stuck. Just wait a minute."

Reed positioned his hands under him, thinking about the fact that he had just referred to a piece of metal as his foot.

He pushed himself more upright, braced his right foot flat against the bridge, slid back just a bit until his prosthetic knee bent. Then, as he had done before, but now from the security of lying on a nearly flat surface, he leaned slowly one way, pivoting his stump outward, feeling the stump push against the side of the prosthetic socket, but not worrying about sparking a wave of phantom pain, not fighting the prosthesis, just levering it, working it, sensing somehow through the metal tubes and mechanical joint and plastic socket the pressure necessary to twist his Flex-Foot free. He heard the thin metal sides of the artificial foot scraping, turning in the crevice . . . he levered his stump a bit more and again the Flex-Foot pulled free.

He let out a grunt of relief, and without another word, scrambled and crawled up the rest of the slight incline, not stopping, not saying anything, ignoring Angela's outstretched hand.

She moved alongside him, reaching for his left arm, helping Reed stand once he finally made it onto the shoulder. Two more steps and Reed finally stood on the road. Only then did he reach for Angela, gripping her forearm, holding on to her as he walked toward the Trooper.

He leaned back against Angela's beat-up, old SUV, gripped her upper arm, then her shoulder, straightening up, he turned to face her, left hand on her shoulder, feeling the height of her and the strength of her, smiling now.

"You climbed up that?"

"Yeah."

"With your—"

"Turns out the damn thing is really worth something."

"I don't believe it."

"Neither do I," said Reed.

He lifted his prosthesis, bending the knee joint, placing the Flex-Foot back down on the asphalt as if to demonstrate. Angela just looked at him, her brow furrowed, a little surprised by the metal foot Reed stood on, still unable to grasp the fact that he had somehow plowed down that embankment in his car, survived the plunge, then climbed back up.

Reed smiled, feeling exhilarated now. "Actually, I was about to call you. What brought you here? And don't tell me you have a rope that could've reached down there."

"No, no, I don't have a rope," said Angela. "Do you want to explain any of this?"

Reed opened the door of the Trooper and started to get into the SUV.

"Not until I'm a hell of a lot warmer. Get in."

Reed looked for the fan control on the dashboard as Angela walked around to the driver's side. He found the knob, twisting it to high. The door slammed behind Angela as she climbed into the driver's seat. Reed already had his gloves off and his hands turning in front the hot air blowing out of the vents.

"What made you come here?" he asked.

Angela's face tightened. "Ullmann."

"Ullmann?"

"I didn't tell you. I should have told you. I went looking for you when my shift ended to tell you."

"Tell me what?"

"About Ullmann."

"What about him?"

"He came into the restaurant earlier." She hesitated. "He was nasty, ugly . . . it had to do with you."

"What? What did he say?"

"Said to make sure you did your drinking at the inn. He wanted me to keep tabs on you."

"Make sure I did my drinking at the inn?"

"Yes."

"What does he know about my drinking?"

"I don't know. I guess he knew about the Lincoln Tavern."

"He wanted you to feed me drinks, didn't he?"

"Yes. I'm sorry. He made it sound like he just wanted you kept at the inn. So you wouldn't be out there making trouble. I knew that was bullshit. I didn't know exactly what he had in mind, but I knew that was bullshit. He ordered me to do it. Like he owned me." Angela quickly shook her head as if she could dispel the feeling. "I don't know. I was worried about you so I tried to find you after my shift and then I heard you'd been called to the hospital."

Reed shook his head. "Bastard had it all figured."

"What? What did he have figured?"

"How to get me out here so they could drive me off the goddamn road. They tried to run me off over there, but I managed to prevent that."

Angela peered over at the dark abyss on the left side of the bridge.

"My God, you would've been killed."

"No shit."

"What about the hospital? Is it your cousin?"

"That's what Ullmann said. I don't know if it was just to get me out here, but I can't take that chance. Can you drive me to the hospital?"

"Yeah. Sure."

"Now."

Angela put the Trooper in gear and started off.

Reed rubbed his hands together, flexed his fingers.

"Angela, do me a favor."

"What?"

"Drive as fast as you can."

Angela glanced back at Reed.

"What the hell is going on?"

"I think they're going to try to kill him."

"Your cousin? Why?" She was almost shouting.

"I don't know."

"Why would they want to kill him?"

"Why would they try to kill me?"

"In a hospital?"

Reed's voice raised in emphasis. "You know how many people die in hospitals? I couldn't think of a better place."

"That was Ray's truck back there. He tried to run you off?"

"Yeah. And McAndrews and the sheriff."

Angela glanced at Reed, still unable to take it all in. Reed didn't try to explain any further. She watched him reach back under his coat and pull out the Colt Commander. He popped the magazine out of the handle and checked the number of rounds left.

Angela turned back, keeping her eyes on the road, but she couldn't help glancing over at Reed and the gun. The pistol looked enormous to her.

"What are you doing?" she asked.

Reed finished checking the magazine, then popped it back into the handle, talking to Angela as he slid back the chamber, set the safety, slipped the semiautomatic into his hip holster.

"Angela, you can drop me off at the hospital. And then I think you should leave."

"Leave?"

"Yes."

"What are you going to do?"

"Whatever I have to. You should stay out of it."

"This is crazy. Why don't you just call the state police or something?"

"How far are we from the hospital?"

"You can't do this yourself."

"I can't do it with the state police. I'll be arrested before I can do anything."

"What the hell are you going to do?"

"Get my cousin out of there." Reed paused before he asked, "Listen, when we get into town, I could really use this car. Would it be terrible for you if I dropped you off somewhere, a gas station or something, and maybe you can get a cab back to your place, or some kind of ride. I'm sorry I'm asking this of you. I'll get this car back to you as soon as I can. That's probably the best thing for you to do."

Angela looked at Reed. "This is crazy."

"It is what it is."

"I'm not leaving you alone. How can you get him out of there and away all by yourself?"

"I'll manage," said Reed.

She yelled at him, glancing away from the road to get his attention, to force him to look at her.

"Hey . . . don't give me some macho bullshit. I want to know if you think you really need me or not. Just tell me the fucking truth and let me decide."

"It doesn't matter if I think I need you or not. You have to decide for yourself."

"Bullshit. It matters. Tell me," she yelled.

Reed yelled back, "Yes, yes. I need you. Of course I need you."

That was it. Angela nodded her head once and looked back to the road. The decision had been made.

THIRTY-FOUR

George Prentice drove to the hospital faster than he usually drove. Fast enough to arrive before the ambulance carrying Johnny Boy. Prentice wanted to make sure that Dr. Singh, the emergency-room doctor, didn't get in his way. He pulled into the emergency parking lot just as the ambulance arrived.

Prentice walked into the ER behind the gurney carrying the doubled-over Johnny Boy, his screams having devolved into whining, guttural moans. Prentice told the ER nurse the Ullmann Institute had called him and began giving orders.

Most of what Prentice did during the next half hour had been rehearsed in his mind during the hours he had waited at home after his dinner with Ullmann. The trick was not making it obvious that he already knew the reason Johnny Boy Reed was coming. Prentice could have immediately wheeled him into the OR, but he went through all the procedures, even listening to the ER nurse suggest it might be a burst appendix, and Dr. Singh opine that it was acute pancreatitis.

Prentice performed a thorough exam, ordered blood work, X rays, and notified the operating room to set up for abdominal surgery, all while Johnny Boy lay doubled over, moaning from the sharp, insistent pain twisting inside his abdomen.

Prentice's orders were clear and definite, given so as to create a medical record that would read correctly. And then, despite the fact that Johnny Boy's agonized, stifled screams were enough to prove to every single medical person in the ER that he needed some kind of emergency intervention, Prentice patiently waited for the X rays and test results.

Sheriff Ralph Malone stood at the intake desk, signing off on the ambulance report and making notes in his logbook. He tried to remember the exact time the ambulance had arrived and realized he had no clear recollection of the time because he and Ullmann had sat in Ullmann's office while they wheeled Johnny Boy into the ambulance. Only when they heard the ambulance doors close on Johnny Boy's screaming had Malone stood up to leave. Ullmann hadn't even bothered to walk outside to see the ambulance off. But as Malone walked out of the office, Ullmann called out to him.

"Oh, Ralph, one other thing."

"Yes?"

"When you get to the hospital . . ." Ullmann's voice trailed off.

"When I get to the hospital, what?"

"Uh, make sure you speak to George Prentice. Tell him I said I'm expecting a good job."

"A good job," Malone repeated.

"Yes. And tell him to make sure and keep track of everything."

Ullmann made a motion with his hands as if he were gathering something together floating in the air in front of him.

"Keep track of everything?"

"Yeah. He knows what I mean."

"Okay."

Malone's digital watch read 1:48 A.M. He estimated when the ambulance must have arrived, wrote in the time, and stuffed his logbook in his back pocket. He wanted to simply leave and be done with all this, but he braced himself and headed back toward the intake area to find Prentice and deliver Ullmann's message.

All the examining areas were curtained off, but Malone knew exactly where to go. He could easily hear Johnny Boy, whose cries of pain had turned into mewling sounds that reminded Malone of a beaten dog. At nearly two in the morning in a rural hospital, there were no other patients in the emergency area.

Malone pulled the curtain aside. Johnny Boy lay on an examining table stripped down to his socks and dingy underwear. A blue hospital gown had been slipped over his arms but not tied at the neck. A nurse stood next to Johnny Boy adjusting an IV line. Dr. Singh stood opposite her, palpating Johnny Boy's abdomen, adding to Johnny Boy's agony. Prentice stood away from the group in front of a rack of light boxes attached to the wall. He slid one X ray after another into clips at the top of the light boxes. Even from where he stood at the parted curtain, Malone could see the dark mass embedded in the twisting black and white shape on the illuminated X ray film.

Malone did not want to see this. He was tired, annoyed, and growing tense at the expectation that his radio would crackle at any moment with a report about an accident on Crossville Road, just south of the bridge. The prospect of dealing with two dead bodies, two wrecked vehicles, one at the bottom of an embankment, didn't improve his mood any.

He cleared his throat. "Dr. Prentice."

Prentice turned away from the X rays. The sight of Ralph Malone scowling at him surprised and discomfited him.

"Yes?" he asked, a testy edge to his voice.

Malone's face twitched and grew hard. He motioned with his head for Prentice to come to the other side of the curtain. Prentice hesitated, as if he might defy Malone, but then decided against it and quickly walked over. He came close enough to Malone so that they would not have to speak loudly.

"Yes?"

"A message from Ullmann," Malone said, his voice hard.

"A message?"

"Yeah. Do a good job. Clean it up. Keep track of everything. Nice and neat."

Prentice frowned, but didn't say anything.

Malone pressed, forcing an answer. "Understand?"

Prentice answered quickly, "Yes. Yes, of course. I know."

Malone nodded, glaring at Prentice for just a moment more. He was about to say something when he heard the voice of the nurse at intake yelling, "You can't go back there. It's restricted. Sir! Sir!"

Malone heard the clackety-clack of Reed's Flex-Foot hitting the tiled floor and turned to see Bill Reed striding toward him. Reed, too, had simply followed the disturbing sound of Johnny Boy's guttural moans.

Malone stared at the mechanical foot, at Reed's ungainly stride, and only then at Reed's right hand pressed tight against the side of his right leg, holding the nine-millimeter Colt Commander.

Prentice stepped back.

The intake nurse was five or six paces behind Reed, still yelling for him to stop.

Malone reached for his gun. Too late. Reed had already closed the distance. As the sheriff fumbled with the snap holding his Beretta in its holster, Reed's right hand snapped up, the barrel of the Colt Commander slashed across Malone's face, cracking the thick cartilage in Malone's nose and splitting open his forehead just above his left eye.

Malone's head whipped left, but only for a fraction of a second before Reed backhanded the Colt across the right side of Malone's face, cracking his cheekbone, tearing open a three-inch-long gash.

The steel barrel against bone and flesh made two huge wet cracking sounds. Prentice flinched even though nothing had hit him except flecks of Malone's blood.

Malone sagged to his right, losing consciousness. Reed grabbed him by the hair and yanked him down hard. Malone's head hit the tiled floor with a sickening thud, knocking him out completely.

Prentice had recovered enough from the surprise attack to step back and begin yelling for help. Reed pointed the Colt at him and yelled, "Shut up or I'll shoot you. Don't fucking move."

Prentice squelched a scream, turning it into a yelp, and stood frozen, his hands raised defensively in front of his chest and face, paralyzed by the sight of the big gun pointing at him.

The curtains separating the examining area flew open and Dr. Singh stepped out, the nurse and an orderly close behind him. Reed could see Johnny Boy now, his face twisted with pain, slowly writhing on the emergency-room gurney. Reed looked away and quickly stepped around to Malone's right side, awkwardly lowered his good knee into the middle of Malone's back, the Flex-Foot slipping on the linoleum floor. Holding the Colt in his left hand, Reed unsnapped Malone's handcuff case on the back of his belt and pulled out Malone's cuffs. He snapped a cuff onto Malone's right wrist, but Malone's other hand lay under him. Reed shoved the Colt into his belt and pulled Malone's left wrist out from under him, snapped the cuff tight.

Dr. Singh yelled, "What is going on here? What is going on?" But everyone ignored him.

Once Malone's wrists were cuffed behind his back, Reed squeezed them as tight as possible over Malone's wrist bones. And then, very quickly, Reed pulled out Malone's police baton and threaded it over and under Malone's elbows. The whole time he did this, Reed kept his gaze on Prentice and the others, freezing them in place.

Reed stood up, trying to balance himself, wary of the metal Flex-Foot on the floor, and pulled out his gun. Malone started to come around, unaware that his hands had been cuffed and his arms skewered with the baton. So much blood streamed from his forehead and cheek that Malone's face lay in a puddle of it. When he exhaled, the blood on the floor bubbled. He twisted around to look up at Reed, smearing blood across the floor and his face. Blinking away the gore, he tried to get up, realizing now he was handcuffed, rolled on his side to get his legs under him, but Reed bent down and grabbed the baton, pulling up sharply, forcing Malone facedown onto the bloody floor.

"Don't fucking move," Reed snarled. "You're under arrest."

Reed straightened up and stepped toward Johnny Boy. The others instinctively moved away from him. As Reed came closer, seeing Johnny Boy's twisted face, hearing the grunting wails, he yelled at Prentice, "What did you do to my cousin? What's wrong with him?"

Prentice, out of fear, yelled back, panicked, "Nothing. We did nothing. He's very sick."

Johnny Boy had curled back into a fetal position, his legs writhing involuntarily. Reed stepped to Johnny Boy's side and laid a hand on his shoulder, trying to gently push him onto his back. Reed bent closer, putting his face near Johnny Boy's.

"John. John, it's okay. I'm here. It's me, Bill."

Johnny Boy could not focus through the pain. He looked at Reed, but it seemed as if he could not see him.

Reed straightened up and turned to Prentice who had started to back out of the treatment area.

"What the hell is the matter with him?" Reed demanded.

Prentice's hands fluttered toward the X rays hanging from the light boxes.

"He's got a tumor. It's blocked his colon. Nothing can pass through. He's impacted. It has to be removed. He'll die if we don't do it. Look, can't you see? Look."

Prentice stepped toward the X rays, frantically pointing.

Reed squinted at the X rays. "A tumor? What the hell are you talking about?"

Johnny Boy's guttural moans made it difficult for Reed to concentrate. He squeezed Johnny Boy's shoulder as if he could assuage his pain and stop the maddening grunts of pain.

Prentice kept pointing at the dark mass on the X ray.

"It's here. Look, look," Prentice yelled over Johnny Boy's moans.

Reed felt Johnny Boy clutch at his hand. He looked down and saw Johnny Boy's teary eyes staring at him, seeming now to recognize Reed.

"It's all right, John. It's all right."

Reed tried to smile at Johnny Boy, but his face tightened into a grimace. The antiseptic hospital smells, the bright lights, the medical personnel, the memories of his own trauma and hospitalization, and Johnny Boy's agonized grunts made Reed feel as if his head were going to explode.

Reed grabbed the gurney and started to push it out of the examining area. Prentice remained frozen near the X rays, but Dr. Singh, a stocky, dark-skinned man with thick glasses, grabbed the foot of the gurney and yelled in his refined Pakistani accent, "What are you doing? Stop. Stop now. This patient cannot be moved."

Reed pushed again. His Flex-Foot slipped on the hard floor. He felt off balance, weak, confused.

Prentice joined in, "We have to operate. There's no choice."

"Where are you going?" said Dr. Singh. "This is nonsense."

Reed shoved the gurney at Dr. Singh and released his grip, as if he were handing over Johnny Boy. He bent down close to Johnny Boy and gently grabbed his face, feeling the stubble of Johnny Boy's slight beard, the softness of his skin, the wet of his tears. He put his face close to his cousin's and said softly but enunciating each word. "John. It's going to be okay, John. It's going to be okay."

Reed kept repeating it until he made eye contact, until he was sure Johnny Boy heard him, understood him. Johnny Boy blinked, holding back his wails, twisting his broad face in an effort to squelch his pain and fear. He managed to nod at Reed. Reed managed to smile, feeling his own eyes stinging with tears. He squeezed Johnny Boy's face and said, "Don't worry. You'll be okay. Promise."

Then he gently released his grip on Johnny Boy and turned toward George Prentice. Reed moved awkwardly around the gurney, ignoring the pain of his sore stump, banishing the sounds of Johnny Boy's pain. Somewhere far off to his left voices yelled. He sensed footsteps running his way, but Reed ignored everything, locking eyes with Prentice, advancing toward him until Prentice stepped backward and bumped up against the light boxes. Reed stepped close enough to George Prentice so that their faces almost touched, his eyes boring into Prentice's.

"You going to take it out?"

"Yes."

"You?"

"Yes."

"What are you going to do?" he asked, each word slowly enunciating through clenched teeth.

Prentice's voice shook slightly. "We excise the tumor,

biopsy it while we're in the operating room, eliminate the blockage, take out the impacted fecal matter, check for any metastasis of the tumor, check for loss of blood supply to the colon, take out what we have to . . . a section of his colon, lymph nodes. Devise a colostomy. Or reattach the colon. I'll have to see. But we have to operate. There's no choice."

"You said there was nothing wrong with him."

Prentice stammered, "I didn't know."

Reed yelled, "I don't believe you."

His face still inches from Prentice's, Reed slowly, carefully, took out his nine-millimeter Colt Commander and pressed the muzzle of the gun firmly against George Prentice's temple, pushing it hard enough so that Prentice bent away from the muzzle.

"You do it right, Doctor. You take care of this man. You don't make any mistakes. Do you understand?"

Prentice nodded.

"He dies, you die. Anything happens to him, I will find you and I will kill you. Do you believe me?"

"Yes," Prentice said.

Reed yelled, "Do you?!" as he jabbed the gun into Prentice's temple.

"Yes! Yes!" Prentice yelled, his face constricted by fear.

Slowly, Reed eased up the pressure on the gun. When he finally pulled away, the muzzle left an indentation on the side of Prentice's head.

Reed stepped away, looking around him now, seeing the others staring at him, shocked, immobilized by fear.

Malone had managed to roll onto his side, blinking away the blood dripping into his eyes, but he only glared at Reed saying nothing.

Reed felt the anger flow out of him, replaced by concern and a strange feeling of sadness and resignation. He knew he had no choice. Reed looked at the nurse, frightened but standing her ground. "It's going to be okay, isn't it?" It sounded more like a command than a question.

She nodded.

Reed prompted. "He's going to be fine, right?"

"Yes," she said. "Yes. We'll take good care of him."

Reed looked at Dr. Singh, the emergency-room doctor. "He's going to be fine, right, Doc?"

"Yes, yes, of course."

Reed nodded, stepped back, and kissed Johnny Boy's forehead. Then he walked out of the examining area, his gait offset, favoring his left side, feeling now every painful step.

THIRTY-FIVE

Angela Quist had done as Reed instructed, remaining parked on the street across from the emergency-room entrance, engine on, lights off. Angela looked away from the emergency-room doors to glance at her watch. It seemed to her as if Reed had been in the hospital for at least a half hour, but the watch told her it had only been fifteen minutes. The urge to drive up to the entrance and see what was happening almost overwhelmed her, but just then she saw Reed backing out of the entrance, his gun extended in front of him, stepping awkwardly.

She immediately pulled the gearshift into drive, but kept her foot on the brake, staying put, waiting for Reed's signal.

He was yelling something at somebody inside the hospital, pointing his gun at them. Angela had the impression he was warning someone to stay inside.

Finally, he turned, but he still didn't signal her. He walked across the parking area hop/stepping quickly but awkwardly, heading through the parking lot and across a strip of lawn between the lot and the street. Even from where she sat, Angela could hear Reed's metal foot clacking on the pavement. Still, Reed did not signal her, but Angela knew that the fastest way out of the area lay in the other direction, so keeping her lights off she drove into a slow U-turn that would bring her to Reed's side of the street, facing the opposite direction.

She saw Reed watch her move as he came closer, nodding his head. She pulled up in front of him just as he reached the street, the passenger side door now facing him. Reed quickly climbed into the Trooper saying, "Keep your lights off and let's get the hell out of here."

Angela accelerated, swerving slightly as she pulled away from the curb.

"Was your cousin in there?"

Reed answered grimly, "Yes."

"Is he . . . ?"

"No. He's not okay. He's a mess, but I had to leave him there." Reed shook his head. "I'll tell you about it later. Listen, I think pulling across the street like that might have let someone see your vehicle."

"I had my lights off. They couldn't get my plate."

"What's the connection between me and an Isuzu Trooper?"

Angela winced. "Shit. What did you do in there?"

"Never mind. As far as you know, I asked you to drive me to the hospital because my cousin was in there. That's all."

Angela shook her head. "You didn't shoot anybody, did you?"

"No." Reed motioned toward the dashboard. "Turn your lights on and drive normally. How many deputy sheriffs does Malone have?"

"I don't know. Ten, twelve, I don't know."

Reed grunted, thinking. "However many there are, they'll all be out soon. At this time of night there won't be much other traffic. I think you'd better get off this main road."

Angela braked almost immediately and turned right onto a side road.

"Dammit, what did you do in there?"

"Do you know where you are?" Reed asked.

"Vaguely."

"You have a map of this area?"

"Yeah. There's a map of the county in the glove compartment."

"When you get to the next crossroad, let's stop and figure out where we are."

"What happened in there?"

Reed shuffled through the maps in Angela's glove compartment until he found the right one, unfolding it, waiting for Angela to stop the car.

"Goddammit, are you going to tell me?" she asked.

Reed did not answer, staring straight ahead, his face blank as if he were lost in thought.

Angela said, "Bill, I want to know what I'm facing."

Reed pointed ahead and said, "Hey, there's a crossroad. Let's pull over. See if there are signs for these roads."

Angela steered the Trooper onto the shoulder of the narrow road, parallel to a set of signs reading Reservoir Street and Water Street.

Reed peered at the signs, then turned on the overhead light and began checking the map.

Angela yelled, "Reed. *Answer* me."

"I'd like to get you out of this. Find a motel where you can drop me off, then you go home and make like this never happened."

"You sure they're not going to come after me?"

"No. But so what? Nobody saw you there. Nobody saw you with me. You go home, if they come to your door you deny everything."

"And they just go away. They try to kill you, but me, they'll just leave alone."

"You haven't done anything to them."

"What did *you* do back there?"

Reed turned to Angela, speaking evenly. "I pistol-whipped and handcuffed that fucking sheriff and put a gun to Dr. George Prentice's head and told him I'd kill him if he did anything to hurt my cousin."

Angela turned away, shaking her head slowly.

"Go home, Angela. Tell them the truth. Tell them you didn't know."

"And what did I do with you? Where did I drop you off? If I say I dropped you off in Greenport, and they find you someplace else, they'll know you couldn't have gotten there any other way. They'll catch me lying. They'll throw me in jail. Ullmann will throw my sister out of there. They'll ruin me."

Reed grimaced, seeing now how the string of lies would entrap Angela. He muttered a curse, trying to think his way out of it. "I'll take you back to the main road. Wait for a deputy. Tell them you gave me a ride, I came out of the hospital crazed, forced you out of your car—"

"How did I hook up with you in the first place? What was I doing out on Crossville Road in the middle of the night picking you up off the side of the road? Ralph Malone will catch the lies. He'll bury me."

Finally, Reed just said, "I'm sorry. I don't know what to tell you. I'm sorry."

Angela shook her head. "No. I don't want your apologies. I want you to get me out of this. If that sheriff tried to kill you tonight, if you think they're trying to harm your cousin, you call in the state police or the FBI or whoever you think can stop them. I'm not leaving your side until those people are locked up, you understand?"

Reed looked at Angela, returning her intense gaze. "I understand. Do you understand what you're saying?"

"What do you mean?"

"I can't call in any law enforcement until I've got evidence. Right now, I'm the one they'll arrest first."

Angela stared at Reed, taking in what he had said.

Reed continued, "I won't be able to do anything if I'm locked up. I won't be able to do anything for me or you or your sister or my cousin if I'm locked up."

Reed could see the anger well up in her, but recede as she thought it through.

"All right. All right. What do you want to do right now?"

"Find someplace we can hide out. I need a place where there's a phone, where I can operate."

Angela reached over. "Give me that map for a second. I know where we are better than you."

Reed handed her the map and watched her quickly zero in on their location, tracing a route from there with her index finger. She checked her watch and grimaced at the time. "Two o'clock, shit, we're going to have to wake up this guy."

"What guy?" asked Reed.

"His name is Tim Koons. He owns a set of condos back toward Dumphy. I built some mantelpieces for him last spring. Nice guy."

"What can he do for us?"

"He has a bunch of condos he rents during ski season. Maybe he'll open one of them for us tonight."

"Will he do that for you?"

"Might as well ask."

"Will he lie for you?"

"What do you mean?"

"If the sheriff's department calls and asks if anybody checked in, will he say no?"

Angela thought about it for a second, then said, "I don't know. Maybe. His operation is closed until ski season starts up. I don't even see why they'd check him. Plus, he's back near Dumphy, but west on the other side of the county line."

Reed nodded.

"It's the only place I can think of."

"Okay. How long will it take us to get there?"

"We can use back roads most of the way, about thirty, forty minutes."

"Hmmm."

"Do you have cash? I don't think he'll want to mess around with credit cards."

"I have cash." Reed grimaced, realizing that his cash was at the inn, along with everything else he needed. "Shit. I need the stuff in my room."

"You really have to go back there?"

"Yeah. My computer, money, clothes"—Reed raised his prosthesis—"another shoe for this thing. All of it."

Angela dropped the map on the floor of the Trooper, switched off the overhead light, and drove off. Reed watched Angela consider the problem. She looked at her watch again.

"Don't you think the sheriff's people will be over there?"

"Yeah. Eventually, but if I were Malone, I'd have all my men out on the roads leading away from that hospital. No way I could have gotten back there yet."

Angela said, "All right. We'll call Brian. Tell him there's a family emergency, you have to check out. Leave your stuff at the service entrance. Tell him you'll call him to open up the door. But I have a key. We'll just go in and get it in case any of Malone's men are watching."

Reed pulled out the Colt and chambered a round, set the safety and shoved it back in his holster.

"I don't give a shit who's watching. I need my stuff. What about you? You need clothes or anything?"

"I'm not going anywhere near my house. There's a washer and dryer in the condo, that's all I need."

Reed nodded, then leaned forward and opened the glove box, grabbed the long tube that ran from his knee joint to the Flex-Foot and pulled the prosthesis toward him, folding it tightly, pitching his stump upward. He shoved the mechanical foot into the glove box to hold his stump in place.

Angela glanced at Reed's maneuvering.

"Don't worry," said Reed. "There's not much weight on the box. I just have to prop my stump up, try to keep it from swelling. It's really started to swell in the socket."

"Why don't you just take it off for a while?"

"It's not that easy to get back on."

"Oh."

Reed laid his head back on the headrest, trying to sound friendly he asked, "So you figure what, about a half hour?"

Angela's eyes never left the road. "About that."

"You okay?" Reed asked.

"Yeah."

Just before Reed's eyes fluttered closed, he said, "Thanks."

By the time Matthew Ullmann stormed into Clearbrook Hospital's emergency room, George Prentice had just finished stitching up Ralph Malone's face. Johnny Boy was being prepped and readied for surgery. And George Prentice was showing signs of emotional exhaustion.

Ullmann found Prentice and Malone in a small side office down the hall from the main emergency intake area. Ullmann made sure to close the door after him before he spoke, but when he turned toward Malone, the sight silenced him.

Malone sat on the edge of an examining table giving orders into his police radio. His unbuttoned sheriff's shirt was still wet with blood, enough blood to soak through and stain the white T-shirt underneath. Two ragged trails of black stitches had pulled closed the gashes on Malone's forehead and cheek, but the skin on either side of the bloody black stitches had already begun to discolor into ugly purplish bruises. Malone's nose had swelled to the point where he had difficulty breathing, and the skin under his eyes had darkened. He looked like he'd been in a car accident.

Prentice stood near a sink off to the side, dropping bloody pieces of gauze, a syringe, needle, and suture thread into a stainless-steel pan.

"I didn't expect to be called here," said Ullmann.

Malone finished speaking into his radio and looked up. "I didn't expect to get pistol-whipped and handcuffed."

"May I ask what the hell is going on?"

"Your friend Mr. Reed. I don't know how he did it. I left him at the bottom of that ravine in a wreck, but somehow he managed to show up here and get the drop on me. Maybe somebody pulled him up out of there. Doesn't matter. This isn't just between you and him anymore. Everybody here seen it. Now it's sheriff's department business. Now I'm going to kill him personally. Me. You can keep your idiot proctors and yourself well out of it now, sir. Your plan didn't work, Mr. Ullmann."

Ullmann lifted his chin. "My plan?"

"Yes, sir. And I paid the price for it."

"I see." Ullmann turned to Prentice who had remained

standing off to the side. "And what about you, George? How has your side of this gone?"

"He's up in the OR. Being prepped. They're probably ready for me now."

"Then what are you doing here?"

"We have a problem, Matthew. A rather significant one as far as I'm concerned."

"What's that?"

"That man Reed put a gun to my head. He promised to kill me if anything happens to his cousin. I have no doubt he'll try to make good on his threat."

Ullmann twitched a smile, looking back and forth at Malone and Prentice. "So that's it." He pointed to them one by one. "You paid the price. And you have a problem."

Neither of the men responded.

Ullmann stepped forward, his voice constricting as he struggled to keep from screaming at them. "Let me tell you something. Let me explain this very, very carefully." Pointing again at Malone, "If you don't do what you're supposed to do and get rid of Bill Reed"—he pointed to Prentice—"and if you don't get up into that operating room and slice whatever you have to slice to get rid of Johnny Boy Reed, we will *all* be dead. The people involved here will not hesitate to eliminate any connections to them if this gets one scintilla more out of hand."

Ullmann's eyes began bulging from the suppressed rage. Struggling to contain himself, he had started speaking in a low voice to keep from shouting. "Do you realize how close you are to losing everything? We have years of effort at stake. *Years.* I can't have this; *we* can't have this. I don't give a damn if my plan didn't work. Make up your own plan. You had him at the bottom of a ravine and you left him there? Why didn't you go down and put a bullet in his head? Or in his gas tank. Something. Anything. You let him walk away from it and you blame me?

"And you, you dare stand there whining to me about a threat? Do you realize what our associates will do to you if any problem, *any* problem shows itself? I've already notified them for God's sake. They're coming to pick up a body and the tissue samples in the morning. In six, seven hours!"

"Matthew, why is everything so rushed? The poor man is going to die in a matter of weeks, a month or two at the outside. You're putting us in terrible jeopardy doing this."

"You're already in jeopardy, you idiot! The man is retarded. He has a relative who knows something is terribly wrong with this picture. An armed, ex–FBI agent. Are you crazy? How many more times do you think he can see his cousin before Johnny Boy says something and he figures out what's going on here? How many more times must I explain this to you? Go up there and get rid of him. Now!"

"But the staff, they heard it. They saw that man warn me, threaten me. He threatened them, too. He made them swear—"

Ullmann's voice raised a level. "There's no discussion, George. No choice. Go. Now. Do it."

Prentice opened his mouth once, then closed it, realizing there was nothing he could say to Ullmann. Ullmann pointed his finger at Prentice, "Don't even think about not doing you're part, George, or *I'll* kill you. Go."

Prentice, tight-lipped, left without another word.

When the door shut, Ullmann turned to Malone. "I can't have this man out there running loose, Ralph."

"Like I already said, it'll be done."

"You think Reed is going to go to the state police?"

"I doubt it. He'd be the first one arrested." Malone pointed to his face. "You think I need any more evidence than this? And he's the one who shot up Ray's truck. Might even be one of his bullets in Boggs for all I know. Nothing connects me to that accident except his accusations."

Ullmann spun away from Malone, pacing in the small office. "How the hell did he get out of that wreck? You said he was thirty feet down."

"Wasn't that steep on the east side of the bridge. The car made it down in one piece. Maybe he climbed up."

"On one leg?" Ullmann yelled.

"He looked like he had two legs when he came in here. Had an artificial leg on."

"This is unbelievable," said Ullmann. "How did he get to the hospital? Did he carry his car up, too?"

"Security guy out front said he thinks he saw a Jeep pick Reed up out in front of the hospital."

"A Jeep?"

"Saw somethin'. Reed held 'em back in the ER at gunpoint when he left. But they looked out as soon as he walked off."

"Who has a Jeep?"

"Angela Quist drives a Trooper. And old one. Boxy, like a Jeep. I figure it was her. He met with her this morning."

"How do you know?"

"I staked out the road leading from her house. I saw him comin' away from her place."

"You didn't think you should have told me about that?"

Malone shrugged.

Ullmann shook his head. "I don't believe this. You think she helped him out of that ravine? I don't believe it! How did she even know he was there? Why? How stupid can she be?"

Malone didn't answer.

"You have someone over there checking on her?"

"I will as soon as I get enough of my people on the road looking for her car. We'll get to it. If she's home, she ain't goin' anywhere. If she's on the road, we'll find her."

Ullmann continued pacing. "Reed wouldn't be stupid enough to go back to the inn."

"Not likely. But I'll get someone over there to check it out."

Ullmann stopped pacing.

"All right. All right. Obviously, we've underestimated Mr. Reed. But it's not that bad. In fact, now it's better. Have they called in the accident yet?"

"I have one of my deputies coming over on that road. He'll see it."

"Good. Good thinking. So we have Mr. Reed shooting at Ray Boggs, causing his truck to overturn, maybe killing him. We have him coming in here, assaulting you, armed, threatening to kill Prentice and the others."

Malone interrupted, "He didn't threaten to kill the others."

"Whatever. We have more than we need. You give your people orders to shoot this man on sight. He's armed. He's dangerous. There'll be no doubt it was justified."

"No doubt whatsoever. If they don't shoot 'im, I will."

"But how are you going to find him?" asked Ullmann.

"We'll find him," said Malone. "How far is he going to go? He's got to be around to see about his cousin. Prentice does his cousin tonight, the man will come looking for him."

"Good. That's fine. Let him. Let Prentice be the bait. We kill him coming after George Prentice. Perfect. What do we do in the meantime?"

"Check Angela Quist's house. Check every motel and hotel in the area. You want to get your proctors in on that, be my guest. You just keep them on a short leash. You tell me if they find him, they call me in. Nobody goes near him. Even my men find him, they have orders to wait for me unless he starts shooting. No more mistakes."

"No. Right. Okay. And what about Ms. Quist, that fucking whore?" Ullmann growled.

Malone shrugged. "She gets caught in the line of fire, too bad. She shouldn't be hanging around people like Mr. Reed. If it wasn't her helped him"—Malone shrugged—"she's not a factor."

"Okay," said Ullmann. "Okay. We've got to wrap this up, Ralph. Tonight."

"Understood."

"Fine." Ullmann paused, looking at Malone. He squinted, trying to project concern. "Sorry about . . . your face."

Malone. "You haven't seen sorry, yet, Mr. Ullmann."

THIRTY-SIX

The phone call that had summoned Matthew Ullmann to Clearbrook Hospital had disturbed his wife Madeleine. Ralph Malone hadn't said much over the phone, but it had been very clear that there were problems. Matthew had grumbled his way out of bed, refusing to explain anything, which had left Madeleine to wonder what had gone wrong.

Such things, however, never kept Madeleine Ullmann awake. She simply resorted to a fantasy that always relaxed her, never failed to occupy her mind, and pleased her so much that she always forgot her troubles and fell into a blissful sleep.

The fantasy began with her calculating the amount of her present holdings spread out over fifteen different accounts at the brokerage company. She would total up all the accounts, then Madeleine would imagine investing everything, margined to the hilt on an incredibly successful stock investment. It was easy to imagine. In the last few years, so many stocks had increased two, three, four, five hundred percent. She settled on a return of one thousand percent. Why not? She would add the zeroes to her millions. Like counting sheep, she would count the dollars, multiplying and multiplying with each successful investment, all margined to the hilt until the numbers rose from tens of millions to hundreds of millions to a thousand million . . . to one billion dollars.

She would stop at a billion. The number suited her perfectly.

But the fantasy didn't stop with acquiring the billion. That was just the beginning. After she pictured the thousand million dollars, Madeleine would mentally divide the thousand million into five lots of two hundred million dollars. Then she would imagine herself meeting with avaricious money managers who would compliment her and fawn over her as they vied over the right to manage her millions, making grandiose but measured promises, calculating the huge management fees and commissions they would earn on two hundred million dollars, and all the while Madeleine Ullmann would never let any of the managers know she controlled not one pile of two hundred million, but five!

She saw herself in their lavish conference rooms, demanding more and more financial plans be presented to her, forcing them to dig deeper and deeper for compliments and flattery. And then, as she felt herself relaxing in her bed under the wonderful fantasy, she would begin to imagine the best part. She always saved that part for just before she nodded off to sleep—what the money would buy.

She would start by being very, very conservative in estimating the overall return from her carefully invested billion dollars. Ten percent. She would calculate ten percent, but underneath relish the conviction that the return would be more like fifteen or twenty percent, or even thirty percent in a good year. Maybe even thirty-five or forty percent.

She would toy with this notion of a large return, and then she would settle on ten percent. It made the rest of the fantasy that much more real. Even at only a paltry ten percent, she thought, that would amount to one hundred million dollars a year in income. The very notion of it enthralled her so much that her mind would be released from every single one of her concerns . . . the constant disgust she felt dealing with all the idiots she had to order around each day. The ignominy of caring for the retarded residents of the Ullmann Institute, people she considered barely human with their grotesque faces and bodies, their speech impediments and impossible hygiene and insufferable retardation . . . all of her cares vanished, even the late night phone call from Ralph Malone, all of it vanished under the power of her fantasy.

Madeleine would fall blissfully asleep thinking about all the things she could do with that money, one hundred million dollars, coming into her account every single year. She would picture the luxuriously furnished condominium overlooking the Charles River in Boston, the ocean-front home on seven-mile beach in Grand Cayman—the tax-free haven where she and Matthew would hide a portion of their millions, a warm place that would be the antidote for the endless days of bitter cold she had suffered through in the North Country. Her favorite residence, however, was the palatial apartment in Paris. Not to mention the elegant hotel suites in all the major capitals of the world where she would be fawned over by obsequious hotel staff and concierges. One hundred million dollars a year, every year, could buy a great deal of service and comfort.

The restaurants, the fine foods, museums, theater, openings, and galas . . . she would picture herself enjoying all of it. And the money spent on it would mean nothing to her, nothing, because she would have so much more pouring in, accumulating faster than she could spend it.

And, of course, they would donate to charities. Serve on various boards. They would only have to give away one or two million a year, a pittance, and they would be welcomed by any number of prestigious groups and famous people . . . all of them grateful, thankful to Madeleine Ullmann for her wonderful generosity and humanitarianism.

Such a lovely, welcoming, wonderful fantasy. Made all the more wonderful by the fact that Madeleine Ullmann knew she wasn't really all that far away from making most of her fantasy come true. Of course, she would never have the billion, never be able to sit back and watch the incredible one hundred million dollars a year pour in. But soon, within the next couple of years, before her sixtieth birthday, Madeleine Ullmann promised herself she would have enough millions to buy the reality of her fantasy. Enough millions to reach her dream destinations, enough millions to live her dream lifestyle every day of her life until she died. She had calculated that soon she would have enough to last her until she was at least ninety years old. She would spend it all, every penny. She would be fat and happy and coddled and rich. Soon. Soon.

The fantasy made her so happy. And it made the electronic bleating of the phone so cruel when it suddenly shattered Madeleine's fanciful dreams.

She fairly snarled into the phone, "What?"

Matthew Ullmann hadn't expected less.

"Sorry to wake you, dear. No choice."

Madeleine cleared her throat, remembering now that Matthew had been called out earlier.

"Yes, right. What's the matter? What time is it?"

"A little after three I'm afraid."

"Problems?"

"Several, actually. No need to discuss them now. I want you to call Eddie. Tell him to get a few of the fellows he can trust and meet me at the lumberyard warehouse in about an hour."

Madeleine grimaced at the effort it took to not ask questions. "Okay. An hour."

"And if he gives you any problem or says he can't get the others—"

Madeleine interrupted sharply. "He's not going to give me any trouble." After a pause she blurted out, "How bad is it, Matthew?"

"It's not good. But nothing we can't handle. If everyone does as they're told. And one other thing."

"What?"

"About Orenberg. It might be wise to call him and give him a slightly revised time schedule. Don't say anything to alarm him. Just try to push your meeting back a bit."

"How far back?"

"See if you can buy a day."

"A day? No, that's too much. He won't tolerate that."

"All right, all right, Madeleine, do what you can. It's already been a long night. I don't want to argue about it. Call Eddie, go back to sleep, call Orenberg in the morning. Good night."

Madeleine Ullmann's right cheek twitched with tension and her face twisted as if she had just tasted something slightly rotten. She dialed Eddie McAndrews's phone number, almost hoping he would complain about being called out again.

Dr. George Prentice stood under the intense, full-spectrum glare of the operating room overhead light. Prentice always sweated during surgery. It usually took about thirty or forty minutes before the sweat began to soak through his green surgical mask. But this time, Prentice hadn't even cut down through the final layers of fat and viscera, he had not even exposed the outside wall of Johnny Boy's colon, and his surgical mask already bore a half-moon crescent of sweat. The work of surgery was bad enough, but coupled with the strain of choosing between Reed's bullet and Ullmann's threat it was nearly impossible for Prentice to concentrate on his work.

He had to perform major surgery while trying to figure a way to escape from an impossible situation. At one moment, he decided to kill Johnny Boy, and would begin thinking about how to do it. The rural hospital could not provide a large surgical staff, particularly in the middle of the night, but there was still a surgical nurse standing next to him and an anesthesiologist just a few feet away. He could do it. He could get away with it.

And then he would change his mind, thinking it was crazy to try this. They would know. And that man Reed would come after him. Sure, he'd have to get past Ralph Malone and his men, but why take that chance?

Prentice forced it out of his mind. Watch what you're doing, he told himself. See what you're dealing with first, he told himself. Maybe this cancer will solve your problem for you.

Reed woke with a start when Angela tapped his shoulder. They were parked on a residential street behind the Maple Inn. Angela had turned off the SUV's engine.

Reed blinked himself to full awake. It seemed startlingly

quiet to him . . . no traffic sounds, no birds or insects in the cold night air, no far-off barking dog. Not even any wind stirring the limbs of trees in the quiet neighborhood. Reed pulled his Flex-Foot out of the glove compartment and sat up. He peered at the back of the Maple Inn, seeing nothing but a single light fixture illuminating the back entrance.

"No sign of any deputies?" Reed asked.

"No," said Angela. "At least not back here."

Reed pulled the Colt out of his hip holster and stuck it under his belt in front. "How long've you been parked here?"

"Just pulled up."

"Okay, drive up to the door. We'll load the damn trunk and my chair and get the hell out of here."

They had the trunk loaded up and in the Isuzu in less than thirty seconds. It took another ten seconds to disassemble and load the wheelchair.

Angela drove away from the inn along back streets until she reached the edge of town. She pulled up to the main road and looked around.

"We're going to have to make a run for it on this road for a while. There's no other way over there."

"You sure this guy is going to open up a place for us?"

"He said he would."

"Why is he being so cooperative?"

Angela looked at Reed as if it were a stupid question. He repeated it anyway.

"Why?"

"He likes me that's why. Is that so hard to understand?"

Reed squinted one eye at her. "Is there any guy in this county that you don't have wrapped around your finger?"

Angela said, "Yeah, you and Matthew Ullmann for starters. What're you complaining about?" She pulled out onto the highway and accelerated. "He's renting us a two-bedroom condo in the middle of the night and waiting up to give us the key."

"Who's complaining?"

Prentice continued, cutting, clamping, working his way down into the depths of Johnny Boy's abdominal cavity. He forced himself to put the prospect of murder out of his mind, compartmentalize it, defer his decision, just forget about it until he had the first part done . . . removing the tumor. No matter what he decided, they needed the tumor.

He had worked methodically, following a well-planned procedure, exposing the intestinal tract, clamping off the section affected, ready now to slice open the colon and expose the cancerous mass growing inside. Prentice had seen many, many cancerous tumors . . . horrifying, ugly growths whose presence were such an invariable harbinger of pain and death.

He made the incision. Began clearing out the impacted fecal matter. Irrigating the area. Probing, cutting, peeling back the viscera, getting ready to expose the tumor. He was prepared for the deadly sight again, but this time was different. The cancerous growth appeared so unusual that for the first time in almost two hours, he stopped thinking about anything but the surgery.

He had never seen a cancerous growth quite like it . . . one discrete tumor with a small finger extending from the main mass, almost like a tentative offshoot or root. But the mass had none of the ragged, unruly, infesting aspects of most of the tumors Prentice had seen. It seemed unusually hardened and contained, obviously the result of the experimental cancer drug that had been used to treat Johnny Boy. If Prentice hadn't known for sure that cancer cells had originally been planted at this very spot in Johnny Boy's colon, he might have hoped the growth was benign.

Fascinating, he thought, the drug seems to have worked. The doctors in Boston will be very anxious to see this. Prentice excised a slice of the amazing tumor, leaving most of the mass attached to the wall of the colon. Normally, a pathologist would be on call to examine the tissue for malignancy. At this time of night, there was no pathologist on duty. Prentice would do the examination himself under the microscope next door. So much the better. Don't want this falling into the wrong hands. Don't need anybody getting all worked up about this.

Prentice excised the six-inch section of Johnny Boy's cancerous colon containing the tumor, laying it carefully on a tray behind him. He turned back to the open, prostrate figure. With the tumor so compact, he could easily reattach the colon. Neither of the ends were inflamed or compromised, so there would be nothing suspicious about foregoing a colostomy. And just then, as he envisioned the procedure to reattach the colon, a plan came to him.

So simple. So obvious. A way out of this dilemma, a way out of the whole horrible mess, came to him all at once. He had been thinking about a way to kill Johnny Boy. He had considered nicking an artery, but ruled it out as too clumsy. He'd not only have to appear as if he made a blunder, he would have to compound it by working too slowly to fix it. No. Not his style. He had considered introducing air into the venous system via the liver, but it would have meant using a syringe . . . something that didn't belong during this procedure. The surgical nurse might easily see it.

He told himself he had missed the obvious because he had been thinking too small, too narrow. He could see that now. He had let that stupid bully Ullmann set the parameters. Ridiculous. There was more to be done here, thought Prentice. Handle this thing the right way, with some style, some intelligence. A little finesse.

Of course, this isn't without risk, he told himself. But now realizing a way out, knowing what it meant, Prentice believed it was the best way. Eat your cake and have it, too, he thought. Silly phrase. Doesn't mean anything. It's really the opposite. If you have it, you can eat it. But if you eat it, you can't have it. You can't have it all, thought Prentice. But I don't want it all. I just want a small piece of happiness. I want Alan. And he wants me. Alan will go along with my plan. He loves me and I love him. A private, protected, secret love. So why not? It won't be as comfortable as it might have been if all had gone as planned, but so what? We'll survive. Together.

It's time, thought Prentice, definitely time.

Prentice left the operating room with his tissue sample to use the office next door. Too bad about the patient. He could have probably survived the whole thing. Ah well, someone lives, someone dies. I do regret it's going to be so painful for him.

Thirty-seven

The condominium development consisted of fifteen two-story buildings, each one containing from two to six units built in scattershot clumps up the side of a mountain ridge. The condo assigned to Reed and Angela lay halfway up the ridge on the far edge of the property, a two-unit structure with their unit facing away from the service road.

Angela stopped at a house about a half mile from the condominium to get the key from the owner. Reed stayed in the Trooper, watching a tall man, barefoot in jeans, wearing a down vest, silhouetted at his front door. He handed Angela a set of keys and a brown paper bag of groceries. Their conversation was brief, Reed watching to see if it ended with a handshake or a kiss on the cheek. It ended with neither. Angela simply turned away from the closing door and came back to the driver's seat.

As she settled into the Trooper, Reed asked, "You think he'll cover for us if he gets a call?"

"I doubt if he'll have to. He's shutting off his phone ringer until the morning. But like I said, there's no reason to call him. He isn't even open for the season yet."

"Right."

"He's a good guy. He even gave me some stuff for breakfast tomorrow."

"That's nice."

"He said there might be some canned goods in the kitchen up there."

"Are you hungry?" Reed asked.

"I'm goddamn starving," said Angela. "I get hungry when I get nervous."

Angela found the condominium unit without a missed turn, drove the Isuzu around back out of sight. They both climbed out into the cold night air.

Reed waited outside while Angela walked around front to open the door, then come through and let him in the back door. He shifted his weight, gingerly checking the feel of his stump in the prosthetic socket. Not too bad, he thought. The time spent elevated seemed to have settled it down a bit. Reed rolled his head. His neck had become increasingly stiff since the terrifying plunge down the embankment, and his left collarbone and lower right ribs felt tender from the impact against his seat belt, but other than that, the plunge down hadn't done much damage. And the climb up had only added muscle strains and sore fingers to the other strains and bruises he had absorbed in the last forty-eight hours. The two quick naps he had grabbed while Angela drove had taken the edge off his exhaustion.

Reed looked up into the night sky and breathed in the cold, crisp air. The moon had set, the air was clear, and with no artificial light anywhere around him, the stars overhead seemed to fill the dark void above him. Familiar constellations gleamed brilliantly, but Reed could also see countless more stars, so many of them that they seemed to be painted in continuous streams against the velvet of dark overhead. Reed found himself struck more deeply than he could remember at how many stars shone in the sky, stars that he never saw while under the canopy of city lights that usually surrounded him. For a strange, shining moment Reed felt liberated from the pain and worry and evil that had fallen on him. But more than that, he felt released from something that had oppressed him for months, something he couldn't articulate but now realized had been buried inside him.

He knew the feeling he was experiencing had to do with climbing the side of that embankment, with surviving the attempt on his life and the crash, but he wanted to grasp it, clearly discern it, wrap his mind and attention around the power of whatever pulsed inside him right now as he stood under the star-filled sky.

Maybe it was simply that for the first time in months, maybe years, yes, Reed thought, years, that he was doing something that made his life pulse hard at the core. One way or another, he was going to save his cousin John Boyd. He thought about that doctor, remembering the look in his eyes when he had the gun pressed to his head. He wasn't going to hurt his cousin. Reed knew it. At least not tonight.

The rear door of the condo popped open as Angela shoved at it with her hip. Incandescent light flooded out from the interior. Reed lowered his gaze and watched Angela walk toward him with graceful, long-legged strides. She popped open the back of the Trooper and said, "Come on, I'll help you with your trunk."

Reed set the groceries down next to the trunk and said, "Hang on a second. I want to get my other shoes out of there. Walking on this bare metal isn't the best thing."

Angela waited for Reed to rummage to the bottom of his trunk to find his second pair of shoes, the left one fitted for the Flex-Foot. He pulled out a brown, nondescript tie shoe and slipped it over the prosthesis, leaving the running shoe on his right foot. Reed set the small bag of groceries on top of the trunk and they carried the trunk in the back door, Angela leading the way.

They entered a brightly lit kitchen.

"Come on," said Angela, "no sense putting it down. You can have the bigger bedroom. It's got a desk and phone in there."

The extra weight and tenderness of his stump made walking with the trunk quite difficult for Reed. He would have preferred dropping the trunk and dragging it out by himself, but instead he just said, "Okay, but go slow."

Angela turned and seeing the way Reed walked made her stop and say, "Oh, sorry. Sorry."

"No, go ahead. Just not too fast."

They continued through an inexpensively furnished living room large enough for two sleep sofas and a dining area. A hallway led to a large bedroom on the left and a smaller bedroom on the right with a bathroom at the end of the hall.

They dropped the trunk on Reed's bed.

Angela turned and left the bedroom, almost as if she didn't want to be in that room with Reed, saying, "Tom told me I have to turn on the circuit breakers in the utility room to get the water heater on. Won't have hot water for about a half hour."

Reed was anxious to get the prosthesis off, but had to walk back out to the Trooper for his crutches. Coming back through the kitchen Angela announced, "I found a can of chili and three beers in the fridge." She held up the grocery bag. "Or eggs and instant coffee."

Reed absentmindedly rubbed his stomach. He didn't feel hungry, but he felt tired, drained. He needed the food more than he wanted it.

"I'll go for chili and beer."

"Me, too."

Reed headed for his bedroom and shut the door behind him. He dropped his pants, sat down on the edge of the bed, and quickly released the suction valve on the prosthesis, but his stump had swelled to the point that he had to gently but firmly ease it out of the socket.

As soon as the stump was free, he lay on his back and elevated it, trying to forestall any rush of blood that might send shocks of phantom pain running through the limb. But to Reed's surprise, as he rolled off his Alpha liner sock, the stump felt fine, as if the crash and brutal climb up the embankment had toughened it and expunged the stump's sensitivity. The skin was red, there was definite tenderness on the front and back where it had rubbed on the socket, but there were no blisters. Reed rummaged around the trunk for his skin cream and a fresh pressure sock, wishing he could take a hot bath and then sleep, but knowing that would have to wait.

Reed took out his cell phone, but checked to see if the phone near the bed had a dial tone. Thankfully, the familiar tone sounded after a click. Reed squinted at the phone's number written on a label affixed to the handset, memorizing it almost as quickly as he saw it. At this time of night, he assumed Irwin would have his cell phone off, so he punched in Irwin Barker's beeper number from memory, then the condo's phone number followed by three nines, his code to Irwin that the call was from him.

Reed knew that Irwin kept his beeper in a metal tray filled with pennies so that when it buzzed and vibrated against the coins it would cause enough racket to wake him. Reed knew there weren't many people Irwin would call back at this time of night, but he was one of them.

He smelled the tangy odor of the chili heating in the kitchen; heard quick footsteps outside his closed door, and then the sound of the toilet flushing.

Reed checked his watch. Three-thirty. In all the years he had known Irwin, Reed had never seen him home asleep, but he imagined Irwin Barker to be the type who slept in T-shirt and boxer shorts.

Reed was just about to beep him again when the condo phone rang loud enough to startle Reed. He snatched the receiver before the second ring ended.

"Irwin."

"What's up, boss?"

"Sorry to roust you at this time of night. Did I wake you?"

"That's what it feels like. What do you need?"

"Quite a bit, as a matter of fact."

"Shoot."

"I'm going to need you up here."

Without any hesitation, Irwin asked, *"When and where?"*

"Now."

"Okay. How long does it take to get up there?"

"This late, with you driving, about five hours."

"What about hunting down your cousin's trust?"

"I'll have to put Adele or Charles on it."

"Okay."

"Get a pen. I'll give you directions in a minute. Risk the speeding ticket. If your badges don't get you out of it, I'll pay your tickets."

"You sound like you got trouble."

"Someone tried to kill me tonight."

"Shit. What dumb son of a bitch did that?"

"Several dumb sons of bitches."

"You get to shoot any of them?"

"Sort of."

"Cops up there involved?"

"Sort of. I'll explain it all when you get here. Just make sure you come armed, and bring your backup piece. In fact, bring a couple of your shotguns. We may need them."

"This is sounding better and better. What else do you need?"

"You find our cyberspace friend?"

"Yeah. He got in touch with me, the crazy bastard. He's more paranoid than ever. You wouldn't believe the bullshit you have to go through to talk to him."

"I can imagine. Before you come up here, get one of his connectors and tell him I want him on-call."

"Starting?"

"Tomorrow morning. This morning. Say starting after nine A.M. You have a number I can reach him at?"

"It's a pain in the ass, Bill. He's buggier than ever about how people find him. He's got his own phone system set up with some sort of super-black-box-caller-ID scanner. All his incoming calls get processed. Only authorized phone numbers get connected. I had to give him my cell phone number. You call from any other source, it won't go through. I'll have to call him about a connector. If you want, I can have him call you."

"Crazy fuck. Give him my cell phone number. I'm going to be on this land line for a while."

"Fine. If he doesn't call you in the next hour, call me back."

"Pain in the ass."

"Hey, that's the way these guys are. SR is very careful. So where am I going and what do you want me to do?"

"You've got to get to a hospital up here and guard my cousin. He's being operated on tonight, right now, as a matter of fact. He should be okay, but I don't want anything to happen to him when he comes out from under the knife."

"Anything like what?"

"Anything like anything at all. I don't want him moved. I don't want him bothered. I don't want anybody but the doctors and nurses at the hospital to see him . . . except for a doctor named Prentice. Keep him away. I want John safe until I make arrangements to get him out of there to my own doctors."

"Okay. I got it."

"You get up there, call me at this number and don't let the guy out of your sight. John won't know who you are, but just tell him I sent you. Cousin Bill."

"Got it."

"If the hospital gives you any shit about it . . ."

"Don't worry, I know what to do. I'll leave now and run down SR on my way out of town."

"Okay, here's where I want you to go."

George Prentice smiled under his surgical mask. This will keep that Reed fellow off me. And if Ullmann doesn't like it, tough. Although if he has any sense, he should like it just fine. It'll be perfect for him.

Prentice had moved through each step of the final phase of the surgery, working quickly, flawlessly, his fingers now rapidly making the last few stitches that connected the ends of Johnny Boy Reed's colon. He had gone through the motions of cleaning the peritoneum, resetting the intestines, essentially reversing all he had done to remove the section of Johnny Boy's colon.

Prentice went through the motions, making sure it appeared that he had left no part of the surgical procedure undone. Except for the last two stitches. No one would ever notice. Not even the surgical nurse standing at his side. Not even if she bent down and looked into the abdominal cavity. Prentice knew one stitch would be sufficient, but just to make sure he made two very delicate, very deceptive stitches, stitches that would come loose and spill waste from Johnny Boy's intestinal tract into the peritoneum. Until that moment, Johnny Boy would appear to be fine. The hospital staff would have no cause for alarm. But certainly during the next twenty-four hours, the faux stitches would open. Moments after that, a virulent infection would start as intestinal tract waste invaded the abdominal cavity. The infection would escalate rapidly to general sepsis throughout the body, and within twenty-four to forty-eight hours, unless Johnny Boy Reed was reopened, cleaned up, and restitched, he would die.

Perfect, thought George Prentice. Actually, just perfect.

Thirty-eight

Bill Reed felt strangely reluctant to get back on his crutches, but he knew that his stump needed time free of the prosthesis to recover from the stress incurred during the climb up from the river. And he could not resist the scent of the chili and the desire for a cold beer, so he struggled up onto the crutches, ignoring the pain and discomfort it caused to his sore hands and strained arms and back.

He slowly hop/stepped his way out to the living room. Reed made his way to the kitchen, opened up the refrigerator, and pulled out two beers, then turned and watched Angela stir the chili in a small pot. He placed a beer next to her, but she didn't seem to notice it. He cracked his can open and leaned back against the refrigerator, watching her from behind. Even in her less-than-flattering, black waitress slacks her rear end and legs looked good. Being on the run with her, standing in a kitchen while she prepared food, watching her without speaking . . . all lent a feeling of intimacy.

Angela divided the contents of the pot onto two plates. Angela placed the beers on the plates and carried everything into the dining room as Reed followed on his crutches.

They sat at the small, round dining table across from each other.

"You eat fast, too," said Angela.

"Yeah, I guess."

"I noticed that when you took me to dinner."

"I didn't notice that about you."

"You were too busy copping looks at my chest."

Reed looked at her skeptically.

"What?" Angela asked. "You deny it?"

"No. I just deny I was so obvious about it."

"Yeah, sure," said Angela. "There's a third beer in there. You want to split it?"

"All right."

Angela returned with the last can, pouring half for each of them. She asked Reed, "You think you're going to sleep tonight?"

"No. I'll have to lay down at some point, but not until I know my cousin came out of his surgery okay. Plus, I have more work to do. What about you?"

"It's doubtful. Too nervous."

"You'll be all right."

"Think so?"

Reed nodded. "Sure."

"What about your cousin? What the hell is going on with him?"

As he considered his answer, Reed wiped his lips with his thumb and forefinger, trying to clean off the greasy feel of the chili.

"I don't know."

"Why'd they take him to the hospital?"

"Probably because they couldn't stand his screaming."

"What?"

"I walk in there, I'm thinking how do I find him? Hell, I heard him moaning and screaming from out near the entrance. The poor guy was in horrible pain. They said he had a tumor blocking his colon."

Angela winced as if she could feel the pain. "A tumor?"

"Yeah."

"How can you have a tumor and not know it?"

Reed pushed away his empty dinner plate.

"Exactly. All of a sudden, my cousin has a tumor big enough to block his colon? Nobody noticed he was sick? That's ridiculous. When I was at that place, his girlfriend told me he had stomachaches. And those assholes running the place didn't know? They knew. They knew all along. And they lied. All of them lied."

"Why would they lie about that?"

"You tell me."

Angela shrugged. "I don't know. Maybe they just didn't want you jumping all over them because they didn't take care of it."

"Then why call me and tell me they're taking him to the hospital?"

"Well—"

"They called me to that hospital because they wanted to run me off the road. They wanted to get rid of me, and probably my cousin."

"Christ," said Angela. "This is crazy. None of it makes sense."

"Only if you don't know why."

"Why then?"

"Money. Most times it's money. I'm thinking it might have something to do with his trust fund."

Angela frowned. "His trust fund?"

"There's more than one way for Ullmann to raid it. It's not

the most obvious thing, but I can't figure out how Ullmann could make the obvious work with John. But somewhere, somehow, Ullmann's figured out some way to make a hell of a lot of money."

"How much is a hell of a lot?"

"So far, what I've uncovered is mostly his businesses and the real estate they occupy. I'd say, just looking at that stuff, at present market value Ullmann's worth over four million."

Reed saw Angela's eyes widen.

"Four million?"

"Over four million. And that's just the stuff on public record. I haven't found any bank accounts or brokerage accounts . . . liquid assets. He's worth more. I know."

"How do you know?"

"It's my job. The patterns. The way the assets have been accrued. The way he runs it."

Angela stood up, pacing over to the window. She crossed her arms and stared out into the black night. Reed watched, seeing now how upset she had become. She turned back to Reed.

"You think these people are actually murderers?"

"I know people who have killed for a lot less."

"What the hell are you going to do?"

Reed didn't answer.

Angela let Reed take the first shower, preferring to clean up after their quick meal and be by herself.

Alone, standing at the kitchen sink, Angela let her mind drift over her situation. She had known Matthew Ullmann was rich, powerful, arrogant, and greedy. But she had never imagined him capable of murder. And she certainly did not want to admit that she had looked the other way so that she could get what she wanted for herself and her sister, Lizzie.

She didn't want to even consider what it might mean if she had to move, to take Lizzie out of the institute and start another life all over again, someplace else. She couldn't stand the thought of how confused and anxious that would make her sister. And where would she take her? To some ratty old group home in a community that didn't want people like her sister around? And what would she do? She'd have to pick up and move with her, leave everything behind ... the beautiful, peaceful house and her studio. Her friends. Everything. It hit Angela suddenly just how much of her life Matthew Ullmann controlled. She felt trapped. Standing at the kitchen sink, she actually found it hard to breathe.

"You better get yourself together, Angela. You might just have to pack up your tools, your clothes, get Lizzie and leave. Just fucking leave."

But the thought of it overwhelmed her. She had a grand total of four thousand six hundred dollars in savings. How long would that last? Where would we go? What would we do? Alone. Fending for ourselves.

And then Angela thought about Bill Reed. He shows up from nowhere and my whole life gets turned over. Can I depend on Reed to help me? Will he feel any obligation toward me? Toward Lizzie? Will he help? He obviously has some money. And then Angela told herself, Get real. He has enough trouble worrying about himself and his cousin. He isn't going to take on you and all your problems.

But Angela knew he was attracted to her. It was obvious. But at the same time, there was no denying that Reed kept his distance from her. At first, she assumed it was because of his amputation. Now she wondered if perhaps Reed was one of those smart, handsome men who had always had it so easy with women that he just never worried much about it—picking up and dropping women at will—always knowing he could replace one with another if the relationship didn't work out.

Or did Reed keep his distance because he had been burned by a woman who was his match? His ex-wife, perhaps.

Or maybe, she thought, maybe the guy is just too jaded by life to form any relationships. It was obvious his work didn't build much trust and respect for his fellow human being.

Or maybe it was just the leg that made him keep his distance.

Who the hell knows? she thought. And then it hit her how much Reed frustrated her. How much she wanted him to make a move for her. As Angela soaped up the dinner plates and let the hot water fill the chili pot, she thought about how Reed's intensity frightened her and attracted her at the same time. He didn't seem to have any doubts. Matthew Ullmann did not scare him. Not even Ralph Malone scared him.

What the hell is he going to do? she wondered. With that look in his eyes and that gun of his? If he went after Ullmann, they'd definitely come down hard on him. Arrest him. And yes, maybe even kill him. How could he possibly go up against Ullmann and the sheriff and all Ullmann's proctors and all the sheriff's deputies?

And once they took care of Reed, what would they do to her?

She didn't want anything more to happen to Reed. Or to herself. But what should she do? For a moment, she had a fierce urge to leave the dishes in the sink, wipe her hands, and just leave. Get in her Isuzu and disappear. Drive to one of her friend's houses and come back in a week when this was all over.

But her mind kept returning to Reed. She couldn't see herself sneaking out on him while he stood under a shower in a condo stuck on the side of a hill in the middle of nowhere.

Lathering the glass in her hand, feeling the soap-slick warm water flow over her hands, thinking about Reed, Angela found herself imagining the hot soapy water flowing over Reed's body in the shower.

That's a hard body, there, she told herself. She could almost see him in the shower lathering the soap over his muscular chest and arms.

Suddenly she had an urge to seduce Reed, to bring him under her power, to eliminate the separation between them so she could influence him, direct him, keep him from acting too crazy, make him care about her and worry about her and protect her. She smiled, standing at the kitchen sink, washing the glass, thinking of standing naked in the shower, soaping up

Reed instead of the glass. She almost laughed out loud. He'd go crazy. He'd forget about that damn stump if I did that. Angela felt the enticing heat in her chest, felt her heartbeat increase, the pulse of it, the lust rising to her throat and back dōwn between her legs. She was horny. She knew it, and Reed knew it. Their pheromones or whatever were so thick in the air between them it sometimes made her head fog. Both of them hadn't been with a member of the opposite sex in a good long time.

I'll bet it would go for hours, she thought.

Angela's imaginings began to make her feel uncomfortably deprived. She reached forward and shut off the water, gripping the front of the sink, pushing her pelvis against the countertop to stem the erotic feelings coursing through her, but finding that the pressure actually stimulated her more.

She backed away from the sink counter, bent forward, resting her weight on her arms, trying to calm herself down, to think rationally.

"Don't be stupid," she said out loud.

Angela shook her head, biting her top lip as she exhaled slowly through her nose. What good will that do? she asked herself.

You know goddamn well what good it will do. You sleep with him tonight, and he'll feel a lot less like leaving you behind to fend for yourself once he takes care of his cousin.

And then she shook her head in a tight series of *no*'s, taking the other side of the argument. The rational side. The smarter side.

No, no, don't fucking do it. He's not going to respect you if you suddenly come on like some horny, deprived North Country nympho. That's stupid. He'll look on you like a disposable piece of ass that he'd better get rid of as soon as he can. You keep your distance, girl. But you keep him looking at you and thinking about it. You keep him interested until you know what's right.

God, thought Angela, what the hell is right? What are you doing here? What should you be doing?

Angela heard the bathroom door open. She stood up straight, looking for something to wipe her wet hands on, feeling guilty for no good reason. She had become so engrossed in her thoughts that she hadn't heard the shower go off. She took a deep breath, trying to relax. She heard Reed's bedroom door close behind him without a word. That was it. For just a few seconds, she had heard him moving, felt his far-off presence, and then she was alone again. Alone in a strange place, hiding in the dark before the dawn, trying to figure out the right thing to do. And knowing she'd be thinking about what to do, mulling it over and over, for whatever was left of the night.

THIRTY-NINE

When Matthew Ullmann entered his house, he saw the lights on out in the kitchen. Madeleine would be sitting in her robe, at the table in the breakfast nook, waiting for him.

Ullmann entered the kitchen and walked over to the breakfast nook, unbuttoning his coat.

Madeleine tried not to sound too shrill, too accusatory, but waiting without any word from him for almost three hours made that impossible.

"Any news, yet?" she asked.

Her question grated on Ullmann.

"What do you think?" he shot back.

"I think you're upset. I think things are not going well."

"No, Madeleine, they are not."

"How so, Matthew?"

"Mr. Reed is nowhere to be found. One of our employees from the inn has apparently helped him check out under the noses of two sheriff's deputies sitting in the lobby looking for him. And driven him off somewhere."

Her eyes squinted. "What employee would that be?"

Ullmann refused to avoid her gaze.

"It appears to be Angela Quist."

"What?"

"I think you heard me. Angela Quist."

"That trashy waitress you're always mooning over?"

"I do not moon over anybody, Madeleine."

"This is infuriating."

"Yes. It is."

"Where did they go, Matthew?"

"I've spent the last two hours riding around with the sheriff, listening to him talk on that stupid radio of his, trying to find out. Eddie and some of the others are looking, too. They haven't gone far. Unless, of course, they've decided to abandon their beloved relatives, which I seriously doubt."

"What are you going to do when you find them?"

"I'll decide when it's time." Ullmann shrugged off his stadium coat and dropped it across the back of the chair. "Now would you like to hear the bad news?"

"The *bad* news?" she shrieked. "Was what I just heard good news?"

"Comparatively. I just stopped by the hospital, intending to meet with Prentice. Pick up the tissue samples and the body for Orenberg."

"Yes?"

"He's nowhere to be found. Nor are the tissue samples. And Johnny Boy is lying in the recovery room, breathing like a sow."

Madeleine hissed through clenched teeth, "What?"

"Prentice has reneged and disappeared. Johnny Boy is still alive, presumably without his tumor. The cousin, Mr. Reed the ex-FBI agent, is on the loose after having killed Ray Boggs, pistol-whipped Ralph Malone, and terrified George Prentice. Apparently aided and abetted by our employee, Angela Quist. I think that's a fair summary."

Matthew Ullmann watched his wife's squinty ferretlike eyes squeezing shut against the anger welling up. Ullmann lowered his voice, matching his wife's effort to contain herself. "What time did you plan on calling Orenberg?"

"Seven. Our original appointment was for lunch. I'll have to catch him before he leaves. You said I should buy a day. But like I said, I think that's going to set off alarms."

Ullmann rubbed his face, trying to dispel his fatigue.

"We need time, Madeleine. But you're right, we can't risk making Orenberg suspicious. He has a very low tolerance for any complications."

"There's always room for some idiot screwing things up. Why don't we just tell them somebody made a mistake at the hospital?"

"What kind of mistake?" Ullmann asked, seeing now that Madeleine had already given this some thought.

"We call and tell him that there was a screwup with the pathologist. That he got called out on an accident. I was thinking about what you said, you know, with Ray Boggs being killed out there, so the pathologist, Hartford or Hartman, whatever his name is, he got called out to the accident. We'll explain that he goes to accident scenes and helps with the investigations. So he left and locked up the pathology office before Prentice could get back in and gather all the samples."

"Would that cause a delay of a day?"

"No, but it could explain a few hours. So let's tell Orenberg to come for dinner instead of lunch."

"Dinner." Ullmann considered it for a moment. "All right, dinner. But it puts an absolute deadline on things. We have a lot of loose ends to clean up by dinnertime."

"So?" said Madeleine. "We're not losers, Matthew. We'll do what we have to do."

Ullmann smiled at his wife, suddenly gazing at her fondly.

"You know, my dear, you are really the only person I can rely on."

"You're just finding that out?"

"No. I'm just realizing it once again. When was the last time I told you I loved you?"

Madeleine smiled back at her husband, a flattered, ferret-faced smile, and said, "I think it was this morning. Or maybe it was last night? I can't quite remember."

Ullmann leaned back in his chair and spoke calmly. He checked his watch.

"There is the contingency plan, you know."

"You mean—"

"Just in case this goes badly. If we call Orenberg, say around seven o'clock, ask him to make it dinner instead of lunch at say six o'clock, that would give us eleven hours. If things didn't go right, we'd still have time to pull the plug on all of it."

"All of it?"

Ullmann leaned forward, trying to sound persuasive and reasonable at the same time. "We've come too far to lose everything now, dear. We can transfer our assets where no one would find them. I've already set up the accounts. Pack up and leave. Leave this whole mess behind. I can liquidate things here from wherever we land."

"At a fire-sale price."

"Maybe. Maybe not. It doesn't matter. We don't really need any of this, Madeleine. It'd just be icing. Certainly, we'd take care of Johnny Boy first, cash that chip in. He's worth over three million to us."

"Take care of him?"

Ullmann wagged a playful finger at his wife. "You know very well what I mean. Go over to the hospital and do what the dolt Prentice couldn't do. You can manage that, can't you, Madeleine? There are ways you know about, I'm sure. People often die after major surgery."

Madeleine groused, "Of course, if I have to. It just annoys me that I have to do that bastard Prentice's dirty work. What's he getting paid for?"

Ullmann's voice rose, taking on an edge.

"He's getting paid nothing for nothing. I'm going to find him, strip him, and have Ralph take him in the forest and put a bullet in his head."

"Find him . . . find them, you keep saying that, Matthew. There seems to be an awful lot of people out there you have to find."

Matthew waved a hand. "I've made Mr. Reed a distant second priority. It's Prentice I want right now. Ralph and Eddie and their minions are out there looking for him, but I have a feeling he's going to be contacting us."

"Why?"

"Because he has the tissue samples. He knows the situation. He's just terrified that I'm going to rip his head off because he didn't take care of Johnny Boy. He's going to try to negotiate with me. He's making a very big mistake, but I'll play along until I get those samples for Orenberg. That's the first priority. We get the tissue samples. We get Johnny Boy back. Take care of Orenberg. Then we'll deal with the rest. There's too much at stake to give in to any emotions right now."

"And you're going to forget about that Bill Reed? After all the aggravation he's caused?"

"Oh, hell, I'm not worried about him. Ralph is so mad, I'm sure he'll take care of that himself."

"And if he doesn't?"

"All right, worst-case scenario, Johnny Boy dies and his cousin raises a big stink. But what is he going to say? His cousin has cancer for God's sake. It's not our fault."

At this Madeleine smiled, but didn't say anything.

"And who is he going to complain to?" Matthew continued. "Eventually, it will end up with Carl Roth. He's the district attorney in the county, right?"

"Yes. Not exactly the sharpest knife in the drawer, old Carl."

"Exactly. And Roth knows where his campaign contributions come from. What's he going to do? Nothing."

"He won't even be able to figure out what the crime is."

"Not unless someone draws him a map. If then."

"But that's the problem, Matthew. Our Mr. Reed might just be the type who can do that."

"Not if Ralph Malone shoots him first."

"I would feel much better if that man were out of the picture, Matthew."

"So would I. We have eleven hours, dear." Ullmann lowered his voice, reached out, and took his wife's hand in his. "We do what we can. Most likely, we'll take care of everything. All I'm saying is there may come a point, this very day, that we simply do our own disappearing act. Almost everything that we wanted to do has been done. We may have to leave a couple of chips on the table, some big chips to be sure, but so be it. Pigs go to market, dear. Hogs get slaughtered."

Madeleine shifted in her chair.

"It's not fair. Not after all our efforts."

Ullmann leaned back. "It never is, dear. It never is, but I for one wouldn't mind leaving this all behind. It might just be time."

Time. Every moment that Angela Quist sat awake throughout the dark morning hours, she kept worrying that Ralph Malone and his men would be barging in on them any second. She hated just sitting, hiding, waiting. She'd washed her clothes and now sat wrapped in a blanket, waiting for them to dry, feeling even more vulnerable.

She knew she could never side with Ullmann and Malone against Bill Reed. But as she sat alone, worried, restless, she ached to do something. She believed that if Malone found them, Reed couldn't possibly survive. They'd shoot him and quite possibly shoot her, too. There would be too many of them. And they had the law on their side.

But what could she do? Convince Reed to call the state police. And ask them to do what? Reed had no proof of anything. And for sure, Malone would demand that they arrest Reed.

Should she try to convince Reed to make a run for it? He'd never leave his cousin. Get the cousin, get Lizzie, and go? Could the cousin be moved? How could Reed get him out of the hospital without being arrested. Where would they all go? What would they do?

She heard the clothes dryer signal beep, startling her to her feet. She pulled out her fresh, dry clothes, reveling in the warmth of them as she dressed in the small utility room.

For what seemed like the hundredth time she checked her watch. At a little before six o'clock in the morning. The nearly tasteless instant coffee she had been drinking sent Angela on her third trip down the hallway to the bathroom. This time, Angela saw the light leaking out from under Reed's door. She knocked quietly, her ear turned closely to the door, waiting for a response.

"Yes?" Reed called out.

"Are you decent?"

"Yeah, come in."

Angela opened the door only partially, and then all the way when she saw Reed sitting at the desk on the far side of the room, his back facing her. He wore jeans and only a T-shirt, the shirt tight enough on him so that Angela could see the outlines of the large muscles running across his shoulders and back. She saw cables and lines and the printer, but Reed's broad back blocked her view of his laptop computer.

Without turning around, he said, "Just a moment, please," as he closed down his modem connection. Turning toward her, Reed asked, "Did you sleep?"

"No. What about you?"

"I think I dozed off for about an hour. Too worried. I called the hospital three times. John just got out of surgery. He's alive."

"Thank God. Now what?"

"A friend of mine is on his way over there to watch over him. Should be there in a few hours."

"A friend? Who?"

"A guy who works for me."

"Is he going to get your cousin out of the hospital?"

"I've got a call in to my lawyer. He should be getting back to me around eight. I have to find out what my rights are. I don't know if the Ullmann Institute has guardianship or something over John or not. Not that I give a shit. I just like to know what I have to do."

"But you're not letting him go back to the institute."

"No."

"Do you know where you're going to take him?"

"To another hospital. After that, I'll see."

Angela nodded, reacting to Reed's terse answer.

"So he's okay?" Angela asked.

"For now. Yes."

"Listen," she said, stepping farther into the room. "I can't shake this feeling that Malone and his deputies are going to come charging in here any minute."

Reed nodded.

Angela said, "I don't think it's going to take any genius to figure out I helped you. Brian knows I went out after you. Someone had to give you the key to that service door to get your stuff from the inn."

"Yes."

"I'm sure they've checked my house."

"I'm sure Ullmann has the key."

"Yeah, right. He's probably already changed the locks. I have this image of him throwing Lizzie out of her dorm room."

"I'd say Ullmann is a little too preoccupied to worry about your sister."

"Yeah, I guess." Angela was too keyed up to sit. She kept moving. Leaning against the dresser. Walking to the window, her hands thrust in the back pockets of her slacks. "What do you mean exactly? Preoccupied with what?"

"My cousin John is still alive. And Dr. George Prentice is nowhere to be found. I asked for him when I called the hospital. I wanted to know about what happened when he opened John up. The guy's disappeared."

"Meaning?"

"Meaning he's probably on the run from Ullmann. He didn't follow the plan."

"You have no doubt he was supposed to kill your cousin."

"Not much."

"Right. So what's *your* plan? What are you going to do? I mean . . . just sitting here waiting is driving me nuts."

Reed turned to his improvised desk and picked up a pile of printouts.

"I need a little more time to find out what I need to know about Ullmann. And I've got to wait until John recovers enough to be moved. My office is sending a medevac ambulance and making arrangements at a hospital not too far from here."

Angela began pacing, again, rubbing a thumb nervously against the palm of her hand.

"The more time goes by, the more I worry about Lizzie. If Ullmann doesn't find me, he . . ."

"He what?"

"I don't know. It's going to bounce back on Lizzie eventually."

"What do you want to do? You want to go over there and take her out?"

"Not unless I have to. It would be very upsetting to her."

"What do you want to do, Angela?"

She stopped pacing and turned to him.

"Just listen to my idea. If you think it's the wrong thing to do, tell me. But just listen. I think it might help us both."

Reed nodded. "I'll do anything you want, Angela. As long as it doesn't hurt John."

"Good." Angela nodded. "Good."

The phone answered on the second ring and a message recorded in the grating voice of Madeleine Ullmann clicked on: *"You've reached the Ullmann residence. Leave a message, and we will call you back as soon as possible."*

Angela's first response was to hang up, but the beep sounded almost immediately, jarring her into a response.

"Matthew, this is Angela Quist. Are you there? I want to talk to you about—"

Before Angela could finish her sentence, she heard the phone snatched off the receiver at the other end. This time, Madeleine Ullmann spoke in person, actually trying to sound pleasant.

"Angela, this is Mrs. Ullmann. Matthew is sleeping right now. He was up most of the night. What was it you wanted to talk about?"

"Bill Reed," said Angela.

"Yes? What about him?"

"I know where he is. Apparently you people are looking for him."

"People? What do you mean by 'you people'?"

Angela's voice hardened. "I mean Ralph Malone, Eddie McAndrews, your husband. Tell me they don't want to find Bill Reed."

"I hear that man attacked the sheriff, of course they're looking for him. What does that have to do with us?"

"You're not interested?"

"Do you know where he is? Is he with you?"

"Yes."

There was a pause on the other end of the line before Madeleine continued, *"Well, I suggest you call the sheriff. Or tell me where you are and I'll call him."*

Angela heard a muffled sound and then Matthew's voice came on the line.

"Ms. Quist, where are you?"

"Mr. Ullmann."

"Yes."

"I'm with Bill Reed. You told me to keep track of him, didn't you?"

"I don't think that included being his chauffeur and helping him avoid arrest."

"Who said I did that?"

"Don't play games with me. I'm not in the mood. Where are you?"

"Not anyplace you or that creep Ralph Malone are going to find us."

"I'm going to ask you one more time, Angela. Don't make a mistake here."

"That's what I'm trying to avoid. Making a mistake. I'm hearing some pretty strange accusations about you from Mr. Reed."

"I'm not interested. And it has nothing to do with you."

"Really? So I shouldn't worry about repercussions against me and my sister."

"If you don't clear up your loyalties, there will be repercussions. Serious ones. Where is he?"

"I need guarantees that nothing will happen to me and my sister."

"I guarantee it."

"Not good enough. I'm ready to give you what you want, but I think you're very angry right now, Matthew. I think you might lash out."

Ullmann's throat tightened with rage, but he kept his voice soft and reasonable. *"I'm not angry. Not yet."*

Angela lowered her voice and began speaking rapidly.

"Look, I have to hang up. I'll call you back in an hour or so. Just convince me that nothing is going to happen to me or my sister over this, and I'll deliver Reed."

Reed watched Angela hang up and nodded, smiling.

"What do you think?" she asked.

Reed shrugged. "I don't know. I'm pretty sure it pissed him off. That's good enough for me."

Angela smiled a rueful grin.

"Don't worry about it," said Reed. "If he figures you might come through for him and he puts me on the back burner for a few hours, that's all I need. Three, four hours and I finish this thing."

"Finish it?"

"One way or another."

George Prentice had taken all precautions he could think of, but he too had the anxious feeling that Ralph Malone would sweep down on him any second. He looked at the kitchen clock in his lover's bungalow. He remembered buying it for Alan at Zabar's during his trip to New York. The ceramic face of the clock looked like a plate of two sunny-side-up eggs. The minute and hour hands were a knife and fork. Alan said the clock always made him happy to check the time. Looking at it now made Prentice anxious. Nine-twenty. Perhaps he should call Ullmann now. No, he thought, let him stew. But if he gets too mad, he'll be completely unreasonable. I'll wait an hour. I'll wait until ten-thirty.

George wished Alan were with him. Alan Molina, one of the male nurses at Clearbrook Hospital, was the tougher of them. He could picture Alan, standing with him in the kitchen, a young muscular man in his nursing greens, saying, fuck him. Let him wait.

George took courage from Alan. He knew that without him, without the chance to be with him, he would never have had the courage to defy Matthew Ullmann.

The relationship with Alan had started as a tryst, a dalliance that had frightened George Prentice as much as it had excited him. Up until he met Alan Molina, Prentice had always kept his sexual contacts confined to places far from home. For many years, George Prentice had satisfied his sexual urges with extended weekend trips to Boston, Montreal, sometimes Buffalo, and once New York, although the gay scene in New York overwhelmed him. Most of the bars there were so crowded and intense. He remembered wishing he could find the places where the old queers hung out, something more sedate. Not that the brazen, aggressive young men who populated the New York gay scene didn't excite him. Excited and frightened him, much like Alan did.

That first time with Alan, a casual, surreptitious grope in the surgeons' locker room, had terrified George Prentice as much as it had thrilled him. Alan had been so cool, so bold. He had simply come up next to Prentice, their hips barely touching, casually turned, and looked at him, looked around, then ran the palm of his hand slowly up Prentice's thigh and across his hardening cock. Despite himself, Prentice had smiled and kept eye contact as Alan casually walked out of the locker room. The next day he told Alan to please forget it ever happened. He implored him to be discreet.

Alan had agreed, but only to mollify George Prentice. He had been admiring the doctor for months, he knew what he wanted, and Alan Molina proved to have enough patience to persevere until he got it. Gradually, very gradually, Alan had won over George's confidence. It had taken weeks, but Alan had persisted, both in his passion and in his discretion. Alan never told anybody, not even his mother, that he had found the man he would love forever.

George Prentice was certain that nobody knew about the nights he had spent at Alan Molina's small lakeside bungalow. And thus he felt sure no one would come looking for him there now.

However, Prentice's certainty did not prevent him from sending Alan to his mother's home in Canton, New York, telling him not to worry, to do this for him, to wait until he called. Prentice had sworn that within a few days, their lives would be forever changed. They would marry and leave Greenport and Clearbrook Hospital and start a new life together in Key West. They would shop for a bungalow of their own, live in a community of loving men. Prentice would come out and face the world as a gay man, a gay physician, surgeon. He would build a new practice. If it thrived, fine. If not, he would have enough money to support them for a long time. Alan would work. He would work. They would survive.

Prentice had planned it for over a year. The only change now was that he and Alan would be moving sooner than expected.

He looked at the breakfast-plate clock over Alan's sink. The time crept so slowly. Nine-forty. Prentice thought about eating something, which prompted him to think about Johnny Boy and the tumor attached to the section of Johnny Boy's colon he had excised. The colon, the tumor, and the sliced tissue sample were carefully wrapped in a plastic and placed in a small ice chest, buried in the far corner of Alan's one-acre lot.

Prentice stared out the kitchen window. Damnedest thing

that tumor. Hard, constricted. Contained. The Reed fellow probably would have survived the cancer. Too bad.

Wouldn't mind looking at that tumor again, thought Prentice. And then he laughed a short bark of a laugh. "You're not the only one," he told himself.

Prentice picked up the phone and dialed Clearbrook.

Gwen Higgins, the matronly receptionist at Clearbrook Hospital, read the patient status report to Dr. Prentice, "Recovering from surgery. In satisfactory condition," while watching the dark-haired man in a rumpled brown suit walking her way. The man looked like he needed coffee and a shave and reminded Gwen of her Uncle Warren, one of the last genuine lumberjacks to work the North Country.

Uncle Warren had been bald, but this man had a full head of dark hair and a stubble of beard so black it had a blue tinge to it. And he was even bigger than old Uncle Warren.

Even though Irwin Barker wore a suit and tie, he made Gwen uneasy. And then Irwin smiled at her from about ten feet away and Gwen's unease evaporated. Suddenly she felt as if she shared something with the man.

"Good morning," said Irwin. "How are you today? Busy?"

"Oh, sure," said Gwen, finding herself smiling back at Irwin. "Can I help you?"

"You certainly can," replied Irwin as he pulled out a long leather wallet from the inside pocket of the suit jacket he had been sitting in for the last six hours. He opened the wallet, presenting it to Gwen. On one side were attached a very large star-shaped badge issued to New York State troopers and under it a second badge, the rather ornate gold and blue shield of the New York City detective division. Opposite the badges were identification cards.

"I'm a New York State Investigator," said Irwin. "I'm checking on the status and whereabouts of one of your patients, John Reed. He was admitted last night, early this morning."

"Reed?"

"Yes."

Gwen pursed her lips and nodded to herself.

"You recognize the name," said Irwin, still smiling.

"A lot of people have been calling about him this morning."

"No kidding," said Irwin.

"Yes. Yes. There've been three or four calls already."

"Right," said Irwin. "How is he doing?"

"Recovering from surgery. Satisfactorily."

"Good, good. When can I see him?"

"Oh, I don't know. It's usually six to eight hours after surgery. Once they bring him back on the ward you can usually pop in. But he's not on the ward yet."

"Oh, right," said Irwin. "The recovery room. Where is that? The fifth floor?"

"Fourth floor," answered Gwen.

"Right," said Irwin. "Say, is there anywhere I can have breakfast while I'm waiting?"

"Basement. One floor down. The cafeteria."

"Thanks," said Irwin with a smile. He ambled off toward the elevators with no intention of going to the cafeteria. Gwen watched him thinking, I'm glad I don't have to make breakfast for him.

FORTY

Reed paged through his printouts, using them to review the volumes of information he had discovered about Ullmann. The pattern was now clear. Starting eight years earlier Ullmann had made his first acquisitions. Every few years after that, Ullmann acquired another piece of his empire . . . businesses and real estate that all worked in synergy with the institute.

Reed had to make estimates on the profits and income derived from those businesses, but from what Reed could tell, Ullmann had not used those profits to acquire other businesses. The profits had been invested elsewhere. Reed had found Ullmann's local bank. But he assumed it was being used for business transactions. Reed knew there had to be brokerage accounts, investments somewhere built from the profits of Ullmann's enterprises. Those accounts were the last pieces of the puzzle.

Unfortunately, when it came to brokerage accounts, Ullmann's could be virtually anywhere in the world. There didn't even need to be a human interface anymore. Ullmann's contact could be solely through a computerized network sending and receiving electronic blips over phone wires. Reed didn't know where the blips had gone. But he knew they had to pass through Ullmann's bank. And he knew the best way to track those ephemeral electronic impulses.

Reed consolidated the computer files, printed out the last batch of information he needed, and logged onto his E-mail program. SR had called earlier. They'd discussed what was needed. He was ready to receive the data Reed had gathered. Reed zipped the files and sent them to SR's E-mail account. It took almost fifteen minutes at 56K, even with the files compressed.

Finished on-line for the time being, Reed logged off. It was all coming together now. But he knew Angela had been right. Even if her call to Ullmann had bought some time, it wasn't much. They were sitting targets. And John Boyd was still in the hands of his enemies. Reed had to move soon.

The bleat of Reed's cell phone pulled Reed's attention away from his next task.

"*The eagle has landed.*"

"Irwin."

"*Yeah. I'm here at this hospital. Nice place for the middle-of-nowhere.*"

"You made good time."

"*I only got stopped once.*"

"You get a ticket?"

"Nah. The trooper was an okay guy. Just told me to keep it under eighty and be careful. I kicked it back up to eighty-five, no problem."

"Did you see John?"

"Just briefly. He's still in the recovery room. I'm up here on the floor where they're keeping him. I bullshitted around with the nurses. One of 'em let me slip in to take a quick look at him. He's still out, sleeping off the anesthesia."

"Are they watching after him?"

"Yeah, the nurses are right in the recovery room. It seems like they're taking good care of him."

"Did they give you an idea when he'll come around?"

"Nah."

"Any doctors around? Any sign of a Dr. Prentice?"

"No sign of any doctors. The nurse said the residents make rounds again after ten. I'll see what they have to say."

"Nobody else around?"

"Nada, boss. It's quiet up here."

"Don't count on it staying that way. If I hadn't showed up there last night and raised hell, I don't think John would be alive now."

"So what's the plan?"

"You watch him until I can get him out of there. Adele is sending up a medevac team to take him to a hospital in Canton which is about an hour away. The medevac ambulance should be on the way now. As soon as he can be moved, I'm going to get him the fuck out of there."

"Okay."

"The main thing is, don't let anybody else move him first. Don't let anybody else get near him."

"Mind if I ask why these people want to kill your cousin?"

"Why does anybody want someone dead? Money. I haven't got all the pieces together yet, but I will. Irwin, you fucking be careful if that sheriff or his deputies show up."

"Let 'em. I like the idea of drawing down in a hospital. You get dinged you don't have to travel far for medical attention."

"Don't get crazy, Irwin. They show up, you call in the state police and just stay with John. Pull out your credentials and try to keep it a standoff."

"Okay. Be nice to just get him the hell out of here before it gets nasty."

"Nothing we can do for at least a couple of hours. I'll be there to meet that medevac ambulance."

"Okay."

"Just in case, Irwin, did you bring shotguns?"

"In the trunk of my car, parked outside."

"Where's the key?"

"Sitting on the rear left tire."

"Okay."

"You hear from SR?"

"Yeah, we're hooked up."

"You give him your cell phone number so you can get through to him directly?"

"Yeah. What's this new thing of his?"

"You mean answering everything with lines from his favorite movies?"

"Is that what he's doing?"

"Who can tell, huh? Who the hell knows any of those movies?"

"Makes for short conversations. He said you got a connector."

"In my pocket. There's a disk that goes with it."

"Good. Stay alert. Keep your ears open about this Dr. Prentice. Maybe get a lead on him."

"All right. I'll see if I can bullshit something out of these nurses up here."

"You okay? You tired from the drive? Need sleep?"

"I'm good," Irwin replied. *"I'll call you if anything happens."*

"Irwin."

"What?"

"Thanks."

"For what?"

"For everything."

Reed ended the call, realizing now that he smelled frying eggs.

He had been working at the small desk in the larger bedroom, sitting on a hard-backed wooden chair in his jeans and T-shirt. His crutches lay behind him on the bed, the prosthesis propped at the foot of the bed. He thought about putting on the prosthesis, but the aroma of food pulled too insistently.

He picked up a flannel shirt he'd tossed on the bed and shrugged into it. Grabbed his crutches from the bed and headed for the kitchen.

Everything felt stiff. His hands were still sore, his fingers swollen, his bruises and muscles still aching. But nothing was broken or torn. And he had massaged his stump earlier, checking it carefully and assessing that it had not swelled much. It was in better shape than Reed had expected after the brutal climb. There was still tenderness at the front and back where the stump had levered back and forth against the socket, but Reed knew he could deal with it, along with everything else.

More importantly, after the climb Reed had much greater confidence in the artificial limb. Reed felt he could do just about anything in it. But for now, it would stay at the foot of the bed, giving his stump a break from the constricting socket.

As Reed hop/stepped into the kitchen, Angela dropped toasted English muffins onto two plates, and flipped eggs in a skillet moving like a short order cook.

She turned and looked at Reed.

"I hope you like your eggs over easy. Dumped on a muffin. That's all my friend put in his little care package. Plus lousy instant coffee."

"Fine with me," said Reed. He motioned out to the dining area. "You want to eat out there?"

Angela nodded toward the counter that ran behind the sink and separated the kitchen from the living room.

"The counter is easier. You all right with one of those stools?"

"Yeah."

Reed took a seat at one of the stools, watching Angela scoop out the eggs and slide them on top of the muffins.

She wore the same clothes she had worn the night before, her white waitress shirt and black slacks. The clothes were cleaner, but more wrinkled. She had pulled her hair back into a ponytail and she wore absolutely no makeup, which Reed thought made her look younger, fresher. But he did notice her brow furrowed slightly. He couldn't tell if she had something on her mind, or if she was concentrating on her work. Her sleeves were rolled up and as usual Reed took pleasure in watching her graceful movements.

"Where'd you get that tattoo?"

Angela held up her wrist and turned it for Reed. "This?"

"Yeah."

Angela poured instant coffee.

"I got it in London, in Soho. A friend of mine did it. He used a really fine needle. Did a nice job, but he took his time and it hurt like hell. Too close to the bone."

"Who designed it?"

"Me. But he made a few improvements."

Angela picked up the coffee mugs in one hand and the plates in the other, again reminding Reed of her waitress skills, and placed everything on the counter.

Angela sat in the stool next to Reed and took a sip from her mug. "The coffee isn't great, but . . ."

Reed tested his. "It's hot. That's most of it."

They ate in silence for a while. But Angela was clearly anxious. She picked at her food. Mostly, she drank the acrid coffee. Suddenly they both shifted positions on their stools and their shoulders bumped.

"Sorry," they both muttered at the same time.

Reed turned to Angela.

"Are you all right?" he asked.

Angela dropped her fork on the plate.

"No. I'm going slowly crazy. When are we going to get the hell out of here?"

Reed looked at his watch.

"An hour."

"Then what? You get your cousin out of the hospital and then what?"

The challenge in Angela's voice made Reed pause.

"What's the matter?"

Angela pushed her plate away.

"Look, this grim-faced determination act is getting to me. I don't know what you're planning, what you're up to. It feels like it's time I started thinking about myself."

Angela stood up and leaned over the counter, splashed the dregs of her coffee into the sink, and walked away. Reed grabbed his crutches.

"Hey," he called out. "Wait a minute."

She continued heading for the bedroom. Reed struggled up onto his crutches, heading after her.

Angela had already crossed the living room, but she stopped at the entrance to the hallway and turned toward him, speaking in a rush, not giving Reed a chance to say anything.

"Listen, I'm not stupid. Your first priority is your cousin. I understand that. You're going to get him out of that hospital and you're going to disappear with him. Maybe you'll do something about Malone and Ullmann, maybe not, but so what? I can't imagine anybody arresting them or making any charges stick. You've been stuck behind that computer of yours for hours . . . is that really going to prove anything about Ullmann? Is it?"

Reed had almost reached her. He started to answer, but Angela talked over him.

"From the moment I picked you up off that road, I was done for in this county. Ullmann knows I'm with you. When you run off with your cousin, what do I say? Uh, sorry, Matthew, he's gone." Reed opened his mouth, but Angela was talking too fast. "Ullmann is going to come after me. Malone will be knocking on my door, or maybe they'll just send Eddie McAndrews and some of his charming pals, one way or another, I'm screwed. I've got to get back to my house and pack up my life and get my sister and get the hell out of here. God knows where I'm going to—"

Finally, Reed shouted back at Angela, "No."

"What?"

"I said, no. You're not running. I'm not letting anything happen to you or your sister."

Reed moved closer to Angela, coming right up to her side. She refused to look at him. He stood on his one leg and crutches six inches from her shoulder, staring at her, waiting for her to turn to him, but Angela simply stared at the wall opposite her, shaking her head.

Reed leaned toward her, his voice rising to force her to hear him, to look at him. "Hey!"

Still, Angela would not meet his gaze.

"Angela, is that what you think I'd do? Just leave, just leave you here to face them alone? After all you've done for me? Is that who you think I am?"

Angela mumbled, "I don't know." Then she said, "How am I supposed to know?"

"Just listen to me."

"Listen to what? What can you do?"

"You don't understand, do you?"

"Understand what, for God's sake?"

"What Matthew Ullmann and his wife are doing?"

"What?" Angela shouted back. "What are they doing?"

Reed yelled, "They are killing innocent retarded people for money."

Finally, Angela turned and met his gaze, but instead of belief, Reed only saw confusion in her eyes.

"Angela, I can't tell you exactly who and when and how, but I'll bet you my life that if I go back into the records of that institute, I'll find residents who died every time Matthew Ullmann came into money."

Angela's mouth moved, but no words came out.

"Angela, this is murder for money. Murder of helpless, innocent people. The most innocent people imaginable. You think I'm going to get my cousin and run? Turn my back on you and leave you to those monsters? You think I'm going to let them get away with this?"

She muttered, "I don't know."

Still standing in his crutches, Reed reached out to grab Angela's arm.

"Please, Angela, listen to me. There's no turning back. Not for me, not for you. You came after me. You picked me up off that road. You got me to that hospital. You saved my cousin. You saved an abandoned, sick, retarded man who never did anything worse than smile at people and try to be brave in a world he couldn't possibly understand or comprehend. Because of you, he's alive. Do you really think I'd just leave you to these, these murderers?"

Angela finally turned toward Reed.

"Why? Because I'm some assistant-girl-crime-fighter helping you against the bad guys?"

"No. You know damn well that's not it."

Angela raised her chin. "Then what is it?"

Reed met her gaze, his mouth a tight line.

"What?" she pressed.

Reed glared at her.

"*What?*" she said again, nearly shouting the question.

Reed pivoted on his right foot, coming around to face Angela, leaning in on her.

"You know why," he said.

Angela tried to stand her ground, but she was no match for Reed's size and strength. She stepped back from him until she bumped into the hallway wall, but she continued to challenge him.

"Why?" she asked. "Tell me. Why?"

Reed pressed in on her, pinning her to the wall, his face so close he could feel her breath on his cheek. Reed's voice felt constricted as he spoke, his words coming out almost as a growl. "You must know. Don't you?"

Angela made eye contact with Reed, looking at him almost defiantly, saying nothing, doing nothing, looking him in the eyes, waiting. Suddenly Reed dropped his crutches, slammed his hand against the wall above her, wrapped his right arm around Angela, and pulled her against him, arching her backward, her face tilting to him. Reed bowed slightly, gently pressing his forehead against hers, and with eyes closed he whispered, "I can't imagine myself ever leaving you, and I can't imagine ever having you."

And then suddenly, Angela had her long arms around him, clinging to him.

"Oh, God," she said, "why is this so goddamned hard?"

"I don't know," said Reed. "All I know is that I don't want to leave you."

"I didn't see any of this coming. I don't understand any of it. I don't know what to do."

And then suddenly they were kissing each other, their lips everywhere, on cheeks, eyes, foreheads. Reed wobbled, caught himself, leaned into Angela, casting aside every fear or worry for the moment, not even caring if he lost his balance and fell. He pressed into her, his right arm wrapped around her, feeling her slim waist and hips, his hand running up her side, feeling her ribs, her breast, her back, trying to feel all of her at once, balancing on one foot, one hand against the wall, but Reed didn't care, didn't care anymore about anything because somehow, some way, he was holding Angela Quist and kissing her, the woman he had wanted from the first moment he'd seen her, but never let himself believe he would ever have.

Reed felt Angela holding the back of his head, pulling him down to her. He wanted to talk, to say something, but her lips would not let him. He felt awkward. He wanted to be lying next to her, holding her against him, taking her.

And then Angela gently eased away from him, pressing her face against his shoulder. He felt her tremble, then, feeling the wetness through his shirt, he realized she had burst into tears. He held on to her, trying to comfort her, trying to convey through his touch that it was all right. Then suddenly, fiercely, she pulled away from him, angrily wiping the tears from her face, forcing herself to stop.

"I'm sorry. It's just, just too much."

Reed reached out, but she put up a hand. He stood mute, afraid to say anything.

She stared at Reed defiantly. "I hope to hell, Bill Reed, I hope to hell you know how I feel about you."

Reed nodded.

"When this is over," she said, "when I know what the next ten minutes in my life are going to be, you and I are going to . . ."

"To what?"

"To see."

"About what?" asked Reed.

"About everything. Everything."

FORTY-ONE

The more Sheriff Ralph Malone stalked the halls of Clearbrook Hospital, the angrier he became.

Almost every person he questioned about George Prentice's whereabouts ended up asking him about his facial wounds. The doctors, nurses, orderlies, all knew the sheriff, and they seemed to take a sly pleasure in asking Malone what happened to him instead of answering his questions.

Malone quickly came up with a cryptic answer, "Line of duty," which only elicited quizzical looks, or knowing looks. One of the doctors even had the effrontery to say, "Line of duty, huh? Well I hope the other guy looks worse than you, Sheriff."

Malone's mood had become so black that he began having fantasies about slapping an answer out of the hospital staff.

Shortly before nine o'clock, Malone found himself standing alone in the second-floor surgeons' lounge, frowning, running an internal monologue in his head, forcing himself to leave his anger behind enough so that he could think clearly.

All right, Prentice is obviously hiding out. Where does someone hide? With friends and relatives. A mother, a brother. A wife, a girlfriend, a boyfriend. As Malone tested the possibilities for George Prentice, the idea of a boyfriend floated so naturally into his consciousness that Malone knew it had eluded him only because of his previous anger.

From the surgeons' lounge to the personnel office took Malone only ten minutes of wandering through halls, asking directions. He arrived at just after nine o'clock. The personnel office was open, but the manager not at his desk.

Malone sat at the desk waiting patiently until a slight man in his forties, dressed in pressed blue jeans, wearing a green shirt and plaid tie, came into the office carrying a sixteen-ounce cup of coffee and a blueberry muffin.

The man was taken aback by the presence of the county sheriff waiting for him, not to mention his battered appearance. But Malone was at his best now, apologizing, putting the man at ease, explaining his appearance and what he was after quickly and efficiently before the man could ask or wonder about the answers.

It took clearing away a few excuses and gently forcing the man, Mr. Pritzker, to call several department heads, but within thirty minutes Ralph Malone had the names of all the people at Clearbrook Hospital who were on scheduled vacation or had called in sick or had simply not shown up to work. The list amounted to fourteen people. Malone eliminated the eight females and received the ages and jobs of the remaining six males. Phone calls eliminated four. A call back from the fifth employee brought it down to one possibility, Alan Molina of 51 Tottenville Road.

Out in his police cruiser, Malone carefully checked a map for the location of Tottenville Road. It ran between Highways 16 and 11, about six miles east of Greenport and ten miles south of Dumphy. Just as Malone was about to start the car engine, his cellular phone rang.

"Malone here."

"Ullmann."

"Yessir."

"Where are you?"

"About twenty minutes away from where Prentice might be hiding."

"Is that so? Well the pansy bastard just called me."

"From where?"

"Oh, Dr. Prentice is being clever. He won't tell me. All he's saying is that he has a proposition for me. Told me to calm down, have an open mind. Said he'd call back in ten minutes."

"Stall him. I may find him first."

"I have no intention of waiting for his call. Go see if you can find him. But don't do anything to him. Get a hold of Eddie and wait. If you find him, call me back. I'm going to the hospital to take away some of his negotiating leverage."

"Okay."

"More good news. I think I've got a lead on Mr. Bill Reed."

"What might that be?"

"Angela Quist called. She sounds like she wants to make some sort of deal."

"Make it," said Malone.

"Oh, I certainly will," said Ullmann. *"I most certainly will. With any luck we'll have this whole thing wrapped up by tonight. It hasn't been easy. I know you're working very hard on this. Rest assured your efforts are appreciated, Ralph."*

"Mr. Ullmann, that's nice of you to say. But I think we both know none of us are in this for anything much but the money. I'll tell you straight out, I'm expecting Prentice's share after we're done with him."

"And why not, Ralph? I think you deserve his share. I assure you Dr. Prentice won't be needing it."

"I'll call you."

Just as Matthew Ullmann hung up the kitchen phone, Madeleine entered, dressed for the day wearing a print blouse, black, pleated wool skirt, and one of the long cardigan sweaters she wore to camouflage her ample hips.

Matthew asked, "Did Orenberg buy the delay?"

"Yes. Although I could tell that his radar was turned on."

"Why?"

"He mentioned he'll want to talk to Prentice. That's the first time I've ever heard him make that request."

"What did you say?"

"I asked if he wanted Prentice to meet us for dinner."

"Very good, Madeleine. What did he say to that?"

"Maybe after dinner."

"Fine. Fine. I'll serve him Prentice's head for dessert along with Johnny Boy's colon and tumor. Are you ready?"

Madeleine patted one of her skirt pockets and said, "Yes. There is a percentage of people who experience heart attacks after general anesthesia and major surgery."

"Really?" Matthew smiled.

"I haven't decided whether to just shoot a syringe full of potassium chloride into his IV shunt, or just a great big bolus of air. One's more certain, but the other leaves less trace."

Ullmann stood up from the table in their breakfast nook and wrestled on his stadium coat.

"Why not do both?"

Madeleine brightened, surprised at herself for not thinking of it.

Matthew said, "I wouldn't worry about leaving traces. His body won't be around for long." Ullmann looked at his watch. "We've got a lot to get done today, and I'm exhausted."

"You'll make it."

"Indeed I will. After we finish up with Johnny Boy, would you like to help me torture information out of George Prentice?"

Madeleine's eyes lit up. "Are you serious?"

"Yes."

"What do you need to know?"

"Not much. The whereabouts of my tissue samples."

"That shouldn't be too hard."

"I don't know. He seems to have suddenly acquired a pair of balls."

"What do you attribute that to?"

"I have no idea."

"Mmmm," said Madeleine. "Balls. That reminds me of a book I once read where the villains wrapped one of those wire garrote things around a man's scrotum sack and penis. They pulled it very tight, then asked questions. He told them everything."

"Don't tell me you have a wire garrote."

"We could improvise."

Madeleine and Matthew looked at each other, seeing the glint in each other's eyes.

Madeleine said, "Did Ralph find him? Are we going to see Prentice after the hospital?"

"It looks like it."

"Let me go get my medical bag."

"All right, dear, but hurry up."

Eddie McAndrews had been rummaging through the file cabinet in Angela Quist's studio when Ralph Malone's call came through. The insistent beeping of the cellular phone surprised him, but he kept looking at her papers as he answered the phone.

"Yeah."

"It's me," said Ralph Malone.

"What's up, Sheriff? How's your face feel?"

"Like hell. Where are you?"

"Standing in Angela Quist's house."

"Doing what?"

"Number one, making sure that bitch isn't here. Number two, looking through her stuff to see if I can find out where she might be."

"What stuff would that be?"

"Oh, letters and bills, stuff like that. Records of folks she did work for. That fucking bitch gets paid a lot for her shit, do you know that?"

"No, and I don't care. We'll find her soon enough. I need you now on Prentice. I told you Prentice was the priority."

"And I told you, Sheriff, I want to find Bill Reed and shoot his face off after what he did to Ray. He's *my* priority."

"He'll have to wait. I want you to meet me now. I found Prentice: I'm parked outside a place on Tottenville Road. His car is behind the garage."

"What do you need me for?"

"I don't need you for anything. Ullmann wants you here."

"Fuck."

"You want me to tell him you're too busy?"

"No, fucking take it easy. Where are you? Give me directions."

FORTY-TWO

When Johnny Boy awoke in the dimly lit recovery room, groggy and confused, his mind did not process information quickly enough to take in the strange environment, remember why he was there and what had happened to him.

At first, the confusion paralyzed him, and then within moments, the pain from the surgical procedure and nausea from the anesthesia overwhelmed him, increasing his confusion and bringing on a panic reaction.

Johnny Boy blinked his eyes, turning his head from side to side, the taste of the anesthesia in his mouth making him feel like he had to vomit. He tried to sit up and felt a sudden piercing, tearing pain in his right side. He looked down and saw a bulge under his hospital gown. He reached down to feel the bulge and realized it was a bandage. A very thick pad of gauze and tape nearly circled him from his abdomen to his chest. He tried to sit up again, as if he'd forgotten the pain it had caused moments ago and grunted, lying back down.

The sound awakened Irwin Barker who had been dozing in a chair set next to Johnny Boy's hospital bed. Irwin had convinced the nurse to let him sit next to Johnny Boy. Irwin knew he might doze off in the dimly lit recovery room, but only allowed himself the rest because he knew he was right next to his charge.

Irwin stood up quickly, looming over Johnny Boy as if he had appeared out of nowhere.

Normally, the sight of a stranger, a stranger as big and formidable as Irwin Barker, would have alarmed Johnny Boy, but this time, just because Irwin was another human being, it helped assuage Johnny Boy's panic. Irwin's soothing voice and manner also helped, as did the fact he knew Johnny Boy's name, although that also confused Johnny Boy.

Irwin reached out to gently pat Johnny Boy's shoulder, making sure not to jar him or cause any pain. "Hey, John, take it easy, guy. Take it easy."

Johnny Boy looked at Irwin with a wide-eyed stare. Irwin kept talking, trying to bring Johnny Boy down from his fear and confusion.

"John, everything is all right. Your Cousin Bill sent me to look after you."

Irwin watched Johnny Boy react to the mention of Cousin Bill.

"Yeah, Cousin Bill sent me."

Johnny Boy continued to stare at Irwin uncomprehending, but dry-mouthed and groggy he managed to repeat the name, "Cuz'n Bill."

"Yeah. My name is Irwin. Bill knows me. He called me. I'm going to look after you. They operated on you. Everything is okay. You're in the hospital. I'm going to get the nurse over here now, okay?"

Irwin felt Johnny Boy grab for his wrist, as if to prevent him from leaving. Irwin patted his shoulder again.

"Don't worry, fella. I'm just going to tell the nurse you're awake. I'll be right back. I know you're brave, John, so you just hang in. I'll be right back. Don't worry. You just relax. Relax and take it easy, okay?"

Johnny Boy mustered the wherewithal to answer Irwin with a nod.

"Good. Be right back."

The transfer of Johnny Boy from the surgical recovery room to the ward happened just as Matthew and Madeleine Ullmann entered Clearbrook Hospital. By the time they arrived at the sixth floor, after having been sent to the fourth floor, they were in no mood for any more delays.

Madeleine led the way to the nurses' station and said to the first nurse who looked up, "Where's Johnny Reed? What room?" Just like that, demanding an answer.

As with most people assaulted by Madeleine, the nurse was too stunned to answer right away.

"Come on, girlie," said Madeleine, "I've been jerked around here for half an hour trying to find him. What room? Johnny Reed. The room number."

The nurse looked down at her list and mumbled, "Six oh three, but he—"

"But nothing," said Madeleine. "We're from the Ullmann Institute. We're in charge of him. We want to see that he's being taken care of properly." And before the nurse could say another word, Madeleine stormed off toward Johnny Boy's room, her heels clacking hard on the hospital's tiled floor, Matthew scurrying behind her.

Matthew caught up to his wife, grabbed her arm firmly, slowing her to a stop.

He said quietly, but firmly, "Just a moment, dear."

He waited for Madeleine to calm down and focus on him.

"I think we should do something that won't take effect immediately. We don't want to be standing there when he dies, do we?"

"I couldn't care less," said Madeleine. "I'm sure it'll be a while before these dimwits around here even notice. I doubt if anybody is going to check on a retarded patient every fifteen minutes. It's not like they can talk to him or ask him how he feels."

"Just a moment," said Matthew. "We show up. We leave. He's dead. That's not acceptable."

Madeleine's eyes squinted nearly shut.

"Well what do you want me to do?"

"Hang on," said Matthew as he considered the problem. "We'll do just the opposite. Do it quickly. Very quickly. Then we'll come out yelling that he's dead. He died before we even walked into the room."

Madeleine smiled. "That's good. Good. Then we can stay and make the arrangements for the body to be shipped back to the institute for burial."

"Perfect. Let's go. Are your ready?"

"I'm ready, I'm ready."

Matthew Ullmann looked closely at his wife. He had never seen her quite like this before. Her eyes glistened. She glowed with anticipation, listing toward the door to Johnny Boy's room as if the opportunity to kill someone pulled her like a giant magnet. Just looking at her made Ullmann feel a pulse of excitement, a titillation gather in his throat and chest, a visceral, almost sexual wallop of emotion.

With one hand on the syringe in her skirt pocket, Madeleine pushed open the door to Johnny Boy's room, pulling Matthew along in her wake.

When Madeleine Ullmann saw Irwin Barker stand up as she entered, she almost choked on the effort it took to stop herself and deal with the emotional backlash. She had already anticipated inserting her syringe into Johnny Boy's IV line. She was already in the grip of excitement at the prospect of pushing death into his veins and watching him die, not to mention the anticipated pleasure she looked forward to from yelling and screaming at the nurses and doctors for allowing one of her precious residents to die.

When Irwin stood up smiling, saying pleasantly, "Excuse me, but Mr. Reed is not seeing any visitors," Madeleine's face constricted in frustration and rage. Her left cheek began to twitch at the effort it took her not to scream. She emitted a noise that sounded like small chewed-up words from deep in her throat.

Matthew Ullmann stepped in front of her and demanded of Irwin, "Who are you, and why are you in this room?"

Irwin pulled out his wallet of credentials.

"I'm the personal, armed bodyguard of Mr. John Boyd Reed. My name is Irwin Barker. And you are?"

"I'm—I'm Matthew Ullmann, the head of the Ullmann Institute. Johnny Reed is one of my residents."

"And?"

"And you're going to have to leave while we check on our patient."

"Your resident or your patient?"

"Both," said Madeleine Ullmann. "I'm a nurse practitioner. I've been looking after Johnny Boy Reed for years."

Irwin nodded. "But not today. Not anymore."

Ullmann didn't have to look behind him to know that Madeleine was probably on the verge of screaming at Irwin, possibly lunging at him. Ullmann assumed a very quiet and reasonable voice.

"May I ask who requested that you be here?"

"Sure," said Irwin.

"Who?"

"None of your business."

Ullmann flashed a tight smile. "Oh, is that so. I see. Well, we'll see about this, Mr. Parker."

"Barker."

"Barker. Fine. I'll remember." Ullmann turned to Madeleine and said, "Come, dear, we'll have our visit later." He took her by the arm and led her out of the hospital room.

When they reached the hall, Madeleine began to speak, but Ullmann hissed, "Not here."

Ignoring him, she snarled, "What are we going to do?"

"Prentice is still his doctor. We'll find him and drag him back here and have him transfer Johnny Boy back to the institute. We'll have Ralph enforce his order if need be. Come on."

Madeleine could not contain herself.

"Did you see him?" she asked.

"Who?"

"Johnny Boy."

"What do you mean?"

"He was smirking. I swear to you that idiot was smirking at me."

"Don't be ridiculous, dear. Let's go."

FORTY-THREE

Bill Reed had almost finished packing up his trunk. He heard Angela Quist out in the kitchen tidying up. He knew she was keeping her distance. They had never been closer, and yet it seemed more important than ever that they keep their distance. Reed shoved the last of his clothes into his trunk, just as he shoved his feelings somewhere deeper inside him.

He walked into the living room. Angela stood by the kitchen window, smoking.

"You ready?" he asked.

"Yeah. Sure. What's the number?"

She dialed the phone. Reed stood on the other side of the kitchen counter, listening.

"Hello," Angela said, making her voice sound businesslike. "This is Gladys Richards calling for Matthew Ullmann. He'd like to speak to the person who handles his account." After a pause, she continued, "Right, Ms. Winston. What?" She looked at Reed when she said, "Oh, Ms. Winston is not in today?"

Reed indicated that Angela should keep going.

"Perhaps you can help Mr. Ullmann. . . . uh-huh, and you are?" She looked at Reed as she repeated the name she heard. "Mr. Washington. Lionel Washington. Thank you, Mr. Washington. Please hold for Mr. Ullmann."

Angela looked at Reed who nodded and gave her a thumbs up sign as she handed him the phone.

Reed took the phone and began speaking in a manner that mimicked Matthew Ullmann. It wasn't that Reed tried to sound like Ullmann. It was as if he had taken on the persona of Ullmann, speaking in an officious yet unctuous manner like a man who deigned to act courteous only because it suited him.

"Ms. Winston?" said Reed. "Oh, excuse me, Mr. Washington. Refresh my memory, Mr. Washington, have we spoken before?"

"I don't think so," said Washington.

"Right. I didn't recall. I usually deal with Winston. My assistant said she was out today."

"Yes, sir."

"Right. Well, I need your help, Mr. Washington. Here's the situation. I'm in a bit of a hassle with my accountant about last year's tax returns. I don't even want to say the word . . . but he got a notice that the goddamn IRS is asking for some verification that has to do with my quarterly estimates. It's a little complicated, but my records show one thing, his another, and I damn well want this sorted out before we end up with an audit."

"Oh, boy," said Washington.

"Oh, boy is right," said Reed. "Here's what I need. I want to confirm checks and wire transfers to my brokerage account from my account there at BancOne. Here's my account number." Reed rattled off the number, repeating it for Washington until he got it. "I'm looking at the time around May of last year, through the end of the year. Can you pull up my records?"

"Hang on a second," said Washington.

Reed stopped talking, listening to the click of a keyboard at the other end of the line.

"Which account is it?" asked Washington.

"Are you looking at oh, six, four nine, or oh, six, six, seven?" asked Reed.

"Uh, let me see," said Washington.

"That's the last four digits," said Reed, making himself sound annoyed.

"Ah, right . . . oh, six, four, nine," said Washington.

"Let's do that one first, then we'll do the other. What wire transfers do you show to my brokerage accounts?"

"Uh, let's see, here's one in June for one hundred twenty-four thousand and change to U.S. E-Trade, account eight, nine, two, dash, six, four, seven, three, one—"

"Right. What's the exact date you have for that one, Mr. Washington?"

"June sixth."

"Which bank transfer number did you use? Just so I can track it back with them."

Angela watched Reed alternate between being demanding and helpful, conspiratorial and pushy, talking quickly when he had to prompt Washington, slowly when he had his own information to provide. Reed blended in the information he had gathered on Ullmann so skillfully that he even had Angela believing he already knew what Washington would tell him and simply wanted it verified.

After five minutes, Reed hung up the phone and spun around, smiling at Angela.

"Done. U.S. E-Trade. Got it. You were great," he said. "Great setup."

"Was that legal?"

"It mostly depends on who your lawyer is."

"Jeezus, he didn't do much to verify you were Ullmann."

"Why should he? It sounded like the call was coming from his office. Thanks to you."

"Yeah, right."

"It wouldn't have mattered. I have Ullmann's bank account number, social security number, his address, his phone, zip code, and mother's maiden name. I wasn't asking him to actually do anything with my money. Just fill in a few blanks."

"How'd you get all that?"

"A combination of paying for it and knowing where to look."

"Now what?" said Angela.

"How are you at cutting hair?" said Reed.

"Huh?"

Matthew Ullmann called Ralph Malone just before Malone was about to call him.

The acid in Ullmann's voice alerted Malone to Ullmann's mood so he spoke first. "I was just about to call you. We have Prentice."

"You do?"

"Yes. I'm outside the place where he's hiding. McAndrews is in there with him. I told him to mind his manners."

"Perfect. Perfect. Let me have exact directions. I'm on my way."

Ullmann listened carefully as he drove. Madeleine watched him as he repeated the directions.

Ullmann said, "I'll be there in ten minutes," and cut off the call.

"You think he'll do what you want?" Madeleine asked.

Ullmann turned to her with a pained expression. "Oh, please. Don't be ridiculous."

"Then what?"

"Then I'm done with Prentice. For good."

"Malone?"

"He'll do it. For the right price. Or Eddie. Or both of them."

"Malone is going to have quite a bit on you."

"No one is going to have anything on us. They won't even have us."

"We're ending it?"

"Yes. All of it."

Madeleine nodded, but not in acquiescence, only at hearing her husband finally admit to her what he intended to do.

"You're sure?"

"Madeleine, it's time. We finish our business here, and then you and I are going to disappear. As soon as we get done with Prentice and Johnny Boy and Orenberg, I'll get on-line and transfer our holdings where they can't be found. I set up accounts long ago: Grand Cayman, Liechtenstein, Switzerland. It'll take me fifteen, twenty minutes to do the transactions. All of the forms have been filed at the brokerage for wire transfers. We'll process the insurance claims from wherever we land. That'll tide us over easily no matter what we want to do. We'll sit back and watch our stocks soar over the next few years and leave our cares behind."

"You think Orenberg and his bunch will be successful?"

"For God's sake, Madeleine, how many bodies did we give them, six, seven? How many of their damn drugs did they try out? You were in charge of that."

"We gave them nine, Matthew. Six didn't make it. Three did. Four Down syndrome, three brain damaged, one normal intelligent palsy victim. They tried forty-seven experimental drugs."

"How many were any good?"

"Assuming the new cancer drug they tried on Johnny Boy worked as expected, that would make seven out of forty-seven that showed promise."

"That's forty experimental drugs they didn't have to waste money on to qualify them for human trials. You know how many millions that adds to the bottom line? You realize how good their numbers are going to look to the analysts. That alone will make the stock soar. If one or two of the seven actually make it through phase one clinicals, the stock will jump another two, three, four times value at least. We'll make more than we'll ever need. The whole thing is getting too risky. They're getting crazier with this stuff every time they do another experiment. You know that. They almost killed Johnny Boy implanting those cancer cells into his colon."

"The drugs they gave him to stop his rejection might have invalidated everything."

Matthew turned to her, speaking in a level voice. "It's not

our problem, dear. The stock will do fine. More than fine. But it's time to get out. We've gone far enough with this. Even if we just get a decent bump in the stock price, we'll have enough. Maybe we won't get all that we could have; maybe we will. Why push it?"

"I know, I know . . . pigs go to market, hogs get slaughtered."

"Yes. And we're going to market, Madeleine. Right after a final bit of slaughter."

Ullmann opened the front door of Alan Molina's bungalow without knocking. He and Madeleine stepped into a small foyer that opened onto a compact living room from which they could see a comfortable sunny kitchen. From the foyer, a single run of stairs led up to where Ullmann assumed were the bedrooms.

The bungalow had been tastefully furnished with what looked to Ullmann like very good acquisitions from local country auctions and estate sales. The small house was impeccably maintained. Even the magazines on the coffee table in the living room were fanned out at just the right angles.

Ullmann entered the small living room, bent forward, head down, a scowl on his face, giving the impression that he was in a hurry and had no time for any resistance from anyone.

Ralph Malone sat with his usual upright posture on a half-size couch set against the left wall. The sutures and bruises on his face made him look more angry and formidable than usual.

Eddie McAndrews, wearing jeans, a thermal underwear shirt, and a down vest, slouched in a comfortable armchair opposite George Prentice who sat in another armchair facing the fireplace. Prentice wore the clothes he had worn to the hospital, khaki slacks, blue blazer, blue shirt, and a stylish yellow tie. He tried to appear as if he weren't intimidated.

Ullmann unbuttoned his stadium coat and motioned for Eddie to get up so he could sit opposite Prentice. Madeleine left her coat buttoned and sat on the couch next to Malone.

Ullmann flashed one of his grimacing smiles at McAndrews and said, "Eddie, would you mind waiting outside for us. Have a smoke. You probably would be better off not witnessing any of this."

McAndrews raised his eyebrows and smiled. "Now you got me curious."

"Please, Eddie."

"Sure, boss. Call me if you need me. You know, to break something up or haul out the trash."

"I will," said Ullmann.

As soon as the front door closed behind Eddie McAndrews, Ullmann turned to Prentice and said, "Whose house is this, George?"

"A friend's," answered Prentice.

"Do I know him?" asked Ullmann.

"No."

Ullmann studied Prentice for a few moments, measuring the defiance in him.

"Where is your friend?"

"Visiting his relatives. Quite far from here, actually."

Ullmann nodded and turned to Malone.

"Do we know the name of this friend?" emphasizing the word *friend* so as to convey to Prentice he understood exactly the nature of the friendship.

"Alan Molina," Malone answered dryly.

Ullmann turned to stare at Prentice, saying nothing, just looking at him, making it clear by his expression that finding Prentice's friend would be as easy as it had been to find the friend's house.

Ullmann watched the concern etch across the doctor's face, even though he tried to conceal it. At just the right moment, his voice sounding conciliatory, Ullmann said, "George, what are you doing?"

Prentice answered quickly, "I'm doing what I have to do."

"Which is what, exactly?"

"I'm going to make you an offer that I'm sure you will find quite satisfactory. Then I'm getting out of this mess once and for all. It's simply not something I wish to be involved with anymore."

Ullmann raised an eyebrow. "Anymore."

"Yes."

"So you're getting out?"

"I expect to pay for my early exit."

"Ah," said Ullmann, tipping his head back. "I see."

Madeleine Ullmann leaned forward to speak, but one quick look from Matthew made her clamp her mouth shut.

"You have to admit, Matthew, this situation is far beyond what you described."

"How so?"

"I didn't expect a crazed lunatic to put a gun to my head and tell me he'd kill me if anything happened to his relative, particularly in front of witnesses. How would it have looked if I'd let that poor retarded man die on my operating table? There would have been all sorts of inquiries. That wouldn't have been good for me or for you."

Ullmann nodded, sitting back in the comfortable armchair, his hands steepled under his chin.

Prentice continued, gaining confidence in his argument.

"Putting aside the death threat, do you think that cousin of Johnny Boy's wouldn't have raised all kinds of hell if Johnny Boy hadn't survived the surgery? I think I came up with a solution that accomplishes what you want and will also prevent a great many problems."

Ullmann looked at Prentice and thought about smashing his face with the lamp that sat on the table next to him, but he simply nodded, cleared his throat to alleviate the tension constricting it, and said, "A solution?"

"Yes."

"And I presume something that would compensate for your failure to perform your side of the bargain."

Prentice nodded, trying to keep his voice from quivering. He pictured Alan, pictured them together in their home in Key West, away from all this, safe.

"I've done everything you've asked. Just a little differently than you've asked."

"That's funny. Was that a dead man I just visited? He looked alive to me."

"Not for long."

"Care to explain that?"

"I fixed it so that he'll die within twenty-four to forty-eight hours."

Ullmann raised his eyebrows. "What do you mean?"

"I didn't exactly complete the surgery. You see, I was trying to devise a way that would ensure his death, but not cause too much suspicion. I kept struggling with that, Matthew, and I finally came up with the idea that I would finish off the closure of the colon in such a way—"

Ullmann interrupted impatiently, "What the hell are you talking about?"

"A couple of stitches. I didn't quite finish them off. If they haven't already opened they soon will and that will be the end of it. Within twenty-four to forty-eight hours he'll be dead unless they go back in and fix it. So you see, I really have killed him."

"Uh-huh."

"Maybe not quite according to your time schedule, but just as certainly and, I think, in a much better way."

"*You* think."

"Yes, Matthew."

"And *you* thought that would be better for me."

"Yes. For you, for all concerned."

Ullmann nodded, now imagining himself hitting Prentice with the lamp until his face was bloody. He pursed his lips and said, "What's your proposal, George?"

Prentice leaned forward, ready now to make his pitch.

"You have told us all along, Matthew"—Prentice nodded toward Malone and Madeleine—"all of us here, that our stock would be ten times the value when we bought it. It's taken three years, three years of very risky efforts, for it to rise just a little under fifty percent. According to your estimates, the vast majority of the value is yet to come." Again, Prentice looked at Malone and Madeleine. "As you know, I own fifty thousand of those shares. They're worth a little over six dollars a share." Prentice motioned to the others in the room. "I'll sell you my shares right now, at market value. Transfer them to your account. I assume you have enough operating capital to purchase them. I know you won't have to worry about cash flow once Johnny Boy dies. Give me half the purchase price now, I'll give you the tissue samples for Orenberg. I've already examined the tumor. I guarantee you those samples are going to be very well received. The shares you'll get from me will be worth much, much more than they are now. For the opportunity to get out now, I'll sacrifice my future profits. I think that's more than fair for any inconvenience I've caused. Although as I said, I think I've saved you a lot of trouble."

"Hmm," muttered Matthew. "What about Johnny Boy? I have to wait twenty-four to forty-eight hours? And the hospital staff is just going to sit around and watch him die?"

"That's not a problem. I doubt if he's showing any signs of infection yet. I'll go to the hospital with you. You pay me my second half, I'll have him discharged to your clinic. Give him to Orenberg in any condition you choose. You'll have my stock. Orenberg will have his body for autopsy, his tissue samples, all his test results. Everybody is happy. I go away, you'll never see or hear from me again."

Ullmann cocked his head to one side as if he was considering Prentice's offer. After a moment, he said in a quiet voice, measuring his words, "I don't suppose I have to point out that unless we get the tumor and the colon and the rest of Johnny Boy Reed into the hands of our associates, the value of the stock will be put in serious jeopardy, thus nullifying much of your offer's value."

"I understand that," said Prentice. "But obviously, I need assurances. I can get you the tissue samples almost immediately."

"Where are they?" Ullmann pointed with his chin. "Out there in the refrigerator?"

"No, certainly not. The temperature outside is just under

forty degrees. Perfect for storing the samples. So obviously they could be hidden anywhere between here and the hospital. It'll take us less than a half hour to drive to the bank, cut two cashier's checks. Give me a check, I tell you the location of the tissue samples. Then I'll go to the hospital and make arrangements for Johnny Boy to be discharged to your clinic, or to the research company's hospital of choice in Boston, or anywhere you like. You pay me the balance, I sign him out. You have everything you need. I lose most of what I've worked for, but I'm willing to take the loss to get out of this situation."

"And go live happily ever after with Mr. Alan Molina?"

"I'll admit that's my plan. I'll be very far away from here. Someplace you won't easily find me. And if you do, harming me will only result in information being divulged that will harm all of you. If you harm Alan, I won't care about divulging information that will hurt me. I won't want to live without him."

"How very touching," said Ullmann. "So that's your offer?"

"Yes."

Ullmann leaned forward, finally allowing his anger and venom to spill out.

"Here's my counteroffer. I'll give you seventy-five thousand for the tumor and colon parts. I'll give you another seventy-five thousand once Johnny Boy Reed is out of that hospital in my hands. I hear one mincing word out of your mouth other than . . . thank you, I call Eddie back in here and have him break fingers and toes while Madeleine sticks needles in you until you scream out the location of my tissue samples. Then I have Ralph put a bullet in your head and bury you somewhere so deep your little gay friend won't even be able to find what's left of you. Then I go to that goddamn hospital with Ralph and his deputies and Eddie driving an ambulance and haul that dying retard out of there myself."

Ullmann inclined his head, speaking softly. "All I need you for is to make it a little faster and easier. That's my offer, George, and a generous one at that . . . a hundred fifty thousand to just get rid of you and be done with this so I can make a dinner appointment." Ullmann leaned forward, even closer to Prentice, and spoke slowly, the acid in his voice burning a deep impression on Prentice. "It's a onetime offer, George, good for five seconds. In five seconds I want to hear the location of the tissue samples. And make damn sure you say thank you first."

Madeleine Ullmann sitting primly on Alan Molina's sofa smiled and began counting slowly, starting with two.

FORTY-FOUR

A minute after Angela Quist began cutting Bill Reed's hair, the phone rang. He talked while Angela snipped away. She had been chopping away at his thick brown hair for ten minutes when he finished his phone conversation with SR.

Reed handed her the phone. She replaced it on the receiver, stepping back to look at her handiwork.

"This looks terrible."

"Good," said Reed. "I don't want it looking like a sixty-dollar haircut."

"How much?"

"Sixty. And that's a bargain in my neighborhood."

"That's insane." Angela held a small pair of scissors up and asked, "Where'd you get these scissors?"

"And that's not including tips. I don't remember where I got them."

"They're pretty good scissors."

"You sound like you know."

"There was a time when I cut hair."

"Yeah, the way you handle the comb and scissors it feels like it. How much do you charge?"

"A hundred."

Reed checked his watch.

"You finish in the next five minutes, you're on."

His cell phone rang again. Reed hit the talk button.

"Yeah?"

"Bill, it's me."

"Irwin. What's up?"

"A spot of trouble. Your friends the Ullmanns showed up. Charming couple."

"What happened?"

"Nothing. They walked in the room here with me and John. They weren't happy to see me."

"What did they want?"

"I don't know. I shooed them away. The woman looked like she was about to spit."

"When was that?"

"About a half hour ago. Both your lines have been busy."

"I was downloading files and talking to SR."

"Talking to SR? No wonder it took so long."

"No, he's coming around. This thing has got him interested. The more I explain, the more he focuses and stops quoting film dialogue to me. Have the medevac people shown up yet?"

"No."

"It should be within the next hour. I'm about thirty minutes away."

"Okay."

"Just hang in, Irwin."

"Yeah, listen, Bill, I have the feeling those people aren't giving up."

"I understand. Just hold the fort."

Reed clicked off the cell phone, ran a hand through what was left of his hair.

"We're finished."

"Wait," said Angela. She quickly ran the comb through his hair from forehead straight back and cut furiously.

"Angela, we don't have much time."

"Wait just a second. Why are you doing this anyhow?"

"I just want to look different enough so that I don't get recognized immediately."

Angela squinted at him.

"When was the last time you shaved?"

"Saturday."

"Yeah. You look a lot more like one of these lowlifes up here."

"Good."

Reed grabbed his crutch and hop/stepped into the bathroom.

He called over his shoulder, "Can you be ready to leave in five minutes?"

"Sure. We going to the hospital?"

"Yeah."

"Are we packing up?"

"Yeah. Five minutes and we're gone."

George Prentice sat next to Ralph Malone in the front seat of the sheriff's patrol car. Matthew and Madeleine Ullmann sat in the rear seat.

Ullmann leaned forward and said, "You're just goddamn lucky, George, that the bank is on the way to the hospital."

"I would have thought you'd have enough cash to just transfer the funds at the brokerage."

"That account isn't for cash."

Prentice mumbled, "I don't know what you're complaining about. I've given you the tissue samples and you've given me nothing yet."

"My, my," said Ullmann. "Look at brave George. Isn't love grand?" Nobody in the car answered Ullmann's rhetorical question. "Ralph, what do you think? Should we just rid the world of Dr. Prentice and call it a day?"

Malone turned left into the bank parking lot.

"Mr. Ullmann, it's been thirty-six, thirty-seven hours I've been at it. I'm not looking for any extra work. Doctor wants to take his money and call it quits, as long as he delivers, I'm not going to argue the point."

"Isn't that interesting?" said Ullmann. "George Prentice gets a hundred and fifty thousand dollars and a chance to ride off into the sunset with his newfound love because good old Ralph here is tired." Ullmann shrugged. "Well, so be it." He looked at his watch. "Almost eleven o'clock. Where has the day gone? I suppose you're right, Ralph. Madeleine? Any objections?"

Madeleine answered through a clenched jaw. "You do what you think is right, dear."

Ullmann turned back to Prentice.

"Okay, George, I'll get you your checks. You get the first one to deposit now and the second one after I have Johnny Boy back. But, George, I'm telling you this . . . if there is a line at the customer service desk, you can forget the whole deal. I'm not waiting. You'll just have to die."

FORTY-FIVE

Bill Reed, sporting his new close-cropped hairstyle, emerged from the bedroom dragging his trunk. He wore his jeans, plain tie-shoes, a plaid shirt, his prosthesis, and a gray, cable-knit sweater with a hole above the stomach that Angela Quist had brought in from the Trooper.

"You look like you fit right in around here," said Angela.

"You mean a one-legged guy in a wheelchair wearing an expensive coat and driving a BMW didn't fit in?"

"Go figure." Angela asked, "Are we coming back here?"

"I doubt it. Lock up, but keep the key, just in case."

"You need help with that trunk?"

"No thanks."

"Hell, my stuff is already in the car. Let me help you."

"Okay, but wait until I drag it outside."

In five minutes, they were on the road, Angela driving.

"When we get to the hospital, what do you want me to do?"

Reed didn't answer at first, then said, "You must be worried about your sister."

"I am and I'm not. I called over there just before we left."

"They put you through?"

"No. But Bridget, the woman who answers the phones, she knows me. She said as far as she knows Lizzie is okay."

"Anything going on there?"

"Lunchtime. Everything is pretty quiet. The Ullmanns aren't there."

"I hope they're still out looking for George Prentice."

"How are you going to get your cousin out of the hospital?"

"There's a doctor with the medevac team. We'll manage. What do you want to do about your sister?"

"Well, once you've got Johnny, maybe I could, I don't know. I think I should go over to the institute, at least check on her."

"Once John is on his way to the hospital, I'll go with you. You're not going over there alone."

"Okay, but don't you want to stay with John?"

"When I get John on his way, I'll have my guy Irwin stay with him. He can take care of him better than I can. Once we see about your sister, I'll hook up with John wherever they take him."

Angela looked at Reed. "See about my sister? What does that mean?"

"Right now, probably nothing. Maybe we'll take her out. She can travel, can't she?"

"She's a little slow moving, but sure. It's going to upset her to leave that place. She's used to it."

Reed paused. "Let's just take it a step at a time, Angela. Let's just see what happens."

Gwen Higgins sat at her reception desk and watched the entourage entering Clearbrook Hospital: Sheriff Ralph Malone, two deputies, Dr. George Prentice, Matthew Ullmann and his wife, Madeleine. She thought she might call up to the ward to let the nurses know, but just then her switchboard console lit up with two incoming calls.

As he entered the hospital, George Prentice lapsed into his doctor mode, feeling as if he were in charge. He asked Ullmann, "Was that Eddie McAndrews waiting outside in the volunteer ambulance?"

"Yes," said Ullmann. "He's been here over a half hour. Killing time while we did our goddamn banking."

"It won't be long now," said Prentice. "I need to stop at the admission's office to sign the discharge orders. You can get the clearance from the accounts office and we're done here. Should we send Ralph and his men up to get him ready?"

"No," said Ullmann. "Let's get all the paperwork done first."

Irwin stood next to Johnny Boy's bedside as the resident doctor finished making notes in a chart. A petite Filipino nurse stood next to the doctor awaiting instructions.

Irwin asked, "Everything all right?"

The doctor answered without looking up, "Yes. Things look quite normal." He handed the chart to the nurse and said, "Keep an eye on his fluids. I'll see you this afternoon." He left the hospital room without another word.

The nurse stood reading the doctor's notes. When she put the chart back into the rack at the foot of the hospital bed back, Irwin asked, "How long before our patient will be up and about?"

She glanced at Johnny Boy lying flat, but his head propped up with a pillow. His face blank, but staring at the nurse, Johnny Boy listened for her answer. She looked away from Johnny Boy to Irwin and said, "Well, he can get up for the bathroom and things, but it'll be a couple of weeks before he's really out of bed."

"Doctor seemed kind of busy."

"We don't have a big staff."

"That wasn't Dr. Prentice, was it?"

"No. Excuse me, are you a relative?"

"Yep. I'm John's brother. I'm staying with him until he's back on his feet."

"Oh, I see."

"So where is Dr. Prentice? I was hoping to talk to him."

"I don't know."

Irwin screwed his face up in an exaggerated look of confusion.

"Isn't that a little weird . . . the surgeon who did the operation never checks on his patient."

The nurse stared at Irwin, declining to answer.

Irwin smiled and raised his hands. "Hey, I'm not trying to get anybody in trouble."

The nurse nodded.

"Do you know where he is?"

"No. I have to go," she said and headed for the door. The small Filipino woman waved a hand and walked out of the room.

No more than a minute after the nurse left Johnny Boy's room, George Prentice led an entourage into the hospital room. Behind him a tall young man in hospital whites pushed a gurney into the hospital room, followed by Ralph Malone and one of his younger deputies, David Proctor, a twenty-six-year-old whose doughboy physique filled his gray deputy sheriff's uniform to the point where almost every wrinkle and line was stretched out of his shirt.

Matthew and Madeleine Ullmann waited in the hallway, and behind them, peering around into the room, the Filipino nurse.

Irwin stood up, stopping Prentice in midstep. Ullmann had given him no warning about Irwin. But Malone had been prepared. He tapped Prentice on the shoulder, nodded toward Johnny Boy, and said, "Go on, Doc, let's get this done."

With the sheriff and his deputy backing him up, Prentice took on an air of authority and announced breezily, as if Irwin hardly deserved the information, "I'm Dr. Prentice. We're moving this patient."

Irwin said, "I'm Dr. Barker, and no, you're not."

"What?"

"You're not moving Mr. Reed. He's under my care. Don't take another step toward him. I don't even want you in this room."

Prentice raised his voice. "Who do you think you are?"

"Get out," said Irwin, taking a step toward Prentice.

Prentice turned to Ralph Malone.

Malone held a hand up and spoke casually, "Sir, just take it easy. The patient here needs some treatment. Why don't you just back off and let these folks do their jobs?"

Irwin reached out and nonchalantly put a hand on the railing of Johnny Boy's hospital bed. Johnny Boy looked over at Irwin and said to him, "No."

Irwin said to Johnny Boy, "Relax. You're not going anywhere." He turned to Malone and said, "This man is under my care. We're not allowing any more contact with this doctor or anybody else. He's being moved to another hospital. Leave now or I'm calling in the state police."

Malone said, "I don't think that'll be necessary."

Irwin waited, phone in hand, watching Malone.

Malone nodded, as if thinking it over. Then he turned to Prentice and said, "All right, Doc, leave us alone for a minute, will you?" Malone told the hospital orderly, "Leave that there and go with the doctor, please."

Prentice hesitated. Malone said to him, "Go on. Give us a minute here."

Prentice hesitated a moment longer, then walked, followed by the orderly who left the gurney near the side of Johnny Boy's bed.

Malone turned around and spoke to his deputy standing behind him, "Dave, go on outside and shut the door behind you. Make sure no one comes in until I tell you."

Malone watched his deputy leave, his back to Irwin. As the door opened, Irwin saw the Ullmanns standing out in the hall, glaring at him, but they didn't try to intervene. As soon as the door closed behind his deputy, Malone drew his Beretta, turned, and shot Irwin Barker square in the chest.

Johnny Boy flinched. Irwin slammed against the wall next to Johnny Boy's bed.

Malone yelled over his shoulder toward the door, "Stay out. No one comes in until I say so." He quickly stepped over to Irwin, pushed aside Irwin's suit coat, and looked around for Irwin's gun. He reached down and pulled out a Smith & Wesson .45, and wrapped the big man's right hand around the butt of the gun. It was only then, when Malone stood up to examine his work that he noticed there was no blood on Irwin.

Suddenly Irwin lurched forward, struggling for breath. Malone stepped back, startled, then quickly stepped forward and stomped a heel sharply into Irwin's solar plexus, sending Irwin back down on the floor. Malone stepped back, understanding now. He had felt the Kevlar vest under his heel.

"Shit." For a moment, Malone thought about shooting Irwin in the head, but too much time had elapsed. The deputy would remember. Holding his Beretta on Irwin, Malone yelled out, "All right, Dave, get in here."

Malone's deputy burst into the smoke-filled room.

"He drew down on me. Get his gun. Put the cuffs on him. Man's still alive. Look at the hole in his shirt, Deputy. Center shot. See how a vest can save you."

The deputy grabbed the Smith & Wesson out of Irwin's hand and shoved it in his pants, panicky, trying to get the gun past his girth.

Irwin struggled back to consciousness, gasping for air, pawed at David Proctor's head. The young man, clearly unnerved, reached for his own gun and yelled, "Don't move. Don't move."

Malone snarled, "Goddammit, don't worry about drawing. I got him covered. Just get your cuffs on him."

Malone, his gun still trained on Irwin, yelled over his shoulder, "Come on, Doc, get in here and get your patient and let's go."

Prentice rushed in, the orderly coming in fast behind him. Suddenly the room was filled with movement. Malone's deputy snapping a cuff on Irwin's right wrist. Prentice rushing toward the bed. The orderly positioning the gurney next to the bed. Matthew Ullmann bursting into the room, heading for Johnny Boy.

Irwin struggled up into a sitting position, leaned back against the wall. The deputy awkwardly tried to maneuver Irwin's arms behind his back to handcuff him properly, but couldn't pull Irwin away from the wall. Malone ignored everyone else, keeping his gun trained on Irwin. He yelled at the deputy, "Just cuff him in front. Front ways is good enough for now."

Prentice yelled at the orderly, "Get over here and help me. Help me. We have to get this patient out of here."

Ullmann added his commands to the din, "Come on, come on. Let's go."

The deputy finished handcuffing Irwin and stood back. Irwin struggled to his feet, but Malone stepped forward and shoved him down into the chair next to Johnny Boy's bed.

Pointing his Beretta at Irwin's face he said, "Settle down, don't move. Sit there and don't move."

Prentice and Ullmann had finally positioned themselves at the head and foot of Johnny Boy's bed. The orderly bent across the gurney and grabbed the middle of Johnny Boy's sheet.

Prentice said, "All right, Matthew, just grab the sheet there and slide him over. Easy, if you want him in shape for Orenberg at six. Easy now."

The orderly, Prentice, and Ullmann lifted and slid Johnny Boy onto the gurney. Prentice repeating, "Easy, easy. Don't rupture his stitches now."

Irwin sat hunched over in his chair, watching them, still recovering from the bullet to his chest. Malone's deputy stood back a few paces, keeping an eye on Irwin.

The sheriff kept his Beretta trained on Irwin, glancing over to the three loading Johnny Boy. Once they had him on the gurney, Malone yelled, "Go on, get him out of here."

As they passed behind Malone, Ullmann grasped Malone's arm and said, "You're coming with us."

"What?"

"You're coming with us. I need you."

Malone turned to Ullmann, the tension twitching in his face. The grimace pulled painfully at the stitches in his face. Pointing to Irwin with his gun he said, "I need to lock up this guy."

Ullmann persisted, speaking in a low, intense voice, "Ralph, let's go. I need you for the other thing now."

Malone muttered a soft curse. He pulled his deputy over to his left, positioning him directly in front of the handcuffed Irwin.

"All right, Dave," said Malone. "Slow and calm, get your gun on him. Step back a bit. Don't get anywhere near him. He moves, you shoot. And make it a head shot. I'll call down and tell Bert to come up here. When he gets here, the two of you take him into the office and lock him in a holding cell."

Dave Proctor drew his gun and pointed at Irwin Barker with a tense, two-handed grip. He asked, "Where you going, Sheriff?"

"Shut up and do what I tell you. Keep him locked up until you hear from me. Understood?"

"Yes, sir."

"Good. Don't hesitate with your weapon. He twitches, shoot him."

"Yes, sir."

As the gurney rolled out to the hall, Madeleine Ullmann gripped the foot of the rolling bed as if she owned it and pulled, turning the gurney so it faced down the hallway.

Irwin watched Malone and Ullmann leave, following the gurney bearing Johnny Boy. As the door swung shut behind them, he leaned forward and coughed. And coughed again, the hacking turned into a wrenching curse.

"Shit. What'd he shoot me with, a nine-millimeter?"

"Shut up."

"Feels like my chest is cracked open." Irwin tried to straighten up and let out another grunt of pain. "God damn, how'd you like to call the nurse in here or a doctor? Christ, I think I need an X ray or something. I can't breathe. Jeezus."

The deputy took an involuntary step toward Irwin.

Irwin's face twisted into a grimace. He started to gasp as if his throat were constricted. Irwin pleaded, "Shit, I got asthma. Can't breathe."

Irwin slumped forward, wheezing, struggling for air.

The deputy stared at him, unsure of what to do.

Irwin pushed himself upright, cuffed hands pressing down on his thigh as if he needed to brace himself in order to breathe. He struggled to suck in air, making a strange high-pitched wheezing sound. His eyes bulged open with the effort.

The deputy's hands started to shake. "Ah, no. No. Shit, what the fuck is wrong with you?" He took a step toward the door, looking as if he were going to call for help. Irwin took one more wheezing gasp, then pitched forward and collapsed, his big body slumping off the chair onto the floor.

The deputy looked at Irwin collapsed in front of him. Instinctively, he stepped toward Irwin to see what had happened. He looked back toward the door, anxious for the other deputy to appear, and two hundred and fifty pounds of a very angry Irwin Barker slammed into him, pile driving him into the opposite wall.

Irwin slammed his forearms down hard on the deputy's wrists, knocking his gun aside, then he drove his forehead into the center of David Proctor's broad face, breaking his nose and sending him into oblivion.

The deputy collapsed, sliding down the wall as Irwin pulled the deputy's nine-millimeter Beretta out of his hands.

"Asshole," said Irwin. He shoved the deputy's gun in his belt, then knelt down and grabbed his own gun out of David Proctor's belt, quickly working it into his holster.

His hands were still cuffed in front of him. He flipped the unconscious deputy over and pulled the handcuff keys off his belt ring. Irwin stood up and propped his foot against the door while he uncuffed himself, working quickly, expecting the second deputy any second.

He dragged the deputy over to the hospital bed and quickly handcuffed him to the frame, keeping his eyes on the door.

The deputy's head lolled back. His breaths came in erratic gasps, splattering the blood that streamed out of his broken nose.

Irwin heard the crackle of a police radio out in the hall and sprang up for the door. He grabbed the inside door handle just as the door started to open and wrenched open the door, pulling the second deputy into the room. The deputy never even had a chance to go for his gun before Irwin snapped a hard, right fist into his temple.

Irwin shouldered the door shut and kicked the man's feet out from under him. The deputy went down hard, all his weight slamming into the tile floor, cracking his tailbone. He let out a yelp of pain, cut short when Irwin kicked once, hard, to the side of the deputy's head, knocking him out.

Irwin dragged the second deputy over to the bed and quickly handcuffed him to the foot of the hospital bed. He ripped a pillowcase from the bedding, gathered up the deputies' guns, handcuff keys, key rings, and police radios, dumping everything into the pillowcase, then casually dropped the loaded pillowcase out the window. He stood up and looked at his victims.

"You guys want to be cops, you'd better fucking learn how."

Irwin stepped forward and said, "Sorry, guys," then swiftly kicked both men in the solar plexus, paralyzing them.

Irwin straightened his tie, ran a hand through his hair, and nonchalantly walked out of the hospital room. He saw several security guards and a pack of hospital personnel standing in the hall. Most tried to see into the room behind Irwin, but he quickly pulled the door shut behind him. He smiled and said to no one in particular, "They want to have a little privacy, if you don't mind."

Irwin walked quickly to the elevator at the end of the hall, never looking back.

FORTY-SIX

As the rear door of the ambulance opened, Eddie McAndrews peered around from the driver's seat.

"Well, well, the gang's all here."

Matthew and Madeleine Ullmann awkwardly made their way to a bench seat bolted on one side of the ambulance. George Prentice and Ralph Malone slid the stretcher bearing Johnny Boy onto the floor of the ambulance. Prentice climbed in behind Johnny Boy and sat opposite the Ullmanns. Malone said, "I'll follow behind," and slammed the ambulance door.

Ullmann leaned over and yelled toward the front cab, "Let's go, Eddie, and please, no sirens."

McAndrews shoved the ambulance into gear and drove out of the parking lot.

Prentice said, "I hope you realize, of course, those stitches are gone."

"What do you mean?"

"Good Lord, Matthew, pulling him out of bed like we did? Slamming the gurney into the elevator? Banging into the curb? I assumed you were doing that on purpose."

Ullmann wanted to scream at Prentice . . . you idiot. Do you think I can wait forty-eight hours for this pathetic retard to die? Orenberg is coming with a station wagon and a body bag, you dolt. But instead, Ullmann winced a smile and said, "Oh, right."

Prentice closed his mouth, looking away as if to separate himself from everything happening in the small enclosed space in which he sat. After a moment, he turned to Ullmann and asked, "Do you think you might want to give Orenberg the option of keeping him alive?"

Ullmann made a face, annoyed by the question. "What do you mean?"

"There's no reason he can't survive," said Prentice. "Assuming the stitches have already popped, the infection can be stopped. As for the cancer, whatever experimental drugs they gave him worked beautifully on his tumor. It was quite contained, even though you stopped treatment and it continued to grow, it was very contained. I'd bet there wasn't any spread at all."

Ullmann answered dryly, "Well that's very good news for medical science. And for our stock. Will that mess in the Styrofoam cooler you gave us show all that?"

"Absolutely. I removed the turmor and colon intact. They'll want to biopsy his lymph system and do other tests I'm sure. But the tissue samples are really all they need to confirm they have something viable. I would venture to say that they are on the verge of a very large, very profitable success."

"Fine. That's all I need to know. Does it matter if their patient is dead or alive for whatever else they might want to look at?"

"Well . . . I suppose not."

Ullmann grunted in response.

Neither Prentice nor Ullmann had noticed that Johnny Boy Reed had been watching them talk about him, eyeing them back and forth as they spoke. But Madeleine had noticed.

"How are you feeling, Johnny Boy?" she asked in her usual shrill, unpleasant voice.

Johnny Boy turned his attention to Madeleine Ullmann sitting stiffly on the bench seat alongside Matthew. She watched him focus his eyes on her, but she saw no attempt by him to answer her question. She peered at him, seeing his face contorted, but not sure if Johnny Boy's face had twisted from pain or fear.

She raised her voice. "I said, how are you, Johnny Boy?"

Matthew Ullmann and George Prentice looked down at Johnny Boy, seeing him now for the first time since they had loaded him into the ambulance. A bump in the road sent a shiver through the vehicle. They watched Johnny Boy wince.

He still made no attempt to answer Madeleine's question.

She started to repeat the question, to demand an answer, but something in Johnny Boy's expression made her stop. Madeleine Ullmann peered at the short, middle-aged Down syndrome man lying at her feet. He returned her gaze unflinchingly. It wasn't pain or fear she saw, it was pure, simple revulsion, revulsion stemming from a primordial perception beyond intelligence, beyond even time or circumstance.

The sudden silence attracted Matthew's and George Prentice's attention. They all saw it now . . . unmistakable, visceral, instinctive revulsion that Johnny Boy could not hide, would not hide. Johnny Boy Reed knew. Somehow, in some deep, basic part of him, Johnny Boy Reed sensed the evil that surrounded him, felt what their corruption, what their complete disregard for his life had done to him. And for the first time in the fifteen years that Matthew and Madeleine Ullmann had dominated Johnny Boy Reed, they turned away from him, unwilling, at least for the moment, to impose their terrible will on him.

Awkward silence continued to fill the ambulance. A silence so pervasive that Eddie McAndrews peered around from the driver's seat to see why it had suddenly become so quiet. Ullmann gazed up at him, their eyes meeting, but nothing was said. Eddie turned back to his driving.

Prentice cleared his throat and finally broke the silence.

"Well," he said, "I've lived up to my end of the bargain. You'll be passing my house in a few minutes. I'd like you to give me my check and drop me off if you don't mind."

Ullmann raised his chin and gazed at Prentice for a moment and said, "Drop you off?"

"Yes."

"You're not coming to the clinic?"

"I see no need."

Ullmann nodded. "Yes, yes. I guess you're right. We'll drop you. That will be fine."

He reached into the breast pocket of his coat and extracted the second cashier's check. He started to hand it to Prentice, but retracted his hand. Prentice had leaned forward over

Johnny Boy to take his money, his hand out. He dropped his hand, but remained awkwardly bent toward Ullmann.

Ullmann leaned back and spoke in a tired voice. "Do you mind, George, if I give this to you in your house? There's just one other thing I'd like to go over with you. If you don't mind."

Ullmann had spoken so cordially that Prentice's innate sense of politeness took over and he answered, "What?"

"Just, one issue . . ." Ullmann's voice trailed off. "I think you'd prefer talking in your house."

"All right," said Prentice. "Fine."

The three of them lapsed into silence.

Johnny Boy laid his head back, dropping deeper into himself.

Five minutes later, the ambulance pulled into George Prentice's driveway.

Reed's cell phone rang just as Angela Quist turned into the Clearbrook Hospital parking lot. As he answered the phone, Reed spotted Irwin standing in the middle of the lot next to his maroon Lincoln Town Car.

"Irwin?"

"Yeah."

"Stay where you are, I'm just pulling into the lot."

Reed pointed to Irwin and Angela steered toward him, pulling up sharply. Reed jumped out of the Trooper as quickly as he could, landing on his right foot, hurrying toward Irwin as quickly as the prosthesis would allow.

"What happened?"

"They got him."

"No. No! When?"

"Ten minutes ago."

"What happened?"

Irwin spread his suit jacket. "That damn sheriff just turned and shot me. Had the vest on, but it knocked me on my ass."

"You all right?"

"I ain't gonna breathe right for a week, but yeah, I'm all

right. Sorry, Bill. I didn't know that sheriff was a stone killer. I wasn't expecting it. They got the cuffs on me and wheeled him out."

"Shit! Wait a minute. I don't want to be standing out here in the open. Let's get in your car." Irwin headed for the Lincoln. Reed walked quickly to Angela and said, "Hey, pull into that spot will you. Just hang on a second."

"What happened?"

"They got John. Just hang on."

Angela pulled into a parking spot while Reed walked back and climbed into the passenger seat of Irwin's car.

"So what happened, Irwin?"

"They walked in with that Dr. Prentice, the sheriff, a deputy, and the Ullmann couple in the hallway. Shot me, cuffed me, wheeled him out of there."

"How'd you get out?"

"I clocked the deputy they left guarding me. And the second one coming in to help him."

"Malone left you?"

"Yeah. I think he might have stayed to take care of me, but Ullmann told him he had to come with them."

"Where'd they take John?"

"I think they said back to their clinic. I wanted to head there after him, but I don't know where the hell it is."

"Our medevac people ever show up?"

"No."

"Fuck."

"Bill, I don't think your cousin is going anywhere right away. I overheard them say that they had to get your cousin back there for some appointment with somebody at six."

"Who?"

"Oren-something. Orenstein, Orenberg, something like that."

"I don't know who that is. You said, six?"

"Yeah."

"What the hell are they doing to him now?"

"I don't know. Honestly, Bill, it seemed like they were hauling out a specimen or something. I mean, you know, it was like they were retrieving a prize, not a person."

Reed checked his watch.

"Not even two o'clock yet. They're going to hold him until six?"

"Sounded like it."

"It doesn't matter. We're getting him out of there."

"Yeah, but can you move him?"

"Why not?"

"That Prentice guy was yelling, 'Take it easy, take it easy, you'll break his stitches.'"

"When they were moving him?"

"Yeah."

"What the hell does that mean?"

"I don't know. He sounded like he was afraid something might bust loose."

Reed stopped talking, concentrating now, trying to hold his emotions so he could think straight.

"You got that stuff from SR, right?"

"Yeah."

"All right, all right . . . let me think for a second."

Without warning, sirens sounded in the distance.

"That's probably for me," said Irwin.

Reed spat out a curse, "Goddammit. Let's get the hell out of here. Give me your keys. Jump in the backseat. They don't know your car, but they'll be looking for someone who fits your description."

Both men got out. Irwin hustled toward the back of the car and grabbed his keys off the rear tire. Reed waved Angela over, yelling, "Come on."

Angela jumped out of the Trooper and came running over.

"You said they got John?"

"I should have been here sooner." The sirens wailed louder, closer now. "Come on, get in the back of Irwin's car, we have to get out of here."

Reed slipped behind the driver's wheel, grabbed the keys from Irwin, and fired up the big V8 engine. He turned and said,

"Irwin, Angela, Angela, Irwin. Get down out of sight. I'm the only one that might not match a description they're looking for."

Reed drove the Lincoln Town Car out of the Clearbrook lot, just as two sheriff department cruisers came racing in.

Ullmann and Prentice awkwardly climbed out the back door of the ambulance. Ullmann held back a few paces, letting Prentice lead the way toward the house.

Malone had parked a few feet behind the ambulance and remained in his car. He and Ullmann exchanged glances, but said nothing.

When Prentice was about three yards in front of Ullmann, Ullmann looked back over his shoulder. Eddie McAndrews was leaning out from the driver's seat of the volunteer ambulance. Ullmann and McAndrews exchanged nods.

They entered the house. Prentice took off his coat and hung it neatly in his closet, then turned to Ullmann standing in the foyer.

"What is it, Matthew? We transferred my stocks before we left for the bank. You have the samples, the patient, everything. What else do you want?"

Ullmann patted his breast pocket. "Well, I owe you this check." Ullmann motioned toward the living room. "Let's just sit for a moment."

Prentice again led the way, Ullmann following. They sat in front of Prentice's fireplace in the two facing wing-backed chairs. Ullmann clasped his hands and leaned toward Prentice, speaking sincerely with a note of request in his voice.

"George, I'll stand by my end of this bargain." And then Ullmann stopped talking, as if he had just remembered he hadn't given Prentice the second cashier's check. He pulled it out of his pocket and handed it to Prentice saying, "Here. This is yours."

Prentice leaned forward, took the check, and laid it on the end table next to the chair, facedown.

"However, I do have one last request."

"What now?"

"I really have to be able to contact you in case the Boston people want to know something that I can't answer. Some medical question. You don't have to tell me where you're living, where you're going to live, you just have to give me a way to contact you."

Prentice did not answer, but instead observed Ullmann, looking to see if Ullmann was leading up to something.

"What did you have in mind?" asked Prentice.

"Well, I don't know, a third party, a go-between. I call them. They call you. You call me back. Something like that."

"But that would give you someone who could be persuaded to give you my location."

Ullmann suddenly seemed agitated. His voice lost its congenial quality.

"Well, dammit, George, I wouldn't have to know where they are. Just a phone number."

"You know full well that would be all Ralph Malone needs."

"Well then, you think of something. E-mail, or, or I don't know. Something."

Prentice shook his head. "I have no idea how these things are done. I don't even know myself exactly where I'm going . . . why don't you wait until I settle in somewhere, and I'll figure a way to contact you?"

The sound of the front door opening interrupted Ullmann's response. Both men turned to see Eddie McAndrews amble into the living room.

"Sorry to interrupt, fellas, but the sheriff out there got something over the radio. Wants you to come out, Mr. Ullmann."

"Good Christ," muttered Ullmann. He turned to Prentice. "Just a second."

He headed for the front door, but stopped for a moment to talk to Eddie McAndrews, his voice low. Prentice squinted at the two men standing at the entrance to his living room, unable to hear them.

Ullmann, right at McAndrews's shoulder, spoke softly and quickly. "Do it like we said. Up close so Malone can make it right. No screwups, Eddie. I don't want to hear any more complaints from Ralph."

"No problemo."

"Are the keys in the ambulance?"

"Yep."

"Your truck is out back, right?"

"Correcto."

"All right, give us about five minutes to get out of here, then do it. Ralph insists he doesn't want to be around. He'll come back later and find it."

"I know, I know."

"I'll see you at the institute." Ullmann turned toward the door, but quickly turned back. "Oh, and don't forget . . . bring back my check. Remember, ten percent commission if this goes right." Ullmann turned and walked out the front door.

McAndrews ambled into the living room, approaching Prentice. He shrugged and said, "Doubt if it's good news."

Reed accelerated the Town Car quickly, his mind racing, trying to figure all the angles, sort out the next moves. He yelled over his shoulder to Irwin, "You bring the shotguns?"

"Yeah. And I got an extra vest for you."

"Good."

"What are we doing?" yelled Angela.

But before Reed could answer her question, he saw an ambulance coming in their direction, lights flashing but no siren. Reed immediately started flashing his headlights, powered down his window, and extended an arm, flagging down the ambulance.

As the vehicles approached, the ambulance pulled over to the far side of the road. Reed did a hard U-turn and drove up next to the ambulance. He yelled, "Are you going to Clearbrook Hospital for John Reed?"

The driver, a heavyset black woman with an angelic Muhammad Ali face, leaned out and yelled, "Yeah."

The passenger next to her called out past her, "I'm Dr. Price. What's the problem?"

Reed yelled back, "Hang on," and drove the Town Car in front of the ambulance. He turned back toward Angela and Irwin.

"Listen, Angela, can you help me out?"

"Of course."

"Take Irwin and that ambulance over to the Ullmann Institute for me, will you?"

"Where?"

"Don't go onto the grounds. Don't let Ullmann or anybody spot you. Just find a place on the road that runs along the perimeter there and have them wait."

"Where you going, boss?"

"I'm going to take a stab at finding Prentice. I need more information. He has it. And I need to know exactly what they did to John."

Irwin interjected, "I think you're right. I didn't like that comment about stitches popping. Where do you think you'll find him?"

"I'm trying his house. If he's not there, the hell with it."

"Do you know where he lives?" Angela asked.

"I remember his home address is Two Ellenville Road."

"That's right off the highway leading into Dumphy. About two miles this side of town."

"Okay. Irwin, take a shotgun. Stay with the medical team."

Irwin jumped out of the backseat and headed for the trunk. Angela reached out and grabbed Reed's forearm. "Look, once I get over there, I'm checking on my sister. You don't need me to stay with the ambulance, do you?"

"No. No. Just get them there for me. Can you get to her without people seeing you?"

"I know the grounds. I just have to make sure she's all right. I know they're probably looking for me, but I want to see her."

"Do it. They're too busy to worry about you right now.

Once you know she's okay, go find Irwin and the medevac people and stay with them. We're all leaving there together."

"Including my sister?"

"I think we should probably take her with us. We'll go back in and get her when we get John."

"How are you going to get him out of there?"

"Don't worry about it." Reed grabbed Angela's forearm. He looked her in the eyes and said, "Angela, they aren't the ones retaliating anymore. I fucking guarantee you, the Ullmanns won't be hurting anybody anymore." He nodded his head toward the ambulance. "Go on. I'll see you there."

George Prentice heard the unmistakable sound of engines starting and two vehicles pulling out of his driveway. He started to get up from his chair, but Eddie McAndrews stood first, dropped his big hand against Prentice's chest, and said, "Whoa. Don't be troubling yourself, Doc. They're gone." He pushed Prentice back down into his chair.

Prentice asked, "What's going on?"

McAndrews shrugged, casually reached to the small of his back, and pulled out a snub-nosed .38-caliber revolver.

"Now don't get antsy, Doc. And don't worry about this cute little gun."

"What the hell are you doing?"

McAndrews raised his voice. "Goldammit, I said don't worry. Now shut the fuck up or I'll pop you right now."

Prentice sat rigid, McAndrews standing over him. For a moment, it felt like his mind had frozen. And then a rush of panic overwhelmed him. No, no, what is he doing? This was settled, negotiated. For God's sake, I gave away millions.

Prentice's mouth began to move, but no words came out. He thought of Alan Molina, his lover, waiting for word, waiting in his mother's house, anxious, worried. Almost involuntarily, Prentice started to get up out of the chair.

McAndrews pushed him back down again, his voice rising in warning, "Doc . . ."

"I have to call, to call someone."

"No calls, George."

Prentice's eyes widened as he stared at McAndrews.

"Okay, that's better. Now don't get your drawers in a twist. This doesn't have to be nearly as bad as it looks."

Prentice said nothing.

McAndrews snapped his fingers in front of Prentice's eyes. "Hey, Doc, you listenin' to me? Helloooh."

Prentice blinked, trying to focus his attention.

"Listen up, Doc. Here's how it's s'pose to go." McAndrews held up the small revolver. "See this gun? . . . Excuse the term, Doc, but it's kind of faggy. It's a Lady Smith & Wesson. I mean it's a thirty-eight and all. It'll put a hell of a hole in you, but it's a small gun. Sheriff Malone picked it out. It's s'pose to look like your home protection piece. I'm s'pose to shoot you in the head with it, real close like. Then put it in your hand so it looks like you did your own self. Hell, sounded like a pretty good plan to me. I don't know half the shit you boys are into, but it seems a pretty effective way to get rid of a partner. Kinda nasty, but hey, what the fuck?"

McAndrews stared at Prentice, waiting for a reaction, but the doctor said nothing.

"Nah, that's all right. I don't fuckin' wanna know what you all did." McAndrews pointed the gun at Prentice's temple, took a step closer, and cleared his throat. "So, anyhow, like I said, I'm s'pose to shoot you, make it look like a suicide, blah, blah, blah. Malone investigates." McAndrews snorted. "Mr. Sheriff Cover-up. That asshole is startin' to get to me, I'll tell you that. But anyhow, as usual, I'm the one gets to do the dirty work." McAndrews pointed the short barrel at the cashier's check sitting on the end table. "I bring back that check for seventy-five thousand to Mr. Ullmann and I get ten percent. That's seventy-five hundred."

Prentice nodded, seeing it now, but not saying anything.

"Nice piece of change for a couple minutes work, don't you think?"

Still Prentice did not speak.

McAndrews, frowning as if he'd smelled something bad, leaned forward, making Prentice sit back away from him.

"You think seventy-five hundred is enough for that?"

Prentice quickly shook his head, no.

"Neither do I. Fuckin' Ullmann. He's a cheap fuck, ain't he?"

"Yes," said Prentice, his mouth almost too dry to get the one word out.

"You know any rich people ain't cheap, greedy fucks?"

"No."

"Me either. I say fuck 'im. Why not put a little competition into it? I mean I don't really want to shoot you, George. You never did nuthin' to me. You're a pretty nice guy for a fag and all. Plenty a people on the list of who I'd like to shoot ahead of you. So how much you wanna pay me *not* to shoot you?"

"What do you want?"

"Hell, if that check weren't made out to you, I'd just take the seventy-five and say, see ya. I heard that's the second check. I figure I ought to get the whole hundred fifty. If I don't shoot you, I need some bucks 'cuz I'll have to pack it in here. Got to be enough to fund my new lifestyle."

And then, inexplicably, George Prentice smiled ruefully.

McAndrews smiled back. "What's the joke, Doc?"

Prentice looked up at McAndrews, spread his hands palms up, and said, "We both want a new lifestyle."

"Oh, yeah," said McAndrews, "but guess which one gets it?" He extended the revolver toward Prentice and waggled it in his face. "That would be the one with the gun."

"What do you want me to do?"

"Let's go cash this check. Then cash a check for what's in your account. I'm gone. You're alive. We're done. How's that?"

Prentice seemed very relaxed now. "It sounds so simple."

"It is. Let's go to the bank and do it, then we can both be on our way. I got my truck here. Won't take us but twenty, thirty minutes, and you'll be done. I don't expect you'll be hangin' around to report anything, huh? I'll drop you off anywhere you want." McAndrews looked at his watch. "Banks open until three-thirty. Hell it ain't even three, but we better get a move on."

Prentice saw it all now, the feeling hitting him somewhere deep in his stomach, a sick numbness that seemed to spread all the way to his brain.

"I'm tired," said Prentice. "Been up all night. I don't think I'm going anywhere."

McAndrews's voice hardened.

"This ain't no time to be fuckin' around, George."

"Please, spare me. I'd rather you just shoot me now than after a humiliating trip to the bank."

McAndrews paused, looking at Prentice. McAndrews sighed, sucked a quick breath through his teeth.

"For a smart guy you're acting awful stupid."

"Am I?"

"Your life ain't worth a hundred fifty thou?"

"And where do I go after that? Where do I go that Ullmann won't find me and finish what you didn't?"

"That's up to you."

Prentice reached into his pocket and pulled out a thin wad of bills.

"Here. Take this. The rest of what I have doesn't belong to you."

McAndrews stared at the bills. Prentice saw the anger and insult well up in McAndrews. The meanness in him taking over.

"Well, ain't that some shit. You spiteful little prick. I give you a chance and this is what I get."

"A chance? A chance at what?"

McAndrews nodded. "Suit yourself."

Prentice stared straight ahead to someplace beyond Eddie McAndrews and his gun and his hate, beyond threats and schemes and the evil he had wallowed in.

McAndrews looked at him with disgust. A man less than a man who had given up without even trying. He stepped forward, placed the muzzle of the gun against Prentice's temple, muttered, "You're a sorry son of a bitch, you know that?" He cocked the pistol. And then, McAndrews cringed almost comically, and took the gun away.

"Shit."

Prentice had been sitting staring straight ahead, his face ticking with tension, waiting through moments that seemed interminable. Now, with the gun taken away, Prentice looked up, confused.

Eddie leaned over toward the end table. "I almost forgot about the check. Sorry, Doc. Don't want to get any blood on this thing. Ullmann'll have a fit. Don't want any arguments about getting my measly seventy-five hunnert."

McAndrews reached for the cashier's check, but the sound of the front door opening distracted him. He looked toward the entrance hall. And George Prentice grabbed for the revolver.

McAndrews turned back to Prentice and tried to pull the revolver away from his grip.

Bill Reed stepped into the living room just as the Smith & Wesson fired.

A .38-caliber bullet exploded into George Prentice just below his left armpit, ripping through his left lung, smashing into his upper spine where it was deflected just past the back of his heart into the long pad of muscles that made up his latissimus dorsi.

McAndrews had the gun free now, turning toward Reed, but Reed already had his Colt out. He fired two rushed shots. Both missed McAndrews.

George Prentice, even with his lung filling with blood, even though paralyzed from mid-chest down, lunged at McAndrews's revolver again, hitting his arm, sending McAndrews's shot wide of Reed.

Reed fired again, aiming more carefully. A nine-millimeter slug struck Eddie McAndrews in almost the exact center of his right shoulder, obliterating the joint, separating arm from shoulder socket, exiting out the shoulder blade, shattering the flat triangular bone with a muffled cracking sound.

McAndrews spun sideways, crashing into the wing-backed

chair, his right arm useless, but amazingly, he held on to the Smith & Wesson, despite the shattered shoulder.

Reed held his Colt Commander in front of him, stepping carefully through the gun smoke toward McAndrews. He felt himself yelling more than he heard himself.

"Don't." And then, "Drop the gun."

McAndrews pitched himself forward off the arm of the chair, struggling to pull his feet back under him so he could stand. His mouth moved. Reed saw him trying to say something, his face twisted in anger and pain. Reed, still deafened from the Colt Commander, didn't try to hear the words.

Reed brought his left hand to his right, bracing his grip on the Colt. He stopped advancing, not wanting to shoot while moving. He was close enough now, not more than five feet from Eddie McAndrews.

Prentice lay back, his blood staining the rich green fabric of his matching chairs, his mouth open gasping for air, watching Reed and McAndrews.

Reed stepped to his right, spreading his weight, balanced, firm on his Flex-Foot, arms extended, once more, in a normal voice, a voice of resignation, he said, "Don't."

Eddie McAndrews had somehow risen to his feet, forcing it now, reaching with his left hand for the gun in his useless right hand. McAndrews refused to believe Reed had won this. If that fag George Prentice hadn't grabbed for his gun, the bastard would have walked in on him blindly; walked into the room with him holding a cocked .38 revolver. Reed should already be dead.

McAndrews's left hand gripped the Smith & Wesson, almost ready to pull it out of the swinging right hand.

Reed didn't say another word. He waited just another second, then pulled the trigger of the Colt Commander three more times, feeling the gun buck, his eyes involuntarily blinking against the explosions.

Eddie McAndrews disappeared as if an invisible giant hand had grabbed his belt buckle from behind and wrenched him away.

By the time Reed focused, he saw blood on the fireplace wall and Eddie McAndrews, six-foot-four, big-boned, North Country good ol' boy, crumpled on the floor, wedged under the mantelpiece like a very large, bloody broken mannequin.

Reed turned toward Prentice. He took a step toward him, blinking away the sting of the gun smoke, his hearing coming back, his focus returning. He heard a muffled, gurgling wheeze and Prentice retched up a wet blob of blood, most of it landing on his chest. Another half cough sent blood spurting over his chin.

Reed stepped to him, reaching out with his left hand, the Colt still in his right. Prentice weakly grabbed Reed's hand, pulling his closer.

Reed shook his head, muttering a sad curse at the mess George Prentice had become, his mouth and stylish yellow tie and pristine blue shirt all covered in blood.

"Help," said Prentice.

Reed knelt down awkwardly on his right knee, in front of Prentice. Reed said, "You're dying. No one is going to get here in time."

Prentice's mouth moved weakly, but no words came out. And then, mustering his strength, he said, "Help, help me with . . ." Prentice pointed to the cashier's check. "Alan Molina. Elizabeth Molina. Canton, New York. Call." Prentice coughed more blood up, but this time there wasn't enough force to clear it from his mouth and throat. Prentice swallowed it down, willing himself not to choke.

Reed holstered the Colt, picked up the check, looked at it.

"You want me to send this to him?"

"Yes. Joint account."

"What did you do to my cousin?"

Prentice opened his mouth, but could not bring himself to talk.

Reed held the check up in front of Prentice's face, slowly crumpling it, asking again, demanding, "What did you do to my cousin?"

Prentice gasped, "Not me. Ullmanns. Experiments. Medical tests. Drugs."

"What? Drug experiments?"

Prentice nodded. "Stocks. Biotech company."

"What did you do?"

Prentice shook his head. "No. Not the drugs. You have to save him. Colon. Closures are loose. Reattach. Surgery or sepsis."

"What? What the hell are you telling me?"

Prentice wheezed another gurgling breath. "Left stitches undone. Two stitches. Inside. You have a few hours. Until six. Then it's over. Help me. Help my friend."

Reed heard another wheezing gurgle emitted from the hole in Prentice's side. He slowly pulled his hand away from Prentice's weak grip and stood up.

Prentice choked out one last word. "Please."

Reed crumpled the check and dropped it in the bloody gore that covered Prentice's lap.

Bill Reed turned, walked out of the house. He didn't look back.

FORTY-SEVEN

As Matthew Ullmann drove the volunteer ambulance toward the front door of his clinic, he spotted five of Ralph Malone's deputies standing around three sheriff's department patrol cars. The cars were parked in a line, bumper to bumper, blocking the entrance to the clinic.

Mixed in with the five deputies were five of Ullmann's proctors: Lyle and Ronnie Barrett plus Jimmy Suggs, Marvin

Dunn, and Philip Jackson. The proctors were dressed in their institute white shirts and cheap ties and their North Country clothes: jeans, boots, Carhartt coats or down vests. All of them held hunting rifles. All of the sheriff's deputies were armed. Two of them with shotguns.

Ullmann stopped the ambulance directly in front of the entrance. Malone parked his cruiser behind. They climbed out of their vehicles and met at the back door to the ambulance, the deputies and proctors gathering around.

As Ullmann reached for the ambulance door, Malone grabbed his arm and said, "When we were leaving Prentice's house, it came over the radio that the fella at the hospital got loose from my men."

Ullmann grimaced. "What?"

"He's out there. So is Reed. I think you'd better figure on them showing up here. Maybe with state troopers."

"Then arrest them. You're the law. They've certainly committed enough crimes. Try and do one thing right. One damn thing that you don't have to do over and over again."

Ullmann pulled the ambulance door open and helped Madeleine step down.

She looked at the group standing nearby and yelled, "Stop gawking and get him into the clinic. Come on. Hurry up."

Several of the proctors stepped forward. Ullmann pulled Malone aside.

"Look, I need two lousy hours. He isn't going to risk getting the state police involved. Between your men and mine can't we take care of two of them? Can't you? Find them. Or if they show up, you shoot them or arrest them or do whatever you have to do, but by six o'clock I want Johnny Boy Reed lying up in that clinic and I want this place to look normal. That's all, Ralph. Two hours and I promise you, you'll never have to work another day in your life. Two hours."

Malone nodded.

The Barrett brothers pulled the gurney bearing Johnny Boy out of the ambulance and wheeled it toward the clinic. Madeleine Ullmann followed them with Matthew trailing behind as Malone started giving orders to the deputies and proctors.

Johnny Boy lay on the gurney. Every time the Barretts pushed or shoved the gurney, every time the wheels struck an uneven spot in the asphalt, pain ripped through him.

He squinted his eyes shut against the agony, but he didn't need to open them to know he was back at the Ullmann Institute—alone again, away from Cousin Bill, away from Cousin Bill's friend. He knew they were taking him to the clinic. And Johnny Boy knew one more thing—what it felt like just before you died.

Bill Reed came out of George Prentice's house, still wearing only the ragged cable sweater Angela had given him, but he felt no sting from the cold coming on as the day's sunlight faded.

He walked quickly, but did not feel the pressure of the prosthetic socket against his stump, or the pull of the knee joint or the spring of his Flex-Foot. He felt nothing but such an overwhelming sense of rage and disgust that his hands shook as he popped the trunk of Irwin's car.

He knew that he must concentrate, focus, control his actions, but he could only do so intermittently, trying to banish the horrifying truth he had heard from Prentice . . . while he stripped off his sweater and strapped on the Kevlar vest, while he checked the bullpup-style Mossberg shotgun Irwin had brought, and changed the magazine in his Colt for a full clip, he kept hearing the words choked out by Prentice, experimental drugs, sepsis, death.

He didn't really remember filling his pockets with shotgun shells, or shoving the nearly empty nine-millimeter clip in his back pocket. Nor did Reed know how fast he drove. The image of his cousin, the horrifying implications of what Prentice had told him, the guilt and helplessness he had been battling against . . . all rushed over him, swarming through his head, making him feel like he was about to choke.

He kept seeing Prentice garbling out the final revelation. They had used John Boyd like a laboratory animal and left him to die slowly.

As Reed turned onto the dirt road that skirted the Ullmann property, he found himself breathing hard, the rage filling his mouth and throat, making him constantly clench his teeth.

He forced himself to pay attention to his surroundings, to search for the medevac ambulance, to slow down so he wouldn't drive past it.

Reed began to feel anxious, wondering where the hell they had stopped. And then, coming around the same curve he had traversed the first morning he'd driven to the institute, he saw the ambulance parked opposite where he had stopped, on the wide shoulder of road that overlooked the Ullmann Institute.

Irwin, thought Reed. He found the best spot. A view of the enemy, and the medevac positioned perfectly.

Before Reed braked to a halt opposite the ambulance, Irwin Barker had already stepped out of the ambulance, heading toward him. Reed climbed out of the Lincoln to meet him. Irwin nodded as they met in the middle of the road.

"You find out what you needed to know?"

"Yeah," said Reed. "I found out."

Irwin paused, taking in Reed's demeanor.

"That bad?"

"Worse. Those are monsters down there, Irwin. Monsters."

Irwin Barker blinked, not quite sure what to say.

"They're running medical experiments on them, Irwin. On John Boyd."

"What?"

"I can't . . . it's—"

"I don't think I want to hear it anyhow," said Irwin. "We'd better get down there."

"Yes."

Irwin gestured with his head behind him. "What about that medevac crew? That doctor has been looking down there.

Sees all the sheriff cars and such. I think he's about to bail."

Reed broke away from Irwin and walked to the ambulance. He pulled open the driver's side door and pointed at the doctor, ignoring the heavyset black woman sitting behind the wheel.

"Doctor, you stay here. You don't move. Nothing is going to happen to you, but you don't fucking move until I bring your patient to you. Do you understand?"

The doctor took one look at Reed and nodded, but couldn't help himself.

"Don't you think you should—"

"No," said Reed. "Just do as I've asked. Please. Don't make me find you and bring you back here."

Reed looked up at the woman driver and nodded to her. She nodded back.

Reed turned back toward the Lincoln. Irwin stood by the passenger-side door, Kevlar vest under his suit jacket, his shotgun resting on his forearm. Irwin climbed into the car, picked up Reed's shotgun propped against the passenger seat, and positioned both shotguns between his knees as Reed slid into the driver's seat and fired up the car engine.

He pulled out and headed back toward the institute.

"Any plan, here?" Irwin asked.

"Yeah. Take the shotguns, walk in, get my cousin. You see a gun raised at us, shoot. My bet is these dumb-ass yokels won't stand up to someone shooting back at them. If they do, hopefully the vests will catch most of it."

Irwin nodded. After a moment, he spoke softly, "Your lady friend Angela is down there."

"Right." Reed paused. "She's with her sister. She has enough sense not to go near that clinic. Not with the sheriff and his people surrounding the place."

Irwin nodded. He pumped his Mossberg, chambering a shell. The Lincoln slid along the dirt road, but Irwin said nothing about the speed. Suddenly Reed pounded his fist on the steering wheel and braked to a stop, shoving the gearshift into park.

"Shit. We have to know where she is."

Irwin let out a quick breath of relief. "I was wondering when you'd come around. I've seen you pissed once or twice, but nothing like this. Best you get your head on straight before we go in there, Bill."

Reed nodded. "Yeah."

Irwin reached in the breast pocket of his rumpled suit coat and pulled out a computer disk and an attachment designed to plug into a computer's serial port. The connector had a male and female side and was about half the size of a pack of cigarettes.

"You still planning on downloading something for SR? I imagine that information would be helpful. We're going to have to explain our way out of quite a mess before this is over."

Reed took the disk and connector from Irwin and nodded. "You're right. You're right." Reed stared at the computer disk and the connector, then lifted his sweater, shoved his hand behind his Kevlar vest, tucking the items into his shirt pocket. "And I want the records from that clinic. At least, John's records."

"Okay," said Irwin. "Then we'd better do this right."

"Yes. Yes." Reed slipped the car into gear. Talking as much to himself as to Irwin he said, "All right. I'm okay now. We'll drive around the back way. They won't see us from where they're standing. There are three dorms in front of the clinic over there. I know Angela's sister doesn't live in John's dorm so we'll check the two others. Find Angela. Make sure she's safe."

Irwin nodded, then said, "There's ten of them, Bill."

"Yeah, but I'm going to add one to our side that should help even things up."

The Barrett brothers dumped Johnny Boy into the corner bed he had previously occupied. He grunted a short bark of pain. Johnny Boy had taken to holding himself around his stomach and ribs, as much to simply hold on as to fight the agony.

Matthew Ullmann watched them, ignoring Johnny Boy.

When the Barretts turned to him, he noticed that Ronnie Barrett's left eye looked as if it were filled with blood and nearly swollen shut. Black and blue stains covered his face from cheek to forehead, and a rancorous scab disfigured his face from below the eye socket to the bridge of his nose . . . all the result of his fight with Reed.

Ullmann looked away and waved them out of the clinic.

"All right, you two just go on outside with the others."

Madeleine Ullmann walked into the clinic office.

Ullmann glanced at Johnny Boy. He seemed to be breathing harder now, his face flushed, a fevered reaction to the infection now racing through his peritoneum. Ullmann looked away and walked into the office after Madeleine. She stood at a file cabinet pulling folders, piling them on her desk.

"What are you doing?"

"Getting these reports in order. I haven't had time to organize them. You know Orenberg. He's going to sit there and make sure everything is in sequence and complete."

"Is it?"

"It will be. Why don't you go do something besides ask me questions? Don't you want to be on your computer making those transfers?"

"Yes," said Matthew. But he didn't move.

Madeleine stopped pulling file folders and said, "What's the matter?"

"In a couple of hours, we'll probably never see this place again."

Madeleine took a cursory glance around the clinic, then looked back at her husband. "I suppose not. Maybe Orenberg will get here early. Then we can never see it again sooner."

After a moment, Ullmann said, "I want to go someplace warm."

"What?"

Ullmann spoke, but his eyes did not focus on anything. He sounded almost as if he were talking to himself. "We'll go home. Pack one suitcase each. Drive up to Montreal. Fly south. A night flight to someplace warm."

"All right," said Madeleine. "As long as we get first class seats."

"Of course."

She reached out and took her husband's hand, squeezing it to get his attention.

"Go on, Matthew. Go do what you have to do. Then come back here and we'll meet with Orenberg."

Ullmann nodded backward toward the corner bed. "What about him?"

Madeleine pulled out the syringe still in her skirt from their morning trip to Clearbrook.

"I'll take care of it."

"Good," said Matthew, "good."

He walked out of the office, out of the clinic past Malone and his men still strung out in a line behind the patrol cars. Ullmann looked at Malone, nodding, noticing again the ugly stitches holding together the gashes on his face. It seemed as if everywhere he looked, he saw someone marked by Bill Reed. But thoughts of Reed faded quickly. Matthew Ullmann realized he didn't care about Bill Reed anymore. He didn't care about any of it. This was over. The next part of his life was about to begin when he sat down once more at his computer. He would send his hoarded wealth out from its hiding places into new places, and it would pull Matthew Ullmann and his wife after it, taking them away from the Ullmann Institute, away from the isolated enclave in the North Country populated by retarded people Ullmann had avoided for years.

Ullmann wrapped his stadium coat around him, hunched against the day's-end chill surrounding him. The sky rapidly darkening around him, he checked his watch. Ten after four. Ullmann stepped up his pace, moving between Davis Hall and Frost Hall, heading for the broad lawn that separated the dormitories, dining hall, and clinic from the administration building at the other end of the campus.

Ullmann walked past the dorms, thinking nothing about the people who lived there. His thoughts were of his brokerage accounts, his offshore banks, the transactions he would make, reviewing the steps in his mind, estimating yet again the time it would take.

Ullmann had planned it all before. It came down to fifteen transactions. Fifteen transfers to send everything to banks overseas where secrecy laws would give him more than enough time to counter any inquiries while he set up a new life for himself, more than enough time to set up yet another series of new accounts and yet another round of money transfers until he buried everything so deeply no one would ever find it.

Who knows? he thought. If Ralph does his job, if Reed is taken care of, and Orenberg does his job, I could come back and gradually liquidate everything left up here. Or do it from afar. Get a good real estate agent. Give him the whole shebang. Of course, that idiot McAndrews has to be taken care of. Another chip to be cashed in, a small one, but worth something. Better not overburden Ralph, thought Ullmann. He's just about at his limit.

No, Ullmann told himself as he walked toward his office in the administration building, concentrate on the task at hand. Start with the Bermuda bank first. Get that funded.

The credit cards drawn on that bank account were nestled in his top dresser drawer. One in his name. One in Madeleine's name. Charges to those cards would automatically draw down funds on deposit at the Bermuda-based bank. As long as there was money in the account, their credit would be good, anywhere in the world. And there wasn't a governmental agency in existence that could obtain the record of the charges from his Bermudan bank unless they could prove murder or drug dealing were involved. And even then it would take months of filings.

Ullmann quickened his pace, hurrying across the broad expanse of lawn, heading toward his office. I'll put a hundred thousand in. No, two. Two hundred should be fine to start with. Make it two hundred fifty. A quarter million. Ullmann smiled. It might be fun to see how fast Madeleine and I can go through two hundred fifty thousand. Really splurge for a few weeks. Why the hell not?

Thinking of the money brought to mind Eddie McAndrews. Wonder where that ape is? He should have been here by now with my cashier's check. I'll have to leave that account open. Mail it back. Have it credited. Then close it down.

As Ullmann stepped into the administration building, he thought, That idiot is probably sitting in the Lincoln Tavern with my cashier's check stuffed in his pocket celebrating his earnings. Damn him. He'd better get back here before I leave.

Reed and Irwin had found Angela and her sister Lizzie in the first dorm they searched. Reed had slipped into the dorm room while Irwin waited out in the hallway.

Angela sat on the dorm-room bed next to Lizzie, her arm around her sister's shoulder. When Reed entered, she stood, but she kept her hand on her sister's shoulder, as if she didn't want to lose physical contact.

"You're here," she said.

"Yeah." Reed looked down at Lizzie. "This is your sister."

"Yes."

Even sitting, Reed could tell that Elizabeth Quist was a tall woman. Maybe even taller than Angela. Her features were similar, but Elizabeth's neurological impairment had slightly twisted her face, marring her good looks. She had also aged beyond her years and become thin almost to the point of being gaunt. Unlike Angela who seemed to be constantly thinking, calculating, evaluating, Lizzie had a nearly vacant affect. Despite all the differences, Reed could see that Lizzie could have easily become a woman as beautiful and formidable as her sister except for one devastating illness.

Angela stared at the shotgun in Reed's left hand. She thought it might make her sister nervous, but Elizabeth Quist didn't seem to notice.

Angela sat back down on the bed and spoke quietly to her sister, her face inches from Lizzie's cheek.

"Lizzie, this is my friend, Bill."

Reed said, "Hello, Lizzie."

He extended his hand and Elizabeth Quist slowly grasped it, looking up at Reed without expression. Reed took the hand gently, smiled and let go, but Lizzie held on to his hand. He allowed it, feeling somewhat caught, and said to Angela, "They've got John in the clinic. I just wanted to make sure you were all right before I went over there."

"All the male proctors have gone down there. And Malone's deputies are down there, too."

"I know."

Angela could see that Reed was not going to be deterred so she didn't try.

Reed asked, "Have they kept all the residents in their dorms?"

"I think so. A few wandered out to look at the flashing lights, but they shooed them back in. I guess they're all in their rooms."

Reed peered out Lizzie's dorm window, but didn't have a view of the clinic. He did, however, see Matthew Ullmann walk past the dorm and out onto the broad lawn that led to his office.

"Do you have any idea of what you're going to do? There's an awful lot of men guarding that clinic."

"Yeah," said Reed. "I do." He straightened up from the window, knelt down to Lizzie's level, and gently extracted his hand. Looking back and forth between Angela and her sister, he said, "You two stay here. It won't be long. Just stay here. I'll come back and get you. And then we'll go."

"So you think we should go?"

Reed straightened up. "Yes."

He turned for the door and Angela said, "Reed."

"What?"

"Are you sure you—?"

"If I don't make it back, take your sister and get the hell out, Angela. If I don't make it, get the hell out of here and don't look back."

Gladys Richards sat at her desk methodically working out the word jumble puzzle in the local newspaper, waiting quietly for her five o'clock quitting time. Mr. Ullmann had not been in all day. She knew that there was some problem down at the clinic and hoped it would keep him occupied until she left. Ullmann's absence caused a strange combination of relief and dread. Relief that he was gone; dread that he might return any minute.

The dread flashed into reality as she heard Ullmann say, "Is that what I pay you to do?"

Gladys jerked to attention.

Ullmann pointed over his shoulder to the doorway that led to his office and said, "Put that nonsense down and watch my door. I don't want any calls or anyone coming in here, do you understand?"

Gladys, too nervous to talk, simply nodded rapidly.

"Can you do that, Gladys?" He pointed to his office door. "My door is going to be locked. Just bleat or snort or something if someone comes in here, but don't you dare let them knock on my door. Understood."

The insult stung, but as usual Gladys swallowed and said, "Yes, sir."

Ullmann walked into his office without another word and shut the door firmly behind him. Gladys heard the push-button handle lock click shut.

Reed stepped out of Lizzie's dorm dressed in a denim barn jacket he had found in the dorm proctor's office.

He had fashioned a sling for the shotgun with a tie he had also found in the office. The Mossberg hung from Reed's right shoulder under the barn jacket as he set out across the green expanse that separated the north and south ends of the campus.

Reed knew the dorm buildings blocked any view of him from the clinic, but a sheriff's patrol car sat parked on the asphalt driveway between the institute's entrance and the guest parking lot, guarding the entrance to the institute. That meant

Reed would be walking in his direction. All the deputy had to do was glance down and he would see Reed.

Reed started across the lawn, out in the open, trying to keep his gait normal, hoping his bad haircut and barn jacket would make him look enough like a proctor to satisfy the deputy if he spotted him.

Irwin stood back in the doorway of Lizzie's dorm staying out of sight.

Reed kept his peripheral vision on the sheriff's car, but tried to put everything out of his mind except walking across the lawn. The thick grass and wet ground underneath didn't make it easy. Reed ignored the discomfort in his stump, ignored the wet coming through his right shoe, concentrated on keeping his stride going, steadying the Flex-Foot, keeping his steps even, trying not to attract attention with his uneven gait. The Mossberg wedged under his right armpit reminded him of his crutch, but certainly didn't do anything to help his stride. And then Reed realized that he had never walked this far with his prosthesis, with or without a crutch.

Ullmann waited for the interminable boot-up process to end. He banged out his password on his keyboard and set to work.

In the outer office, Gladys Richards looked up and saw a stranger standing in front of her dressed as if he worked at the Ullmann Institute.

Reed put his finger to his lips, making the shush sound.

Gladys's eyes widened.

Reed stepped over to her desk and put out his hand. Gladys raised hers, and Reed grasped the pudgy hand gen-

He said in a whisper, "Bill Reed. You must be Gladys."

She nodded.

"Thanks for your help the other day when I called."

"You're welcome," she whispered back.

Reed continued whispering, as if he and Gladys were conspiring to play a trick on someone.

"Is he in there?"

"Yes."

"I'm going in to see him. He probably won't be happy to see me."

"You're right," said Gladys. "You can't go in."

"Yes I can."

"The door's locked."

Reed made a concerned face and nodded one exaggerated nod. He looked down at Gladys saying nothing. She looked up at him.

Reed whispered, "Do you have a key?"

Gladys nodded.

Reed smiled a very charming smile and said, "Can I have it?"

Gladys sat paralyzed.

"Tell you what," Reed said slowly. "Give me the key, and I'll bet you he never bothers you again. How's that?"

Reed let go of her hand. Gladys had to push her chair back away from the center drawer to get her bulk out of the way. She slid open the drawer and lifted out a ring of keys. Reed watched her carefully pick out a key. She held the ring of keys up by the small key for the handle lock on Ullmann's office door.

Reed whispered, "Thanks," and took the keys from Gladys.

Reed moved past her desk, shrugging out of the barn jacket, tossing it on the floor out of his way. He slid the Mossberg off his shoulder. Carefully, he lined up the key with the door lock, then quickly shoved it home, turned it, opened the door.

Ullmann sat staring intently at his computer screen, the sound of the opening door annoying him, but not enough for him to stop what he was doing. He entered a burst of keystrokes, yelling, "Goddammit, Gladys, I told you—"

Just as he began to turn toward the door, the fat barrel of the Mossberg cracked across the top of his head, a quick, sharp blow, just enough to stifle his yell and knock him away from the computer.

Ullmann instinctively ducked, put his hands up to ward off

another blow, and turned to see Reed standing in front of his desk, the shotgun pointed at him.

"You!"

"Yeah, me. Get up." Reed pointed the barrel at Ullmann's face and yelled, "Get up."

Ullmann stood up, his hands raised. He looked back down at his computer, then back at Reed. Reed moved around the far side of the desk so he could see what was on the screen.

"Move back," Reed yelled.

Ullmann backed up as Reed came around in his direction so he could see the computer screen. Ullmann instinctively moved away from Reed and the shotgun, but when Reed bent toward the computer screen something in Matthew Ullmann snapped.

Reed heard the growl, turned a split second before two hundred thirty pounds of Matthew Ullmann driven by hate, rage, greed, and frustration slammed into Reed with a sudden, unexpected ferocity, buckling the artificial limb, shoving Reed into the side of Ullmann's desk. Two of Reed's floating ribs cracked on the hard desk edge. The pain was so intense, Reed almost passed out.

Ullmann grabbed on to Reed, pinning the shotgun between them. Reed let go of the Mossberg, felt himself being forced down along the desk edge, Ullmann's hands grabbing for his face and neck, a punch landing, another one hitting his throat as he scraped painfully down to the floor, cracking his head on the desk edge, landing on the floor with all of Ullmann's weight on top of him.

Reed heard Ullmann screaming a high-pitched wail. He grabbed Reed's throat with this left hand, reared up with his right to smash it into Reed's face. Reed, tensing his neck muscles against the hand on his throat, blocked the wild punch.

He heard Ullmann screaming, "I'll kill you, I'll kill you." Reed grabbed Ullmann's left wrist with his right hand, a bone crushing grip that paralyzed Ullmann's own grip, neutralizing it. Ullmann swung down again with his right hand. But this time, instead of just blocking the swinging punch, Reed knocked the arm away, and then drove a hard, quick left hand into the underside of Ullmann's jaw. Then another punch to Ullmann's jaw and face, and another and another.

Matthew Ullmann had never been punched anywhere, much less his face. The shocking, stunning force and pain of the blows turned him into jelly. He began toppling off Reed, who twisted off the floor and shoved him away.

Reed rolled to his right, so infuriated that he was up on his artificial left knee before he realized it. Ullmann lay on his back, breathing heavily, semiconscious. Reed reared back and drove his fist into Ullmann's solar plexus nearly rupturing Ullmann's spleen.

Reed cursed, wiped his face, picked up the shotgun, and struggled to his feet, ignoring the sharp pain in his left side.

Gladys Richards stood at the doorway.

"It's all right," said Reed, breathing hard.

Gladys stood and stared at him.

Reed thought for a moment that she might bolt and run, so he said, "Come in. Sit down." Reed pointed to the couch. Gladys slowly took a seat in the corner.

Reed rummaged around Ullmann's desk until he found what he wanted, a roll of packing tape. He quickly wrapped five or six turns around Ullmann's wrists. Gladys Richards watched silently.

Reed pulled out his cell phone and made his call to SR.

"It's me. I'm with the computer."

"All right."

"He's on-line." Reed squinted at his screen. "On his broker-age account site."

"Excellent."

"Okay. What do you want me to do?"

"Can you tell how many accounts he has?"

Reed reached for the computer mouse and peered at the screen. He clicked on the screen portion that said "Home Page." The screen changed and a new page started generating. Reed stared at the list of accounts that began to appear. He had to scroll down to count all of them.

"Fifteen."

"Holy shit, is there a dollar total?"

Reed hesitated before reading it, until he realized that SR would find the total eventually.

"Eighteen million, six hundred eighty thousand, two hundred twelve dollars and eighty-six cents."

"Nice chunk of change. Got my disk and connector?"

"Yeah."

"Tell him he can kiss it good-bye. It'll still be in his name. He'll just never find it. He's on a dial-up connection, right?"

"Yeah."

"Put my connector in the serial port. Then put my disk in the A drive and run it. Watch his screen. It'll tell you when to take his phone line out of the back of his CPU and put it in the back of my connector."

"You don't care if I break his connection?"

"No. After you switch the phone line, hit F11 twice. My program will find his modem and connect to me automatically and start the file transfers. I'll have his whole hard drive and every keystroke he made since he turned on the computer. Just don't turn the damn thing off."

"How long before you can access his accounts?"

"If I'm lucky and he uses the same password for all the accounts, right away. If not, eight, nine hours for each account."

"Shit, eight hours for each account? That long to decipher a password?"

"If they're different. I mean randomly different. Don't worry about it. Just let me get to work."

A quiet voice from across the room asked, "Do you want his passwords?"

Reed looked at Gladys Richards and said into the phone, "Hang on, SR."

She sat forward, perched on the edge of Ullmann's couch, a tentative expression on her face as if she wasn't sure she should be interrupting Reed.

Reed smiled at her, lowered the cell phone, and said, "Yes, actually, I do."

Gladys Richards hefted her bulk up and walked toward Ullmann's desk.

Ullmann, still flat on his back, made a gagging sound, then began sucking in air. He rolled onto his side, moaned, gagged again, sounding like he might vomit.

Gladys headed for the other side of the desk, avoiding Ullmann. She daintily bent over the desk and reached for the slide-out writing table, but then leaned back away from it. She looked at Reed. He glanced at the small handle of the extension easily within his reach, but he didn't touch it.

Gladys said, "Reed and Barton."

"Yes." And then after a pause he said, "Yes," again, realizing now that he had found the person who had helped Johnny Boy mail his message.

Gladys nodded once, as if confirming her decision. She reached over and slid out the extension, revealing a single page of stationery taped to the sliding wood piece bearing a neatly typed list of randomly devised passwords and ID numbers, combinations of letters and numbers that defied memorization.

Reed looked at the page, lifted the cell phone to his ear, and said, "SR, do you have a fax there?"

"No faxes."

"You got a pen?"

"For what?"

"To write with."

Reed handed the phone to Gladys and said, "Could you read those off to the gentleman on the other end of the line."

"Okay," said Gladys in a slightly tremulous voice.

Ullmann had struggled up onto his side, his taped-together hands braced on the floor. He growled, "Gladys . . ." as if he could still threaten her.

Reed turned to him. "Say another word and I'll break your jaw."

Gladys turned back to the phone and began slowly reading. As she read, sometimes repeating a letter or number for clarity, Reed pushed SR's connector into the serial port and inserted the disk. He typed in the commands SR had told him, hit the enter key. The monitor flickered, the modem connected, and within thirty seconds streams of file names scrolled rapidly across the screen, disappearing as fast as they appeared. It was as if a huge invisible vacuum were sucking out the contents of Ullmann's computer.

Gladys Richards's soft, diffident voice droned on, enunciating each password, while Ullmann stared at the computer screen.

Reed lifted Ullmann to his feet and pressed the shotgun barrel into his chest. "I want my cousin."

"You'll never get away with this. That's my money. We'll find it."

"Not if you're dead you won't. You want the chance to stay alive, give me my cousin."

Ullmann sneered, "You're not going to shoot me."

Reed pressed the barrel harder. "I'll shoot you in a fucking heartbeat. Then I'll go get John Boyd by myself."

Ullmann swallowed hard, wincing at the pressure of the Mossberg against his chest. Reed felt Ullmann's heartbeat pulsing through the shotgun. He pushed once more. "Now."

Ullmann said, "Fine. You want him, you can have him. What's left of him."

FORTY-EIGHT

The sheriff's deputy manning the patrol car near the entrance could have been the first to see Bill Reed and Matthew Ullmann slowly walking across the expanse of lawn, heading toward the clinic, but he never looked in that direction.

Irwin Barker remained inside the doorway of Lizzie's dormitory, so had no view of Reed.

Inside the clinic, Madeleine Ullmann worked steadily sorting her files, unaware of anything that had transpired in Matthew's office.

Nor did Ralph Malone, his deputies, and the proctors who stood guarding the front and back entrances to the clinic know that Reed and Ullmann were approaching.

Johnny Boy lay in his hospital bed, rapidly falling under sway of the escalating infection racing through his system.

The view of Lizzie's dorm room gave Angela Quist the first opportunity to spot Reed pushing Ullmann along at the end of his shotgun. The sight brought her to her feet, hurrying closer to the window.

Ullmann walked ploddingly, but his mind raced, fueled by the panic that came from realizing everything he had worked for, everything he had schemed and murdered for, everything he had hoarded over the years had slipped away from his control. Reed followed closely behind Ullmann, step after painful step across the wet lawn. They were approaching the dorms now. One way or another, this would soon be over.

Irwin, who had held his position on the front side of the dorm, saw Reed and Ullmann come into view. He raised his Mossberg to waist level and stepped out from his doorway, looking toward Reed, trying to catch his eye, but Reed never looked his way. They had already talked about it. Nothing more to say.

Irwin turned and headed around the far side so that he would emerge out from between the back end of the dorms, to the left of where Malone and his men stood guarding the clinic. Reed would approach the clinic straight on. Irwin would cover the left flank and secure another angle of fire on Malone and his men.

Malone's deputies had parked all three of their patrol cars bumper to bumper parallel to the clinic entrance. Three of the five deputies and two proctors stood near the patrol cars. Most of them leaned against the cars, facing toward the clinic, away from the approaching Reed and Ullmann.

The Barrett brothers hung back closer to the clinic entrance.

Two deputies and one proctor were on the far side of the clinic guarding the back entrance.

Malone sat in the passenger seat of one patrol car, sipping coffee, trying to stay warm. His head and face ached terribly. He hadn't slept in almost forty-eight hours. Even the blazing hot black coffee one of the men had brought over from the kitchen didn't help much.

Ronnie Barrett, standing with his back to the clinic entrance, was the first to see Matthew Ullmann walking toward them with a shotgun at his back.

"Holy shit," he muttered.

But the others, talking to one another, smoking cigarettes, didn't hear him. They neither looked up nor turned around. And then Ronnie yelled, "Fuck!" pointing behind them.

The men turned around, first one, then another. For a moment, no one moved or said a word, then all at once the yelling started, the ducking and scrambling, the sounds of handguns, shotguns, rifles being hurriedly drawn and cocked, everybody yelling instructions at the same time.

Malone came out of the patrol car barking, "Shut up. Shut up. Take cover. Take cover."

Through all the commotion, Bill Reed just continued walking, pushing Ullmann forward with the barrel of the Mossberg, coming closer, fifteen yards away, closing the distance. Most had scrambled down behind the cars, but another wave of confusion started when the men assigned to guard the back of the clinic came running toward the sounds of commotion.

Malone waved frantically at them, motioning with his arms, yelling at them, "Get down."

Up in the clinic, Madeleine Ullmann heard the muffled shouts. She stopped sorting the files, annoyed at the interruption. She hissed, "Now what?" and stood up from her desk in the clinic office.

And still Reed came, keeping the barrel of the Mossberg pressed against Ullmann's back. He stopped five yards from the settling band of armed men in front of him. Reed prodded Ullmann with the shotgun and said, "Tell them to bring me my cousin."

Angela had seen Reed disappear between the dorm buildings. He was actually going to confront them. Fear and dread hit her so hard that for a moment she felt paralyzed. She found herself hardly able to breathe or swallow. Instinctively, she went to her sister and gently forced her to lie down on her bed, as if to take her out of the line of fire.

"Lizzie," she said, trying to keep her voice from shaking. "Lay down. Don't move. Stay here." She gently patted her older sister's shoulders and forehead. Lizzie looked up at her calmly, following her instructions as if Angela's quiet commands were nothing unusual.

The proctors and deputies behind the cars focused on Reed who stood before them, even as a half-dozen weapons were pointed at him. The Barretts and one of Malone's deputies hung back behind the group, as if forming a second line of defense.

Malone knelt behind the patrol car farthest to Reed's left. Now he stood, extended his Beretta, and yelled to Reed, "Drop that weapon and stand back."

Reed shifted slightly to his right, positioning himself behind the stocky Ullmann whose body provided a good amount of coverage and yelled back at Malone.

"Get my cousin out here now."

Malone yelled back, "Drop that shotgun."

Reed raised the muzzle of the shotgun to the base of Ullmann's skull. "Get him out here now."

"Drop the weapon."

Reed pumped the shotgun, "Now. I want him now," yelling

over Malone, who kept demanding he drop the shotgun. Ull-mann cringed away from the shotgun barrel, raised his hands, and screamed, "Madeleine. Madeleine."

Malone and Reed stopped. Almost all eyes turned to the clinic. Madeleine Ullmann stood at the window shrieking her husband's name, "Matthew."

Angela had come out the back door of the dormitory, stand-ing in the doorway, staring at the standoff in front of the clinic. Reed's back was to her, no more than twenty yards away. She had heard Madeleine and Matthew yelling for each other. She saw Madeleine in the clinic window. Saw her dis-appear and knew that she was running to her husband. And then, Angela saw it all, realizing what Madeleine Ullmann would do, and Angela broke left out of the doorway and be-gan to run.

Ullmann watched his wife disappear from the window. Des-perately, he called out, "No, no."

Reed let him yell, thinking Ullmann was going to try to save himself, try to persuade his wife to bring out John Boyd. He poked the barrel into the back of Ullmann's head and told him, "You tell her to bring him out. Bring out my cousin now."

Malone turned back to face Reed and Ullmann, raising his Beretta in a two-handed grip.

Ullmann yelled at Malone and his men, "Wait. Wait. Don't shoot. Don't shoot."

Suddenly Madeleine Ullmann appeared in the doorway. "Matthew."

Malone held up a hand, palm out to Madeleine, shouting, "Stay back."

She grabbed on to the doorjamb to stop herself from stum-bling out.

Reed snarled, "Tell her."

Ullmann straightened, standing taller, his arms raised,

glasses askew, face puffy, his thick lips split from Reed's punches, but with his eyes gleaming, a fire in him now. He yelled to his wife, "Listen to me, Madeleine, listen to me carefully."

Madeleine Ullmann stood bent over, staring at her husband, oblivious to everything except her husband, their eyes locked. Connected now, waiting.

Ullmann spoke to her, quietly now, but with an intensity that made every word clear. "Go back inside. There's nothing left. He took everything. Everything. Do you understand?"

She stared back at him, uncomprehending.

"He knows everything, Madeleine. He's got the accounts. All of it. All of it is gone!" Matthew Ullmann watched the meaning of his words burn into his wife's consciousness, waiting for the words to penetrate, to ignite the rage in her. In a moment, she might be out of control. This was it. Ullmann yelled, "Go back inside. Go back and kill him!"

Reed yelled, "No!" He slammed the butt of the shotgun into the back of Ullmann's head. He dropped in a heap. Madeleine disappeared back into the clinic. Malone shot at Reed, but missed. Reed blasted off one shot and dropped down behind Ullmann.

Malone ducked behind the car. Reed scrambled up close behind Ullmann's body as every weapon facing him erupted.

Reed, tight up against Ullmann's back, felt the impact of bullets slamming into the body, heard more bullets whizzing overhead. He propped the Mossberg on the dead man's hip, pressed himself up close behind Ullmann's body, his prosthetic leg stretched out behind him, pumped and pulled off three rapid shotgun blasts, not aiming, not even raising his head up to see, but shooting straight out at ground level, sending shotgun pellets at the legs and knees exposed behind the patrol cars.

The screams of two deputies could be heard even over the roar of weapons as their shinbones shattered and they fell back.

And then a dark shape emerged from behind a thick oak

tree, suddenly illuminated by the flashes of shotgun fire blasting out in front of him. Irwin Barker advanced on the deputies and proctors, pumping and firing steadily over their heads and into the cars protecting them. First came confusion at being fired upon from another direction, then terror, and then panic at receiving volley after volley from both Reed and Irwin. One, then another, then all of the proctors ran away from the two blasting shotguns, led by the Barrett brothers.

The remaining deputies cringed behind their cars, shooting blindly, pinned down by the raking blasts of shot smashing into sheet metal, whizzing over their heads, shattering glass.

Johnny Boy saw the flashes of gunfire illuminating the inside of the clinic like strobe lights, winced at the booming explosions and the piercing *crack, crack* of the handguns. He rolled over in the bed, the pain of his surgical wounds somehow buried under his fever. He tried to sit up. He had to get up. Cuz'n Bill. Cuz'n Bill was coming. He had to get up, but it felt like the inside of him had evaporated, robbing him of his strength. Images of his father flashed in his mind, his long-ago mother. Johnny Boy saw them looking at him, shaking their heads as if to say, John, John, what are you doing? What's the matter with you?

Somehow, Johnny Boy managed to get an elbow braced under him, then a hand. He brought his knee toward the edge of the bed. Up, get up, he told himself.

Madeleine Ullmann burst into the clinic, the syringe filled with potassium chloride already in her hand, a growl animating her, propelling her forward. She saw Johnny Boy rising, getting out of the bed. She stopped, her momentum pitching her forward, off balance.

"Don't move," she yelled.

Johnny Boy pushed himself up, sitting up, sliding his legs off the bed, his feet on the floor. He raised an arm against her and said, "No."

Madeleine looked at him, realizing now she'd never get the syringe into a vein. She threw it aside, frustrated, angry. "You," she snarled. "All because of you."

She looked around, momentarily helpless, then she ran into the treatment room, ripped open a drawer, pulling it out of the cabinet. A shower of instruments crashed to the floor, the din mixing with the shotgun blasts outside. She bent down, found what she was looking for, and grabbed it. A scalpel.

Reed saw Irwin slowly, methodically, advancing on his left, shotgun extended, blasting his way toward the deputies, pinning Malone down, step by step closing in on them. Reed scrambled up onto one knee. The clinic, Reed thought, the clinic. She's in there with John. She's in there. He had to get into the clinic.

He stood, started for the entrance, shoving fresh shells into the Mossberg, ready to blast away anything or anybody that tried to stop him, watching Irwin advance fearlessly on his left, and just then a patrol car that had been guarding near the entrance came racing along the asphalt walkway. Reed and Irwin both turned, both opened up with their shotguns. The front radiator blew, the hood flew up, one front tire exploded. The patrol car swerved and slammed right into the middle patrol car blocking the clinic entrance, knocking back everyone behind the cars. In two strides Irwin was on Malone. He levered the butt of the shotgun into Malone's head, walloping him to the ground. Reed stepped around the other side of the barricade and aimed his shotgun at the remaining deputies. He yelled, "Drop your weapons. Drop your weapons."

He saw Irwin bend over Malone, handcuffing him. Then he cracked the butt of the shotgun into Malone's head knocking him cold.

Reed ordered the deputies, "Show me your hands, show me your hands."

Irwin came up behind them, kicking them facedown on the ground, growling, "Face down, face down." He grabbed the handcuffs off their belts and snapped them, cuffing ankle to wrist, one by one, as Reed staggered toward the clinic.

Madeleine Ullmann approached Johnny Boy, concentrating, her head down, the scalpel poised. Johnny Boy, weak, feverish, dazed, and hurting, still managed to ward her off.

Madeleine ducked to see under his upraised arms, focusing, taking aim, ready to punch the scalpel into his neck, into his jugular, to slash across his neck, ready to kill, just as the door to the clinic banged open. Madeleine flinched, turned. Angela Quist rushed in, running full stride, as she had run around the gunfight to the back door of the clinic, up the stairs and down the hall, running furiously, her long legs carrying her, running right at Madeleine Ullmann, who turned and tried to slash at her with the razor-sharp scalpel, except that Johnny Boy Reed had grabbed her arm from behind.

Madeleine ripped her arm free of his weak grip, just as all of Angela Quist crashed into her, driving her back against the bed, into Johnny Boy. Madeleine screamed. Johnny Boy cried out in anguish. Angela, terrified of the gleaming scalpel, grabbed for Madeleine's wrist, pressing her down on Johnny Boy who also grabbed for Madeleine's wrist deflecting another slash aimed at Angela's face.

Angela finally managed to get both hands on Madeleine's wrist. Holding on, keeping the scalpel away, she pulled Madeleine off Johnny Boy, pulled with all the strength her terror gave her, whipping Madeleine into the bed across from Johnny Boy. Still holding Madeleine's wrist, she slung her back against Johnny Boy's bed, then wrenched Madeleine off her feet, dragging her across the floor, twisting like a hammer thrower, whipping Madeleine into the wall, still holding Madeleine's wrist, kicking at Madeleine's arm, shaking, kicking, until finally the scalpel clattered to the floor.

Angela looked down on Madeleine Ullmann, crumpled against the wall. And then, she let go of Madeleine's wrist as if it were tainted, noticing now for the first time, feeling now the burning pain from the slash that ran from her elbow almost to the tattoo on her right wrist. The sight of it made her woozy. She staggered over to one of the hospital beds, grabbing a rail. The lights burst on in the darkened clinic. Angela turned. Bill Reed staggered into the clinic.

Far off in the distance, the sirens of the state police cruisers wailed.

Reed yelled, "John."

Johnny Boy Reed's mouth silently formed the words "Cuz'n Bill."

EPILOGUE

Bill Reed and Irwin Barker met at the same bench near the model boat pond in Central Park where they had met two months before. This time, Reed sat on the bench next to Irwin instead of in his Paraglide wheelchair, which was now gathering dust in his closet.

Christmas had come and gone, leaving the walkways in the park lined with desultory piles of frozen snow that looked like melted candle wax. The boat pond had been drained, making Reed's oasis appear quite bereft. But bright sun and crisp air helped invigorate the day.

Irwin wore one of his usual suits, plus an enormous tweed overcoat left unbuttoned despite the chill. A soft-brimmed fedora and dark green sunglasses in elegant tortoiseshell frames added a bit of raffish style to his look.

Reed wore brown corduroy pants, a beige cashmere polo shirt under a brilliant white down coat, and old-fashioned Ray•Ban aviator sunglasses, which were coming back into style. A knit Irish woolen cap kept his head warm.

Irwin pulled out a folded legal document from his coat pocket and handed it to Reed.

"Charles dropped this off yesterday. Your immunity agreement."

Reed glanced at the folder. "You sign yours?"

"Yep."

"Satisfied with it?"

"Charles and Turkin are satisfied. They're the experts. You know, the usual lawyers' provisos . . . if our proffers don't have any landmines in 'em, we should be fine."

Reed took the document from Irwin and stuffed it in his

coat pocket. He shook his head. "Damn negotiations took much too long."

"What'd you expect? Just a good thing we finally got the evidence admitted."

"There's precedent. Private citizen doesn't need search warrants. Plus, you know Charlie Fox. He didn't get to be federal prosecuting attorney for the Northern District by being a nice guy. I was pretty sure he'd get it all admitted."

Irwin shrugged and lit one of his Pall Malls, sitting back on the bench, gazing out at the empty boat pond. After a moment, he said, "I guess if he can't get the job done, nobody else could. Christ what a pile of shit . . . murder, fraud, what was it a two-hundred-page indictment?"

"Something like that."

"You pretty sure nothing's coming back on you?"

Reed shrugged. "I doubt it. Ullmann was transferring accounts when I busted in. SR found it all and rerouted it so many times they'll never figure out whether or not the money I turned over was all of it. And quite honestly, that's not at the top of Fox's list."

"Tracking it down?"

"Yeah."

Irwin asked, "How many of them do you think he'll end up prosecuting?"

"I don't know. They'll start with Madeleine Ullmann. I saw her at the arraignment. What a wretched thing she is. Standing there with this victim look, wearing a neck brace. Not an ounce of remorse in that woman."

"What'd you expect? She's a maniac."

"I wouldn't have minded seeing that husband of hers standing next to her."

"I don't know. Better he took a few bullets. Better we're rid of him." Irwin shook his head at the memory of Matthew Ullmann, then asked, "So there's the wife and the group at the biotech company. What's that, about a half dozen people who were in on it? And a couple of insurance executives out in Utah?"

"Yeah. Plus, of course, that local sheriff."

"Right. That asshole." Irwin took a last deep drag from his Pall Mall and tossed the burning butt. "So how the hell did they work it? Did you figure it out? The part about the insurance."

Reed pursed his lips and nodded. "Yeah. That was the key. When I was up there unraveling Ullmann's deal, putting the pieces together, there was this nagging hole that I couldn't fill in . . . these blocks of money that appeared every few years. The money that got Ullmann started and kept him going. I thought about insurance, but the numbers were too big. I couldn't believe they could insure people in that institution for such large sums. I didn't believe they could scam insurance companies into issuing such big policies."

"So how'd they do it?"

Reed smiled. "The answer was right in front of me all along. Right from the very beginning."

"Where?"

"On John Boyd's message. The one you delivered to me. Did you see it? Remember all those little numbers and letters pasted on that page."

"Vaguely."

"They were cut from his paycheck."

"His *paycheck*?"

"Yeah. Gladys, Ullmann's secretary, explained what those were to me." Reed stared off in the distance, speaking almost mechanically. "It was right there in front of me. I guess I couldn't connect all the dots because I really had no idea how fucking depraved those two were. Even now, it seems impossible to believe."

Irwin frowned, but did not comment.

Reed pushed the memories of Matthew and Madeleine Ullmann out of his mind and continued. "The insurance ploy was a natural, actually. Ullmann picked out older residents with substantial trust funds. Then he used their trust funds to buy huge policies on them . . . made possible because Ullmann claimed they were employees of his various corporations. He did, in fact, give them jobs, issued them paychecks. It was easy, since everyone at the institute did some sort of work. He paid them a pittance, but he insured them as key corporate executives with COLI policies, corporate life insurance. There's much less scrutiny on corporate life insurance. I assume Dr. Prentice faked the physicals. And Ullmann owned a large interest in the insurance company out in Utah that issued the policies, so the fix was in from the very beginning."

"And every time one of 'em died, it was a jackpot."

"Right. But that wasn't good enough. Those poor people had shorter life expectancies because of their medical problems, but Ullmann didn't like waiting around. Or paying premiums, even though it wasn't his money. Somewhere along the line, the lovely nurse practitioner Madeleine got involved with that biotech company and their drug development program. It didn't take her long to figure out a way to kill them off sooner . . . use them for drug testing. That made the policies much more cost effective. But the real payoff came when they took the insurance money and invested it into the drug company stock. Doing the human drug trials before they filed with the FDA gave them an enormous advantage. Saved them millions. Practically ensured that the stock would explode."

"It all works out nice if you don't give a shit about human life."

"Yeah. Real efficient." Reed shook his head, his disgust apparent. "So what do you say about that? Horrible? Depraved? Inhuman?"

"All of the above, and it still don't nail it."

"No," said Reed, "I guess not."

Irwin Barker crossed his arms, wanting to change the conversation, but somehow determined to see it through. "So how many victims were there?"

Reed sighed, grimacing. "Four that went all the way through to their end. They don't know how many underwent experiments and might have died from the drugs, or before their time. Maybe twenty. John Boyd was supposed to be the fifth with an insurance policy. There were five insured, plus it turns out Prentice and McAndrews."

Irwin's eyebrows raised in surprise. "Son of a bitch. Ullmann was gonna off them, too?"

"Oh, yeah. Ullmann wasn't going to leave any loose ends behind, so he figured he'd make some money when he killed them. Or I guess have that sheriff do it for him."

"That fucking sheriff. I keep thinkin' I should've blown his head off."

"No way, Irwin. You did the right thing. Putting a lawman in prison is the worst punishment imaginable. If we'd've killed anybody it would've been a lot harder to make our deal. You were right. Once we shot back at 'em, they crumbled. That's all we needed."

Irwin shook his head, done with it now. "I guess. So how's my pal, John Boyd? How's he doing?"

Reed cocked his head. "I hope he'll be okay. You know he's getting another scan today. They want to make sure the cancer hasn't spread."

"First one was all right, wasn't it?"

Reed grimaced. "Yes and no. I guess it wasn't completely conclusive." Suddenly Reed felt the sting of tears. The suddenness of the emotion made him shake his head. "Fuck."

"What?"

"It's so crazy. All those years I could have been around him." Reed cleared his throat. "Irwin, I really love that guy."

"I know you do."

Reed smiled. "I have to watch myself that I don't take advantage of him."

"Take advantage?"

Reed rubbed his face as a way to tamp down his emotions. "I don't know if it's me or him, I just find that I'm always messin' around with him. I do it like I'm trying to cheer him up. And he's so good-natured, he gets a kick out of it. I think."

"Sure he does."

Reed sighed. "I just hope we didn't save him so he can go through another round of hell. He went through a terrible thing with that sepsis. Fucking Prentice."

"He made it, that's the important thing. You saved him."

"Not without you. And Angela. By the time I got into that clinic, I was done for. If it hadn't been for you—"

Irwin waved off Reed's comment. "We did what we had to do. No choice."

"If you hadn't gotten him out to that medevac team, told 'em what Prentice told me, if they hadn't—"

"And if you hadn't guarded those files when the troopers came in there, it would've all been for nothing. Like I said, we did what we had to do."

"Right."

Irwin shoved his hands into his overcoat pockets. "Isn't it time you got John Boyd?"

Reed checked his watch. "Yeah. Just about."

"So what's going to be with John?"

"Well, he's trying not to hurt my feelings, but it's pretty clear he'd rather be living with people more like him. Dragging him to the office, hanging out, he knows that's no life. He's living with strangers now. In our world. Not his."

"So what's the plan?"

Reed sat up straighter on the bench, talking intensely, almost as if he was reviewing the plan for himself. "That place I told you about up in Columbia County . . . I think it'll be good for him. A small community, everyone lives in these group houses, like a family, the staff and the residents. They work together, live together. Everyone on equal footing, accepted as individuals. All different levels of retardation, but it's not really an issue. The focus is just on living together and making a life."

"Do they have a spot for him?"

"No, but they will. There are five houses up there, a house for each group of about ten. We're building another house. That is, an anonymous donor is building another house. It'll be big enough for ten new residents. John will be one of them. And I think Angela's sister. Maybe also Pauline Trainor. That's John's paramour."

"Good for him. And your friend, Angela?"

Reed didn't answer right away. He gazed out at the empty model boat basin, obviously not quite sure how to respond.

"Well, it's not my business, really," said Irwin.

Reed said, "No, that's not it. It's just, I don't know, I guess we met in rather unusual circumstances. It wasn't easy for her. She lost the house. Her job. And, of course, her sister's situation changed. We've got some things to work out."

"Sounds like you are."

"Yes. We are."

"And meanwhile she's out from under a couple of ruthless fucking murderers."

Reed winced. "Yeah. She is. We'll work it out. I'm looking at a house up there when John gets settled. A weekend place. She's renting right now. Once I get up there regularly . . ."

Reed's voice trailed off. Irwin sat up, ready to leave, saying, "I know you ain't givin' up on it."

"No. No. I'm not."

"Then it'll work." Irwin dropped a fist on Reed's shoulder. "I'm outta here, boss. Have a good weekend. We'll get on that Chiolla case Monday, huh?"

"Right." Then, as if he had just remembered it, Reed reached into his coat pocket and pulled out an envelope and handed it to Irwin.

"What's this?"

"Knicks tickets. Season tickets. A box."

"What're you kiddin' me?"

"Mid-court, fifteen rows back. Where they have waiter service. You and your cronies can get all the shots and beers you want without moving your fat asses."

"Holy shit. Who'd you have to kill to get these?"

"Hmmm, mostly just pay. An anonymous donor funded it. As long as you want 'em, Irwin, they're yours. Just invite me to a game once in a while."

Irwin shoved the tickets in his suit jacket. "Shit, guess I'll have to live a long time to make that son of a bitch good for something."

"You do that, Irwin. A long time."

Reed suddenly stood up. Irwin Barker roused himself, standing quickly. Reed extended a hand. As they shook, he looked at Irwin Barker, but Irwin spoke first. "Don't start with all the fucking *thank you*'s again." Irwin patted his pocket. "This is plenty. Tell John I said hi."

Reed watched the big man amble off toward the West Side, then turned and headed east toward Fifth Avenue.

Reed arrived before Johnny Boy's CAT scan had finished.

He sat in the waiting room alone, but he watched an old acquaintance huddling with a middle-aged woman and her two teenage children off in the corner. Reed couldn't hear the conversation, but even from across the room, he could tell that Sarah Carpenter, the social worker who had counseled him, was making the family feel better, reassuring them, saying something to help.

Reed continued observing the group sitting together, grateful that no one noticed his attention to them. Before he realized it, a nurse had brought Johnny Boy into the waiting room. Johnny Boy, still thinner than his normal weight, aged even more by his ordeal, smiled when he saw Reed. He nodded to the nurse, at least a head taller than he, and shuffled over to his Cuz'n Bill.

Reed finally saw him, turned, and waved Johnny Boy over. "Hey, everything okay?"

Johnny Boy spoke with his usual nasal tone, perhaps exaggerating his feelings. "Yeah, yeah. Sure. Let's get the hell out of here."

Reed smiled at his cousin's pseudo-tough guy attitude, knowing where his new vocabulary had come from, but also realizing that his cousin had every right to feel threatened and phobic about a medical environment.

The nurse caught up to Johnny Boy. She patted him on the shoulder and said, "He did fine."

"I'm sure he did."

"The doctor will be calling you when the results are analyzed."

"Thanks."

The nurse smiled and left, but Johnny Boy did not look at her or thank her.

"What's the matter, John, you don't like that nurse?"

Head down, Johnny Boy answered with his nasal tone, "No."

"Why not, she likes you."

"So."

"So you should be nice to her."

"I am. C'mon, let's go."

Reed grabbed Johnny Boy's forearm and pulled him down into the chair next to him.

"Sit down, you big baby. I want you to meet a friend of mine."

Johnny Boy sat.

"Who?"

"That woman over there in the white coat."

Johnny Boy looked over at Sarah Carpenter.

"Who's she?"

"Someone who helped me once. In this very hospital."

"With what?"

"My leg thing?"

"What'd she do, cut it off?"

The quip surprised Reed, and made him smile. "You're a real wise guy, aren't you?"

"Yeah."

Reed poked Johnny Boy gently with his elbow. "Just wait a second."

Johnny Boy crossed his arms and sat back in his chair, resigned.

Reed sat with his cousin, watching Sarah Carpenter. He wondered about what she might be saying, assuming that somebody in that family was losing a limb, or had lost a limb, wondering who it might be. Maybe the husband. Why? They were in the cancer wing. Probably cancer. A tumor. In a bone. They'd had to take off a leg. Like him.

After a little longer, the mother and her children began talking to each other. Sarah Carpenter turned and saw Reed sitting across the waiting room. He smiled at her, but could tell that she didn't recognize him. Reed lifted his prosthetic leg and scowled. The scowling face jogged her memory. Sarah

Carpenter smiled, recognizing him now, and nodded.

Reed smiled at her again. She looked at Reed for just a little longer, nodded once more. After a moment, she nodded again, as if in confirmation. And then Sarah Carpenter turned back to the family.

Even across the room, Reed felt it. Her conviction.

He gently elbowed Johnny Boy again and said, "All right, you convinced me. Let's go."

Johnny Boy snapped to attention and said, "Yeah. Come on."

Johnny Boy stood. Reed extended his right hand. "Help me up."

Johnny Boy made a determined face and grabbed Reed's hand. He pulled. Reed didn't budge.

"Come on."

Johnny Boy grimaced, pulled harder, and Reed stood. He wrapped an arm around his much shorter cousin, leaning on him enough so that Johnny Boy felt the weight.

"Hey," said Johnny Boy.

"Hey what? I need help, man. My stump is sore."

"All right."

Reed began walking, leaning on his cousin for a few steps, then slowly he straightened up, walking normally, not leaning anymore, just holding his cousin, smiling at the joke. Just walking and smiling.